FEELING FOR THE AIR

Karen E. Black

Viceroy *Power* **Press**
2014

Published by **Viceroy** *Power* **Press**

If you enjoy this book, please contact me at:
E-mail: karen.black@sympatico.ca
Or post a review on Amazon and/or Goodreads!

Vol 2 of the Devereux Cousins Trilogy

Print edition:
ISBN: 978-0-9879866-4-1
Kindle edition:
ISBN: 978-09879866-6-5

Feeling for the Air

In this captivating sequel to *From the Chrysalis*, cousins Dace and Liza Devereux each face new battles in life while continuing to cope with the lifelong, passionate yearnings forbidden by societal norms.

Dace Devereux has escaped from a maximum-security penitentiary designed to house the most ruthless of criminals. Now the alleged biker leader is on the run, still wanted for his leading role in the biggest prison riot in Canadian history. But it's not the cops or the penal system, that dominate Dace's thoughts. Instead, it's his cousin Liza—a gifted college student, now with child, but still hoping to begin her master's degree at the University of Toronto.

As Dace, filled with thoughts of his cousin, migrates south to Mexico to find where the monarch butterflies spend their winter, Liza faces a new set of challenges at home in Maitland. Forced to balance her studies, the trials of new motherhood, and the consequences of her unconventional situation, she remains passionately in love with Dace—and will go to any lengths to help her soulmate clear his name.

The second of three novels about the Devereux cousins, *Feeling for the Air* combines the electricity of a forbidden romance in the early 1970s with breathtaking plot twists as two lovers who wish to roam as wild and free as butterflies are dealt a difficult and unforgiving fate.

" (This is) a brilliantly written coming-of-age novel. We all make decisions and must live with the consequences. That is where we find Dace and Liza — dealing with the consequences of their decisions. When I first reviewed *Chrysalis*, I compared Dace to James Dean and the roles he played. I still see Dace in that manner…He's trouble, but he's not all bad. Karen Black's characters are highly developed, even the secondary ones. She's not afraid to tackle a social issue and addresses several. I suggest reading this series in order although *Feeling for the Air* can stand well alone. This is a series you will want to savor. " ~Anne Boling from *Readers' Favorite*

"Loved it! Black has written an amazing story with this second book in *The Devereux Cousins* series. It's a twisted tale of forbidden love, monarch butterflies, and living on the lam. The twist and turns in this book took me on one heck of a ride. I love books that are a bit dark and unconventional and *Feeling for the Air* delivered. ~ Read On, *Amazon* reviewer

From the Chrysalis

"Drugs, bikers, prison breaks and incest provide surprising plot twists in this rough-and-tumble romance novel...set in '60s and '70s Ontario...Black has a flair for historical novels...and she shows remarkable storytelling depth..." ~ *Kirkus Reviews*

***** 2012 Readers Favorite Award Winner!***** "Dace...is about 17 when the book begins and the reader knows from the start that he is drawn to trouble. He sort of reminded me of James Dean, handsome, tempting and sure to cause suffering... Black has written a very descriptive account of the prison. She brings the scenes in her book to life and they march off the pages." ~Anne Boling from *Readers' Favorite*

"I'd like to congratulate Karen Black on her new page-turner, *From the Chrysalis*. It tells the twisted and winding tale of Liza and her dashing and dangerous older cousin D'Arcy "Dace" Devereux.

Set in Canada (Toronto's Christie subway station makes an appearance), it is the tale of a relationship blighted by uncomprehending relatives, social conventions, a harrowing stint in Maitland Penitentiary (complete with riots and semi-totalitarian "people's committees"), the well-intentioned galumph Mel, and a conundrum Liza has to bear calling for an ever more inevitable decision. You'll just have to read it if you want to know what I mean by that. I found the prison scenes, with their occasionally stark violence but underlying ethical probity, especially fascinating, but there's also lots of romantic tension, a kind of yearning whose fulfillment seems always out of reach, even when its physical manifestation is realized. What a potent novel! I spent the rest of the day shooting mysterious dark looks at people."--Julian Fauth, 2009 JUNO Award *Blues Album of the Year*

For all the men in my life: John "Jack" H. Black, John R. Allen, Jesse John Black-Allen and the boys coming after them: Harrison Allen and Finn and Riley Morrell. I lucked out.

Devereux Descendants of Randallstown, Wexford, Ireland and southern Ontario, Canada 1788-1973*

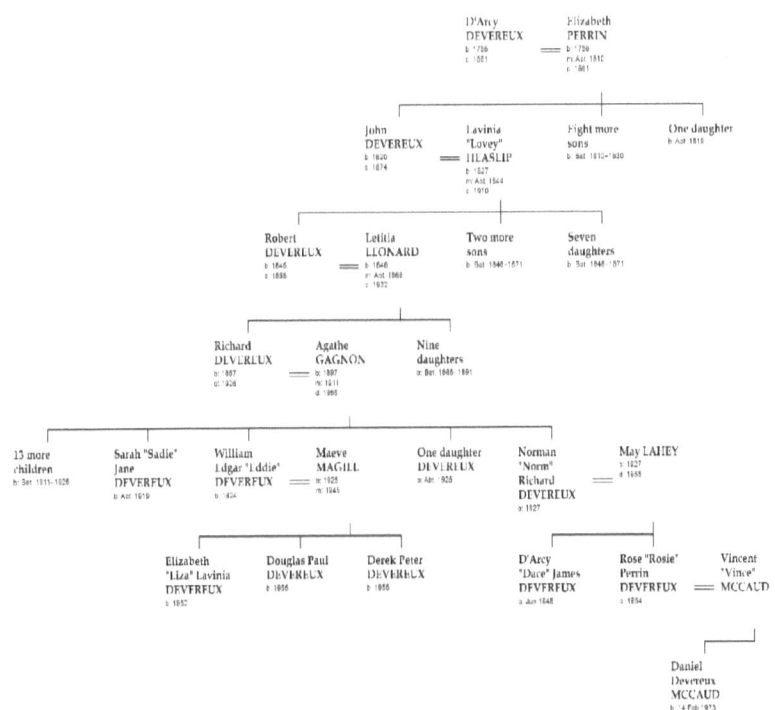

*As told to Liza Devereux by her Aunt Sadie.

My cocoon tightens, colors tease,
I'm feeling for the air…
"From the Chrysalis," by Emily Dickinson

PROLOGUE

Ontario Provincial Police are asking for the public's help in Finding D'Arcy "Dace" James Devereux, a full patch member of the Wolfhounds motorcycle gang. Devereux escaped from Maitland Super Maximum Penitentiary on Christmas Day.

Devereux had been incarcerated for among other charges, his part in the September 1971 Maitland Penitentiary Riot. He was one of thirteen men charged in the torture-murder of two of his fellow inmates. Twelve of these men subsequently pleaded guilty to manslaughter charges. He was the only one to get off on an assault charge.

"D'Arcy Devereux is a 24-year-old inmate who has spent most of his time in jail since 1966, when he was convicted of manslaughter," said John Humphrey, a spokesman for Correctional Service Canada. "His juvenile records are sealed, but he was up to no good way before 1966.

He was released on mandatory supervision in 1972 after serving two-thirds of his sentence. He is currently serving time for a weapons offence while he was out on parole."

Devereux is the first inmate to escape from Maitland Super Max, custom-built to house the 'worst of the worst' The Super Max was forced to open early to accommodate an overflow of inmates after Maitland Penitentiary suffered heavy damages during the riot.

He is described as white, about 5 feet, 11 inches tall, with a muscular build and dark hair and eyes. He may be wearing a white doctor's coat. Devereux disappeared after overpowering the prison doctor. Questions about why Devereux was left alone with the prison doctor arose when news of his escape broke.

Although police are seeking the public's assistance, they warn people not to approach him. He is considered armed and dangerous.
Maitland Spectator, Dec 27, 1972

Chapter 1
The Dark Side of the Road

Boxing Day, 1972, east from Trenton

The morning sun came up, lit the Ivy Lea Parkway and caught him hiking east along the freshly cleared road. Like any quarry, he'd kept a sharp eye on the horizon all night long.

But it was okay. Because it was too early for anyone else and way too fucking cold. Bundled up in a parka and walking, he knew he wasn't going to freeze, but it sure felt like it. He'd spent the long, dark night hours telling himself that he looked more like an old man than a dangerous, escaped con. But even with his head buttressed against the wind, he couldn't hide his massive shoulders or the bulk of his muscles. If he ran into anybody with half a wit, he was as good as dead. Or they were. He had only one hope. Get out of Canada and fast.

Everything was going to be alright, he kept telling himself. Just go slow and steady and it would all fall into place. He'd clear his name and make a new life with his cousin Liza somewhere down in the States. Sure, he'd promised the prison psych and priest he'd forget her. On account that she was his cousin and it wasn't right. He really wanted to forget her, but he couldn't. Nothing ever really changed. Looking over his shoulder at the road he'd just covered, he still half-expected the past to come up and bite him in the ass.

He scanned the horizon again. The sky was cloudy. The sun wouldn't be out for long. Much as he hated to admit it, he'd formed habits in prison he couldn't break. For years, he'd told himself he marched to the beat of a different drummer, but he didn't. He was just like all the other bastards who'd done time and sworn to make good if they ever got a break. Look what happened the last time he got paroled. It was like he'd gotten punch drunk on freedom or something. Like some nutty politician or a celebrity with everything to lose, he just couldn't stay out of the news.

Liza had tried to help, but she couldn't. A girl like her, she must have thought she could reform him. What a mess. He'd broken her heart and his father's and for what? His chest swelled with a shout, but he didn't let it out. For a moment, he couldn't even breathe.

Maybe if he'd stayed away from the Wolfhounds like he was supposed to, but they were his friends from way back when. It was no secret to those who knew him: he'd loved trouble and excitement since he was in his teens. His friends were all the same. Except for Liza. He'd done a lot of thinking in segregation and there was a pattern here, alright. The same thing had happened in the prison riot, back in 1971. He'd been trying to help his old friend Rick Lowery, yeah, right. Much good that had done. The press had loved Rick, but not him. Herbert Yonge's news stories had helped. It didn't matter, though. Rick was practically a lifer. He'd gotten a transfer and ended up working in another prison library out west. *Ah, Jesus, Rick*, Dace thought, feeling a little rip in his chest.

He shouldn't let these memories destroy him. Because he was out, back on the road again. He'd plotted and connived for months. Never mind that he was still a marked man, inside or out. *It's Cornwall or bust*, he thought, concentrating on his clopping feet.

Sure, they'd tried to break him, but they hadn't gotten to him yet and they never would. He had too much to do.

They, yeah, *they*—the police, the guards, the authorities, the "concerned" public, the fucking press. On the road again, he was everything he'd ever wanted to be—young, unbroken, strong.

Okay and frozen, buck naked cold. Maybe if he burrowed into that bank of snow—like the Eskimos had. Yeah, right. What the hell did he know about Eskimos? They didn't even call them Eskimos anymore. Maybe they had more body fat than him. He had to keep on trucking or he'd freeze.

He tried cheering himself on. Nobody else was going to do it, that's for sure. *C'mon, go for it. Go, go, go. Make it up to Liza, make it up to*

2

Society, come back and tell your story to the Parole Board, what the hell. As if he had time for all this self-analysis crap out here in the freezing ass snow.

His hands tingled, so they weren't frozen yet. If he ran into a stranger, he could still punch him out. Or an enemy. He boxed his way along the Ivy Lea Parkway for the next mile or so, imagining he was socking the head guard's face.

He was a man accused of murder and soon to be on Canada's Most Wanted List, right up there with the likes of FLQ members Marc Charbonneau and Paul Rose and bank robber, Stephen Reid. He didn't know what made them tick and he didn't care, but he hadn't had much choice.

He'd seen the prison psych and the priest once or twice. They thought different. Well, of course they would.

Too bad the temperature had dropped so much overnight. The Melville bomb shelter had been equipped with damn near everything except boots in his size. And he was still way too close to Maitland, courtesy of his little detour to hang out with Liza at Stu Melville's place.

If he hadn't done that, he would have been home free by now. Down in the States, faking a new identity. If the Canadian police and guards caught up with him on this side of the border, they wouldn't fool around. Those guys were all cut from the same cloth, they were the kind of assholes who'd swear he had a weapon and shoot him in the back. Real men.

If he didn't die right away, they'd build a fire, crouch down on their fat haunches and wait. He'd heard stories and seen them in action, so he knew their type. The cold would do their dirty work, while he bled out in the snow. "Just watch," his old nemesis Savage would crow to his cronies while he rubbed his hands in glee, "I bet he's blood and water like the rest of us. I'm just going to sit myself down here and watch the boy freeze."

Dace's breath puffed out in front of him, but hey, that was good. He was still breathing. Anything to get his mind off freezing. For the next hour or so, he counted trees, boxed the empty air with his fists and drew them back up into his sleeves. Just like he did when he pumped iron or punched an exercise bag. Except it didn't work.

The worst place in the Super Max — the digger, the hole — had been a sauna compared to this. It was crazy. Rounding the next bend in the road, he almost missed his cellmates, the protection of the herd. He'd forgotten about winter. It was spring last time he'd gotten out and by then, he'd been inside for several years.

If he hadn't nicked a fur-lined parka from the Melville house, he'd have been dead by now, a frozen Ice Age man at the side of the road. Liza had made him put the parka on. Petty theft wasn't his style, but what the hell. They both knew he was a marked man in the prison doc's clothes.

The Melvilles' bomb shelter had been stocked with money, clothes and food. And booze. Liza had met him there, thank God. He'd worried for a while that they'd gotten their wires crossed. But she had hitchhiked from the university, straight to Trenton and the Melville house. Luckily for him, she didn't have anywhere else to go. She'd been so cold on Christmas Day and then so hot. His cousin, his... well, it didn't matter to her. Or him. Why the hell should it? They had more important things to worry about than their blood ties. They always had. It was nobody else's business anyway.

"I want my Christmas present," he'd whispered to her in the Melvilles' dark basement room. Though he couldn't admit it to himself or her, they were both scared. Scared of losing each other again. Scared of the soulless fucks after him, scared of the dark places in their own souls. The Melville residence was in the wrong direction from where he should have gone, but he had. He couldn't help himself and neither could she.

It was the same old dance. At first she didn't want to, but then she did. Well, who could blame her. He'd looked like hell, even after he'd hacked off most of his beard and hair. And she'd looked so small. He had almost felt like a rapist, doing it in a sleeping bag on the cold hard floor.

"I love you," she'd said, holding his face in her hands with her body arching to meet his.

She wanted to leave with him too. *Take me with you,* her eyes had begged with each thrust. He should have taken his time, but he'd rushed her along, like the prison guards, the police or the homeowners were about to burst through the door. As if. The Melville family had been having a party, doing their own thing. Everybody in town was there. Everybody except him and his cousin, his lover, Liza Devereux, of course. From upstairs at the front door, he could hear carolers singing: *Let it snow, let it snow, let it snow. Yeah,* Dace had thought as they launched into Good King

Wenceslas, *let it snow.*

Liza didn't hear the carolers. She was oblivious to everything except him. At first, she had looked prison-pale and wasted, but underneath her clothes, her body was still lush, a bit of a surprise. Visiting and supporting somebody in prison sucked it out of most people, but it hadn't gotten to her.

She would do anything for him and they both knew it. Except tell him the truth, apparently. She'd had a secret and for all he knew, she had been keeping things from him for years. Something for herself. Or maybe she'd just wanted to protect him from something real or imagined — when he should have been the one protecting her — because that's what a real man did.

The snow lay deep in the fields, but it was just a thin dusting on the icy right shoulder of the road. A plough had come through recently. He ran and slid, determined to ignore his soaked shoes.

He'd hitched a ride from Trenton to Maitland, but the dumb cluck had dropped him off in a bank of snow and then had the nerve to look disgusted, a concerned parent. "Where are your boots, fella?" he'd asked, as if a self-respecting, good old Canadian boy came equipped at birth.

Maybe if he got back onto the 401 or Route 2. Some place with lots of other hitchhikers. Holiday people. A busy place where he'd blend in with a legion of losers without wheels: the handicapped, the stupid, the loafers, the kind of people who just didn't pay their bills.

Straight people, people like his Dad, worked so hard to make a living. It floored him, but he was his father's son, so people said he was a good worker too. And he was. When he wanted to be. He didn't want to be another grease monkey, that's all. Cars and engines. Much as they used to fascinate him, they bored him stiff right now. He wanted to do something else. To go crazy, to live wild, just this side of the law. To reach the stars. To travel, to tear off to wide open spaces, the way he had on his bike. To take an airplane way up into the sky. To learn how to fly a plane, for God's sake. To make up, redeem himself, or at least forget about the bad stuff he'd done with his life.

The river on his right, a gleam of silver, caught his eye and from out of nowhere, his grade ten geography came back to him. He could almost see his textbook, which was strange, considering how little time he'd spent in school. He'd always had that kind of mind, though, a cache for odd bits of junk.

He remembered now. The St. Lawrence was like a highway through the heart of Canada. It flowed from Lake Ontario out to the Atlantic Ocean and lots of little places in between. The old guys—the pioneers—had used the river like a road. Especially in wintertime, when the river got rock hard, when and if—ha!—there wasn't too much snow.

Except walking on water—a river overlaid by ice—scared the bejesus out of him. The river looked solid enough, but it was also at least a foot deep in snow and underneath all that white fluff, who knew. *What lies beneath.*

The wind picked up from the river and slapped him in the face. He heard Liza then, clear as a bell. *For God's sake,* she screamed, *Run Dace, just run! I'm alright.*

I can't, he thought. Back in prison, he'd planned to run for days, but he hadn't factored in the extreme cold. The sooner he found shelter, the better. Except the only shelter he'd seen so far was some boarded up tourist cabins on the riverside of the road and a couple of cemeteries on the opposite side, deep in snow. No doubt the Ivy Lea Parkway was quite picturesque in summertime, but the leafless trees—maples and birches— offered little protection now.

Ever since he'd spent the summer with Liza, music had followed him everywhere. He heard it again: *The haunted frightened trees.*

He tucked his head further down on his chest, trying to suck in warmer air, and ended up with a sharp pain in his side.

He had no choice. He had to slow down. His breath came in short gasps while his heart tried to break out of his chest. It made him mad. Why the hell did people live way out here anyway? What were they trying to avoid? With massive granite cliffs to his left and a huge river on his right, he felt like a miner cut off from air. He'd learned lots of stuff from his buddies in jail, so he could break into a cabin, but then what? If he didn't make Cornwall by nightfall, he was as good as dead. Dirt Beard was there.

Their goal was Akwesasne, the Mohawk Indian Reservation. Dirt Beard had hung out in Cornwall since last fall, so he ought to know his way around by now.

The Reservation bordered both banks of the St. Lawrence River. Big as the river was, it froze solid from late December to March. Near

Cornwall, anyway. Dirt Beard said they could walk across the ice, a half a mile or less.

Dirt Beard was a three-pack-a-day smoker and the whacky-tobacky stuff he was dealing, he'd soon be a pothead too. "No problemo," he'd yelled into the phone, laughing and coughing. "It's just a mind game. Any retard could do it. Just pretend you're fucking Jesus Christ and you'll walk over water, I swear to God." That's how his boys got back and forth between Cornwall and Massena, New York, the place where they made the grass. Everybody smoked pot in jail, but it sounded kind of boring. What the hell could go wrong? He'd have to check. Smuggling marijuana sounded more like a misdemeanor than a criminal offence to him. If it had been guns or diamonds or something. Cocaine, maybe.

"Man," Dirt Beard had added, "you could drive a truck across that fucking ice!"

I bet, Dace thought now. Except this year, the best crossing was just outside the good old Cornwall Jail. Built to accommodate just forty to fifty felons, the old-timey jail currently held a hundred prisoners or more.

It sure beat walking across the Cornwall Bridge and messing with the American border guards or slipping through in somebody else's car. The Canadian guards weren't armed, but apparently the Americans had been packing guns since the War of 1812. A war Dace hadn't even heard of until now. God, who the hell had? *What a bunch of sore losers*, he thought, after he'd brushed snow off an historical plaque and read what it had to say.

He knew guards — knew all their slimy, conniving ways. "Why'd you come all the way up from Trenton?" the border pigs would ask him. "When you could cross at Hill Island or Johnstown?"

Unless they'd already gotten that picture, the stupid mugshot they'd taken when he got sent up at eighteen.

God help him, he hoped his face had changed.

Akwesasne, he repeated to himself, liking the sound of the name, though that's not what the locals called it. The Reservation went by many names. To his fellow Canadians in the provinces of Ontario and Quebec, it was known as Cornwall Island or St. Regis; it was only called Akwesasne on the American side.

Nobody expected him there. And that was the whole point. Some of his biking bros were in Cornwall doing a little of this and that, but few knew about his escape—yet. Judge Silverton and his cronies were such a fucking bunch of clueless saps. What the hell did Silverton expect when he kicked Dirt Beard and his Wolfhounds out of Maitland—that they'd just go away?

Whatever the Authorities—the coppers, the jailhouse administration and their flunkies, those pigheaded guards—thought about his "likelihood to reoffend," Dace was no fool. Well, not yet anyway. He couldn't stop shivering though. The son-of-a-bitch cold had settled into his bones. And why were there so many cemeteries? It looked like people just came here, plopped down and never left.

Hitchhiking past the Army base out of Trenton had been nerve wracking enough. He'd even seen an insane asylum down the road. Odd how so many institutions stacked up along the Canadian-United States border.

Who was trying to keep who out?

At least the 401 hadn't gone right up to the Maitland Supermax. The shiny new prison was located twenty miles outside his hometown, a small city with the same name. Maitland was also home to an army base, in addition to its cluster of jails.

"Let me out here," he'd said to the Montreal bound trucker who'd picked him up, but then the guy said he wasn't going into Maitland either. Claimed his eighteen wheeler was overweight, the liar. Liars always talked too much. If he wasn't freezing his ass off, he would have found out what the guy was really hiding.

So Dace lied too. Told the trucker he'd walk across the bridge near Gananoque, but he hadn't. *Keep them guessing* because the less people knew, the less they blabbed. Not that the driver gave a fuck. He was a long-distance trucker, lived his life on the road, but he was human. He'd wanted some company, that's all.

After getting dropped off near the bridge, Dace had doubled back. More snow had fallen and covered his tracks. With any luck, the trucker had probably taken off along Route 2. He wasn't supposed to, but there weren't any weigh stations there and he must have hoped that on a holiday there'd be no coppers.

Dace did too. He knew he had to keep walking or die, but he wondered about his stamina in this kind of cold. He'd lost some weight in jail. The pigs "forgot" to feed the prisoners in segregation sometimes.

Then trouble came, just like it always did, the sneaky bitch. He heard an engine, so he looked over his shoulder and sure enough, he had a car on his ass. She was slow moving, but still. She was bigger than him and no telling who was driving. A local? The OPP? He felt like taking a running leap into the St. Lawrence, where a bunch of bulrushes still poked through the half frozen water at the river's edge, but he couldn't give up this soon. *Steady, boy*, he coached himself, *steady*. For God's sake, it was probably just some busybody in a stupid old car. It was too soon for the police.

From the shoreline of the river, some overfed Canada geese gazed at him and honked. They were larger than he recalled: at least forty inches in length with distinctive black heads. They probably should have flown south, but they hadn't.

Like me, he thought.

Christ, he didn't have time for comparisons. Or what-ifs. He looked back again. He definitely wasn't imagining things. The car was still there, a blight on the fucking horizon. He ran a couple of yards, but he couldn't keep it up. His hands twitched. Maybe if he hijacked the car. Got the driver's license and registration, that's all he needed. Yeah, and what about the driver and people inside?

He slowed down a bit, so the car could catch up faster and he could think. The car was taking so long that his mind started to wander.

Let's go on down to Mexico, Liza used to say. She'd been thin and hyperactive, all nerves, but real focused too. She'd always wanted to do stuff, write books, go places. Butterfly hunt. Ride her motorbike, when she'd finally learned. And have babies, he kind of suspected — his. Through no fault of her own, she ended up at her grandmother's in Ireland when she was only fourteen. If he'd ditched his friends the bikers, if he'd forgotten about wanting to make just one more big score, she'd have given up everything.

From all her reading, she knew stuff like Canada geese mate for life, but all she'd wanted was him.

He used to think they were halves of the same whole, but they sure weren't twins. She called them soulmates, but it wasn't the same thing. Because she'd always be loyal to him, at least in her heart and mind. Even if she ended up sleeping with that little dick Stuart Melville and she would, she would, if she had any sense. She'd have another protector then and she'd always been so fucking sensible, except when it came to him.

Oh, Christ. He couldn't. Be loyal to her, that is. Physical monogamy appealed to him in theory — it just wasn't that practical. Girls drove him wild. The curve of a cheek, the thrust of a breast, the way they smiled. He'd been like this since he was nine or ten. Maybe if he hadn't spent so much time pulling on his wire inside. *What the hell*, he thought. The cold was really doing a number on his mind. What kind of jackass thought about sex with his balls freezing off and a car on his ass?

A little further out, the river looked less mushy, not that he planned to test the ice and see. Meanwhile, the closer the solitary car got, the more it squealed. When he smelt the car's exhaust, he knew he was in trouble. Big trouble. Maybe if he just stuck out his thumb? It was Boxing Day, so there wasn't a paper, but what if the car had a radio? He'd be on the news. His stomach turned over.

On Christmas Day, a man once wanted for murder escaped from jail.

"Once wanted." What a joke. Everybody — except his lawyer and Liza — thought he was guilty. And they still did. Probably his Dad did too.

With the rattling car almost on top of him, he made out a brown Buick station wagon with a male driver. Several heads bobbled behind him, like a row of jack-in-the-boxes. Just his fucking luck! If the damn driver had been alone, but a family man...

Just then the guy reached out and backhanded the nearest kid. Oh, yeah, he was a family man alright. The car hit gravel, but pulled back onto the road. Like maybe the guy fancied himself an expert driving on a slick road with one hand. Worst case scenario: he ploughed into a ditch or a tree. It was awfully early to be out and about with a bunch of youngsters; they must be headed east to some Boxing Day do.

Where the hell was the mother?

Dace edged closer to the river. If he didn't watch the driver, he was going to end up in the drink. His mind ran on. Police dogs would find him or he'd float out under the ice — all the way out to the Atlantic Ocean, he supposed.

Stories about drowning victims had always fascinated him. Those bodies they never found — had the people really drowned? Well, this was crazy talk. Nobody was going to find him, dead or alive. If he took control, got the hell out of here. Mexico—that's where he'd go, after he slipped across the border at Akwesasne into New York State. Yeah, Mexico—he'd infiltrate the locals and find out where the monarchs swarmed. Just like Liza had always wanted. Why not? He could do it. He could do anything, as long as he stayed out.

Christ, what he'd give to hear Dirt Beard's chopper—but fat chance in the middle of winter on a curvy, icy road like this. Behind him, the station wagon swerved on and off the pavement. Even Dace's own chopper, his Harley, would have a hard time hugging these curves.

Did the stupid bastard really have to drive at ten miles an hour though?

"C'mon, Man," he shouted back at the driver, the sound of his own voice scaring him a little when it echoed off the cliffs. *Stick to the road, Rover.* What an effing Nervous Nellie the guy was. Even Liza had gone faster on her Honda than that!

And then he felt the heat of the car's engine. The driver had gotten way too close, either because he hadn't seen him or he didn't care. The cliffs were on Dace's left and the river was on his right, very close to the road on a scenic route like this. Heated metal side brushed his parka, then the front bumper of the car buffed his rear, but he didn't care.

Let go, something in him said, so he did. One hundred and eighty pounds levitated straight into the air. He flew through the air with his limbs splayed out, a distance of five or six feet, while his mind did its best to protect him from his own mortality. He felt all-powerful and not the least bit afraid, like that daring young man in the old song on a flying trapeze. When he finally landed, it took a minute or so to realize he'd broken through thin ice in the river, where it was still shallow. How had he gotten here? Oh, yeah, that fucking car, that boat, that station wagon had hit him—that's what happened. Where the hell was it now? Had the bastard just taken off—hit and run? Said to his kids: "It's okay...I think I just hit a deer. It was on the wrong side of the road."

Maybe the driver had seen him though. Maybe he was after him! Maybe the coppers had sent him! Shit, he couldn't feel a thing. Not the cold, nothing. He couldn't hear anything either until he shook some water from his ears.

Reaching backwards with one hand, he felt for his parka hood. It had come clean off his head. It floated behind him, an anchor, a makeshift life preserver, tugging on his neck. Water had never felt so heavy. He had trouble lifting his head.

Get up, his dream Liza shouted, *get the fuck up! Christ,* he thought, finally coming to his senses and snatching at some frozen bulrushes near the shore. Several of the brittle plants snapped in his hands, but one or two held and he got out anyway, a sodden mess. His shoes squelched. As far as he could tell, he was still dry under the parka—the goddamn thing was probably waterproof—but his crotch and legs felt wet enough to freeze.

He'd been alone so long that the sound surprised him. "Daddy," a squeaky little voice pleaded, "Water, water, water! Take me home..."

Reluctantly, he turned his head in the direction of the voice, pretty sure what he was going to see. And he was right. The station wagon had ended up in the river too, but about ten feet further out from the shore. Cracks in a larger sheet of ice radiated out beyond the car. She was still upright, but another crack and the momentum of the water, if not the current, would push it and its kiddie cargo downstream.

Maybe. With his heart hammering, he tried to think, but he couldn't even move his feet.

Ah, Christ, it was too late. The small girl in the car took one look at him and screeched. Her voice carried across the water and up and down the empty road. His heart beat so fast, he could hardly breathe. No one could hear the little brat, he reassured himself. *Shush,* he signaled anyway. The car wasn't that far out. The people inside the car could get themselves out. He didn't want to. There was only one problem. If the little girl slipped into the water, they'd never find her.

This time when he opened his mouth, it worked. Something came out. "Stop doing that!" he roared. Moving, he meant. The other two kids looked pretty small too, but their combined weight might be enough to rock the car, even a great big boat like that. It sure as hell wasn't going to float.

Where the hell was the Dad? No way he'd gotten out. He might be knocked out, slumped over the steering wheel.

Oh, Christ, now the mouthy little brat was jumping up and down, a little she-devil with a halo of golden curls. Just as she held out her arms to him, the front of the station wagon took another nosedive. The kids fell back on their rears into a bench seat. When the license plate popped into view, Dace's stomach dropped some more.

Another lurch and the car's rear wheels would be airborne too. This time, the kids would be tossed into the front seat. The lucky ones. The little devils might have a minute or two to open the side windows and get out, if they were smart enough and they didn't freeze. Except the water pressure...and they looked kind of small. Oh, great, another brat had cranked down the window on the tailgate. A boy. He started yelling too.

Just then Dace felt a tingle in his legs and his feet started moving. He ran up the road. For a split second, he hesitated at the shore, but there was no time to test the ice. Placing one foot on the ice and then the other, he started slip-sliding. He reached the car in three slides and grabbed the tailgate, counter balancing it with his weight and hands.

The biggest kid locked eyes with him, like he wanted to grab onto him and pull him down, but Dace was prepared for that too. *Oh, no, you don't*, he thought. The boy's teeth were chattering hard enough to fall out. He wasn't wet yet, so he was probably just scared. He looked about ten or so, old enough and big enough to climb over the tailgate by himself, but maybe he couldn't see through all that damn hair in his eyes. The little girl had stopped screaming, but she was still emitting a kind of high-pitched squeal that pierced Dace's waterlogged ears.

"Mister," the boy begged. "Get us outta here."

Shush, Dace mouthed again. What if just talking rocked the car and they slipped from his grasp? Steadying the tailgate with his left hand, he grabbed the little screamer by the front of her dress and plucked her right out. He half-expected her dress to tear, but it held. Christ, she was light. Even in an oversized red velvet dress and a bulky white sweater, she couldn't have weighed thirty pounds.

Back, back, Dace jerked his head at the other kids, the boy and a second girl who looked a year or two older, but he didn't have to. A healthy sense of self-preservation had kicked in. The older kids either knew exactly what to do, or they were just too petrified to move. They shrank to the opposite side of the wagon and waited, their eyes glued to his face. *Save me, save me*, their eyes said.

The little girl in his arms had good instincts too. First off, she'd tried to strangle him, but when that failed, she tightened her tiny arms around his neck and swung onto his back, determined to get as far away from the whole sinking mess as possible.

Dace figured she'd forgotten her father, but she hadn't. "Daddy," she started whimpering until she summoned something or somebody up from the front seat. Dace wasn't sure it was human until he saw the eyes.

Blood dripped from the man's balding head into his eyes, but that didn't stop him from climbing over the driver's seat into the back with his fist curled and rabbit punching the boy. He looked more mad than scared.

"Get the hell out of here, you little chicken shit," he said, boosting his own flesh and blood over the tailgate with a knee to his rear.

Dace wondered about the kid's head, but it must have happened before because the boy knew how to fall. He slid down the back of the car and landed on his stomach, still in one piece. Dace was impressed. The boy lie there for a moment, looking a bit stunned.

"Crawl," Dace urged the boy when he finally started making little mewling sounds on the ice.

"Take him too," the father grunted, scooping up something else from the floor beside him and thrusting it into Dace's arms, before hauling himself out of the car.

Dace was so surprised that he nearly dropped this second bundle. It looked like a doll, but then the little thing opened its mouth and yawned. Christ, it was another kid—a baby! He'd never held one before. He stared at it and then tucked it under his right arm in a football hold. He needed to get down on the ice like the boy, but he couldn't, not with two squirming children in tow.

At least the little girl on his back had settled down a bit. "That's Vinnie," she said. "The new baby. He's nineteen days old. Our Mommy's sick. She cries more than Vinnie. She's mental, Daddy said."

Dace looked back at the car. The older girl still hadn't moved, but some people froze in a crisis. "What about her?" he asked the Dad.

"She's bad," his larger burden whispered.

"She's big enough to take care of herself," the father said, just before he whistled an old German shepherd from the front seat of the car. The dog scrambled with some difficulty over the bench seat, took one look at Dace and started nudging him between the legs.

"What about the presents?" the girl in the car asked, oblivious to yet another groan from the overburdened ice.

"Never mind them presents," the father yelled. "If you think I'm risking my arse for a BB gun and a couple of Barbie dolls, you're nuts."

Jesus, Dace thought, *this guy is loud enough to crack ice.* "Shush," he begged again, "shush."

The unburdened boy reached land first, but Dace and the man weren't far behind. Dace put the little girl down on a log with the baby in her arms. They weren't even wet. With the dog nestled at their feet, they looked like a Christmas card.

Against Dace's instincts, he almost started back for the older girl, but then he saw her out of the corner of his eye. At the last minute, she had climbed over the tailgate, dropped to the ice and started belly crawling too. She was only using her right forearm and hand to crawl. She wasn't hurt though. In her left hand, she clutched two little lady dolls by their legs. And she was mad, real mad. She had her father's looks for sure and maybe his temper.

That's the girl, Dace thought, watching her slide like a sleek, little otter across the ice.

"You," the father roared at the girl, knocking her back down, the moment she reached him and got to her knees, "I told you to stop fighting with your brother. Didn't I? Didn't I? Look at all the trouble you've caused... You're getting the belt right now!"

Dace and the older children stared, transfixed by spittle dripping from the corner of the man's mouth. For an old guy, he sure had lots of energy.

"Jesus Christ, Mister," Dace muttered. "Take it easy." But with the kids all howling and the dog barking, nobody heard him or another vehicle up a ways.

From the way the man unbuckled his belt and pulled it off with a snap, Dace could tell he'd done it many times before. But somehow in his effort to reach his daughter, he tripped over Dace's foot and pitched forward onto the frozen ground. When he lifted his head, his mouth was bleeding too. Dace felt a jolt of satisfaction. The sight of the blood made him feel like doing a whole lot more.

His oldest girl forgotten, the man glared at Dace. "You..." he said, but he didn't get out another word. He spat out something, a tooth maybe, into his cupped hands. The belt lay discarded, a snake on the road.

Dace looked around. What the hell was he doing here? He'd better get the hell out of here and fast. That car—or whatever it was—was definitely getting closer. He bent down over the smallest girl and spoke real fast. She was only four or five, but she was a smart little thing. She might remember what she heard.

"Don't get Daddy into trouble. Say the accident wasn't his fault because he was drinking," he whispered in her little shell ear.

Chapter 2
Mrs. Melville and the Police

Boxing Day, 1972, Melville residence, Trenton

Mrs. Adelaide Melville seized both police officers by their forearms and pulled them into her hallway. A tall, stout woman, she had the strength. Maybe she recognized them, Liza thought, or maybe she just didn't want to leave them out on the front porch while her neighbors got a good gawk. Trenton was still a pretty small place, less than 15,000 people.

"I know your mother," Mrs. Melville said, staring at the male officer with her protuberant eyes until he turned a mosaic red. "She's from the other side of town, but we were both in the Garden Club a few years back. She was so proud when you got into the police academy. She showed your picture all around."

There were two police officers, a man and woman. The red-faced man was a foot taller than Mrs. Melville, kind of beefy, and they were both younger than her by at least two decades. From the look on the policeman's face, Mrs. Melville could have been Chicken Little, flapping and clucking around her house.

The commotion had just woken Liza up from her short winter's nap. *Good move, Mrs. Addie Melville,* she thought. *Let's put the cops on the defensive for a change.* Bleary eyed and shivering, she'd crawled out of bed and was standing in the doorway of the guest bedroom down the hall. With any luck, nobody would notice her until she figured out exactly what was going on. No point in scaring Mrs. Melville, especially if Mel had neglected to tell his mother that she was there. *Surprise, Mommy!* She scrunched up as tight as she could.

But the policeman was undeterred. "My name is Jerry Mann," he said, ignoring Mrs. Melville's chitchat, "and this is Officer Lois Dempsey."

Liza squirmed a little, feeling like a mouse who'd crept in from the cold. There was only one reason the police would come to the Melville residence. They were looking for her cousin Dace Devereux. Dace, who had left her in the basement less than six hours ago.

Lois Dempsey, the female officer was just a girl herself, a plain looking girl with the waist-less, squared figure of a man, but a girl still. She probably looked a whole lot different in some makeup and a skirt.

Mrs. Melville didn't respond. She didn't ask the police officers into her living room either. She couldn't. She had a habit of speaking with her head cocked to one side, so Liza could see her profile. She looked like she was taking everything in—the badges the police flashed in her face, their names, their stated purpose—but Liza knew she wasn't.

But Mrs. Melville's mouth tried. Her lips twitched until she finally said, "I don't understand. Is something wrong? My husband should be here." A little frantically, she looked behind her like she expected him to spring out from somewhere. *I'm home, honey. I'll take care of you.* The black house phone on her entrance table caught her attention. She picked up the receiver and dialed, but maybe her fingers were greasy. She couldn't get the phone to work. It was just after ten a.m.

"And my son should be here too," she added. "He's almost twenty-one."

Oh, God, Liza thought, *where's Mel?* No way he'd slept through this racket. Judging by the state of the kitchen which Liza could see from the guest bedroom, Mrs. Melville had probably been pulling apart the remains of the Christmas turkey for leftovers when the front doorbell rang. The bell had gone on and on.

Liza had to give the police some credit. They waited patiently. Mrs. Melville tried dialing twice more before she finally gave up and slammed the receiver back down in its cradle. What was she going to do?

"It's okay, Mrs. Melville, it's okay," Lois Dempsey said so soothingly that even Liza believed her for about ten seconds. "We don't need Dr. Melville. We just want to ask you a few questions."

"Dear God," Mrs. Melville muttered, "My husband's over sixty years old. Why does he have to work in Emergency on Boxing Day?"

"Never mind," Jerry Mann said, scratching his bullet-shaped head with a pencil and looking down at a grubby little notebook in his right hand, "Nice man—my mother's been to him a couple of times—but we don't need Dr. Melville. We're looking for an escaped convict called D'Arcy Devereux..."

Liza stuffed her knuckles into her mouth and bit down hard. By this time in the morning, she was sometimes starving and nauseated, but not today. Fear cancelled everything. She was just scared.

"The police bulletin said that he's twenty-four years old with dark brown eyes and hair and that he's about six feet tall. He was wearing a doctor's white jacket when he disappeared. Oh and he's armed and dangerous, he has a knife. Lois," he said to his partner, "show her that picture."

Mrs. Melville looked at the felon's picture—of Liza's cousin, Dace Devereux of course. Liza didn't have to see it. How many escaped convicts matching Dace's description were loose on Boxing Day? In Canada, hey. No doubt the photo made him look desperate enough—like some kind of outlaw biker or a confirmed thug—but Mrs. Melville hadn't seen him before. Not in Trenton anyway.

Mrs. Melville didn't touch the picture. Instead, she shook her head, scrubbing at her hands with a tea towel she had hanging from her waist. "Was his picture in the paper? He looks a bit like one of those men charged in those horrific penitentiary murders last year," she said, "but I don't recall meeting him. Why would I? We don't mix with... And why on earth would he come here?" she asked.

Oh, God, Liza thought. Dace had taken such a risk coming to the Melville house to see her one last time. He was crazy, crazy just like her and a risk taker through and through. Why? And what in hell was he doing now? How far could he have gotten? *Pretty far,* a little voice inside her crowed, *with clowns like these in hot pursuit...*

"Well, he's Liza Devereux's cousin and she's here, right?" Jerry Mann persisted.

Mrs. Melville looked bewildered. "Well, yes, she is, but how did you know that? It certainly was a surprise to *me*. My son dragged the girl home at Halloween, so naturally I thought she'd go home to her family at Christmas, but she didn't..."

Lois Dempsey raised her eyebrows. "Really," she said. "What kind of girl doesn't go home for Christmas?"

A bad one, Liza thought.

"Yes, well," Mrs. Melville continued, "I think she's estranged from her family. Because of a divorce or drink or something, I can't really say. Or maybe it's her mother who's not right in the head. It's unfortunate and I'm sure it's not the poor girl's fault, but still... She's old enough to make her own decisions. She'll just have to pull up her socks and make her own way. I'll give her this much though—she's never breathed a word and it's not the kind of question I like to ask...Mel tried to tell me about her, but it wasn't the kind of thing I wanted to know..."

"Mrs. Melville..." Lois Dempsey said.

"No, well," Mrs. Melville rushed on, "like I said, Liza Devereux just showed up here yesterday—late—very late. I didn't even realize she was here until this morning when I passed the guestroom on my way to the bathroom. I heard something that sounded like a sob, or maybe somebody was retching and the toilet was running, so I..."

Jerry Mann interrupted her with what probably passed for a smile. "We have our ways," he said. "The Maitland police have been searching for both Dace and Liza Devereux high and low since yesterday. Listen, we'd like to talk to both the Devereux girl and your son...uh, your youngest son is Stuart "Mel" Melville, right? Our records indicate both he and Liza are second year students at Maitland U..."

Mrs. Melville stared at her visitors again, on much firmer ground now. Or so it seemed to Liza. Maybe because it was one thing for the police to look for a convicted criminal, quite another for them to investigate Mrs. Melville's son. Her boy had never done anything wrong. She had the family home movies and the school reports to prove it. She and Dr. Melville had shown all their home movies to Liza at Halloween. *See, we're normal.*

"Your records?" she scoffed. "But why are you collecting information on an ordinary citizen like my son?"

20

"Mrs. Melville, can you please just answer the question?"

"Yes, of course," Mrs. Melville said. "My son's a student at Maitland University," she confirmed, standing up a little straighter. "It's the closest university to Trenton, so there was no need for him to go too far from home. His Dad bought him a car so he could get back and forth. A brand new Datsun. It's such a safe car. I don't know what the girl's doing there. At the university, I mean. My son said she got a scholarship, but I find that hard to believe... She's hardly said a word when she was here unless it was some of that Women's Libbers stuff. Drove Dr. Melville nuts."

"Maybe she's doing her Mrs.?" Lois Dempsey winked.

"Yes, maybe," Mrs. Melville agreed, "But not with my son if I can help it." Brightening a little, she must have winked back at the police girl who gave her a small smile. "That boy's going to be a doctor just like his Dad..."

"I'm sure," Lois Dempsey said, bending down to knock some crusted snow off her boots onto to the Melvilles' Oriental runner, while the male officer just stood there and watched his melt. "Well, it's 10:30 a.m. What time does your stellar student get out of bed?"

Mrs. Melville looked down at the spreading puddle on her hardwood floor and sighed. "I'm not sure I care for your tone, Miss. You don't look much older than him," she said, dropping her tea towel to absorb the policeman's melting snow before going to take a look down the hallway.

Or at least that's what it sounded like she was doing from the clip-clop of her shoes. Agitated, Liza had already edged back into the bedroom, taken off the blue jeans she'd slept in and was pulling a rumpled granny dress over her head. What if the police could smell Dace on her? Mel hadn't, but... *Oh, shush,* she told herself. *They're not dogs.*

"Mel," Mrs. Melville called, raising her voice just slightly. "Get up and tell your guest to come out here too."

Liza came back to her post in the doorway, but that was as far as she went. She wasn't going anyplace else in this house without Mel. At least he wanted her here.

The police looked down at the floor and snickered. "You're not letting your son shack up with some girl here, are you?" Jerry Mann said.

"Yeah, my mother certainly wouldn't let me do that," Lois Dempsey said. "Not when I lived at home..."

Mrs. Melville came back to them and picked up the soaked tea towel. "I'm sure," she said, snapping out the towel and then bunching it up in her hands. "Like I said, somebody was in the guestroom the last time I checked and when I went into the bathroom, Mel had left me a little note to say his friend Liza Devereux had arrived and he couldn't get the toilet stopped. He's such a thoughtful boy. Nothing like her. Can you imagine just showing up at somebody's place unannounced?"

"Maybe your son and the girl had just had a lover's spat and she wanted to make up..." Lois Dempsey suggested.

At this point, Mrs. Melville must have given her a look that would have quailed most people—in the past, it certainly had Liza—and shook her head. "I don't think so," she said, "And I don't know what time the girl got here, but it must have been the middle of the night. As you're no doubt perfectly aware—the whole neighborhood was invited and half of Trenton besides—we had a party here last night and my husband and I didn't get to bed until after one ourselves... Sorry, the place is still kind of a mess."

"How much does your son really know about this girl Liza Devereux, though? How long has he been seeing her?" Jerry Mann asked while Lois Dempsey stood there and stared at Mrs. Melville, no doubt so she could evaluate her reactions and get a good read.

Mrs. Melville's profiled nostril flared a little, but she composed her face. "Not for long. I don't know where you're getting this lovers' stuff from, though. They're just friends," she said. "Mel met Liza during Freshman Week, but I don't think he was really "seeing" her. They were both just nineteen." The damp spot on the floor drew her eyes again. "Would you mind taking off your boots?" she asked, just as the police girl started pawing through the mail on her entrance table. "Uh, Miss, I don't think you have the right..."

"Actually, we do," Jerry Mann said, looking like he had every intention of clumping through the entire split-level Melville residence, snowy boots and all. "We have every right if we think a crime is in progress or there's an escaped convict hiding in your house. Was that a backdoor that I just heard slamming? Because it won't do you any good. We've got another officer out in your yard. Nice house, but I don't like the way it backs onto two streets."

"Mel!" Mrs. Melville begged over her shoulder again. She turned

22

back towards the officers with a small, careful smile and addressed her remarks to Jerry Mann. "Kids. You're young, so if you've got a child, he's probably still pretty small. Didn't I hear your mother say that you had one on the way when you got married last year? Yes? Well, at least you weren't a teenager. It's when you're fourteen or so that trouble usually starts. If it does. Mel's been pretty good. Or he was until Liza Devereux came along. He'll be here in just a minute…you'll see…"

As if on cue, Mel came out of the kitchen and into the hall, but his mother didn't hear him.

Liza saw him though and he saw her too. *Stay back*, he motioned her.

"Ma'am," Jerry Mann said when Mel appeared behind his mother's back. "He's here."

Mrs. Melville spun around and regarded her boy. He was wearing his blue jeans, but no shirt. She reddened. "For God's sake, Mel, can't you put a shirt on?" she sputtered.

"I was just letting the dog out the backdoor," he said with an apologetic smile. "You know Liza's allergic, Ma. She's been sneezing all night. What's going on?" Liza knew that he had never been in trouble with the law before, so he turned from his mother and stared at the officers, cheeky and undeterred.

Both the officers and the Melvilles started speaking at the same time, but then Liza emerged from the hall too, barefoot and disheveled. She didn't dare wait any longer. She had thought briefly of fleeing out the backdoor after the dog, but there was no point. She certainly wouldn't get far. Besides, she was in absolutely no condition to run.

Jerry Mann and Lois Dempsey looked her up and down. *That's right, guys, like I'm the scum of the earth*, she thought. She tucked her bare feet under the hem of her dress. She still had dirt on her feet from the cement floor in the basement and she was freezing cold. She had no desire to see anybody—not Mel, not his mother, not the police. In the bedroom mirror, her nose and eyes had looked red, but with any luck, maybe they'd just think she had a cold.

"Is your name Liza Devereux? Are you D'Arcy Devereux's cousin?" Jerry Mann asked.

Lois Dempsey looked genuinely puzzled. "We have your picture, but it's much prettier," she said thoughtfully. "You must be real photogenic."

Yeah, so photogenic that I look better in a picture than I do in person, Liza thought.

"I told you she's not much of a talker," Mrs. Melville said.

"Speak up, girl," the policeman said. "A good thing we didn't have to fetch you because if you had resisted an officer..." He didn't finish his sentence. "Where's D'Arcy Devereux?" he demanded.

I don't know! Liza thought. "I don't know," she said aloud, crossing her thin arms over her chest and immediately drawing his attention to her breasts. "What's he done? He's in lockdown, isn't he? For no good fucking reason at all..."

Standing just behind her, Mrs. Melville gasped. "Liza," she cautioned her, her face paling. "Your language—really, my dear, just answer the officers' questions. They're here to help. And you don't know anything about this cousin, right? Because Mel and I certainly don't..."

"Yeah, Dace is in solitary," Mel volunteered eagerly. "Liza hasn't seen him in months. I haven't either, but it was kind of cool when we visited him last year. I'd never been to a prison before. I had no idea conditions were so primitive. Christ, what an eye opener..."

"Really, dear," Mrs. Melville said, "Surely you don't expect these officers to appreciate this kind of talk. Prison isn't supposed to be comfortable..."

While they were speaking, Jerry Mann had circled Liza. Without warning, he grabbed her by the hair and yanked her head back, forcing her to look in his eyes, but it was Mrs. Melville who yelped.

"You're lying, you little tramp," he said, giving her head a sharp little jerk. "You know where he is. You're his lover, the report said."

Mrs. Melville raised her hands to her mouth, perhaps to stifle another sound. Her eyes widened like either she didn't believe what she was seeing or she couldn't believe what she had just heard. "Cousins?" she repeated.

Lois Dempsey smiled like she was watching a damn good show.

"Stop that, you—!," Mel said, reaching out his hands to Liza and wincing. "So they're cousins, so what. The last time I checked, that wasn't a crime in Ontario and even if it was, I doubt you have any proof..."

"What—it's not a crime to have a relationship with your own

cousin? Well, maybe. But it's not right, dear, it's not right," Mrs. Melville said. "I'm sure it's incest or something."

Mel ignored her. "Let her go," he said to the police. "I think you need a warrant, but suppose my mother and I give you permission to search the house…"

"No," Mrs. Melville said. "We're certainly not going to do that…I'm not having my house torn apart."

"For the sake of due diligence," Mel plowed on while his mother frowned, "Because we certainly don't have anything to hide and this sure looks like police brutality to me. I was just wondering, though. If this is what you guys do when we're here—what do you do when we're not around?"

Jerry Mann snickered again. "Never mind, son. You're the doc's son, so you've got nothing to worry about because you're not a murderer or an escaped convict, right? We're just cooperating with the Maitland police, that's all. Doing our jobs. You want police protection, don't you?"

"Dace isn't a murderer," Liza said, refusing to rub her head though her entire scalp burned and her eyes were watering. "You've got that wrong."

"Well, my boy Mel certainly isn't!" Mrs. Melville said, her voice rising. "The idea that he's even been visiting a common criminal! I don't believe it. He's never even had a traffic ticket! Nobody in our family has."

"We'll take you up on your offer to search the house, though. Just in case. We're pretty sure that the Devereux character came this way…"

"There were a lot of people here last night, but we knew them all and none of them were armed and just for the record, I didn't offer to let you search my house…"

"A trucker dropped off a man matching the escaped convict's description and it turns out that the convict's cousin is here too. How's that for a coincidence? Maybe he stayed and you didn't know it? After all, you didn't know his little rag-tag girlfriend was here…" Jerry Mann grabbed Liza's hair again, but she was ready for him this time and it didn't hurt as much.

"Stop that right now," Mel said again, "Or you'll have to get the hell out of here."

Mrs. Melville grimaced, but then she stepped back to let the police access her house. "Well, as long as you don't break anything, I guess it's alright. Also, I'd really appreciate if you didn't hurt the girl in my house," she said.

"Or anywhere else! Would you mind letting go of her, please?" Mel said.

"Would you like some coffee?" Mrs. Melville asked.

"Yes, that would be grand," Jerry Mann said, suddenly letting go of Liza and shoving her so fast at Mel that they almost banged heads.

Mrs. Melville stared at Liza in Mel's arms with distaste and touched her own carefully coiffed hair. She must have just had it done at the hairdresser's for the party. Every upswept hair was still in place. "It's a good thing you have so much hair," she remarked to Liza while still patting her own.

Mel had wrapped his arms around Liza while she faced forward, with her heart still racing in her chest. She could still feel the policeman's hands on her upper arms.

"I don't think you'll find anything, though," Mel said, looking at the police officers over the top of Liza's head.

"Oh, we always find something," Jerry Mann promised.

"I bet," Liza said.

Lois Dempsey gave Liza a dirty look.

"You're one bold girl," she said. "You really are. We're just doing our jobs, Miss, and we do them good."

Mel and Liza sat down on the edge of the couch in the living room, while his mother fetched two matching mugs of coffee from the kitchen after asking the police how much milk and sugar they would like.

The police searched the living room and the adjacent dining room first. "Don't move," they said as they exited the room with Mrs. Melville bringing up the rear, an anxious expression on her face.

Mel took Liza's hand. "Liza," he whispered in her ear as soon as his mother was out of sight. "He wasn't here, was he? You came in through my window last night with your little bag and you were crying..."

"No, I wasn't," Liza said, jerking out of his grasp and rubbing her scalp. "And Dace wasn't here either. Where do you think I kept him — in your driving shed with that old sled? I couldn't go home for Christmas, that's all and I got lonely. I told you, my mother's place is too small and uh, Uncle Norm's place isn't safe..."

"Not safe?" Mel shook his head. "Why—because the police are looking for Dace there too? So then you knew that Dace had escaped, but you didn't think to mention this to me?"

Liza closed her eyes and folded her hands in her lap. She started out speaking slowly and carefully, but the minute she started to lie, her voice picked up speed. *Careful*, she told herself anyway, *careful*. "Sure I knew," she said. "I was still in the student residence, so when Dace escaped, his lawyer tracked me down there. He said the police were checking out everybody: both my parents, Dace's Dad and that I should turn Dace in. He acted like I had helped Dace, but I hadn't. He...I don't know how he escaped or where he went. Um, they probably checked everybody he knew and you were on his visitor's list. I was frightened, so that's why I came here..."

"That still doesn't explain why you didn't tell me..."

Liza sighed. Oh, God, so many lies. She was going to have trouble keeping them all straight. "It was so late last night," she said. "I was going to mention his escape, but then you fell asleep..." And he had fallen asleep too, with his head in her lap, leaving her to slip away into the next door guestroom a little later.

"And you really don't know where he is?"

"No," Liza said. "And I'm really sorry I brought this trouble on your house... It's the last thing I wanted. Your mother...well, never mind. Please just believe me. "

One hour and twenty minutes later, the officers came back to the living room with Mrs. Melville still trailing them, but looking quite relieved.

Because it didn't look like they had found much until Lois Dempsey suddenly reached into her jacket and pulled out a small plastic bag that contained some tobacco-like matter. She held up her prize and waved it in the air. "Anybody been using that bomb shelter in the basement lately?" she asked.

Mel looked at Liza who stared straight ahead. "No," they said in unison.

Mrs. Melville couldn't help herself then. She started crying. Liza was amazed that she'd held up this long. And impressed. Mrs. Melville was one tough lady. If it had been her mother... Or even herself. She'd probably be bawling her eyes out, telling everything she knew.

"Oh, Mel," Mrs. Melville said, "you know what this means."

Jerry Mann reached behind him and opened the front door. He looked at Mel who still had an arm around Liza and directed his parting shots at him. "Listen to your Mum. You hiding anything, boy and it's bye-bye medical school for you. We found enough pot in that bomb shelter to put you away for a few years."

Lois Dempsey pointedly ignored Liza and spoke to Mel too. "On the other hand, if you suddenly remember anything—or if she tells you anything—just give us a call," she said, holding out her business card.

Liza half hoped Mel would take the card and tear it into tiny bits, but he didn't. Instead, he politely stuffed it into his jeans pocket, just before Lois Dempsey added: "You won't be the first poor sap who's gotten used, but it looks like you've got the most to lose..."

"Don't you want to question the girl down at the police station?" Mrs. Melville asked.

"Mother!" Mel exploded.

Jerry Mann opened the front door. "We'll let ourselves out, but don't tell us how to do our business, Ma'am. We don't have time to question her right now, but if she leaves Trenton without checking with us first, we'll know..."

"Yes," Lois Dempsey said. "We'll know. Sorry, I guess that means you're stuck with her for a few days..."

Mel stood up and pulled Liza to her feet too, but the police were fast. They made it through the front door and pulled it closed behind them.

"Kiss my ass," Mel said, aiming a kick at the door.

Mrs. Melville pulled him back and stuffed a pile of newspapers into his hands. "Really, Mel, your language," she said automatically as she finished tidying the living room, no doubt eager to eradicate any sign of her latest visitors.

Liza's own manners kicked in too. Much as she disliked the woman, she started helping her.

"So," Mrs. Melville said to Liza as they put the room back to rights, including the newspapers and the *Time* magazines that the police had scattered, "what do you really know?"

Liza sucked in her breath. "Nothing," she said as she put her stack of *Time* magazines into date order. "My cousin Dace wasn't here. I didn't even know he'd escaped," she added, ignoring the sharp intake of Mel's breath, echoing hers. "I didn't. Why does everybody keep asking me? Oh, God, I wonder where he is? And also, while we're on this subject, I haven't slept with him. He's my cousin, for God's sake, not that such a thing is a crime in this country anyway, it's just that I wouldn't, he wouldn't and he's a Catholic you know…." *Stop, you're babbling,* she told herself.

Mrs. Melville looked at her, the same way she had looked at the police, like she was an intruder hell bent on destroying her lovely home. *You lie and lie,* her eyes said. *And if there's any justice in the world, you'll pay someday.* "Well, never mind," she said briskly. "I'm sure your family wouldn't put up with such a thing — that they'd talk you into doing what's right."

"If they knew," Mel muttered under his breath.

Chapter 3
Cornwall Bound

The wind roared and sculpted little snow castles, but he kept on walking. As if he had a choice. *Unidentified man freezes to death on Ivy Lea Parkway...* They'd figure out it was him pretty quick and rush to inform his next of kin. *Escaped convict D'Arcy Devereux's father refuses to believe he's dead...* If he was real lucky, the animals would leave him alone because they were hibernating or something. *My son's way too strong, convict's Dad says...It's not him.*

Ah, wintertime in Canada. He was way down in eastern Ontario where the country bordered on New York state, but still. Stuck in solitary, he'd obsessed about his wasting muscles, but his prison built body was still a well-oiled machine. It kept on going and going, doing what it ought to do. Nobody was going to fool with him. He plunged on through the cold, hard darkness, a shaken figurine in a glass globe.

For all he knew, he was walking in a circle, headed straight back to jail. For his own sanity, he stopped at every crossroads, rested a little and tried to memorize the signs. While there was still enough light to see, but not long enough for him to freeze. He almost welcomed the tingling in his fingers. His feet were numb. The cold had the blunt, cutting edge of a dull axe. If he lost a toe, he wouldn't even be able to tell.

Mallorytown Landing was the next dot on his mental map and then Brockville and Prescott. Well, okay. That made sense. Maybe he should cross the border at Prescott, make up some story. Except in all his twenty-four years, he'd never crossed the Canada-US border and he couldn't now—not without a fake ID. Most law abiding Canadians didn't need one in 1973, but he would. Unless he faked out a guard or got a pardon.

Fat chance.

Nobody mentioned stuff like this when you got sent to jail, but it was true. You lost way more than you knew. The Wolfhounds, his biking bros could help him get a fake ID, but he wouldn't need one at Akwesasne. That's what the guys said and they ought to know. He liked that.

Akwesasne, the Indian reservation—that twenty hectare maze of islands and hidden inlets spanning the Ontario, Quebec and New York state borders—was sprawling and notoriously hard-to-police. Hard-to-police! He liked that too.

He still had the two hundred bucks his cousin Liza had lifted for him from the Melville house, but it was a long way to Mexico and an even longer time before he dared contact his Dad. He scowled just thinking how that conversation would go. *Yeah, Happy New Year, Dad.*

His father would help him, though, no matter what the cost. He always had. *You've got the wrong boy. My son's not like that. He was with me the whole time...*

Liza would lie too.

It must be nearly noon now, but the sun looked like it was still struggling to come up. The more he walked, the dizzier he felt. Maybe if he just lie down for a moment and slept... But he couldn't. And he didn't need to, he reminded himself. Out of sheer exhaustion, he'd copped a couple of hours of sleep with Liza last night in a stranger's house. *Go,* he thought he heard her say, but she was back in Trenton with baby face Mel, just where she ought to be.

He watched himself, as if from a distance, putting one foot in front of another. As long as he didn't think about it, his feet moved. What was wrong with him? Liza was safe in Trenton, safer than she'd ever been with him. She was a marshmallow, a...well, just on the outside. She was a lot stronger than she looked. She'd stuck by him for years.

He'd pulled the fur-edged hood so closely around his face that he had almost no peripheral vision, but he could still see straight ahead. A white clapboard house with red trim popped into view. The place looked more promising than all the lonesome cabins and cemeteries he'd passed so far. There was nothing coming from the chimney and no dog barking in the yard. No cars either. If anybody was inside the house, they were in there alone. The tumbledown barn beside the house didn't look too cozy, but it might do. He sure as hell didn't want to get caught breaking into somebody's house and add that to his rap sheet, which was already half a mile long. Mostly bullshit institutional charges, not that he gave a fuck.

Just a little sleep and then when it got dark again at four thirty or five, he'd hitch another ride. Traveling on the main highway, he'd hit Cornwall by seven. He expected a lot more traffic on the road by then, people coming back early to get ready for what was left of their work week, Wednesday through Friday and on Saturday, all those big New Year's Eve parties.

Christ, it was a long time since he'd had a drink. He'd never felt so dry in his life. Every now and then, he scooped some clean snow from a low hanging tree branch and packed it into his mouth, but it didn't help much. Nothing would be open on Boxing Day either. Maybe in Brockville or Cornwall, before he got to Akwesasne, he'd find a bar or a liquor store, an LCBO. They'd open up tomorrow for sure. Both towns were almost big enough to get lost in. He'd have to change his looks, though.

Maybe if he bleached his hair and got a cowboy hat.

For now, he was just going to try and get into that barn, burrow down into some hay and sleep. *Christ,* he thought, irritated by a jolt of adrenalin when he stumbled over a rock hidden in the snowy field, would they shoot him or just handcuff him or what? *What do you think, dumbass! They'll nail you with a bullet in the back or the gut.* Red blood on white snow, white snow on... He looked up and tried to focus on the barn, almost blinded by the snow's reflective light.

Crossing the road and cutting across an open field in the snow took longer than it should have, but the door to the barn opened easily enough. Once inside and out of the wind, he felt dumb with warmth. The hay, even the remnants of some ancient manure, smelled pretty good too. Sweetish, like the field at the family farm where he'd first met Liza.

Wait, what the hell was that? It sounded like a girl's laughter. He looked around, all through the cattle stalls and up in the hayloft, but no one was there, just a family of field mice that scattered and ran. He lie down, burrowed deep into the hay until he was almost on the bare floorboards and was instantly asleep.

But he didn't sleep well. *Dace!* the police screamed, *Yeah, you, D'Arcy Devereux! We got you surrounded. And we got your little cousin too.*

******

He slept longer than he should have. His feet had worked their way up and were poking out of the hay. An old woman woke him up. What was she doing here in the hayloft? What was he? He rolled over and eyed the bottle in her hands, forty ounces of Seagram's Gold. It sparkled. Was she going to hide her bottle in the hay or crown him with it? He couldn't tell from the look on her face. People never behaved like he expected.

She looked the belligerent sort, not quite savvy enough to be scared, but used to taking care of her own place. The man she lived with — if she did — was bound to be the useless, feckless sort. He knew that kind of man. Prison was full of them.

The old lady glowered at him, like a mouse she had trapped with her broom. "Go on, you. Git out of here. Just git," she screeched, prodding him in his rear with the stick end of her broom. Dace was used to the noise men make, but he couldn't stand hers. Her shrill woman's voice hurt his ears. And it made him mad. Something was wrong here. She was supposed to be scared of him.

He jumped to his feet and tried to stare her down, but it didn't work. She staggered a little, but held her ground. His own grandmother came to mind, though Granny Debo had certainly been a much tidier sort. He hadn't seen a real old woman for a long, long time. Few people got old Inside.

Playing for time, he took a closer look at her and any resemblance to Granny Debo vanished. Why did the old girl's skin look so papery thin? And why did she have so many broken veins interspersed with the wrinkles on her face? As she tightened a heavy man's coat around her, a smell of alcohol wafted off her and then he knew. She was a big time boozer for sure. She might even be younger than she looked, a fine figure of a woman wasted inside her ballooning coat. Inside his zippered parka, he felt himself stiffening while the blades of a stolen pair of scissors grazed his chest. *Down boy*, he scolded himself, *down. Smarten up*. Ah, shit, he'd miscalculated. Somebody else must be in the house. Why the hell else would the old woman come out here to hide her Christmas chug?

"Get out of here," she repeated, coming closer, her breath steaming

34

out of her horsey face. He couldn't help himself then. Everything he'd learned in prison took over. *Mind your back, guys.* Without thinking, he grabbed the bottle from her, leapt from the hayloft and ran.

In outraged disbelief, "He took my bottle," she told everybody, the police first, with their dogs sniffing at the hay and then the reporters with their pens and papers and their eyes all lit up. "I fell down. No, he didn't knock me down, but he left me flat on my arse! Just in case you're wondering, I'm no spring chicken anymore. My bones are like chalk. And he looked like such a nice boy too. At first I thought it was young Sammy from down the road, sleeping off some stuff he got off his Mum and Dad, so "git out" I said and he got…"

"Did he hurt you?" somebody in the crowd of reporters asked.

"What? Well, no," she said derisively, "of course, he didn't hurt me — he wasn't going to hurt me — or I wouldn't have spoken to him at all. I get a feeling about somebody and I'm usually right. What? Can you just speak up one at a time — kind of take turns like you used to do in school? That's right, I used to be a schoolteacher before I — what's it to you? No, like I already told you — it was dark; I couldn't see which way he went. It looked like he streaked straight across the road to the river, but that can't be right. That river might look frozen, but you'd be a damn fool to walk on it even at this time of year, especially around here. If he went that way, he's a goner. That's the St. Lawrence Seaway for God's sake, not some piss piddling little stream. That there river has swallowed up whole villages and cemeteries. It almost got this farm in '59. Don't worry; it'll take care of the likes of him."

Karen E. Black

Chapter 4
Mr. Larry Savage

The Wheel Tavern, Cornwall, Ontario, December 28, 1972

Staring into the bottom of his beer glass, Larry Savage talked to himself, mostly about how much he hated damn Dace Devereux. And always had, ever since he first laid eyes on the kid. Dace had been a cocky, full of shit kind of boy, the kind of kid any decent person just ached to knock up the side of the head. And he still was. Larry recalled with pleasure his first time alone with the boy. He'd shown him what's what, yes, sirree.

And then the kid started pumping weights and stirring up trouble, like the shit disturber he was. Yes, sirree, everything was fine — just fine — when Devereux wasn't around. So it had been excellent booting him into solitary where there were no snoops and a man, a real man, could do whatever the hell he pleased. In Larry's version of a recent pop song, the deputy had survived. *I shot the sheriff, but I did not shoot the deputy!* Larry could be the deputy. One of these days he was going to catch Dace Devereux (number 2909, D'Arcy James Devereux, yeah, that was his full resplendent name) and bring him back to justice, dead or alive.

It sure helped that Devereux--or Debrex as Larry liked calling him ---had gone a little local last time. The kid hadn't been thinking straight. Boohoo, he'd shaken it rough when they nabbed him on a phony weapons charge and played right into Larry's hands. Better still, he'd lost his visiting privileges and couldn't see his little slut cousin no more.

And that was another thing. It pissed off Larry that a jailbird like Dace Devereux got all the girls. It wasn't fair. Dace wasn't even that good-looking. As for that little co-ed Liza, she was the creep's cousin! If Dace had left the stupid little bitch alone, an older, more mature man like Larry might've stood a chance.

Yes, sirree, Devereux deserved everything he got and more.

The last time Larry had so much fun was with a little neighborhood dog, a cocker spaniel. He'd used a pocket knife on her too, done what he wanted to the bitch and she'd kept coming back for more.

Just like a couple of little sluts he'd known.

Debrex had made a fool of him in the riot, taken his friends hostage and nearly gotten away with it too. Oh, yeah and killed a couple of guys. Okay, so they were perverts and the jail staff didn't care and there was some yap that Devereux hadn't really done it, but still. Dace was no fucking hero, that's for sure, not like his friend, Rick what's-his-name Lowery.

For sure, Larry Savage wasn't the only person after the escaped convict, but he was the only one who had the time, the only one who'd never give up. He'd lost his job when the bastard escaped and he had no family to keep him back. *No wife and no kids, anyway*, he thought sourly.

"Yoo-hoo," he said to the pansy bartender who was standing there doing absolutely fucking nothing, "Gimme another."

How the hell was he supposed to find a wife when he worked twelve hour shifts? He downed two thirds of his draft beer and stared into the bottom of the glass again, as if he half-expected to find a busty blonde there. He didn't drink much, but when he did, he did.

Damn it, he'd given his life to the Pen, worked his arse off until he made Head Guard and was making twenty-one bucks an hour and now this. His old lady Barb didn't count. She never had. Why he still lived with his mother, he didn't know. It had just happened. At age forty-two, he figured he was doing the old bat a huge favor by sharing the apartment over the pet shop with her. Barb was only fifty-eight herself, but the old girl hadn't gotten up off her fat arse in years. She looked eighty with her sparse, blondish hair scraped backed into a teensy ponytail. People had taken her for his grandmother, the few times he'd taken somebody home.

Barb said she had a hip problem or something, but the doctor said it was her weight. Larry had offered to get her a cane or one of those little shopping carts to hang onto, but no, she was lazy, lazy to the bone. Worse than some of the goddamn cons! She didn't even cook. They ate Kraft dinner and ordered in pizza the rest of the time. Near as he could figure, they'd kept the pizza delivery guy in business for twenty-four years because little Larry always had another paycheck on the way. Yes, sirree. She drove him crazy. He stayed with her because it was too much work to move, that's all.

But when Dace Devereux flew the coop on Christmas Day, the new Director had called him into his office and fired him. Just like that. Waited for him to get back from his so-called holiday and then bang, he was out! Said he'd read his personnel record and sorry, man, but he'd already gotten way too many chances.

Larry had stared at him open-mouthed for a minute, unable to believe what he was hearing, his stomach roiling, his head reeling. What the hell did the Director even mean? Was this some kind of sick joke? Larry played the scene over and over again in his mind. To his shame, he'd practically gotten down on his knees and cried.

Come to think about it, they blamed him for the riot too. Said he should have had supervised the guards better and had better control of the cons. After he'd warned them and warned them. True, Larry had had a few drinks at the guards' party and he might have closed his eyes for just a minute, but for this last fiasco—Dace's Christmas Day prison break—they should have fired the Doc instead of him, except they hadn't. Yes, the guy had worked at the Pen almost as long as Larry had, but he must have had some hoity-toity connections or something. All those educated types did.

Besides, it was Larry people were always after. Just like in school. He was always the one getting the strap, hard on the palms of his hands. First from the principal—a fag, if he ever saw one—and then from his mother when he got back. Two of his fingers were still bent. The vice-principal claimed he'd bullied the younger kids, but it was all made-up stuff. He was just trying to make friends.

If only he could get a break, he thought as he sat in the bar in Cornwall, his haunches straddling the sides of the stool, but it was the same old crap.

When he'd first got hired on at the Pen, he thought he was set for life. It was only minimum wage—that's what you got if you didn't finish high school even in those days—but there were annual salary increments, health benefits and a nice little pension if you didn't get yourself killed or fired. Life looked pretty damn good. It wasn't like in school. When he first started, he was tall and not too fat and people had mostly respected him. He'd stayed with it, gotten promoted, well, not too fast, until finally some shuffling old guard got shanked and Larry got his chance.

And for the most part, his co-workers had appreciated him keeping order and making sure people behaved right, served their time. He'd liked his work, at least until that bastard Devereux came along. To get paid for kicking ass and doing your civic duty—who could ask for anything more?

His mother had thought he had it made too. She still did. He hadn't told he'd been fired, just that he wanted to take a little vacation down south. She'd squawked enough at that. The mouth on the woman. Always yapping that life was unfair, that her son was doing way better than her, in spite of all the sacrifices she'd made. If he'd just pulled some more overtime, they would have been able to buy a house in that new suburb over Confederation way.

When she was younger and kind of cute, she'd had lots of boyfriends to help her out. In fact, she had a boyfriend back in 1951—one of several phlegmy drinkers who lasted a month or two and picked up a couple of bills—so that winter, she'd threatened to cut her overgrown son loose. Larry was over eighteen and she'd looked after him long enough, but then he'd come home, waving a government job offer in his hand and everything was lovey-dovey again. She quit her job at Stedman's, booted out her latest man friend and settled down with him.

She made Larry sick. He would have cheerfully paid somebody to fuck her to get rid of her, but that wasn't going to happen any time soon. How the hell could it? She never went anyplace. She got fresh air by leaving her apartment door open.

He wouldn't have gone anyplace either—he never had—except he'd seen a confidential police report that they thought Devereux was headed for Cornwall of all places. Apparently some of Dace's old gang, the Wolfhounds, were there. That young constable sure had been eager to spill the beans. He wouldn't have lasted a week in the Pen.

40

"I don't care if you've lost your job at the Pen," the cop told him, that and a lot of other things, some of which he'd already forgotten. Once Larry had heard Dace Devereux's name, he'd blanked out. The bastard had that kind of effect on him. He always had.

Larry had started listening again when the cop said, "The more people looking for this bastard the better and if you do find the guy, they'll have to give you your old job back. That's what the Director said, didn't he? We've got the Cornwall police looking out for him and the feds down in the States, but it would be nice to have a local guy there too."

Well, that's not exactly what the Director had said, Larry thought. But he might change his tune if he brought back Dace Devereux dead or alive.

Larry checked the gun, a hard lump in his pocket, the one he'd brought on a day trip to Buffalo. There was nothing to stop him from being a kind of bounty hunter, he supposed. Ex-lawmen (on television) did that in the States, all the Jesus fucking time. It probably worked the same way here.

"And so here we are," he said to the old guy who'd just slid onto to the stool next to him. The bartender with the ring in his left ear was down at the other end of the bar, chatting up some young ladies. Surprise, surprise. When he'd first come in, he'd taken the bartender for a homo.

The old guy looked at the girls briefly, but he wasn't too interested. Larry was though. He ran his crooked fingers through his thinning brown hair and stared. It jarred him to see girls here. The last time he'd frequented bars (while he was still an under aged teen in Maitland), it was men only. Females had their own drinking room. Could it be that Cornwall was a little wilder than Maitland? They were both basically border towns. Well, at least he'd gotten here.

The new guy focused on him, perhaps assuming or just hoping that Larry was good for a free beer. As if.

"My name's Bill Morton," the old guy said, holding out his hand. "And I'm Mr. Savage," Larry said, ignoring the man's veiny hand.

Bill Morton, who looked like he was at least sixty-five and judging by his bulbous nose, a longtime boozer, was undeterred. He put down his hand and tapped his dirty fingernails on the bar. "Ah, Savage, an interesting old English name," he said. "I know all the bars along this strip. You're not from around here. Where you from?" he tried again.

Larry felt like getting up and going, but he couldn't. He hadn't finished his beer. "Maitland," he finally said, rolling his eyes west.

"Funny," Bill said. "I met another guy here last night. He didn't exactly say where he was from, but you know, he kind of reminded me of that guy in the newspaper, the one who busted out of Maitland Pen, the one who they think ran that family off the road..."

Larry wasn't too interested at first. Bill was just a barfly for God's sake and he really doubted that he knew anything, but he played along. "What are you talking about?" he asked as casually as he could.

"You know, that news story about the father and the four kids who landed in the river on Boxing Day. Hey, hey, take it easy, you almost spilled your beer. Nobody drowned and Social Services took the kids. On account that the mother's whacko and the father can't cope. The father was taking the kids to their grandmother, but she can't look after them either. Going by their picture in the paper, the little girls were real pretty, some nice family will take them in and lots of people want babies. The youngest kid was only a couple of weeks old—can you imagine? The father was alone in the car with all those kids. I don't know about the boy though...nobody wants a half grown boy..."

"Look, I'm not real interested in some stupid bugger who doesn't even know how to drive," Larry interrupted. "But I am interested in the guy who reminded you of that escaped con—I'm kind of a bounty hunter, you know."

"A bounty hunter? That's real interesting. I didn't think we had them in Canada. Yeah, well, like I said, this guy kind of looked like that escaped con, same age, same build, except he had yellow hair. It could have been bleached, I suppose."

"Bartender," Larry shouted over the giggling girls, "Bring my friend a beer."

So smartass Dace Devereux wasn't as smart as he thought. Imagine hanging out with some barfly! And the Wolfhounds—double fool, double shit if he reckoned on going back to them! Because if Dace could find them—and they could find Dace—Larry could too. How the hell hard could it be, especially with their big, old noisy machines? Although what the hell they did with their Harleys in wintertime, he neither knew nor cared. He had his Camaro with him—a real little muscle car—with its

42

jacked up wheels. He'd be fine.

When he left the bar, Bill Morton was passed out with his head down on the counter. *Ugh*, Larry thought, almost gagging at the sight of the dandruff on the man's shiny head and neck

Chapter 5
Dirt Beard

*A man in his twenties is dead after a police shooting
in the parking lot of the Motel 8t on Water St.
There was an "interaction" between three Cornwall
police officers and the unidentified man, who wielded
a large knife. The shooting took place just before 11 p.m.,
when an officer discharged his service revolver, fatally
injuring the man. Officers had been called to the motel
to investigate a reported sighting of escaped convict,
D'Arcy James Devereux, age 24. A second man, possibly
a member of the Wolfhounds motorcycle gang, escaped
from the scene. Police spokesmen have not confirmed the
identity of either man, pending notification of next of kin.*
Cornwall Expositor, Dec 29, 1972.

Motel 8, Cornwall, December 28, 1972

Somehow Dace had gotten to Cornwall in the cold and the dark and ended up at a little place on Water Street, the Motel 8, exactly as planned. He'd been there for three days. Amazing, even if the minute he got there, things started to go wrong. He'd unlocked the room, taken one look at the full-length mirror inside the door and almost bolted. He'd looked like a wild man with his ripped pant knees, but he'd had enough money left to check into the motel, no questions asked. The desk man hadn't even asked for ID. No wonder. The place had been empty and it was still empty, except for him.

As for Cornwall, it was just another crappy little border town, an

American wannabe. That didn't make it safe though, so he'd better stay sharp. Unless he'd flown here, he'd passed through Brockville, but he hadn't stopped. No doubt the Seagram's had helped. Too bad it hadn't lasted. The first day in Cornwall, he'd headed straight to the closest liquor store. Across the border and into Quebec, you could buy booze in the local stores, but not here. People in Ontario were so goddamned straight-laced.

A city of 40,000 plus people, Cornwall smelled bad even in wintertime. The riverfront was contaminated by mercury, zinc, lead and copper and the soil by coal tar and byproducts, the legacy of several decades of industrial pollution. Dace had gotten the lowdown from a barfly hanging out at the first drinking hole he'd hit.

Not that stink bothered him. He'd gotten used to it, first in a priest-run kind of reform school and then in prison. Both places had had their share of whack jobs, the kind of guys who liked to mark their territory by smearing their own shit on the walls. Best to hang out by the riverfront, no matter what and pray for a breath of fresh air.

Akwesasne—or St. Regis as the locals said to distinguish it from the American side of the reservation— was just across the way. *Ah, freedom,* he thought, imagining a Hollywood set with an Indian village full of Braves (though he knew that natives weren't like that anymore). Still, the sooner he got there, the better.

Dirt Beard was supposed to meet him at the Motel 8, but when? Dace had reached him before he left Trenton, but then the next time he called his place, the guy's phone had been dead. Something might have happened to him, but Dace wasn't too worried. Dirt Beard had probably just forgotten to pay his bill.

Dace hadn't realized Cornwall was so big. *Corn-wall.* Somehow the city's name made it sound small. Going into the third day at the Motel 8 and enjoying another surprisingly good shower—at least compared to prison plumbing—he wondered how long he should wait. Was it New Year's yet? No, only December twenty-eighth according to the last newsstand he'd seen, with a face on the front of the *Cornwall Expositor* that looked a bit too much like him.

At least he had blond hair now and a brush cut—that should throw them off! After he'd gone to the liquor store, he'd brought some hair bleach at the drugstore down the street. His new hair style didn't suit him.

46

He looked like a hick, a country bumpkin out on the town.

The bad guys would have gotten to Liza by now—pulled her hair and yelled in her face, if she wasn't at Doc Melville's place. Dace would kill the bastard who hurt her. Liza would figure out something though. She'd been pretending all her life—that she really had a home—that she could save him. The only smart thing he'd done was leave her behind. But what wasn't she telling him? His stomach tightened, in spite of the hot water needling his face. It was bad, real bad, what had happened, the way he'd left, but he'd had to go.

Maybe another drink… He could go back to the bar or stay here and drink himself to sleep in the double bed pushed up against the wall while he watched more reruns on Channel 3. Stupid stuff like *Gilligan's Island* and *The Three Stooges*, so he didn't have to think. He turned off the shower, stepped out of the murky water pooling on the plastic floor and scrubbed his torso with a towel until it fell apart in his hands.

And Savage, the head guard, if they'd let him, he would have been even worse. The silly bugger hated Liza almost as much as he hated him. Hated her for loving him. What the hell was he up to now? Dace really had to get Savage out of his head. The last time he carved his chest, it wouldn't have been enough. If the bastard ever got his hands on Liza—well, he'd better not. The fat old vulture was always hungry for blood.

Ah, but straight shooter Mel and his fine upstanding doctor Dad would have stopped Savage, with their rock-hard certainty that a twenty-year-old girl who looked like brainy little Liza had to be blessed. As long as they were home.

Mel's mother was something else, the kind of fine, upstanding woman who'd throw somebody else's girl to the dogs to protect her own flesh and blood. Dace grinned at himself in the mirror and shook his head. Life sure wasn't fair. Because in addition to everything else the future Dr. Stuart "Mel" Melville had going for him, he had a mother like her.

A knock on the door soon wiped the grin off his face. Who the hell was it, the scrawny little guy from the motel office bringing more towels? He'd told him not to bother cleaning the room. He'd been here three days and every morning, he'd paid up front, twenty bucks for the night. The motel guy didn't know he'd gotten hair bleach on the orange flocked wallpaper outside the bathroom door. And surely to God Dirt Beard wouldn't be so fucking stupid as to just knock on his door!

He scrambled into his pants and shirt and pulled on his boots, but he had a hard time keeping his balance. He stumbled a bit and almost fell flat on his face. The last time he'd dressed so fast, he'd ended up in a prison riot. His head reeled and he staggered a little more. Shit, he must have drunk too much tonight. *Think,* he urged himself, *think!*

He checked—he had left the scissors in the side of his new right boot, with the remaining cash wedged into his left. He grabbed the pilfered parka too. Too bad he'd hung the hand-knit sweater on a peg by the door. He'd have to let it go. Damn, those reindeer had grown on him, they really had.

"It's me," a raspy voice finally whispered, "Dirt Beard..."

Dace couldn't answer. He was too busy busting out the open window in the bathroom into a convenient dumpster, Superman in a free fall. Luckily he didn't have to fall too far. He yanked the parka after him. He'd be an idiot to go near that flimsy motel room door, bulky coat or not.

By the time he'd donned the parka and rounded the motel, somebody who looked a lot like Dirt Beard was pummeling on the door to his vacant room and shouting, all caution aside: "Listen, you freaking mother fucker, I know you're in there, so open up..."

Dace knew it really was Dirt Beard then. A cop would be more cool, at least for now. And there would be more than one. Why hadn't Dirt Beard brought some backup? What the hell had happened to the rest of the Wolfhounds? Coppers were smart that way. He'd give them that much credit. Yeah, the bastards were coyote-smart, always traveled in packs. And most bikers did too.

Dace scanned the almost empty parking lot behind Dirt Beard just in case, but he couldn't see anybody else.

Dirt Beard didn't see him coming. Natch. Swatches of matted black hair had escaped the greasy bandanna on his head and covered his face. Knowing him, he'd probably been partying with his family since Christmas. There were a bunch of them; they went back in Cornwall a long way. Dirt Beard sported a three-day-old beard and he was all dressed in black. He stood there, staggering, an open Jack Daniels bottle swinging from one hand and a knife in his other.

Dace tackled him from behind. They hit the pavement on their sides, but ended up on their knees. In the melee, Dirt Beard lost both the

48

bottle and his knife. "Sorry..." Dace started to say. He lunged sideways for the bottle, but it slithered out of his reach. The shiny bottle rolled under the only vehicle in the motel parking lot, a dump truck, thank God.

Dirt Beard still didn't have a clue what was going on. His head spun around. "What the fuck...what the fuck...?" he kept saying.

"Where the hell have you been? Where's everybody else?" Dace asked, doing his best not to laugh at the look of utter panic on his friend's face, but inside he was thinking, *How's this idiot supposed to get me across at Akwesasne?*

They didn't get a chance to say anything else. A light flashed, something popped and he was in trouble again, Dirt Beard too. Dace ducked his head and froze. He was still on his knees. And so was Dirt Beard at first, but then he wasn't. Dace hadn't heard a real gun in years, but he hadn't forgotten the sound. *Shoot now, ask questions later,* so it had to be a cop...

"Cop," he said quickly, all that he could articulate, while Dirt Beard slumped against him and slid flat out on the ground. Everything told him to dump the guy and run, but he couldn't just leave him behind. Dirt Beard had been trying to help him, for God's sake.

And where the hell were the fucking cops? He couldn't see them yet, but he could hear them alright. They were arguing and then somebody started running towards them, probably to get a better shot.

Quick, quick, he thought.

"Dirt Beard..." he shouted, half rising and pulling at the body. He saw the small hole in Dirt Beard's chest, but it didn't register.

Nothing did. Even after the life he'd lived, he still couldn't believe it. Lights out — death — always happened so fast. That's all folks, just one shot and Dirt Beard was silenced, gone.

Just then, a second bullet whizzed through his brush cut hair and somebody bellowed, "Put your hands up."

Yeah, sure, he thought. *I'll help you kill me.* That hole in Dirt Beard's chest — any minute now and it would start pumping out blood. They'd have to be a little more creative with him. They'd aim for his head and zap him in the face instead. Let the crafty bullet find its own way to his brain. He started crawling out of sight, following the liquid trail Dirt Beard's bottle had left. He didn't feel the glass cutting into his knees. He didn't feel anything. He was too busy concentrating on crawling and too busy thanking God for the dark, moonless night.

And for the little bit of strength he still had left in his arms. For several seconds, he crouched under the dump truck, holding his breath and listening. Then he reached up under the truck and grabbed. Footsteps pounded alongside the truck. He counted two men, maybe more. Somebody looked underneath the truck, but they missed him, hanging upside down from the underbelly. *Hurrah!* he thought. He was weak, though. Weak from jail and four days on the run. If only he hadn't drunk so much. Christ, he was stupid. In no time at all, his back and arms started to ache.

Fuck off, he prayed, wondering how much more he could take.

"That him?" a cop-sounding voice asked. He couldn't have described a cop voice, but he knew one when he heard one. There was just something about the guy's tone.

"I think so," somebody else grunted. "That fellow he ran into the river was kind of mixed up—and a bit pie-eyed by the time we got to him— so right now I'm just going by the news bulletin. This guy here certainly looks dark and hairy enough, except he's got a tattoo on his chest, just above the bullet wound. I can't tell what of because it's covered with blood. Look how it's starting to gush out! What a geyser. Watch out or you'll make a mess of your shoes. Our man D'Arcy Devereux's been gone a few days, though. Looks like he got himself some new boots and a tattoo while he was on the run. Something with a girl's name—did you ever? The effing broads probably think he's cute, but he's got kind of a gorilla looking brow to me. You got him good, Brucie. Right through the heart. The kid's lucky he got such a good break."

"Well, let's hope you bagged the right one, guys," another voice said. "Because Blondie got away. If there was any moonlight tonight, I could have nabbed the bugger by his hair."

*****

Over by Brookdale Street, Dace waited an hour or so under the bridge. He really wanted to climb a trestle hand over hand and walk straight into the good old USA. *Yeah*, he told himself—*straight into the arms of a New York state trooper, a man with a broad-brimmed hat*. At least he had some company under the bridge, a bum nursing a bottle in a paper bag and a couple of kids, a boy and a girl. The boy was keeping his hands warm inside the girl's coat and dress. What the hell else did kids do in this hick town? *Good*, he thought, *good*. He didn't say anything to them. Nobody was interested in him.

Plus, he was having trouble moving. Every time he tried, he saw Dirt Bag lying dead on the ground, then his stomach heaved and a couple of times he barfed—but eventually he edged back over to the riverfront, a short block, and followed a moving shadow across the ice.

When the dark cloaked figure finally turned back and glanced at him, he asked: "You got some smokes, Man? Some of that Indian stuff?"
It was definitely the right question to ask somebody pulling a sled, not that the fellow wanted to take a chance out here on the ice. Without looking directly at Dace, he checked him out.

"Yeah, Man, " he finally said. "and I might know where we can get some real good grass."

Chapter 6
Larry Savage's Superiors

Riverside Motel, Cornwall, January 2, 1973

They were wrong, I tell you! That dead guy's somebody else. No way they got Dace 'Debrex' Devereux, the son-of-a-bitch is too damn hard to kill," Larry Savage sputtered into the pay phone. The motel room they'd put him up in was too cheap to have a bedside phone, so he was outside the main office, freezing his balls off. It had taken several collect calls to get through to his cop friend at the Maitland Police Station.

"Harry — Harry Who?" the dame on the other end had kept saying. Christ, he couldn't believe how stupid some people were.

There was a pause and when the cop at the other end finally took the phone, he sounded kind of flat. Larry didn't know the guy so he wasn't sure. Also, somebody was yelling or maybe there was just an awful lot of static on the line. Larry shivered. As long as nobody was yelling at him.

"Yeah, yeah, smartass, his old man said the same thing. Dace Devereux's father Norm made a trip to the morgue in Cornwall the day after New Year's. Almost collapsed over the body, but he said it wasn't his son. So where the hell is he then?" the cop asked.

"I don't know, but I'll find him if it's the last thing I do. I just need a little more cash."

"Don't you have any family who can float you?" More static. "You're costing us, fella. You sure eat a lot."

"No."

"No, what?"

"No, I don't have any family to support me."

"Trust us," the cop said. "If they didn't get the right guy, then Dace Devereux is still in Cornwall, with the Wolfhounds or holed up with some little wop or frog girl, maybe even a squaw. I hear tell those women on St. Regis are really quite loose."

This was news to Larry. He knew a lot of cheap hooch was made on the Indian reserve because he drank it and he'd heard tell that the res Indians were smuggling a lot of grass and hash, but he'd never once thought about the people who lived there. "They are? How do you know?" he asked, trying not to sound too eager.

"Everybody knows. And remember our boy Dace's cousin; you know his type, somebody just like himself! There's an all-points bulletin out. He's not stupid enough to cross at the border. He'll bide his time and walk across the ice, the minute it's thick enough. Listen, this is what you want to do. Cross the border and go to a town called Massena in New York state. It's on the northern border, less than fifteen miles from Cornwall…"

"What—by myself?"

"Trust me, you won't have any problem. You don't need a passport. Just tell the border people you're visiting family for a week and get your ass to the nearest Western Union. You got that, Man? Go to Western-Union-in-Massena," the cop said, repeating this last phrase very slowly. "We'll wire you some money and get you some 'backup' in a couple of weeks. Judge Si—uh, the guys here at the station know a couple of real discrete types. Guys who'll help us out for a little quid pro quo and they're not bikers either. You'd like that, right? One way or another, Devereux is bound to pass through Massena. That's where the Injuns bag the grass they peddle to the high school kids here. All you got to do is find their warehouse. It's the kind of criminal activity that's right up this jackrabbit's alley."

"Maybe we should just raid the reserve? I bet he's there!"

"What—on suspicion that some white guy might be hiding out? Dace Devereux is dark enough to pass for an Injun anyway. That's another reason we think he might go for one of their girls. We can't just go on the Res. We need 'just cause.' Injuns have rights too, don't you know. Now if you run into any illegal activity, that's another story. Get back to me, hear? And don't be so stingy with the long-distance. Just call collect and ask for me."

"What the hell do you think I just did?" Larry shouted into the phone, but nobody answered. The line had gone dead. He stared at the phone for a couple of minutes, willing it back to life and then bashed it back on the receiver.

The man in the motel office came to the screen door and stared at him. Larry gave him the finger and stalked off to his room.

Chapter 7
Perfect Recall

If only she'd been more conniving, Liza thought during those dark few winter days before she left the student residence and settled into her Uncle Norm's farm. If only she had taken Mel up on his gallant offer.

The conniving little bitch, she could hear his mother saying. Right. As if Mrs. Melville talked that way. If only Liza could have put up with her and small town life. Mel might have grown to resent her, but so what. She and her baby would have been safe for a little while at least. This is what anybody else in her situation would have done. Any sane person, that is.

And Dace — where the hell was he? Well, not in Cornwall anyway where some guy had just gotten himself killed by the police.

For the first few weeks after she'd left Mel, she dreamed she was at his place almost every night. In Trenton, of all places. She'd thought she'd be able to separate herself from him, just like that, but she couldn't. So she loved him a little, that's all. What a mess. The details were always the same: Mel's anguish, the relief on his mother's face, her own despair over Dace and her desire to protect their unborn child, the way she'd felt she had no choice.

The only person she told the whole story to was her roommate Janice, who'd said: "My God, why the hell don't you just marry the doc's son? Are you nuts? The guy's in love with you and hey, get this: he's not your cousin and he'll cheerfully take on your brat! That's good, isn't it?"

Maybe, Liza thought and closed her eyes. For lovers' conversations, she had almost perfect recall. The important ones played like a movie in her head…

Melville residence, Trenton, January 2, 1973:

Surfacing from a deep sleep, Liza squinted at a small leather folding alarm clock in Mel's parents' guestroom. For the first time in three weeks she felt almost rested. Dace was safe. He was listed as one of Canada's Ten Most Wanted Men, according to the *Star*, but safer than he'd ever been in prison, where Savage or one of his henchmen would have gotten him for sure.

Dace's last message, courtesy of a very cold biker passing through Trenton, was in her purse by the bed. "Monarch butterflies make a perilous journey" was all it said. When nobody was looking, she took the paper out of her purse and touched it with her lips, thankful she still had some of his hair in her pockets so that when she closed her eyes and touched it, she could pretend he was there.

Everything was beige in the Melville guestroom except a single-sized corduroy bedspread in a deep, chocolate brown. The clock sat on top of a three tiered metal bookcase crammed with literary erotica Mel's parents must have been too enlightened to purge: *Fanny Hill, Harriet Marwood, Lady Chatterley's Lover, Lolita, My Life and Loves, The Pearl, Tropic of Cancer, Story of O*...The room had belonged to Mel's older brother George, who was a high school librarian in Toronto.

It was nearly 11:30 a.m. on January 2 and they were leaving Trenton to go back to school, though Mel's mother worried about the snow. His father was working in the Outpatient Department at Memorial Hospital. Classes were starting tomorrow and Mel couldn't miss Chemistry, not if he expected to get into Med School in two years.

Surprised to have anything on her mind besides Dace and her pregnancy, Liza found she was still mildly curious about her marks. Somehow she'd met all her deadlines with just a couple of extensions, performing on remote control. The phrase "personal problems" had done the trick. People had their own problems. They didn't need to know anything more. The Sociology professor was the only one who had said he was sorry about her cousin. He'd even suggested another lawyer who could launch an appeal. Dace had been fed up with appealing, though.
"Give him time," Uncle Norm had counselled, but that wasn't what he was really saying. "Where is he, Liza?" He had begged so often that she was

almost afraid to talk to him. He was reckless in love, just like his son, but they had to be careful. At the very least, his phone was tapped.

Stretching her arms and legs, she flexed her toes beneath the comforting weight of wool blankets that smelled of mothballs. Mel had come to visit her during the night. Oh God, how could she say no again when he'd been so kind? But she had so much on her mind.

She pulled the blankets up to her chin and although it was becoming more difficult, she lie on her back and listened to the voices in the next room. Mel's grandmother had been hanging around her son's house all New Year's Day, picking over the carcass of a second seasonal turkey. Why was she back in the kitchen talking to his mother? At almost eighty, Liza thought the old woman should be tucked up under an afghan, watching *All My Children* after doing all that visiting the day before.

Mel's mother looked like a middle-aged woman badly in need of a rest from her mother-in-law and assorted relatives, not to mention her unexpected houseguest, Liza Devereux, who had been there a week. "Thank God they're all gone," she had muttered when the last guest had departed at just after 11:30 p.m. the night before.

"She's getting a belly. She didn't look like that when we saw her at Halloween," Granny announced now, probably louder than she intended because she had lost most of the hearing in her left ear.

Liza held her breath and waited. There was nothing wrong with *her* hearing. Mel's parents lived in a five bedroom split-level house with a swimming pool in the backyard, even though they were quite close to Lake Ontario. The guestroom was only separated from the kitchen by a narrow hallway and a breakfast nook at the back of the house. Grandma had probably entered the kitchen through the rear door from her own yard, which happened to be next door. The Melvilles were always fussing about the possibility of her falling into the pool.

Mel's mother's voice was a little harder to catch. "Oh, I wouldn't say that. She's so thin. Too thin, if you ask me. I could stand to lose a few pounds, but if that girl swallows a cookie, it shows." She was talking louder and more emphatically than usual, though. Liza could almost imagine the poor woman's thoughts: The police came here on Boxing Day looking for an escaped convict and now this?

"Well, somebody has to say something. Didn't you see her picking her way down the steps when we went to the Wagner house for a drink?

She walks like a pregnant woman."

Mel, or somebody, must have come into the kitchen then, because the two women stopped talking. The next thing Liza knew, he had burst into her room and was kneeling by the bed. She would have felt a little frightened, except he was wearing his Levis and nothing else and he looked so earnest and sweet that she just wanted to take him in her arms.

"When were you going to tell me?" he asked, tugging the blankets out of her hands and down to her waist. Although his face was usually easy to read, she had no idea what he was thinking now.

"After the trial. I don't know. Then it was after Christmas. When I was sure it was real," she whispered, placing her hand on her heart. It felt as if it had almost stopped beating, though she could see Mel's kicking in his naked chest. His uncombed hair was wild around his head and he looked like he hadn't shaved for days, probably the result of several New Year's celebrations with his old high school friends rather than anything he'd heard in the kitchen. Her own shoulder-length hair was a knotted mess due to his nocturnal visit.

"I should have known. Your tits are so big," he said, moving his hands up under her flannel pajama top, capturing both breasts and crushing them gently together. The nipples were browner and nearly as large as the tips of his thumbs. When a familiar surge of desire betrayed her, she crossed her legs.

"Oh, how would you know, Mel? We didn't sleep together until well into the fall." And only once, she thought.

"Right. And during the trial you were so burnt out, we didn't make love at all. Actually, I was real surprised when you showed up Christmas night, looking like God knows what ... though I guess with Dace on the lam you got scared." He sighed. "Some doctor I'd make." He tugged her pajama bottoms down and stared hard at the slightly softer belly beneath her navel, although she doubted he could see the slightest bulge, not when she was lying almost flat on her back. If he felt her lower belly though, her uterus was bound to feel enlarged.

"Look at me, Liza," he said. She shivered as he ran his hands over her torso then stopped and squeezed her breasts tighter this time, rolling the tender nipples between his forefingers and his thumbs. She made a small noise, somewhere between a sob and a moan.

"Shhh," he whispered, covering her mouth with his. "They'll hear." She quieted down immediately. The idea of Mel's mother or grandmother knocking on the door or bursting into the room was just too much to bear. "We have options," he told her, and she saw tears in his eyes. "Every problem has a solution."

She was still crying soundlessly, but the word "we" thrilled her immeasurably. Maybe there was a solution. Maybe she didn't have to do this alone. She sat up a little, wrapped her arms around his long, lean body, put her head on his shoulder and sighed.

But she also heard what he hadn't said. "I know abortion is an option," she confessed. "Especially now that it's legal in Ontario. But it's too late."

"Too late? Already? But didn't you have any clues? Missed periods? Nausea? You were sick through that farce of a trial, but I thought—"

"I thought the trial was making me sick. The way those men died ... I didn't want to think." And Dace, she thought, I was so scared. And probably would be now, if my hormones weren't tricking me into this beatific baby calm.

"Jesus, Liza, how could you be so careless with your health? But I suppose it's as much my fault as yours. Maybe the condom leaked at Halloween. We were both kind of out of it." He stroked her hair. "Have you been to the Student Health Services? How many weeks are you?"

She looked away. "About eighteen," she blurted.

Mel was quick, too quick at math, quicker than she ever would be. "Not mine," he confirmed immediately, burying his wet face in her neck.

"Not yours," she agreed.

Still, he got up off the floor and lie beside her on his brother's narrow bed. His tears had stopped hers cold, but she also felt something akin to peace. Even relief. They stared at the ceiling, side by side, until he went through the night table drawer and came up with a pack of Marlboros. Liza was surprised, but she didn't say anything.

The front door to the house slammed. His mother and his grandmother must have gone out to give them some privacy. Finally.

"When you were away in Europe," she started to say.

"I don't need to know everything, Liza. I don't own you now and I didn't then. No wonder you wouldn't sleep with me last year. He's the one who's away, though. A jailbird — or at least he will be when they catch up with him in a few days."

"No."

"And sure, he'll get a little more time. And be out in two or three years. Or less. That's how it goes, isn't it? And what will you do then? What can you do? He's your family as well as your ..."

Liza took a deep breath. "I'll do what I should have done in the first place," she admitted. "And it's not because of the riot, although I know, deep down in my heart, he's innocent of murder. Even his lawyer thinks so. He was quoted as saying as much in the *Spectator* just last week."

"Yeah, yeah, I saw that. So why then?"

"Because he's a recidivist!" She clenched her fingers in her hair with frustration. "God, I hate that word!"

"A what? Oh, you mean you're scared he'll reoffend."

"Well, that's what he's done so far," she whispered, a small sob caught in her throat. "And I still don't know why. I tried to give him up the last time he went to jail, but I couldn't. I had to be there for him during the trial. He had no one else."

"Goddamn it, Liza, he had his father! Maybe he couldn't tolerate the inside of the courtroom as well as you could, but from what you tell me, the man has spent a fortune on him over the years."

Mel smoked two more cigarettes, staring into space. When he spoke again, his voice was soft but decisive. "I'll marry you then. Like you said, you have no choice. You have to give up on him. Your only crime is that you've waited so long to do what's right. But that doesn't mean I have to give up on you. And as for my family, well, it's been done before. We'll put my name on the baby's birth certificate."

"You can't!" she cried, but when she raised herself over his chest and looked into his eyes, she saw that he could. A well-loved boy like Mel, almost twenty-one, probably did have the inner resources to grow up in a blink.

"But what about school?"

He shrugged. "We'll figure something out. Do you think my parents are going to toss my education out the window because of you? Oh, my father might bluster, but they can afford it and they'll pave the way. I'm their baby, their last hope. If we get married right away and move into the Married Students Residence, you can probably finish your year, too. That's what you want, isn't it? You really should. The baby's due in what, June? You can finish your year and maybe take some part-time courses next year. A cakewalk for an ambitious girl like you."

He took a deep draw on his cigarette, letting the smoke circle over their heads, then shook his head gently. "Christ, you were so full of hope when I met you. The way you talked … And you love all that English twaddle, those big fat tomes of books, the stuff nobody else reads, the stories I don't have time for and don't pretend to understand. And you were going to write. That's what you said. Before … I'm sorry. I was going to say before you met him, but he was always there, wasn't he? Your one."

"But I'm pregnant!" Liza almost choked on the words.

"My parents will want us to put the kid up for adoption," Mel said flatly, flicking the ashes off his cigarette into her water glass. He wasn't looking at her now. "Even if they think it's mine. It's just too soon. We're too young."

"Oh, Mel." She reached for her belly and laid her hands flat on it. The swell was larger for sure, and unbelievably taut. She knew exactly when it had happened: the last night, at Uncle Norm's house. In the grass. True, she had got her pills a little mixed up that week, but it had happened because she had willed it. She must have been crazy — crazy with grief and what she feared about Dace — that he wouldn't, or couldn't, change. That he'd be in and out of jail all their lives.

But she was exactly the same as he was. She couldn't change either. Couldn't change who she loved. Maybe nobody could change who they already were. She was just a girl who had wanted a great passion, babies, and a chance to write books. And she had blithely, foolishly, insanely hoped to somehow have it all at once.

Still, I'm a woman now, she thought, liking the sound of that phrase. She could almost think clearly, now that she had passed the three month mark and was no longer so sick. Even if it were just that false hormonal calm, the sacrifice of a girl-woman ensuring the future of the human race. It really didn't matter. Although she had been anxious and would be anxious again, she knew she could do this. She could keep going to school and get a job, maybe even live with her mother for a couple of months after the baby was born. Somebody had to look after the baby. Summertime in the city. It wasn't a perfect solution, but it was the only one she had come up with so far, in between exams and letters of appeal. Because in her experience, mothers and grandmothers came through in the end, even if their only solution was poison.

Poison. Well, she had briefly considered that. But it had never really been a possibility. She had known all along she wanted Dace's baby if she couldn't have him. It might be an unreasonable choice, a crazy choice, but it was the right thing for her.

Still. How wonderful if she could have wanted Mel too, a boy so loving and so breathlessly uncomplicated. Sometimes she felt like she had come home. Especially now that he wanted her, even when he knew. But, clamored a practical little voice, belatedly born of necessity, *how long will that last?*

"Something tells me you don't want to do that."

"Not this, no. I mean, no, although if you'd asked when I was so sick ..."

"So we'll keep the kid. We'll both be old enough. What the hell's wrong now?"

She hesitated. "It's just that ... stepfathers. You know."

"What do you think I am, Liza? A lion?" Mel looked so indignant she nearly laughed. "Do you think I'm going to eat Dace's kid?"

"Some do."

"Look, anyone can see you and Dace were connected. Did you think I was blind? The thing about him was anyone who knew him was attracted to him. Even men. That's both his weakness and his strength. I don't know why. It was just him. And I don't know why he can't stay out of trouble. Do you?"

"No. Well, I have some idea, but it all amounts to the same thing. He didn't really have any choice. Maybe he was programmed. Maybe it was something innate."

"Aw, Jesus Christ, Liza. Everybody has choices."

"Not always good ones."

"Well, tell me again. If he showed up right now, would you go with him?"

But he did and I didn't, she thought. If it hadn't been for the baby, she would never have been able to let go, to let him go alone. She wouldn't have had the strength. Jesus. Did she get pregnant just so she would be trapped?

"Of course not!" she said out loud. "It's not an option. Even if it were, I've got the baby to think about now. If he gets sent back to prison, my baby's daddy will be in jail."

"He will."

"Well," she said and sighed. "It's not like he's been trained for anything else. But I will not take my kid, even if it is his kid, into a prison visiting room. Some people might think they were doing the child a favor, letting him get to know his Dad, but I don't. Dace wouldn't either."

"You haven't told him?"

"No. What's the point? He'd go nuts. Worse, he might have stayed."

"Are you sure?" Mel asked slowly. Then his eyes widened. "Wait a minute. What do you mean he might have stayed? Did you talk to him before he left? Did you lie to the police?" He sat up, grabbing her by the shoulders and giving her a little shake.

"No, of course not," she lied again. "Let go of me!"

"They'll get him. Extradite him if he's gone down to the States."

Liza shrugged. Maybe not, she thought, unless he commits another crime. And he won't, now that he's away. It's only at home he wasn't safe — where he should have been safe, where all his troubles began. "Besides, Dace and I, we've had our chances. Now it's all about the baby once he's born."

"'He'. So you think it's a boy. Right. Makes sense. Dace would have a boy for sure."

She lie back down on the bed, thinking. She was going to need help. She had always known that. Even if she got a job, she couldn't work and look after the baby, too. And Mel was so dear. But she couldn't. He deserved his own child, not another man's.

But there was somebody else who might not mind. Why hadn't she thought of this before? All along she had wanted to help her Uncle Norm, to protect him ...

"Liza?" Mel asked. He'd turned his head on the pillow and now eyed her suspiciously. "What's happening?"

"Um, I've just thought of something. And you're the reason," she said, running her fingers down his chest, her eyes briefly alight. "If you're willing to help me, and you're a man ..."

He flicked one eyebrow. "A mere man."

"Oh, don't look at me like that, you know what I mean. The thing is, I bet Uncle Norm would help me too."

"Dace's father? Are you nuts? What's he going to do with a baby? Jesus, don't you think the poor bastard might need a rest?"

"But it's his grandchild, Mel. He was never able to help Dace, which is a terrible torture for any parent. You heard me talking to him yesterday. He's heartsick about Dace."

"His guilt is hardly your concern. I bet he regrets leaving him at that school, though."

"I could probably finish school while I lived at his place. It's only twenty miles outside of Maitland. If he loaned me a car …"

"And the baby? What are you going to do, lug him to class?"

"They have those carrier things now, although I'm sure my uncle would pay his housekeeper a little extra to watch the baby while I went to school." Dace said Uncle Norm would help me, told me to go to him for anything, she almost added.

"But if you and I got married, Liza, you wouldn't have to rely on anyone. How about next week? We'll go to City Hall in Maitland and tell everybody later. Face the music. Maybe we can have a little party on Valentine's Day."

"I'd still be relying on you," Liza said. She tried to hug him, but he was board stiff on his back, both hands locked behind his head. She sat up and really looked at him. Oh God. This wasn't right.

"Sweet boy, I can't get married and live like this," she muttered, her eyes filling with tears she tried to hide by fumbling on the floor for her clothes. "I want to. I want to, so much. I want a normal life and I'm scared, but …" She pulled a paisley granny dress over her head, a garment she now wore most of the time. She'd been able to secure the zipper of her jeans with a safety pin just last week, but after several days of three square Melville meals, she couldn't anymore.

"Like this? What's wrong with this?"

"It's too … I don't know," she said weakly. "It's too not me."

For the first time, Mel looked slightly angry. "You mean it's too easy here, I suppose," he replied, removing one hand from behind his head. He reached towards her, looking like he couldn't believe she would

66

be stupid enough to let go of the lifeline he was tossing her way. "Do you think you'll be riding a motorcycle when you have a kid?"

She shook her head. "Oh, I don't think it would be easy living here. Not for me. What do you think would happen if your people found out more about Dace?" she asked. She came back and took his hand, holding it like a prayer book between hers.

"Well, we'd never let on it was Dace's kid."

"Still ..."

"Okay, so you're related to a convict. Who the fuck cares? They'll get over it. Everybody has a few bad apples on their family tree."

"But he's not a bad apple, he's not! Oh, I don't know. People don't know anything about him. Not really. Except that he got away with murder, or so they think," she said softly, turning away and poking through her purse on the desk.

Mel sat up and swung his legs over the edge of the bed, his eyes intent. "It doesn't matter what they think. I could help you, Liza. And you, you would love me in the end."

"Probably," she agreed, securing her growing hair with an elastic band. "And I'd love to have your help, but it wouldn't be fair. Besides, your family hates me. They didn't like me in the first place and they liked me even less after the police came," she reminded him, tossing the rest of her clothes into the small duffel bag at the foot of the bed. She headed for her coat and boots in the front hall. "Your grandmother—"

Mel followed her, pulling a T-shirt over his head in case his mother came back. "—will probably be dead in a couple of years," he said ruthlessly. "Liza, if you walk out now ..." His expression hardened. "You're going to find him, aren't you? Jesus Christ, you really are a reckless girl. Reckless, reckless, just like him." He stopped, jamming the heels of his fists into his eyes and watching her unlock his front door.

"Liza," he warned, "you can't go anywhere in this storm. There's already a foot of snow on the ground. And I'm not driving you. Jesus fucking Christ. You're not planning to hitchhike again, are you? You were half-dead last week when you showed up here like some stray cat."

He was never going to stop asking her. *Do you still love him, Liza? Do you still love him more than you love me?*

"No. Please believe me. I'm not going back to him. How the hell can I? I'm a liability to him. Jesus, I don't even know where he is." Not to mention he doesn't want me, she thought, feeling a great tear rip inside her chest.

Mel folded his arms across his chest, staring down at the Oriental runner in the hall, dark and intricate, on the shiny oak floor. "But you'll find out. You've romanticized your relationship with him because of the drama. That's what you've done all along."

"You're right. It's probably all because of those books I've read," she said, awkwardly maneuvering herself and her bag out the front door and onto the snow-dusted porch.

She paused to take a deep breath, bracing herself for the terrible journey ahead. God, it was so beautiful in the open air: the bulky, cloudy sky, the fresh snow on the trees, even the dry, brown wisps of a climbing rose on the arbor at the side. Why had she stayed inside so long? Everything would bloom again, given time. Like Eliot's lilacs out of a dead land.

And the monarchs would come back too. Because somehow they knew where they belonged. Lucky them, they didn't care with whom. She would have to hurry, though. A door opened and closed across the street. Mel's mother was on her way back.

"C'mon, Liza. You're pregnant. You can't do this by yourself," Mel said, shoving his bare feet into boots.

"I know. I'll stay at Uncle Norm's for a couple of months, even a year if he lets me, and I think he will. When Dace shows up, if he shows up, I'll be gone. Long gone. Me and the baby." She shook her head. "No, Mel, really, it's okay. Please don't put your jacket on. I promise not to hitchhike. Really. The bus station's just down the street. I'll wait there until the storm is over," she said, pushing her hands against his chest.

Suddenly she was glowing with so much vitality, she thought her eyes must look feverish. She distinctly felt two bright red spots burning on her cheeks. For weeks she hadn't been cold, with the baby growing inside her, millimeters every day. All his organs were developed now, she exulted. He weighed half a pound and he could cry. Her baby. Dace, Dace's son. Their Devereux boy.

"Maybe I should call my father," Mel said coolly. "Get something to calm you down."

He thinks I'm insane. Well, maybe she was. If she didn't leave right

68

now they would sit around all day, arguing until they were both weak and broken down — a tedious argument of insidious intent. His parents and his grandmother would get in on the act, too. How ironic that Dace, the escaped convict, had been spared all this. For a moment she felt a pang of envy so sharp for her renegade cousin that she almost stayed.

But in the end she couldn't. She was busting to get out of this place. Looping her purse around her neck, she lifted both her bag and her coat and glided down the porch steps. She made it down the Melvilles' recently shoveled front walk to the road, although she could tell by the look on Mel's face that he didn't think she would. Maybe he even hoped she would fall. He watched her go, his high forehead pressed against the frame of the open door. But when she looked back over her shoulder and smiled, he closed his eyes. The snow, big, wet flakes, had temporarily stopped, and his mother, still across the street, hung back, her expression palpably relieved.

Yes, I'll wait again. And Dace's baby and me, we'll both have a life. Without you, she thought, following tire tracks in the snow down the street to the bus station.

And oh my God, without Dace.

****

I made the right decision, she kept telling herself at her uncle's farm. She had to or she would have gone insane.

Chapter 8
Summer in St. Regis

Summer's Trailer, St. Regis, December 30, 1972-February 3, 1973

Dace felt warmer in the smuggler's tinny little trailer, but he kept the parka on. The trailer was home to at least three people and a dog, except it was about the size of a refrigerator and damn near as cold.

He tried to deep-six his brain too, but he couldn't. Dirt Beard kept falling in slow motion to the ground.

The guy's sister, a compact eighteen-year-old with the kind of face he couldn't read, was frying eggs and white Wonder Bread in some bacon grease on a woodstove. The bacon was all gone. A baby slept in a splayed wicker laundry basket by her feet. In the long nights ahead, he would play this homey little scene in his head over and over. Dace stared at the child until the girl caught him looking like he could be a kidnapper or something. The baby pulled at him, he didn't know why. He hadn't been around kids much. He didn't think he liked them. But this one was kind of cute with all that spiky black hair. The family belonged to the Mohawk tribe, Dace found out later, with a couple of blood infusions from European explorers and settlers in the 1600s. It was hard to say what had percolated down the generations, but some said that the Dutch and the French had been pretty busy in those days.

"Shush," the girl said, pointing to the basket, the kind of place he wouldn't have stashed a litter of pups.

Another girl might have offered him a blanket, but she didn't. It put him off a little. Well, maybe she didn't have one to spare. He looked around the trailer again. The brother and sister must be working for somebody else. If they were working for themselves, they weren't doing too well. They didn't have much, that's for sure. They were just kids, really.

For a couple of moments, the sizzling eggs made the only sound in the room. They smelled good, but he didn't want any, not right now. Just some sleep, that's all. Through half closed eyes, he studied the girl in the dim, smoky room, still trying to figure her out. *Keep your friends close and your enemies closer.* She might go either way. She was short with unwashed black hair, but her skin was taut and smooth. He recalled a couple of sixteen-year-olds who'd gotten pregnant in school. This one had weathered her youthful pregnancy well. If she ran hollering out the door, he wasn't sure what he'd do. Let her go? Or tackle her—a little girl, a mother— to the ice? *Oh, sure.* That was him alright.

But that first night, the alternative—that she might show some interest in him felt even worse. *Please don't come on to me,* he caught himself praying for the first time in his life. *Not now. Not tonight.* And the hollow way he felt inside, maybe never. After a couple of moments of just standing there and not even being asked to sit down, he collapsed into an aluminum lawn chair in the corner, wrapped his arms around himself and turned his face into the wall. No time for politeness. Before the girl took the pan of eggs off the stove, he'd fallen into a light sleep.

He could still hear her, though. Jesus, she was getting on his nerves. His hand itched a little, but he'd never hit a woman before and he didn't plan to start now.

"What's he doing here, Mac?" the girl asked her brother, who was just standing there, puffing on a cigarette and scratching the dog's head while he waited for his food. "We don't have enough eggs and we don't need no heat. If there's one thing I know when I see it, it's trouble. He's got jail eyes, just like Daddy did and you know what happened to him. Literally broke Mom's heart."

"Literally," Mac mimicked. "Ah, Summer, don't get started," he said, dropping his cigarette and grinding it out with his heel on the trailer

72

floor. "You know it wasn't Dad's fault. Another effing cop spotted me tonight. The same one maybe. I could feel the cop's eyes on my back. I had to get off the ice."

"Ah, shit, so you didn't get that grass across? How we going to get some food? The baby's teething, he's been crying all day."

Mac snickered. "Looks like you'll have to do it, Sis."

"Get your own eggs," she said, tossing down her fork with a loud clatter onto the stove.

******

The very next night, Dace slept with Summer. Mac had gone out on one of his contraband runs. Dace hadn't planned to, but he had his reasons. He'd listed them to himself with every stroke.

First off, Summer wanted to. And he liked being wanted. Who the hell didn't? He'd met some guys in prison who didn't, but they were few and far between. Next, it was effing freezing and this would help keep them both warm. The propane they used to heat the trailer was expensive, so no doubt they used it sparingly. He was willing to bet that the temperature outside the trailer often fell below zero.

It was the first in a long string of nights. Sometimes they took the baby into bed with them too. The kid's name was Justin. When Dace first arrived, he had just turned ten months old. He learned to walk while he was there. Summer's brother Mac slept on a couch — when he was there — but she had a three-quarter bed that folded down from the wall, so they managed. The bed had a patchwork cover, pieced together from her father's old clothes. Her mother had made the quilt before she died.

"Don't worry, White Boy," she'd told him straightaway. "You're safe from me. I don't need a commitment from you or anybody else. I'm not into that. Besides, if I marry a non-Indian, I lose my status and then my kid's screwed."

Summer had finished grade thirteen, a remarkable feat on the reservation, especially for a girl. She could have moved into Cornwall and gotten a job, but everything she loved was here: her brother Mac, her parents in the Catholic churchyard and a huge extended family, never mind that they all pulled her down. She got a little welfare subsidy for her baby, so a cousin (and her cousins were legion) or an aunt or uncle "borrowed" money from her all the time. They also shared their problems with her. An educated girl had all the answers, or should have, since they'd sent her to school for so long. They gave her no credit for her academic success. She was a lucky one, that's all. They could have done it, if they'd been so inclined, but most of them had wanted to get out to work as soon as possible. It was the only legit way to get ahead. The factories in Cornwall had paid good money before they closed down. Summer didn't say much, but Dace could tell it wore her down. If it had been him, he would have taken off long ago.

She never said who had fathered her baby either, but there was a good possibility he was dead—dead like so many of the boys from the reserve who drank and went out on the ice and froze or got tangled up with the law. Or worse—just last month, one young father had stayed up all night drinking and let his toddler children outside to freeze. Summer's saving grace was that she didn't drink. If she couldn't pull herself out, maybe, just maybe, she'd pull out her son.

The weeks passed. Sure he knew he wasn't doing her much good, but he felt sorry for her and it wasn't like he had much choice. Not if he wanted to stay there, that is.

The more time he spent there, the more he wanted to do something for her. *Yeah,* he could almost hear the prison psych saying: *and you can't even help yourself.*

"Hey, little girl," he'd say as he buried himself in her body. She spoke tough, but oh, God, she was so pretty without her clothes on and so girly. She didn't believe him, though. She'd always hunted and fished and cooked and looked after everyone else.

"I'm not pretty," she'd frown damn nearly every time, flipping her razor straight hair off her shoulders and pointing to a tiny stretch mark, her small, milk laden breasts or the slight curvature in her underbelly, where her baby had so recently housed.

******

Summer wasn't as rabid about Indian rights as her brother Mac— she had baby Justin to think about—but Dace drew the line at getting involved in reservation politics anyway. He owed Summer and her brother big time, but he had to stay out of it. He had other fish to fry and besides, too many people might have recognized his face.

Mac was a bit of a problem, though. He liked to tease people and he wouldn't leave Dace alone—especially when he drank. He sounded a lot like the guys Dace had known in jail and look where that had got him.

"You could be a real asset to the Tribe," Mac kept yapping.

And where have I heard that before? Dace thought. Mac wanted the help of a strong man like him, especially if the Tribe ever had to form a blockade, something many of the young men plotted. The Mohawks and the people who ran with them—the white opportunists who called themselves businessmen—could do exactly what they wanted with all the marijuana from Massena then. The Saint Regis Mohawk Tribe wanted to administer its own programs too.

There was also some talk about the reservation finally getting government funding, so it might have just been talk, but who the hell knew? Dace couldn't afford to take any chances. *Jesus*, he kept reminding himself, *I'm an escaped con.*

Within a week, he started to go stir crazy inside the little trailer. He'd occupied bigger jail cells.

He waited a bit, but one day during a brief February thaw, he finally told Summer he had to leave.

She was fiddling with the pilot light on the stove. "It's the baby, right?" she said.

"No," he said, trying to hug her close while she elbowed him away. Justin had just started getting his eyeteeth and he'd cried all night, but that definitely wasn't the reason. Dace had nearly slipped away in the night, but he couldn't. Though he hadn't exactly told her about his stints in Maitland Penitentiary, she knew he was on the run. If and when somebody came snooping around, he needed her on his side.

He was sure going to miss her though—her compact body and the happy little baby who bicycled his sturdy legs whenever he saw Dace.

Backing away from him, Summer picked up her baby and looked over his head at Dace solemnly, but she was true to her word. She hadn't wanted a commitment after all. But she must have gotten used to having him around. Still, if she'd hoped he might stay a little longer, she didn't say.

Christ, he loved a strong woman—a dark eyed woman, with a baby on her hip. Kind of like Liza. He thought of all the long nights ahead on the road, the nights he'd sleep alone. Maybe he could take her and the kid along with him...

He shifted his shoulders, anticipating the weight, the additional responsibility of a woman and her child. Well, it might work. It would get warmer as they went south, way warmer than it was here. Just the thought of the sultry heat revived him. And baby Justin wouldn't need much. He was still feeding from his mother.

As if he'd read his mind, the baby smiled at him and held out his little arms. "Da," he said, just like he did to every man.

"You know," Summer said, smiling a little, "most of the women here on the res are on their own. Maybe all women are. You play nice with Justin, but I don't need a man."

"You don't?" he asked, feeling a little wounded.

"I got this," she said, jabbing her right index finger up into the air. "I can take care of my own needs."

Dace caught her finger and kissed it. He didn't know if she was serious or not, but God she was so cute. If only he didn't have to leave her behind. If only he could have her and Liza, the whole damn shooting match.

"But if you ever come back again, I won't turn you away. You just can't stay."

"Ah, Summer," he said, "you're all heart. I love you too." And in his own way, he did.

She wasn't his cousin Liza though. Liza who knew him through and through and still loved him, no matter what he'd done. Liza who wasn't encumbered with a son.

Chapter 9
Dace and the Butterfly Girl

The Aztec believed an adult Monarch butterfly
to be the incarnation of a fallen warrior, wearing
the colors of battle.

Plattsburgh, New York, Molly Maguire's, February 5, 1973

She knew he was watching her. There, out of the corner of his eye, while he perched on a bar stool and avoided the lowlifes to his left and right. Well, maybe it was hard not to—she, Mary "Kathleen" Aldous was the only woman at Molly Maguire's Tavern in upper New York state. And he, the handsome bastard, was indisputably a man—and from the looks of it, the kind who liked women too. For Kathleen, a man's good looks and his interest in women hadn't always gone hand-in-hand, but she had them pretty well figured out now.

Lucky, lucky me, she thought. Exhausted from her fearsome and unaccustomed journey across the Canada–U.S. border, she'd already forgotten the name of the town she was in. She'd had a license ever since she was eighteen, but she never drove outside her little Montreal neighborhood if she could help it. She'd never driven in Toronto at all, though she had practically grown up there. Both cities made her crazy. She couldn't say which one was worse.

Don't be so hard on yourself, her psych Hazel always said. For an agoraphobic, she did pretty darn well. She'd always been afraid of wide open spaces, so she made herself, that's all.

What was with these small towns, though? All the men—skinny, lone wolves—seem to do was drink. After work, if they worked—at the local pickle factory yet!—and from the looks of it, there wasn't much else to do in this town. No college, no hospital, no theatre, no stadium, just this bar and a couple of churches, the Third Methodist and a United Baptist down the street. If you were Catholic like her—too bad. You either hiked to the next town over or went out-of-state. Ditto, if you were nonwhite. Or anything different, like you even had a brain and you could think. There wasn't even a park, unless you counted the bit of turf around a Great War cenotaph in the middle of town. And a baseball field.

Growing up in a place like this, she would have died. She couldn't imagine it. As far as mental stimulation went, the children's tuberculosis sanatorium in Toronto had been the Sorbonne compared to this.

No wonder by 5:30 p.m. on a Wednesday, the good-looking guy on the bar stool, lean and muscle bound, was into his fourth draft. She knew because she'd been watching him too, ever since he walked in, cased the joint and plunked himself down at the bar. He had bleached his thick hair blond, several weeks ago judging by his half inch roots. She wondered why. She preferred blonds, but it didn't suit this guy at all. His eyes and brows were much too dark, almost black. He reminded her of a monarch butterfly, a bit. *Uh, oh,* she mentally kicked herself, *no, you don't. Ah, me,* she thought, *I'm still a sucker for anything to do with monarch butterflies.*

Reluctant to get caught looking at him, she looked down at the gin and tonic in her hand, her third. Because she was on holiday. A working holiday, but still. *You drink too much,* her mother always said. *Grrr.* It had definitely been a mistake to go back home to live. At her age! Why— gulp—she was twenty-nine. The sooner she moved out, the better. If she had to, she could always sleep in her office at the university. Yes, that's what she'd do when she went back, at least until she got her own place. She had some friends, but everybody else her age was married and living on their own, usually with a kid or two. Or three or four. Ugh. Some of them were on their second or third marriages as well. She didn't envy them all that. Really. She had way better things to do with her life than put up with a man. Irritably, she scooped her yellow hair into a ponytail and secured it with a rubber band. Sometimes she wondered where the hell she'd be without alcohol. It gave her the confidence a clever, educated person like her should have had.

The man she was talking to, Professor Francis Murphy, immediately and predictably lowered his eyes to her chest. She hated when men did this. It made her feel like a butterfly mounted in a frame. A late bloomer, she didn't have much, but maybe Murph liked them small. Some guys did, though only one had. She had come late to sex and then spent her mid-twenties making up for lost time, mostly with the same man. Perfect and perky, Francis-Prancis no doubt thought. He was twice her age, a portly, balding man with a greying beard, but that wouldn't stop a guy like him. It never had.

Once upon a time in academia, Francis had been a departmental enemy, but they'd agreed to meet here. With three generous gin and tonics in her, she'd almost forgotten why, though with her dissertation in shreds, there was nothing to keep her back in Montreal. She'd hoped to jumpstart her dissertation by moving from the U of T to McGill—a move that had cost her dearly, both academically and in her personal life—but no dice. The face of her former advisor, Dr. Gene Sheridan's assistant Percy Meadowvale, came to mind. And Percy looked real mad.

Too bad, Percy and Genie, she thought. *It's your fault I'm here anyway.* She felt such a horrible traitor, though, as she glanced around. All that bad blood between Gene and Francis. She'd been so much on Gene's side— helped him write a couple of articles refuting Francis's theories about the monarchs, in fact. Well, she wrote some of them and let him publish them under his name. She never would have met Francis here a couple of years ago, but then Percy… "Ah, look at all the lonely people," the jukebox sang. Not that she was vengeful or anything. She was a lepidopterist, or almost one, and she wanted to find the monarch hideout, that's all. Everybody remotely connected to Biology did, no matter what their professed passion.

Thank God nobody else knew she was here. Well, why should they? It was crazy, this dream of hers to find the monarchs' wintering ground. Crazy, unless you were like her and Dr. Sheridan and Percy Meadowvale and Francis Murphy and had studied the miraculous little devils for years.

Francis raised his heavy eyebrows and cocked his head, like he was cute or something. *Oh, God,* she thought, suppressing a smirk. Men were such simpletons. It was all her fault though. She was smart, she knew better and if she hadn't smiled so much, he wouldn't be acting this way. For years, she'd scorned girls who behaved like she was now. She glanced at his left hand. She couldn't see a ring, but that didn't mean anything. He'd probably already taken it off.

"You know, we could cut costs by sharing a room," he suggested as if the thought had just occurred to him. "I'll sleep on the floor."

The floor—now that was an interesting offer. Did all professors do it on the floor? And what costs? He had tenure at Princeton; surely his traveling expenses were paid. Whereas hers... Well, better if the Faculty didn't know she was here. She might get another go at her dissertation in the fall. If she stopped chasing Percy. Stopped annoying Gene. My God, she was almost thirty, or she would be by then. Where the hell had time gone? And what did she have to show for all the work she'd done? Once, she'd been the youngest student in her class, but now...

"I don't think that would work," she replied, boldly staring into Murphy's bespectacled eyes. It was difficult, though. For one thing, she felt a little wobbly. She hadn't eaten since noon. She'd been afraid to stop on the road—afraid if she got out of the car, she'd collapse on the road in some stupid girlish swoon. And she just wasn't that kind of girl. A swooner. A ditzy little girl whose life depended on a man. She liked men, what they could do for her, that's all.

She hid her mouth behind her hand. She wouldn't have had to get out of the car at a drive-thru and risk her heart trying to thump out of her chest, but she loathed those yellow arched McDonald places springing up all over the road. She hadn't noticed them so much in Canada, but here in the States.... *My God*, she kept telling herself, *you're agoraphobic, you're lucky you got this far.*

She'd wanted to trace the monarchs' migratory route for years, but it had been one thing and then another. First she was a child sick with TB, then when she finally got out of the sanatorium and went to a proper school, she'd gotten busy with Percy. Maybe it was a good thing he'd been married, or she probably would have ended up just like her mother, a sad sack trapped with a child. My God, all that stuff about her art ("I need some time to myself, Mary Kathleen!"). Her mother had never done one damn thing except wait hand and foot on the men in her life. Like a woman in Africa or Asia or something. It really annoyed her. Why did her

80

mother, a privileged North American, behave like that in this day and age? What possessed the woman? It didn't make any sense.

Murph tried again. "Oh, c'mon, I've got a map. We could do a little more work on the route the monarchs take…"

Yes, those monarchs she thought. *The super generation.* The ones who flew south were big and strong and lived longer than those born in the spring — six to eight months compared to four to six weeks. The first time she'd seen them migrating, she'd been a tuberculosis patient, a nine-year-old at the Children's Sanatorium in Toronto. The sight had changed her life. In those days, people had thought monarchs went to Florida, for a variety of reasons, which no longer made any sense.

Dr. Gene Sheridan, the Canadian scientist, had tagged the monarchs, so now they knew they went to Mexico, but where? If only she could find out where they really went in Mexico! For Gene and Percy. For her, so they'd think she was still a clever little schoolgirl and love her all over again.

"Routes," she corrected, wanting to be right.

"There's only one route, little lady, if you're starting from upper New York state. I vote we start on 87 and wind our way down through the Atlantic states. I'll drive. We'll stash your car around here someplace."

The driving part sounded real good, but she looked away. The deer head up on the wall was smarter and sexier than this man. Besides, she wasn't that little. She was a half a head taller than him in fact.

To her horror, she blurted, "You're married, aren't you?" Oh, Christ, they had warned her about this in staff meetings before. *Miss Aldous, sometimes you're a bit too blunt.*

"It depends what you mean by 'married.' We don't…well, you know."

Have sex anymore, she thought. *Well, neither do I. What am I going to do — sleep with all the married men on my faculty and yours?* She didn't like sex that much anyway. Too messy and gooey and she hadn't… Maybe if Percy had kept it up longer. But he hadn't. He couldn't. They'd tried everything, gotten hold of a copy of the *Kama Sutra* but he was still good for ninety seconds at best. Not that she'd minded at first. She'd liked the closeness, the affection, the power she had over him.

What do you think I am? A monarch? Percy had joked. *I'm human. I can't keep it up for sixteen hours, little girl. And you, it's not right that you want it this much.* Yes, it had been her fault alright. She loved him for other reasons, though. She'd always loved men for other reasons—their bravado for one—that profound and endearing little boy ignorance they concealed so they could brave the world. She just hadn't loved any of them for long. Now that she thought about it, maybe it was Percy's passion for monarch butterflies that had so obsessed her, not him.

"I can't, Francis," she said earnestly to her bar companion. "We're working."

He'd been fine up to now—mostly—a jovial gentleman, but he slammed his whiskey down on the little table between them, sloshing some pungent liquid over the rim. Even though she'd half-expected this, adrenalin surged through her. Fortunately they weren't sitting down, just standing and leaning on a tall table, so she jumped out of the way. She really didn't want the smell of his awful whiskey on her clothes, a yellow sweater set she'd brought to wear with her black velvet pants. She checked the other customers' reactions and then stared at the dribbled alcohol, mesmerized by the way it pooled like pee on the table and the floor.

"That never stopped you before," her former friend muttered not quite under his breath.

Damn, so they'd heard about her affair with Dr. Percy Meadowvale, all the way down in Princeton, for God's sake. Well, the academic world was small and on a personal level, a married professor who slept with a PhD candidate was definitely big news. Academic people were no different than anybody else. They loved gossip. Loved hating people who did what they wouldn't have dared.

If Kathleen had been back in Montreal, she would have turned around and walked out the door, but she wasn't sure about anything in this hole of a town, so she backed up—too far it seemed. One of her little stack heels caught in a knot in the wooden floor. *Shit*, she thought, almost toppling, *that's what happens when you're clumsy with embarrassment and drink.* She was also good and mad now and that made things even worse, it always had. She'd better get hold of her temper or else. She stumbled a little, almost falling back on her rear.

"Sorry, little darling," the bleached blond guy on the bar stool automatically said, reaching out a steadying hand.

Ah, but his hand felt so good on her back. *So he's Canadian, too,* she thought, recognizing his accent. *How strange, two Canucks in this dreary little Yankee place.*

"Sorry," she offered simultaneously to somebody who suddenly didn't look half bad. She liked the way he kept looking at her, so she checked him out again too. Yes, he was muscle-bound and hairy—not her type at all—she much preferred hairless men with more muscle between their ears—but oh, my God, he was young.

And the darkness in his eyes didn't bother her a bit; it just made him more interesting.

Suddenly she felt even more tired of men whose stories were almost over: the doctors who had followed her childhood illness, her stepfather back in high school and dear, dear Dr. Percy Meadowvale, the only one she'd actually had time to sleep with.

The stranger on the bar stool gave her strength. She looked back down at Francis. She felt like shaking him, the old geezer, he really had some nerve! She didn't need this. For the moment, she hated all this self-analysis crap (she got enough of it when she talked to her therapist) and she hated old men. Maybe she'd got his hopes up meeting him here like this, though. To discuss butterflies yet! What if he thought she was some kind of tease? What if he told other people? And why the hell did she even care?

She looked over her shoulder. *Help me*, her big blue eyes said.

The stranger on the bar stool cracked the briefest smile. "You're doing just fine," he said.

"Yeah," Francis Murphy slurred. "But you'll do better with me, oh, yes, you will. Do you think Mr. Beefcake here is going to help you find the monarchs? D'you think he has the goddamn brains? I'm the one who knows their habits—that stupid fuck Sheridan didn't even know they ate milkweed. And you, you skinny little bitch, you'll never find them on your own."

So be it, she thought, shrugging at the boy on the bar stool who looked as if he might have decked Francis Murphy if she hadn't smiled her best I-don't-give-a-shit smile and taken his hand.

Chapter 10
Rabbit, Run

You do things and do things and nobody really has a clue. ~**Rabbit, Run** by John Updike

February 5, 1973

D ace and Kathleen drove for hours while she sat on the edge of the bench seat with her hands on her bony knees, her ankles twisted like giant pretzels, the kind you buy at a fair. Her little Datsun reeked of coffee and lavender. He'd expected — well, hoped she'd fall asleep in the car after last night because they'd been up half the night, but she hadn't. Man, the girl could talk.

"My name's Mary Kathleen Aldous," she'd said, like somebody who expected to see her name up in lights or at least on a book cover. She gave off a lot of confidence for a girl — overplayed it maybe — but something in her still seemed afraid. "I've always been called Kathleen, though. There were too many Marys where I stayed."

And where was that — at some exclusive girls' school? he wondered, though he certainly didn't ask. You just didn't ask personal questions in jail and besides, what if she asked him where he'd grown up? *In downtown Toronto and Maitland* he'd say, leaving out the part about the school he'd gone to in Maitland. Girls didn't want to hear stuff like that, no matter what they said.

Mary Kathleen Aldous. He liked her name. She reminded him of a little rabbit, so edgy, so alert. Nobody would believe he was on the run with a girl like this. A smart girl, an educated girl, a PhD candidate, whatever the hell that was, though it sounded like something his cousin Liza might do if she had the chance. Kathleen had talked about butterfly paths and her career path for a good half hour last night, while he'd just lain there with his hands behind his head and stared. Because she was pretty good-looking too, if you didn't mind a tall, lanky girl and he didn't. Her breasts had fit so nicely in his hands and her secret place, her tight little snatch, was perfect. He got hard just thinking about it. Well, they wouldn't have believed he was on the lam with a girl like Liza, either, except she was his cousin—a known companion of his— and they always checked out family first.

"Watch the road," Kathleen said for the umpteenth time that day. Her cautiousness puzzled him. He'd seen less wary men in Segregation with a shiv pointed at their backs. She'd refused to drive her own car, a grubby little blue Datsun with a McGill University sticker stuck to its rear. How she'd crossed the Canadian-American border, he didn't know. With him around this morning, she couldn't even get into the driver's seat. She'd just stood there and shook, a butterfly of a girl, trembling against the trunk of a tree.

"Maybe later," she'd said. "It's funny, but I really drive better when I've had a drink and I don't want to drink now. It's way too early." What the hell was she so frightened about? Not him. For one thing, she knew almost nothing about him, except what she'd seen of his body last night. She'd asked about the scars—who wouldn't?—but her interest was doctor-like, clinical. He'd never met anybody like her before, except on the Parole Board maybe. And he never had the chance to sleep with one of those women of course. Or any woman with such icy blue eyes. It scared him a little, the way Kathleen could look so detached.

As for the story he'd spun—well, it was all lies. If only he could keep it straight.

Those eyes—she was starting to spook him again. He doubted she'd recognize him from the papers back home—it had been awhile and he'd been one of thirteen men—but you never knew. "Shut your eyes, baby girl," he said. "You're scaring yourself again." He'd never met a girl who didn't want somebody to take care of her, at least part time.

Drawing her sweater tighter around her thin frame, she stared. He knew she liked looking at him, but still. "You're so damn good-looking," she'd said last night. "Though it's kind of wasted on a man." She'd bitten down all the nails on her left hand, he noticed, although the nails on her right hand were still intact.

"You know I can't do that. Close my eyes. We might...." she said.

"Crash into a transport truck? Fall off a bridge?"

"Or run over some more bunny rabbits like we did this morning…"

"Jesus, don't start that again. It was an accident! Christ, there were rabbits all over the place. Aren't they supposed to hibernate or something?"

"No," she replied, chewing on her left forefinger again. "As a matter of fact, we don't think monarch butterflies do either. They do a kind of suspended animation during the winter months instead—torpor, it's called."

"Well, how am I supposed to know all that?" Dace interrupted. He didn't mind listening to her in bed, but it bothered him while he drove. When he really had to focus on something, he tried to keep everything else out. The stuff he did in bed was pure instinct, so she could yap there all she wanted. "You're the academic, Miss Smarty Pants! I'm just a mechanic, a bike mechanic while you're a lepidopterist—a butterfly specialist of all the goddamn things," he enunciated, pleased to actually remember the fucking term, "and a research assistant… to who—to whom— did you say?" he asked, hoping to distract her.

And it worked.

"To Dr. Percy Meadowvale," she replied listlessly, her little shoulders slumping under her yellow sweater. "At least I was. He was an assistant to Dr. Gene Sheridan at the U of T, but then we both got transferred to Montreal. Uh, it was a personnel problem. You know how conservative some of these workplaces can be."

Dace didn't have a clue what she was talking about, but he nodded anyway.

"Plus it's the same old story," she elaborated, "what's sauce for the gander isn't always sauce for the goose. You must have heard about Sheridan though. He's always in the news.. He's done tons of groundbreaking research."

Dace glanced at her quickly. That tone. It sounded like she was torn between pride and scorn. He was always wary of what people didn't say. *I'll bet her doctor friend's married,* he thought, with a girl like her on the side. *Some guys had all the luck. Jesus, just look at her.* She had everything going for her, but she'd given it up to a married man. Couldn't she have found somebody else? What was with some girls? Why did they do that? Their subservience, their acquiescence, the shit they put up with, yeah, the way they endured. It astounded him sometimes. They acted so powerless. Why—because they were smaller? Oh, hell, why did anybody do anything? He didn't understand why he did a lot of things. Next time around he'd be a psych and figure everybody out.

"I never heard of him," he shrugged, "but my cousin Liza might have. She's at Maitland U and she's always been crazy about monarchs too," he volunteered proudly. Too much information! What the hell was he doing? Christ, he'd better shut up. "C'mon just lie back there, shut your eyes and take a rest. You're tired. It's a long way to Mexico. We aren't anywhere yet."

Kathleen hadn't asked about Liza last night and she didn't now. She had zero interest in other women, which was kind of odd. Maybe they bored her or something. Well, who cared! She liked men or what they could do for her anyway. She liked him. "I must have stayed up too late last night trying to figure you out," she smirked, knowing that definitely wasn't why she had stayed up. "Tell me your story again."

Mind your own business, Dace felt like saying, but that would only egg her on. Most guys took you at face value, but so many girls were like a priest and the Parole Board combined. Always wanting to know. And this girl was the kind of person who really wanted to know things. All those degrees. Just look at that double crease between her eyes. Her finely tuned mind worked overtime. No doubt it had since she was a tiny girl, while his—he prayed for sleep and oblivion most of the time, although they rarely came.

What exactly had he said back in the hotel with the mice in the walls and old man Murphy in a creaky bed next door? The old bugger had probably had a glass up to the wall. She'd been so insatiable, he could tell she hadn't had sex for a long time.

"I told you. Somebody took my car for a joyride and used it to rob a bank. The manager got shot…"

She shuddered, the way girls do. "I hate guns," she said. "They say that everybody down here in the States keeps a loaded rifle by their front door. This happened back in Ontario? I didn't hear about a bank manager getting shot in the news."

"Because he didn't die! You know what newspapers are like. That's good, isn't it? And it was in the kind of place nobody cares about..." Dace paused, trying to think of some hick northern Ontario town. "Uh, Cobalt or something..." he finally dredged up, remembering a guy in jail who'd come from there, a skinny little Irish guy.

"Or something?" she echoed, her eyes burrowing right through him. "I thought you said Timmins. Don't you know?"

Jesus, he thought, starting to sweat a little. Did Cobalt even have a bank? Had she ever been there? "No, it was Cobalt. Besides, what kind of Ontario news do you get out there in Quebec?" he asked, still trying to divert her. "Just Frenchy stuff, right? And we certainly won't get any Canadian news down here."

"Well, the *Gazette's* in English, but it is kind of provincial. I might have missed it on a back page," she said doubtfully. "I usually read *Le Devoir*, too, though and it's well, more sensational. I love newspapers; they're so gossipy." If she'd just shut up and let them get on with wherever the hell they were going, but of course she didn't. "You don't think that maybe you should go back? Try and put things right?"

At first Dace thought he'd misheard her and that she was talking about herself again, but no. He waited, watching her out of the corner of his eye.

"It's not like you're really guilty of anything....unless...." She stopped speaking and stared out her window at a cavalcade of trucks gas guzzling by.

"Unless what?" Dace asked, choosing that moment to pull out of his lane and whip around the first in a line of poky little sedans up ahead.

Kathleen's head snapped back against the seat and she covered her eyes with her hands, like a child playing peek-a-boo. "Unless you already have a record?" she asked in a rush, although she still didn't look at him.

Dace took a deep breath. Oh, God, she was a sharp little thing, another Liza. Just his luck. So fucking sharp she'd never had to be street smart. No wonder she could barely take care of herself. "What the hell kind of record would I have?" he demanded, striving to sound as innocent and injured as possible.

"I don't know," she said unhappily. "Calm down."

"I'm not a bank robber, so do I look like a murderer or something?"

"Why would you even say a thing like that, if..."

"If I wasn't guilty of something....is that what you mean? Ah, fuck!"

Behind them, the lights of a police cruiser flashed. Dace's first thought was that he didn't he even have a valid driver's license.

"What?" Kathleen asked, at the same time as he hit the brakes and put out his right arm to protect her little face. She had already grabbed the dashboard and was looking wildly around.

Dace blanked out momentarily, but his body took over. They were in the passing lane, in a cursedly long snake of closely spaced cars. If they hadn't been in such heavy traffic, he would have floored the gas pedal and run. If only he'd had his Harley, he could have weaved in and out. He felt like such a wimp. Best to play innocent, though. Just because some guy in a police vehicle wanted to pull them over, it didn't mean he knew anything about him. It was probably just the goddamn muffler.

"There's a state trooper right behind us," he said while he maneuvered the car into the right lane and onto the shoulder.

As if she doubted him, Kathleen looked over her shoulder at the flashing red lights, but then she flipped into high gear. "Let me do the talking. I'll tell him you only speak French," she said, pulling and practically pushing him to the passenger side at the same time as she crawled across his lap. Dace's head spun. Where the hell did such a skinny little girl get so much strength?

Chapter 11
The Trooper

Somewhere in Kentucky

D ace could tell just by the way the trooper walked that he was a real jerk, but so what. Cops always looked like jerks to a guy on the wrong side of the law. The man sauntered slowly over to their vehicle, tucked his tiny head into his neck and looked in the driver's seat.

"Sit still," Dace whispered to Kathleen, so of course she didn't. She'd bow to authority and listen to the fucking trooper though, just watch. Her hand crept to the handle on her door. *Don't open that*, he signaled with a little sideways motion of his lowered hand.

Why the hell had the trooper stopped them? They weren't doing anything wrong, unless... Dace's right hand gripped the side of his seat. It took all his strength not to just open the car door and run.

"Don't get out," the trooper said.

Yeah, don't get out, Dace thought, *unless you want him to cop a free feel.* What the hell was wrong with her? Had the girl never been stopped by the police before? How was that even possible?

The trooper wore a wide-brimmed hat. Dace was in the middle of the bench seat by now, his left hand on Kathleen's thigh. How he'd ended up there, he wasn't sure. The trooper had probably just noticed their loose muffler, but still.... Shit, he'd meant to fix it at the last service center, but just being with Kathleen had distracted him.

Dace looked like he couldn't keep his hands off Kathleen, but murder beat in his heart—the same way it always did when he felt threatened. Maybe if he hadn't spent so much time with murderers and cutthroats, but he had. And this tall, tree-like man was definitely a threat. To Kathleen, if not to him. The man's head and shoulders filled the window. *Ah, Christ, just look at his eyes!* Small, muddy and mean. *My knife,* Dace thought with a pang, but it wouldn't be any match for a bullet. Besides, lovely little Kathleen was in the way. At another signal from the trooper, she rolled her window down all the way.

"Hi, sir!" she said with a forced, bright smile, from her in-charge position behind the wheel. Dace breathed a small, premature sigh of relief. Oh, she was a good little girl all right. And a babe. From where he sat, she had enough going for her to distract any man.

Except this man appeared immune to Kathleen's charm. Weird. And then it came to Dace, the way these things sometimes do. *Son-of-a-bitch,* he thought in rising panic, *maybe he doesn't like girls.*

"I thought you were driving," the trooper said, while Dace just kept sitting there, trying his best to look deaf, dumb and blanker.

"Oh, no," Kathleen said, her confidence fading almost as fast as her smile. During the man's approach to the car, she'd pulled a crumbling cigarette from somewhere under the seat, but from the looks of it, she'd never smoked. She couldn't decide which end to put in her mouth. "He can't," she elaborated while brushing dry tobacco from the sweater stretched tight over her small breasts. "He doesn't have a license. That was me, sir. I just had my head down a moment, trying to do two things at once—you know, my boyfriend, um!— and light this darn cigarette…"

The trooper looked her up and down with distaste. When Kathleen's little throat quivered and turned red, Dace understood her affinity for rabbits. She looked like a white one in the jaws of a nasty dog. Her eyes dropped to her lap.

For a couple of seconds, the cop just let them stew. "Yeah, I bet," he finally said.

The registration, Dace thought, *give him your license and the registration and get it over with.* Jesus, she hadn't stolen the goddamn car.

"…and you know, my boyfriend—Claude, Claude Monet, uh, I mean Claude Manon— he was steadying the wheel," Kathleen soldiered on. "This is my car. The registration, Sir, would you like to see the registration? It's in the glove compartment, I think…"

Dace stopped his hand from reaching towards the glove compartment just in time. For God's sake, he was worse than Kathleen. *Easy, Mac,* he told himself. *Don't get too helpful.*

"You think? Your license, Miss," the trooper spat.

Kathleen's cool vanished completely. Dace had never seen a girl look so terrified. It made him even madder. He nearly lunged across her and grabbed the trooper by the throat. "Oh, that. It's in my purse behind his back…" she stammered. She looked at Dace, but she wasn't seeing him.

The trooper nodded — barely — but he kept his eyes on Dace while Kathleen retrieved the license from her purse. Her hair flashed in the light, a shoulder length helmet of gold. Neither Kathleen's license nor the attention-grabbing color of her hair interested the trooper much. He dropped the license back in her lap after the briefest glance and looked over at Dace.

"Did you know the muffler on this automobile is loose, boy?" he asked. "It's a hazard if you lose it out on the parkway."

"Yes, sir," Kathleen volunteered eagerly. "He does. We're just driving to the next service center. My boyfriend is a whiz with cars, but he needs, uh, some tools…"

"Shut up, girlie," the trooper said. "You deaf, boy?" he asked Dace, while still holding onto the car door. The Datsun shook whenever he moved. The man weighed at least two hundred and thirty pounds. "How come you're letting a silly little skirt like this drive and do all the talking?"

Kathleen pulled her chewed fingernail out of her mouth and tried again. "He's French, sir…uh, French-Canadian, I mean," she said. "He doesn't understand you."

Dace had already noticed the vein throbbing in the trooper's forehead, but now his nostrils flared too and his right hand brushed the holstered gun on his hip. Fortunately, a passing car honked at them and he forgot the gun. *There's too many witnesses*, Dace could almost hear him thinking.

"A frog, eh?" the cop said, suddenly losing interest in Dace too. "Well, make him good for something," he said to Kathleen. "Tell him to get your auto fixed pronto. If I catch you down the road again, it's a big fine. You could do better, Miss," he added as he walked away.

A stunned Kathleen sat still, but not for long. Before Dace could stop her, she stuck her head out of the window and shouted at the retreating uniform, "And just what do you mean by *that*?!" And no doubt she would have said plenty more if he hadn't clamped his hand over her mouth and dragged her wriggling little butt back into the car.

Just keep on walking, Dace thought, *don't listen to her.* He didn`t have time for this shit. If he played hero, he'd end up either dead or in jail.

Kathleen struggled briefly in his arms, but then complied, just like she had last night in bed. *Sweet,* he thought, burying his face in her breasts and tugging at the nipples with his teeth. Like she had no choice, like he was the last man, the most important man, the most virile man on earth.

Somewhere in a nearby big city, it was the evening rush hour. People wanted to get home to their spouses and kiddies or catch the game at a local bar. If the commuters hadn't been in such a hurry, somebody might have stopped to strip the car. Kathleen's dirty Datsun looked empty enough, a derelict on the side of the road.

"Don't tell me anything," she said as she shoved off her pants and grabbed his upper arms. "Just put it into me," she cried, without looking at his face.

Chapter 12
Threes

But at my back I always hear Time's winged chariot hurrying near.
~Andrew Marvell

Maitland University Campus, February 7, 1973

At first, everything went better than Liza had hoped, but life was like that, hers anyway, a lie. Just like her cycles used to be when she wasn't pregnant, just like her moods. A lovely lull, then a precipitous decline. It irritated her to realize she was so controlled by her hormones, but she wasn't thinking about that now. She couldn't. She was only twenty, but she still felt time rushing at her side.

Judging from the yard and his garage, Uncle Norm owned every vehicle he'd ever driven and most of them still worked. After he`d cleaned it out completely and equipped it with new brakes (and seatbelts which were compulsory now), he gave her the old station wagon he'd had when his wife was alive and Liza went back to university, her secret life, the bulk in her belly hidden under one of her uncle's overcoats. Just like that. In her heart, she knew life couldn't continue this way—calm and hope-filled even with Dace months gone—but she wished it could. Her baby was going to need all the calm he could get.

Her uncle hadn't said one damn word about the baby so far, but that was okay, it was just his way. And he worked all the time. She had never seen anybody work so hard, unless it was the women she'd lived with, her mother, her Gran and now Millie. The sight of Norm's busy big hands always made her feel a little sad, the way they kept going even if nothing else was going right. Even if his only son had screwed up big time and was now on the run.

Yes, Norm was a dear man who had been dealt a bad hand and she wasn't helping things, either. Though he still tried to make the best of things, to do what was right. He'd done right by his wife, his children and he'd do right by his grandchild too. Even if he couldn't acknowledge him right now. What else had she expected? He was a man of few words, that's all, just like his son.

She'd come by the house herself the first time, then gone back to the university residence in Maitland to fetch her suitcases and a couple of boxes the next day. Her roommate Janice had cried, but not her. She couldn't. She didn't have time for tears. She'd wasted days crying and now she had to do what was best for her unborn son—carry him, nurture him and find him shelter.

"So you'll come stay with us awhile," Uncle Norm had said in a kind of offhand way, but he wanted her alright. Especially after he came back from Cornwall and found her at the farmhouse, the last link to his son Dace, who definitely wasn't the boy in the morgue.

And he knew what had happened to her. What she'd done. He just didn't like to admit it. Well, she had a hard time facing it herself. And sometimes if he didn't talk about things, they went away.

Not that the baby was going away. The baby—well, the fetus— was the size of a cantaloupe now. He had all his fingers and his toes and he could probably hear and see. Six weeks ago, he had been scarcely formed and ten weeks ago barely more than a fertilized egg, but there was absolutely no turning back now. It was almost like he was growing at the speed of light. Liza had felt movement for the first time on January 8 and when the midwife had put the stethoscope against the lowest portion of her abdomen, a drum roll of the baby's heartbeat had filled the room.

In spite of all the uncertainty in her life—Uncle Norm's housekeeper Millie-What's- Her-Face hated her and she didn't know what the hell Dace was doing oh God where was he, was he alright?—she had been almost happy through January. *It's just my hormones* she thought more than once. *Is that all I am? My body is so busy gearing up for the birth—*

my biological destiny — it doesn't care what the hell happens to me next.

She missed Dace terribly and Mel too if the truth be told, but it came as a relief to have nothing to do except go to school. Life was so simple when you didn't have to worry about where to throw up next, when you weren't completely obsessed with food and so exhausted that you craved sleep at least twenty hours a day. From what she'd read about mid-pregnancy, this sense of wellbeing would also pass, but she sure had a ton of energy right now.

Isolated on the Devereux farm with no roommates to distract her and little to do, she'd caught up on all her courses. She might even pull ahead. Yes, she'd make it, maybe even sail through the rest of the school year, win that third year English prize, who knew. If she didn't specialize, she could graduate with a general BA. Write a book along the way! The baby wasn't due until mid-June, a couple of seasons away. She'd worry about it then. She had tons of time.

Then February came.

"Where the hell did you learn to drive?" Mel scowled when he ran into her in the parking lot near the Sciences Building, a place where she would never make the mistake of parking again. She had parked there because it had snowed last night and the other lots were still not ploughed.

Liza's body changed daily. She didn't want Mel to see her ballooning figure, but she had no choice, so she climbed awkwardly out of the wagon and pressed down the lock on the door. Her nose prickled with an unspent sneeze as soon as her face hit the cold. But she couldn't just sit there and freeze, or idle and burn gas. *This is what a pregnant woman looks like*, she thought angrily. But her cheeks also burned with shame, remembering how she'd walked out on him at Christmastime. She'd mailed him the money she had taken for Dace — after getting a partial fee refund from the university residence— but that still didn't make it right. Oh, God, Mel's mother... Not that she cared what old Mrs. Melville thought. What on earth had ever gone wrong in her life? Oh, well, her older son hadn't gotten into medical school and she was a woman, so she'd might have forfeited a couple of dreams along the way.

"You should have kept the fucking money," Mel had phoned Liza to say while Norm's housekeeper Millie fussed in the shadows. "They never would have missed it. I've dipped into it myself a couple of times."

It felt good to see Mel though. Safe, safer than she had ever felt with Dace. Another dear man, well still a boy really.

"Uncle Norm showed me how to drive," she said a little proudly. "It was easier than learning to ride a motorbike." She grimaced a little, recalling how long it had taken Dace to teach her how to ride one. Christ, she'd been so scared. It was a miracle really. She'd never thought she could do it, but she had.

"I got my license too," she said now. *Shut up*, she told herself. *Shut up!* So what if Mel thought she was lawless enough to drive around without one. When she'd done much worse, like harbor a criminal in his parents' house. Thank God he only suspected that—he didn't know for sure.

She needn't have worried, though. Mel no longer cared what the hell she did. Snow stiles bordered the parking lot. Always the gentleman, he didn't offer to help her over them now. From the looks of it, he wanted to get away from her as fast as possible. Not that she blamed him. Within seconds, he was on the outskirts of the parking lot, headed off to his class, coatless, except for a denim army jacket, in the falling snow. His birthday was February 5, so he'd just turned twenty-one. Bluish black stubble glistened on his chin and his glasses were fogged. Liza fought the urge to run out of the parking lot and warm him in her arms. *Oh, God, I already feel like a mother*, she thought. At least he had a university scarf, the one she'd given him for Christmas, wrapped around his neck.

"Well, it's not like you can ride a bike in the wintertime and in your condition," he flung over his shoulder. He stopped then and really looked at her for a moment and then at her car. His uncut hair, a wiry stack of curls, blew back into his face, a face she nearly smacked when he suddenly smirked and said: "And did Uncle Norm show you how to turn off the lights?"

"Shit," Liza said and turned back to the station wagon. She couldn't afford to drain the battery; she'd already done that once. *Please, please, don't ask about Dace.* Who was old news now, she felt certain. Six weeks had passed since he'd escaped from Maitland Super Max. Life moved on; other miscreants stepped into the limelight; other news stories took hold.

But of course Mel didn't ask her anything about Dace, not then,

98

nor would he ever. She knew that. And by the time she'd finally found her car key again in the numbing wind, opened the door and flicked off the lights, he was gone. *He's got more important stuff to think about*, she thought a little sadly. *Like getting into medicine. And Dace isn't his problem, his lover, his kin. He's mine.*

Rushing to her Communications class in the Journalism Department with her head straight into the wind, loneliness hit her so hard that she almost buckled at the knees. She had to face it. She was going to be an unwed mother, the kind of girl she used to look down on. How could a girl make such a mistake and then go through it? But she had and now her life was practically over. She'd never see Mel or Dace again.

She had on knee high boots under another long, loose granny dress, but no tights, so her bare thighs stung with the cold. The doors of the Social Sciences Faculty looked so far away. She gritted her teeth.
Buck up, she chattered to herself, *Remember Dublin. What the hell do you expect? Dace isn't coming back — he can't — and nobody else will want you in your condition. Ever. It's time to grow up and be the mother you always wanted. You've got to find a way to look after this baby and make it on your own.*

****

Joe Armitage was more difficult to deal with than Mel. He always had been. During her first year at Maitland University, he'd just been a pest, but now Liza recognized in him a predator, a man who lusted after what he couldn't have, but who would also lose interest the minute he got what he wanted. She'd seen it happen. Six weeks into the winter semester, he'd already bedded and booted out two naïve young girls. He couldn't afford to get "involved," he told the people he called his friends, a comment confirmed by one of the girls. Both girls were virgins when he lured them to his den, a campus office on the third floor of the Social Sciences Building, but not for long. They did it on the floor. Or so people said.

Nobody — especially Liza — blamed the girls. For much as she and his many detractors were loath to admit it, Joe Armitage had a certain charm. Part of this charm was that he read and "understood" people in a flash and to be understood, well, that was good.

For the first couple of weeks, Joe and Liza just observed each other in the advanced Communications class — *Sexual Media Exploits* — that he co-taught with the new American professor, Dr. Jack Diamond.

Not that Joe taught much. He stood at the podium, a tall, thin man except for a small pouch of loose skin sagging over his belt and showed the class pictures of questionable advertising practices on an overhead projector. Curse those advertisers; they had imbedded subliminal sexual messages everywhere. And just look at those magazine ads! What, they couldn't see them? Well, trust him, trust his new mentor, Dr. Jack Diamond who had written several books on the topic of subliminal advertising. If they just sat back and relaxed, they'd see that they were really there.

But when the classroom got really hot and Liza finally had to open her coat or die, he zeroed in on her swelling belly right away. It was hard not to notice, she supposed. Other people stared too, the girls especially, some of them with a little grin. *When I walk out, I am a great event*, Liza thought. Her stomach had been concave before, but just look at her now, making a spectacle of herself. When she'd first come to Maitland University from her grandmother's in Dublin, she had mourned Dace so much that she'd lost tons of weight. This year, in all her classes, but especially this one, she sat in the back row, but it didn't help. She was the center of attention, but not in a good way. And wherever she went, whatever she did, Joe found her. He had just smiled at her at first, but that was enough. Christ, he had an irritating smile. She was beginning to really hate his guts.

Yes, most people smiled at her. With her chosen transformation, this takeover of her body, her willingness to take such a stupid leap of faith, she had become public property. Nobody else was pregnant at university. Nobody. If you got pregnant and you wanted the baby, you went home. If you couldn't have the baby, you had a therapeutic abortion and nobody knew. Except the Hospital Board of course, who had to approve, though that was just a formality in southern Ontario anyway. Thank God—it had been like that in Canada for the last year or two.

Liza couldn't even think of Ireland. It hurt too much. To commit such an act of desperation had cost her and her grandmother so much. The terrible despair Liza had felt, the risks they had both taken and the guilt her grandmother had felt about the termination of an embryonic pregnancy.

"I can never do this," her grandmother had said, but in the end she

100

had, for Liza, her responsibility and her kin and for her own sanity too. Meanwhile, abortion was still illegal in Ireland and it looked like it would be for years to come. All those Catholics, Liza supposed and the fact that Ireland had lost so many due to forced immigration, hunger and murder over the years. Of course, richer girls could go to England for a termination, they always had. For that reason alone, abortion shouldn't be illegal in Ireland, it shouldn't be, she thought, marveling how she could even think about such a thing while Dace's seed quickened in her womb.

People—girls mostly— came right up and asked if she planned to have the baby "naturally" and if she really thought she could finish the year. *Yes,* she assured them with a confidence she didn't feel. By a stroke of luck, Liza's midwife, a Mennonite woman in early middle age, lived just down the road from Uncle Norm with her husband, a houseful of children and another on the way. Her name was Mary Bergen. Before January was out, Liza had put a ring on her left hand to forestall a fresh set of questions: who's the father and what do you plan to do?

Fortunately another freshman—one of the few married students— came along and distracted Joe Armitage for a time. Perhaps the girl's looks and marital status had attracted Joe who had so far shown a marked preference for what wasn't his. She was an animated little thing, a smart whip of a white girl with a mop of permed "Afro" curls. Lovely, really. She reminded Liza of the prime minister's young wife, Margaret Sinclair Trudeau. Joe drank coffee and smoked cigarettes with the girl in the Social Sciences cafeteria on the ground floor until one day the girl's husband, a big, burly red-faced boy showed up and started blowing smoke in his face. Liza despised the jealousy she felt, but couples always annoyed her these days. Even Uncle Norm and his housekeeper, for God's sake!

Joe backed off, but he caught up with Liza later that same day, exiting the lecture hall when she did. When she should have ducked and run, she looked at him gravely and sighed. Her mistake. Nothing was ever his fault. He was temporarily at loose ends, she supposed, so she was fair game.

He backed her into a closed doorway to the left while the rest of the class—seventy of them— stampeded past. Liza had no choice. She had always disliked crowds, and she hated them even more now, fearful as she was for the life she carried inside her. On a daily basis, she grew less nimble, less able to protect herself. It was ridiculous, really. She'd read somewhere that women were most likely to be killed when they got pregnant. Mostly by their partners, though, and she didn't have one, so she was probably safe. Lucky, lucky her. Oh, Christ, she hated, hated feeling so fucking helpless.

Sweat broke out on her brow when he pinned her in the doorway. The urge to vomit had never entirely left her, especially when she got tired. If Joe didn't watch it, she'd throw up on his shiny black leather shoes right now.

I want to go home, she thought, marveling how quickly Uncle Norm's farm had become "home," *I've got a great idea for my paper on Beowulf in Renaissance Lit...if I can just escape this idiot's clutches.*

Joe's hand strayed to her forehead, but she jerked her head away. Tears came to her eyes; they came so damn easily these days.

If your hand goes anywhere else, I'll kill you, she thought. *I'll take my new red ballpoint pen and stab you right between your small, beady eyes.* In the meantime, it was all she could do not to raise her knee and slam it into his crotch. He'd be the one puking then.

Joe could read her alright. "Don't you dare," he growled, but he didn't touch her again. He put a hand up on the wall and hung over her instead. His face looked damp and he had sweat stains in both armpits too. Dr. Diamond rarely let him give the class lecture. Giving the lecture had excited him, she supposed.

"So your renegade cousin, the dashing Dace Devereux is still on the run?" he asked pleasantly enough, his breath uncomfortably close to her face. She smelled cigarettes, stale coffee and some kind of rot and almost gagged again.

Though Liza had to force herself, she lifted her eyes and stared hard at him. *Please*, Dr. Diamond, she thought, *come*. Diamond was no rescuer of damsels in distress though. No doubt he'd left by the backdoor to escape Joe. For the first time, she noticed the way Joe's fleshy lower lip jutted out and then turned down. No wonder he looked so cruel.

"If you mean that they haven't found him, yes, that's right. What do the police say?"

Pleased, Joe smiled. "The police? You act like I have a special line to the coppers..."

"Because you damn well do! The *Spectator*. You're still working for

102

them, aren't you? Part-time?" *And on your book about outlaw bikers*, she supposed. He had better not put Dace in it. Or she'd ... Yeah, just what would she do? "The press, the police, everything is run by the same people in this town," she said. *Your people*, she thought. The Armitages had lived in Maitland for generations. It sounded wonderful, but it wasn't. In her mind's eye, she saw them, a long line of men with the same nasty mouth and a string of hapless, fucked up wives. *May your line die out in this generation*, she prayed. "Or do you find yourself a little pressed for time now that you're finally working on your dissertation?"

"My, my, you'll have to watch your tone, little girl. You don't sound very maternal. Nope—all I know is that lover boy is still on Canada's Most Wanted List and probably the FBI's too. A traffic cop spotted somebody who looked a lot like him in a McGill student's car. Way down in Kentucky or Tennessee, I think. How they met up, nobody knows. Real strange. Well, I guess you can't blame him for wanting to warm up with somebody because, baby, it's cold out there." Her eyes widened and he stopped, evidently pleased with her reaction.

Where? Liza's inner voice shrieked, but it didn't pay to engage in conversation with Joe Armitage about Dace Devereux. It never had. From underneath Joe's rancid armpit, she checked out the hall. Everybody had gone. The image of Dace with another girl popped into her mind. *What the devil*, she thought. He was supposed to be scared, he was supposed to be on the run. Maybe the girl—what girl, what did she look like? what did she do?—was helping him though. Maybe they were after something really important. Thinking of her swollen body, Liza almost despised herself. In her present condition, she wasn't much use. To Dace or anybody else. And she wanted to be useful to Dace so much. She always had.

"I don't believe you," she muttered. "You're making stuff up."

Joe raised an eyebrow. "Well, I'm not making up that belly of yours, girl. And I've got an idea, a theory. It's his, isn't it? Yes, I can see from your face that it is. Your eyes—your lovely dark eyes—just did a telltale shift to the side. Tsk, tsk. And I hear you're living out at his father's farm. Nice of him not to kick you out, like your parents so evidently have. Maybe your old uncle is a bit too nice in fact. How old is he anyway? And what kind of family puts up with something like this? Especially cause you're cousins, yuck."

Liza slid out from under his arm. "Fuck off," she said, nearly biting her tongue in half. She wanted to say more, but dammit, she was still enrolled in his course, a course she had to pass if she really wanted to finish her year. And she had already put in half the year. She had gotten A's first term, even while attending Dace's trial, but Joe had given her a C on her last assignment. Luckily the assignment had only been worth five per cent.

"Oh, by the way, sorry I was so hard on your last paper," he said. My God, he really could read her mind, something he always used to his own advantage, never hers. Of course. "But I had no choice. Your paper wasn't very academic — sort of novelistic, in fact. Like you had baby brain or something. I was a little disappointed. I know you can do better than that."

Liza turned red. To say her paper wasn't academic enough — when all that stuff he'd written for the *Maitland Spectator* was such overblown hyperbole! She'd hate to see his book. He was the worst writer in the world. "Everything Joe Armitage writes is grating, saccharine drivel," his kindest critic had said about his editorials. She had to be ten times smarter than him — she just wasn't old enough to be working on her PhD. Well, unless she was a genius who had started university at fourteen.

She held her tongue, but her mind raced. All Joe's misinformation about pregnancy and how it affected a woman's mind, surely to God it had been debunked by now. But doubt crept into her mind. Because she didn't know. It didn't make sense that a woman would get stupider when she got pregnant, though. How would that further the human race? *Well, never mind,* she told herself, *it's galling, but all you have to do is pass Joe's course.* And he wouldn't fail her, the misogynist, he wouldn't dare.

What the hell had happened to him when he was a child? What crimes had been committed against him? *Please God, don't let babies just be born this way.* She'd go to Diamond, she'd go to the Faculty Head, she'd... well, she'd do something.

She sagged against the wall. The easiest thing to do would be to sleep with Joe, she supposed. She was hardly a virgin. Just once and he'd probably leave her alone. Because that's what he did. What the hell did it matter? He definitely liked the chase more than the kill. It had taken him so long to start his PhD, he didn't have much credibility in the Social Sciences faculty at Maitland right now, but he had all sorts of family connections and he would in time... When it came right down to it, the Armitage family was just like the Devereux family. They took care of their own.

What, just to pass a course? Are you crazy, her inner friend shrieked again. *Come back to me, Dace,* she prayed, with no more hope than Heathcliff trying to scream Cathy from the grave. She put out her hand and pushed against Joe's chest. He staggered back a little. Pregnancy had made her stronger than she thought. She smiled a little, empowered by the weight behind her hand.

Ugh, no, of course, she couldn't sleep with him. Just the smell of him made her sick. It always had—well, mostly. Sometimes when he taught, he had a certain allure. When the rest of the girls looked at him, like he was a man worthy of their respect and a powerful one at that.

Joe chuckled, caught at her hand, and kissed the back of it European style. "Ah, Liza," he said, "you're really, really something. Especially now that you're so lush, so fecund and so safe. Because you're already pregnant, aren't you? I'd love nothing better than to sink myself into your soft, compliant flesh. Or you could struggle, too—absolve yourself of any responsibility. I know how that works and I don't mind. You think I'm weird, don't you, but I'm not the only one who wouldn't mind sleeping with a pregnant woman, a delicious little dish like you. The other profs..."

Oh, God, how he lied and manipulated. "Really?" she said as she walked away. "But you're not a prof, are you." *And won't be if I have any say.*

He chuckled after her, temporarily abandoning the chase.

******

Meanwhile back at the farm, Liza thought while she listened to her uncle and his housekeeper, Mrs. O'Connor—Millie—sort out things in the family room downstairs. God, it had been a long day. Did nothing ever change? Why did bad stuff always happen in threes? Liza ached to retreat to her room, to crawl into bed with the quilt her dead aunt had made and pull it up over her head, but she didn't dare. She had to know what Millie was saying. Better to know her enemy, better to be prepared.

Millie hadn't always been her enemy—well, at least not overtly— but from the bleak, cold day in early January when Liza moved from the student residence out to the farm, she had viewed her with suspicion, like she was a con artist come to cheat her employer Norm Devereux of his fortune. She had taken care of Norm for ten plus years and she wasn't about to stop now. *Millie's like a cartoon of that housekeeper in* Daphne du Maurier's Rebecca, Liza thought.

Millie had also made it her business to keep an eye on Liza. She watched her all the time — her expanding shape, how much she talked on the phone, how clean she kept the bathroom, but mostly how much time she spent alone with her Uncle Norm.

Some sense of decorum — or perhaps the simple desire not to jeopardize her job — had so far prevented the housekeeper from saying anything to Liza's face, but she muttered under her breath a great deal, especially while she ironed Norm's shirts. Liza remembered her mother doing the same thing, while her father sat in the living room and read his newspaper. *Never underestimate the powerless,* she thought, for Millie controlled everything that happened in the house.

Perhaps most telling, she never served Liza any food, though she was always cooking and baking and on her ample hips, it showed. Norm ate dinner promptly at 5:00 pm — ridiculously early — and Liza rarely got home before 6:00, but the housekeeper didn't even deign to save her some overcooked meat and vegetables in the oven on a tinfoil plate.

It had taken her uncle a couple of weeks to even notice. He never bothered with the kitchen. He didn't have the time. Besides, he paid the woman and he paid her good. "Help yourself, dear," he'd finally just shrugged. "Mrs. O'Connor has her ways." At first Liza had almost starved, reluctant as she was to prowl through somebody else's refrigerator and cupboards, but she soon got over that. And the shiny fridge was always full of eggs and cheese and fruit. Though Millie tried her best to guard the kitchen from the adjoining family room, she was usually snoring long before the CBC news came on at 10:00. Too bad she slept over most nights — so she could make Norm a good, hot breakfast, she said, crisp bacon and scrambled eggs, with plenty of white buttered toast and dollops of her homemade strawberry jam.

Thank God, it was almost Millie's bedtime. "They still have homes for girls like her," she yawned.

Uncle Norm never said much and he didn't now, at least nothing

106

Liza could hear from the shadows on the second floor. *Protect me*, she thought. *Protect me from myself and from censure and from shame.* But knowing him, he probably just wanted to sit there and enjoy his beer. She would just have to protect herself, that's all. She felt a little sorry for him though. Would his women folk never leave him alone?

Millie's mind must have been working overtime. She tried a new tack.

"People will talk," she said, "They're already talking, about you and the girl. Maybe if your Rosie and her husband were living here too, but they aren't."

Well, that did it. Uncle Norm started talking too. "Don't be stupid," Liza thought he said. He was always soft spoken, but his voice got harder then. "She's just a kid, my brother's little girl."

"Not so little," Millie said and when that didn't get any response, she added, "It was good between us until she came." There was a soft, little slurping noise then, but it might just have been Uncle Norm sucking on his cigarette. Millie wasn't much of a smoker, but sometimes she had one with him.

Liza closed her eyes and wrapped her arms around her chest. She was on the floor by the heating vent and she wanted to hug her knees, but she couldn't. Her cantaloupe-sized stomach was in the way. The idea of somebody as old as her parents having sex made her feel a little sick, but she also felt shut out. My God, was everybody in the world with somebody except her? She didn't care about the sex, she didn't. In fact, she couldn't even remember…

"She's trouble, Norm, nothing but trouble. The little slut…"

Damn you, Liza thought, while visions of yanking out the woman's hair exploded in her head.

"Nothing but trouble," Millie repeated.

With some difficulty, Liza got up from the floor and crept over to the head of the stairs. She was halfway down the stairs when she saw them through the open door of the family room. They were doing it on the floor, but somehow Millie was still talking. Behind them, the flames in the fireplace leapt.

"Sleeping with him and God knows who. Or what! She has pills, birth control pills. I saw them. They were locked in her suitcase, a half finished package, expired, but I found them because my set of luggage has the same key."

Norm looked like he had collapsed on top of Millie. Judging by the housekeeper's flushed face, they had finished, though Norm was still nuzzling her ear. Thank God they'd pulled the blanket off the couch over them. Liza could see their bare arms, that's all. She started edging back upstairs, then stopped.

"Maybe she got pregnant on the Pill," her uncle said. "It's only been available a couple of years. And maybe he could have used a safe. May and I did and it worked."

Millie took Norm's face in her two hands and kissed his mouth. "Yeah, if she didn't take them! My daughter-in-law told me. She keeps forgetting hers too—accidentally on purpose—but at least she's married. No, Liza didn't have to get herself knocked up. That boy of yours is in enough trouble, isn't he? Not to mention, they're first cousins. The baby could have all sorts of problems, extra fingers, extra toes and who's going to deal with that? I know people used to marry their cousins, but they sure as heck don't now."

Liza started backing upstairs again. She didn't want to see anything more and she could hardly speak to them now. The look of bliss on Millie's face, the evidence of a long-time alliance between the pair bothered her. She wasn't sure, but at this point it sounded like her uncle snorted.

"What will people say?" Millie went on. "It's just not right! You're too soft, Norm, way too soft. Another man... And what's the rest of your family think? You got a bunch of brothers, don't you? What about Liza's father? Where's he in all this? I bet he has some sense!"

She reminds me of somebody, Liza thought, *but who? My father? Yeah, he'd kill me for sure, not that he has any right.*

"And she knows where Dace is too," Mrs. O'Connor rattled on. "She's aided and betted him or abetted him, I think it's called...It means they're in cahoots..."

This time, Norm definitely snorted. "Ah, Millie, you watch way too much television," he said.

"I know you don't want him caught, but it might be better that way...better for him and for you. You'd know where he was if he was in jail! And what if the police turn up here again? What? Well, because I saw some notes in the little slut's room…"

You did not! Liza almost shouted back down the stairs, but she didn`t have the energy. *I give up*, she thought, when she didn't hear Norm say anything more. What was wrong with him? Was he trying to digest what Millie alleged or was he just too pissed off with her — with Liza — to even speak?

Well, she didn't have time for this. She simply didn't. She staggered into her unlit room, shut the door as stealthily as she could and slid into bed. *Someday I'll get you Millie*, she thought, *but I don't have the strength right now.*

With a pillow propped under her knees, she stared at the moonlit ceiling, exhausted, but too keyed up to even close her eyes. Uncle Norm's face flashed before her. He looked thunderous and for the first time she was afraid of him and his big hands, the way she used to be of her father. *Please*, she thought, *don't come up here. Don't ask me…*

Four or five minutes passed, then the backdoor slammed and a car started up. Was it Millie's old beater or one of Uncle Norm's? Dace would have recognized the engine — although he rarely admitted it, he was good with motorbikes and cars, a genius in fact — but Liza didn't. Except for the distinctive noise a Harley engine made, she had no ear for bikes or cars.

There was no point in getting up and looking out the window, even if she could have moved her aching, sleep-deprived legs. Out here in the country, it was way too dark to see. Liza's stomach tightened and down lower, her twenty-four-week-old fetus fluttered in protest. *Please let it be Millie's old Ford,* she prayed. Where the hell would Uncle Norm go at this time of night? What if he got so upset he ended up in a ditch or accidentally ran a little black Mennonite horse and buggy off the road?

Yes, please let it be Millie leaving in a snit, she prayed again. Millie shared a house in Maitland with her son's family, away from the university, on the north side of town. Well, close to the old Pen in fact where her uncle had once worked briefly as a guard, back when he was just getting his auto business off the ground. She'd know that Liza had just heard her little burst of temper. If she'd stayed in the house, she'd never leave Liza alone. She'd want to justify her remarks. She'd come upstairs, ostensibly to complain about a single dish left near the sink and then all hell would break loose.

"Liza!" Uncle Norm roared upstairs and Liza's heart leapt, but she ignored him too, even though she'd never heard him yell so loudly before. She had to. Her whole body trembled in exhaustion. Her pregnancy and the emotional events of the day had totally depleted her. She had nothing, absolutely nothing left to give. And she couldn't give her uncle what he really wanted anyway, what they both wanted. She couldn't give him Dace.

Butterflies, she thought as her uncle started climbing the stairs. *I hope you find the monarchs, Dace. Because I'm stuck here in Canada dealing with this crap and I sure as hell can't.*

******

From what she saw when she passed the family room the next morning, Uncle Norm had continued drinking far into the night. At least ten empty beer bottles littered the coffee table.

She had tried waiting in her room until he left the house for one of his auto shops in Maitland, but perhaps she'd only heard him going in and out, for he was still in the kitchen when she came down. He'd ask about Dace again for sure, or perhaps half apologize for his housekeeper's remarks and that would be even worse. Best to take a page from him and pretend nothing had happened.

She had dressed in her usual loose granny dress and put her hair in a little ponytail. Norm was looking out the picture window over the sink, dressed in his work jeans. Frost extended halfway up the window. He had one huge hand wrapped around a steaming mug of tea. His other hand gripped the kitchen counter tightly.

Go to work, she thought. *Go, just go.*

Without looking at her, he shoved the mug along the counter towards her. He'd actually noticed that she drank her tea clear. It didn't spill. Almost hating herself, she came a little closer and took it. She was dying of thirst. The only thing that kept her in her room last night was the thought that in the morning she would leave this place, although where the hell she would go, she didn't know. She sagged. There was always her mother's, she supposed. *Yeah, sure.* She'd have to leave school, though. She couldn't stay where she wasn't wanted.

Liza couldn't look at her uncle, so she looked out the window too. Cardinals—flashy males—crowded the bird feeder. Maybe if she counted them. Her mind started to go blank. *Don't go there*, she thought. Just for a moment in the moonlight last night her uncle had looked so much like Dace. His hands, his eyes, the shape of his face. Well, no wonder—they were father and son. She took a sip of her tea and swallowed hard. It was too hot, but she wanted the pain. Anything so she didn't have to think— that there might be some truth in the housekeeper's words, that she had wanted Dace's father. Not that she would have…but, there, she'd admitted it, the worst part. Because she was guilty. Guilty of contemplating what surely had to be a sin, by any stretch of the imagination. Even if in the cold light of the day, she didn't want him, would never want him that way.

"I don't know where he is—honest," she said, but then to her horror and somehow this was even worse than when he'd come into her room to ask her about Dace—Norm began to choke back tears.

"You don't know what it's like," he said. "Since May died and then Dace…"

You still have your daughter, Rosie, Liza almost said, but he didn't. For good reason, Rosie had aligned herself with her husband's people. She had to, if she wanted to keep her own unborn baby safe. Or at least that's how she must have felt and Liza didn't blame her. Some of the bikers—the Wolfhounds' enemies were definitely crazy and the so-called good guys in Maitland weren't much better. Rosie had spent both Christmas and New Year's at her in-laws' house. *"It's more fun,"* she'd said. Well, maybe she could have been more tactful, but she was probably a little jealous of Liza living at her father's too.

Would their babies—hers and Rosie's, his grandchildren—ease Norm's pain? Because Liza didn't want him to hurt and she would do anything, almost anything, to make him feel better again. But would he even acknowledge this grandchild, the one she carried?

He had welcomed her into his house just like Dace had said he would, but they never talked about the baby. It was like Norm really didn't believe the baby was there, although maybe when he saw it…

Christ, I can't keep a child here, she thought. What the hell was wrong with her? She was a university student, but Rosie was the smart one when it came to protecting her unborn child. What if Dace came back, a man who drew nothing but danger? Their child, this baby, would never be safe. They—the police, the authorities whatever—would use the baby against her and Dace if they could.

Her hand crept towards her uncle's back, but she snatched it back, irked at both herself and him. God, this was terrible. She would never be able to touch him again, especially if there was nobody else in the room. What the hell was she going to do? And where was Millie O'Connor when she needed her? The woman must have gone back to her son's place last night. *If I stay, I'll have to win her over*, Liza thought. *She's a harpy, but she's got good instincts and she'll protect me from myself.* Why, oh, why, had none of Norm's other love interests ever stuck around? Because of Dace, she supposed. Norm and Liza's father were brothers, but he wasn't like him. Except for those desperate early years when he was a young widower trying to establish his business and pay his bills, he'd always put his children first.

"But I can guess what it's been like," she said. "So why don't you marry Mrs. O'Connor then? She's a widow, isn't she?"

Norm shook his head in mock horror, but his left hand relaxed a little on the counter. She could see that he was thinking about her suggestion. He no longer looked like an old man just trying to hold himself up.

"Oh, God, Liza," he shuddered, "I couldn't do that. I just couldn't."

Chapter 13
The Wrong One

February 13, 1973

When the strong southern light woke Dace at six a.m., his road companion and latest lover, Kathleen Aldous was gone. Gone, except for some of her dumb monarch photographs. Not that these Polaroids looked much like monarch butterflies. They showed the monarchs in their striped pupae and jade green chrysalis stages. Dace nearly ripped them in half, but there was no point in cutting off his nose to spite his face. They might come in handy later. You never knew.

How big of her, he thought. He picked up the pictures from the bedside table. She might have been scared of waking him, but he doubted it. She didn't want these photos anymore. She'd left them behind just like she'd left him. A girl like her — she had a shoebox full of butterfly pictures in her car and back at the university, a truckload of men.

Even with all the lights on, the motel room and its adjoining bathroom were still poorly lit. He tore the room up looking for her just in case. What the hell did he think—that she was hiding or that she'd vaporized? A swampy smell outside the window disoriented him until he remembered he was in Kentucky. On one of the direct routes monarch butterflies took.

And that reminded him of something else. He went over to the metal coat rack where Kathleen had hung up and neatly zipped his parka. Every night she'd put the room back in order before she got into bed. Well, good, so she'd left him another little present too—a penciled diagram of the monarchs' route in autumn. It was still in his coat pocket. Based on her description, he'd drawn it himself. That girl knew all the monarch routes by heart. She knew so much about butterflies, he'd wondered how she had room for anything else in her head. Or heart. Well, maybe she hadn't.

He was a light sleeper, the byproduct of prison life, so he remembered her getting out bed. He'd thought briefly of fucking her again and then went back to sleep. If he was sore, then she probably was too.

When she'd gotten up, she'd pulled the sheet up over his shoulder, a tender little mother wrapped in the filthy flowered motel bedspread. "Shush," she'd said, "I'm going to the bathroom." *Oh, yeah, right.* That bedspread should have been his first clue that she was up to no good. If she could help it, she never let anything like that touch her precious skin.

He took a deep breath. He had to calm down. Get control of himself. He was practically hyperventilating, for Christ's sake. *She's not worth it, she's not,* he raged under his breath. The motel room felt empty, but he double-checked behind the shower curtain in the bathroom anyway and underneath the double bed. All he found was a previous occupant's prescription pill. He put it into his pocket.

What if she blabbed, the little snitch? Half-expecting to see the state police outside, he yanked aside the dirty curtain on a filmy window by the door. No police cars, not even a chambermaid's cart, unless they were hiding behind that whack of pines. The lights of the motel office were already on. Kathleen might have gone there to get some coffee—she drank about ten cups a day—but he doubted it. Because the Datsun was gone too.

Goddamn it, the little she-devil had gone and stranded him without wheels! The only cars left in the parking were a station wagon and a Volkswagen.

Where the hell had she gotten the gumption? She was agoraphobic or something, she'd told him the other night after a couple of drinks. As if he couldn't tell. He'd known some people like her in jail and they had been together for eight days now. Booze gave her a kind of Dutch courage, he supposed. *Oh, shit, she'd been drinking a lot last night. Gin and tonics.* And she'd spent a lot of time in the phone booth yesterday, talking to her mother, she'd said.

Dace kicked the bed so hard he almost cracked his toes. "Her mother, I bet!" he yelled at the walls. A girl like her—she'd probably gone back to that dick Murphy. She'd never struck him as the loyal type and she wasn't looking for true love, that's for sure. She wore her heart on her sleeve, but it wasn't for men. No, she was looking for butterflies—a special kind of monarch butterfly.

Yeah, he got that. He really did. Between PhD student Kathleen and his clever little cousin Liza, he knew more about monarch butterflies than he gave a shit about right now. Liza wouldn't have gone traipsing all over the continent to track them down though. Too poor and in her short lifetime, she'd already done too much. She might have written about them though. Poetry and stuff. But Kathleen wanted what she wanted, so if that American Prof Murphy had some extra knowledge, she'd squeeze it out of him, no matter what she had to do. Yes, she would. She'd fuck the bastard silly if that's what it took.

A moment passed after he finished yelling, then somebody on the other side of the left wall yelled back. It was his own fault. It always was. He was pretty careful with guys these days, but he wasn't with girls. They looked so small and harmless. Like kittens or something, the way they almost purred. And he'd loved Kathleen's blue eyes, her pert ass, her la-di-da talk. Because she talked like Liza. And she'd needed protection—from herself— but what the hell. She wasn't the only one. And that was the problem. A little thing like her—of course he'd wanted to protect her, but he couldn't. Too much heat.

So two nights ago, he'd let down his guard and confessed he really was a wanted man—but for something else, not the bank heist. Yeah, so he'd escaped from jail. He'd had to bust out or the head guard Savage would have killed him, the stupid bugger. Yeah, the guy's name really was Savage.

He'd had to tell her. What the hell else could he do?

Two little parallel lines between her eyes had popped out again. "Did you tell me your real name?" she'd asked.

"Yes," he'd said. And, he added, the stuff he'd told her about the priest at his school had been true too. It had been ridiculously easy to share some of his secrets with her, especially old ones, the kind he didn't think really mattered anymore. After a few weeks on the road, he had been eager — maybe too eager — to connect. *What a fool I was,* he thought now.

After his confession that he was on the lam, she'd looked interested, that's all. Like he was a talking head on educational TV. "What's prison like?" she'd asked after a long pause.

"It's boredom with a capital B, corruption and politics — a real cutthroat organization with everybody trying to get to the top."

She smiled a little then. "I know what that's like," she'd said. They'd even talked about the poster they'd seen in the last town, but that hadn't bothered her either.

"It didn't really look like you," she said loyally, adding that maybe, just maybe, she'd recognized something in the eyes.

"What — desperation?" he quipped. And since she hadn't run for the nearest door, he'd felt safe. Safe about her, anyway. They'd gone back to the motel and fucked like crazy. She could never get enough of him, her lying little body said.

Ah, but she must have been thinking though. She was always thinking, that one. Thinking and conniving, like he was a murderous dick who'd strangle her if she up and left. Whatever he was, she had been real turned on at first. For eight nights, she'd almost made him forget he was on the run. From the police and from Savage and from God knows who else. Kathleen hadn't made him forget Liza, though. Nobody could. It was always Liza he saw when he closed his eyes. Had Kathleen sensed that?

Oh, Kathleen Aldous was a cool little customer alright. Like him in some ways. Institution-raised for some two or three years and he knew what that did. Except his experience had made him into a "criminal" while hers had made her a scholar. All that alone time in a tuberculosis sanatorium, all the time she'd lived in her head.

Well, no one had fiddled with her and she'd never had to look out for somebody else, so she'd just focused on herself. His heart still skipped a little when he thought about his baby sister Rosie. And being super smart

116

had probably helped Kathleen a lot. Yeah, she'd talked about the San, that sanatorium in the Weston end of Toronto in such glowing terms: her awe-inspiring teacher from Quebec of all places, the dedicated nurses, the god-like docs. Said they'd not only saved her life, they'd saved her fine mind. She'd skipped grades and won scholarships all through school. She'd had to—her mother had been too busy looking after her dickhead second husband and dabbling in her "art."

"Is your mom somebody famous?" Dace had asked.

"No," she'd said scornfully. "She's just a dilettante." A phony, a dabbler, she'd meant.

Kathleen had never lived with people who'd thought she was real special, though, who'd loved her just for herself. What the hell did that do to a kid? His parents had idolized him when he was little. He could do no wrong. And they'd adored Rosie too. They would have had a slew of children, if his mother hadn't gotten so sick.

His scalp prickled. If Kathleen hadn't been talking to her mother last night, who the hell had she talked to? The police? Ah, Christ, she wouldn't do that. She wasn't a snitch.

"Shit, shit, shit," he muttered as he walked around the room, gathered up his few clothes and tossed enough money on the dresser for the room. Here he went again. He had to get the hell out of here and fast.

Closing the door to the room softly behind him, he cut through the parking lot to the open road. A bear cub came around the dumpster at the side of the motel and stared at him before ambling away. Cute, but he knew better than to play with one even if its mother wasn't around. The sun was just coming up. The heat hit him square in the face. Right on cue, sweat prickled in his armpits. It looked like another long, hot day.

So she'd left him. The little egghead didn't have a loyal bone in her body. *Just like I knew she would*, he thought as he stood out on another empty highway, hoping for somebody—the right person—to come along. Because if he was wrong for Kathleen, then she was wrong for him too. They both had too much to do. True, he wanted and needed to clear his name, while she just wanted to find out where some silly butterflies went, but it was real important to her and a bunch of other eggheads besides. He just hadn't expected the girl to take off so soon.

Liza wanted to find those butterflies too, but she would have stood by him. *Ah, women*, he thought. *And some guys said they were all the same.*

Chapter 14
Wedding

Devereux Farm, near Maitland, February 23, 1973

Millie O'Connor and Norm Devereux were married two weeks later at City Hall on Friday, February 23. Millie had wanted to get married on Valentine's Day—the same day Mel had offered to marry her, Liza ruefully recalled, but they couldn't. A proper wedding—even a civil ceremony—could only be rushed so much. When Liza heard that the bride had grinned all through the short ceremony, she wasn't at all surprised.

Millie had a brand new set of dentures—uppers—and with Liza, that little devil of a girl in her house, she had also been harried into losing fifteen pounds. Never one to hide her opinions, she had actually bragged about this a couple of times in Liza's hearing. None of her diet pills had ever worked so fast.

Millie was just this side of forty and her first husband, a truck driver had been dead for more than ten years. Almost as long as she'd worked for Norm. And for as long as she'd worked for Norm, people had said that he was using her. She told Norm and Liza that too. None of her friends (or her one true treasure, her boy baby) had believed this day would ever come, but it had, it had!

She'd been so nervous—nervous Norm might change his mind, nervous his criminal son might show up, nervous his niece might go into premature labor, anything to steal the show!—that she'd cut herself shaving her legs that morning. She hoped nobody would be looking at her legs, she'd confided to Liza and Norm. In the hall mirror at the farm, she'd looked quite fetching, especially with her reddish-blonde hair permed around her face.

And even if her employer Norm Devereux was just marrying her to avoid talk about him and his grownup niece, so what? He was marrying her, wasn't he? She'd take him anyway she could.

The groom had gotten a new blue suit to complement the bride's short tulle dress—Millie wouldn't let him wear the grey one he had worn to most of Dace's court appearances—but his expression was much less joyful than hers. Not that his face ever revealed much. Too stoic. He'd walked around Maitland far too long pretending nothing was wrong, Liza supposed. And not that he cared much for pomp and ceremony. He just wanted to get the whole thing over with, that's all. Why the hell did people have to make such a big fuss? For his wartime wedding to pretty little May Lahey, they'd just gone over to the priest's house when Norm was home on leave.

If the police hadn't shown up at City Hall, Norm would have gotten his wish for a quiet ceremony. But they did and so the very next day, Maitlanders woke to this tidbit in the *Spectator*:

> *Norman Richard Devereux, 46, owner of the*
> *Devereux Auto Shop chain and his housekeeper*
> *Mildred Olive O'Connor, nee Smith, 39, had just*
> *finished tying the knot at City Hall when the police*
> *started asking hard questions. Mr. Devereux's only*
> *son, D'Arcy James Devereux has been on the run*
> *since Christmas Day...*

Of course Millie had wanted a church wedding just like her first when she'd been a sixteen-year-old almost virgin in white, but Norm had balked. It wasn't the expense—he had the money and he was generous to a fault— or that most of the gossips in Maitland would worm their way in for a free meal. Or even that Norm hated the parish priest, whom he'd suspected of terrible crimes ever since that long ago incident with his little boy Dace. Maybe the local priest hadn't done anything, but he sure hadn't helped. If he'd just gone after...notified somebody...done something. Well, that was all water under the bridge. When it came right down to it, the priests were just like everybody else. A bunch of buggers who protected their own kind.

"Look at me, Millie," Norm had said when she'd started talking about cathedrals and hotel receptions and white roses and such. "I'm grey — do I look like a groom?"

"Yes," she'd said loyally. "You still have lots of hair."

Norm had been on his own for over fifteen years. He was marrying his housekeeper to make something right — and to make his niece Liza's life easier — but that was all. Millie went to confession regularly, but he had turned Catholic for his first wife May and his religion only went so deep. They hadn't asked their children or their friends to attend the short ceremony. None of Norm's numerous siblings or their families lived in Maitland and if Millie was so adamant that Rosie and Liza with their pregnant bellies not attend, how could she ask her own son and his brood? As it turned out, Rosie couldn't have come anyway. She went into premature labor and gave birth to her first child, Daniel Devereux McCaud, on Valentine's Day.

Liza certainly hadn't minded either. All she could think about was the paper she was presenting that day to her English class, a nerve-wracking affair in spite of the fact that she'd already gotten an A.

Norm said it sure didn't stop the Maitland police, though, from lying in wait for them at City Hall. And, yeah, he probably looked like a man on his way to the gallows, but Millie was carrying a small bouquet of white roses and baby's breath. There was no mistaking that she was a bride.

He stopped when he saw the police and almost turned on his heel, as if he could have just walked away.

"I should have known," he whispered out of the side of his mouth to Millie. "They wait for days like this." He stiffened his spine though. What the hell choice did he have? Besides, he could handle them. He always had. There were just two police officers, seasoned men judging by the size of the guts trying to bust out of their buttoned-down shirts. They were in plain clothing, but their clothes and close-cropped hair styles gave them away.

Millie was always feisty, but she was a woman too. She'd dreamt of this day for years. You just had to see her to know that. Tears came into her eyes, which had made Norm want to sock both cops in the mouth. He could have and still gotten away. "You sons of bitches!" Millie blurted. "You're ruining my day."

According to Millie who related the story to their guests later that day, neither police officer even dignified this with a reply. In fact, they pretty much ignored Millie, who was just a woman after all and a dumpy, middle-aged one at that. Now if she'd been a pretty little blonde girl...
It was Norm they were interested in anyway—Norm and his frigging dangerous son.

D'Arcy James Devereux had been on *Canada's Most Wanted List* for nearly two months now, they said. And nobody had found him! Where the hell could he have gone? There was no way he'd gotten out of the country, he'd never been anywhere, he didn't have the experience, he didn't have that kind of smarts. How could he? He'd grown up in jails.

"He has friends, though," one of the officers said darkly to Norm and Millie, referring to the Wolfhounds, of course. Nothing else was happening in Maitland right now, so no doubt D'Arcy Devereux's escape from a federal penitentiary ate at them all.

Millie had laughed a little when she reported this conversation. Because it had happened right under the cops' noses. Not that they would have blamed themselves, she'd added. *Those guards at the Super Max, what a bunch of losers,* she imagined them saying to each other. *Working to rule on Christmas Day, partying and leaving Devereux – a murderous fucking felon – alone with the prison doctor. Had they learned nothing from the riot? The deadliest riot in Canadian penal history!*

"If you can call any biker a friend," the officer had continued as he opened and downed a thermos of purportedly black coffee. "Judge Silverton tried to get rid of all the Wolfhounds, but they have connections, criminal connections all the way down through the States. The dirty fuckers are into all sorts of stuff—prostitution, drugs—you name it. And they're getting worse."

As for what else had been said back at the police station, Millie could just imagine, but Liza thought she was probably right that it had gone down something like this:

"And Devereux has a family—that college girl he's fucking (no morals there!) plus a father who has no scruples, absolutely no scruples about helping him no matter what he's done. By the way, has anybody checked on her lately? Liza Devereux, his cousin, for fuck's sake! What's the matter with you guys? Let's make sure she's still here. She's not a local girl, she's from Toronto, the big T.O., she could be anywhere. And she spent her teen years in Ireland—she could be mixed up with the IRA for all we know. A girl like that...! You saw her, the way she pranced around town last summer. She couldn't stay away from the Devereux boy. The only mystery is why she didn't go with him...what's that you say, she has a scholarship...an English scholarship? What for? She speaks English, don't she? I wish I could afford to sit around on my ass reading books. Well, so-the-fuck-what. All she cares about is him."

On the steps of the City Hall, the older cop had looked like he ached to grab Norm by his testicles or the lapels of his wedding suit, but didn't quite dare. He'd clenched and unclenched his fists instead. "Where," he'd asked very slowly, rightly suspecting that Norm had already been into some booze, "Where is your son D'Arcy James Devereux? A neighbor swears he's out there at your farm, holed up in your sugar bush..."

"What," Norm had snorted, "At this time of year? He'd freeze to death. It's February, my good man. My boy isn't crazy. And none of my neighbors would do that—they're all good people. Mennonites mind their own business, not yours." Actually, that wasn't strictly true. And not all of his neighbors were Mennonites, but he couldn't see them lying about Dace.

"Well, we'll see about that. We sent a couple of cruisers out that way—hope you weren't planning some big wedding do!"

The whole time the police were talking, Millie had held onto Norm's arm, like they were a bride and groom on top of a wedding cake. But when she'd heard this, she'd let go of Norm and marched right up to the officers. She'd been baking for several days and lined up quite a few treats for the neighbors who were likely to pop in, if only to confirm she and Norm were no longer living in sin.

"What's it to you?" she'd said.

Norm had smiled for the first time that day. He could handle a couple of coppers quite well on his own turf, as long as they didn't get too rough. They had cracked one of his ribs last year when they were searching Dace's room. It hadn't sounded like they'd bother with the house though. They'd have Millie and her broom to contend with for one thing. And good luck to them out in the ass-freezing bush. He'd almost gotten lost in there a few times himself. They'd be thirsty when they got back, though. A little shot of whiskey here, a little shot there — this pair sure didn't look like teetotalers to him.

******

The police were still at the farm when Liza got home that night. The yard blazed with car lights. If she hadn't been so busy watching the darkened country road for Mennonite buggies, she'd have spotted the party from five miles away. Some of the neighbors were in the yard too, nattering to one another and getting in and out of their cars.

Liza parked the station wagon as slowly as she could, stalling for more time. She would have done a three point turn and sped back down the lane, if she had anyplace else to go. *I want my mom*, she thought with a small, sad stab of pain. She'd been thinking a lot about her mother lately. She had to stop. *It's my crazy hormones*, she thought again.

There was no room by the garage, so she parked by the laneway where the daffodils would soon bloom. Her head spun, no doubt from lack of food. She usually forced herself to eat regularly now, but she hadn't eaten for hours. A couple more minutes passed before she summoned up the courage to turn off the engine and get out of the car.

The neighbors' cars puzzled her until she remembered it was Millie's party, the wedding celebration she'd been planning for days. Liza had said she'd come home early, but she'd forgotten and gone out with one of her presentation partners for coffee instead. She liked the intellectual stimulation of campus life, the heady mix of books and ideas, the flash of insight into other worlds and she hated, hated parties. Selfish. And now her first instinct was to run and hide.

But it was so embarrassing to have the police at your house, the jerks, the vultures. She wondered how long they'd been clustered around the backdoor like that, watching Norm's neighbors come and go. She didn't see any buggies though. Had their Mennonite neighbors been here earlier and witnessed their shame too? *Christ*, she thought, as she approached the police, *I really can't take this stuff. It's bad for the baby — please, God, they haven't found him, have they? He can't be dead!*

By the time she reached the cops, they were all grinning, goddamn it. She'd left her books in the car, but she still couldn't hold her coat around her belly and walk at the same time. She was that far gone, but at least she hadn't swollen up like little Rosie. You could still recognize her face. *A baby,* she imagined the police thinking. It was amazing how babies made the most miserable people happy, even if their happiness was short-lived. *Go home*, she thought. *Go home to your kiddies and grandbabies. Stay away from mine.*

"Ah," the youngest officer, a recruit barely out of his teens, said, "So that's why you didn't join him, your cousin, your...You've got a bun in the oven."

Liza tightened her arms around herself and regarded both policemen warily. She remembered how the Trenton officer had grabbed her hair, although these guys weren't likely to pull the same stunt now. Too many witnesses. *Oh, aren't you astute*, she thought. She could hear her uncle at the door behind them, but still.

"Wrong, genius," she said. "It`s just fat."

The pimpled boy bristled. "Watch your mouth, girl, I don't care for your attitude... I'm an officer of the law."

"Somebody ought to slap her silly," the cop standing next to him said.

"A pregnant little girl," a spectator-neighbor said. "Nice."

"She doesn't know where he is either," a second female voice chimed in. "And she doesn't have time for this shit. She's at the university, finishing her, uh, her BA." The backdoor swung open all the way. The speaker, Millie O'Connor now Millie Devereux—none of this Women's Lib keeping-your-own-name stuff for her—came out of the house and stood beside her Norm. She held a tray of intricately decorated cupcakes; her new husband had the beer. To Liza's amazement, they both looked quite relaxed, as if they always entertained the police at this time of year. Well, what did she know? Maybe they did. Millie's morning curls had loosened and were tumbling into her face. For the first time in months, Liza warmed to the older woman. Maybe it was just the drink or Millie's happiness at finally getting Norm, but it sounded like she was on Liza's side.

Good for Norm and Millie, she thought. The more frightened you looked, the meaner the Maitland police got. And she, Liza, had almost lost her cool.

Maybe it was the celebratory drinks he'd already had, but Norm's face also glowed. Well, no wonder. You never knew what the police might turn up when they came onto your property. A body, a shitload of drugs, guns, every goddamn last item planted by them. And no news was good news, so his boy Dace was still safe.

Too bad the police know about the baby, Liza thought. Why hadn't she thought about that while she was sharing her birthing plans with complete strangers, the rest of the students at school? My God, she'd told her presentation partner all about the midwife today. She adored her warm-hearted, nonjudgmental midwife. She'd just wanted to share. What the hell was wrong with her? The girl had thought she was crazy anyway...a homebirth...no drugs. She'd actually turned green.

"Well, aren't you the brave one?" the girl had said. Not that Liza could have hidden her condition from the police or from the rest of Maitland much longer.

It made her vulnerable, though, it made the baby vulnerable. And it made her sick. Sick with fear. What would happen when they got back to the police station and it clicked that Dace was the baby's father? What would they do? Goddamn it, she didn't have to talk to them. She hadn't done anything wrong. She wasn't under arrest. *Oh, God,* she thought as she maneuvered her small bulk past everyone and slipped inside the house. *I should have said the baby was Mel's.* Why the hell hadn't she? Mel's mother might have been upset, but he certainly wouldn't have minded. He probably would have strutted around in fact. The police would have left her and the baby alone then, but no, not her, she'd been too proud to lie.

"Beer anyone?" Norm inquired blandly. "There's lots more in the garage and it's darn good and cold."

Chapter 15
The Ivory Tower

Kathleen raised her nail bitten fist to the door. Her eyes were level with the copper nameplate: Dr. Gregory H. Phillips, Head of Biology. The plate hung just a little too high for a woman of average height, but she wasn't average. She was almost five foot nine, even without heels. She ignored her shaky hand. She was all nerves today. She hadn't made an appointment, but she had a plan. She always had a plan. Sometimes you had to do stuff at university you didn't want to do—labor through boring courses, memorize a bunch of useless facts, praise an associate's derivative paper. Or screw somebody. Yeah, well, she was getting good at that. She used to be so careful, didn't need men all that much, too much to do. But once she'd started with the professor, it was just like her mother had said: she couldn't stop.

Well, what was sex anyway, if it wasn't used for procreation? A touch of skin, an exchange of body fluids, a muscular release to achieve orgasm. All this she'd shared with D'Arcy James Devereux. A jailbird. My, oh, my. His eyes, his... *Watch yourself, Mary Kathleen*, she cautioned herself. What a fool she'd been to make herself so vulnerable! She'd gotten so scared out there in the wide open that she'd lost her head a little and almost fallen in love with the boy. Unbelievable. Because she wasn't like that. She just wasn't.

The minute she'd gotten back to Montreal—thank God!—she'd done what any sane person would have done, especially somebody with a couple of advanced degrees. She'd researched and confirmed Dace Devereux's story. The more she researched the story, the more she'd remembered about the Maitland Penitentiary Riot, she just hadn't remembered Dace and when she reread the accounts mentioning his name, she couldn't reconcile the man she'd met on the road with what she read. *Oh, God, what a horrible story!* The university librarian had stood over her shoulder while she scrolled through the microfilm, so she'd said she was doing it for a friend.

Thank God Kathleen knew Dace's real name, so she didn't have to dig too far. And what a bonanza—an assistant criminology professor at Maitland University had published an article in the *Journal of Criminology* about the riot last May. When she'd found it, she could hardly believe her eyes. If the professor had done his research, Dace had told her the truth; he'd just left out a few things because the article certainly made convict D'Arcy James Devereux sound a whole lot worse. So what. Nobody expected a convict to be totally honest.

Who the hell was? Look at the interview process here at the university.

And no one would ever know she'd helped an escaped prisoner if she didn't tell. She had a hard time believing it herself. When she should have been chasing butterflies, she was on the lam with a jailbird.

All these thoughts went through Kathleen's head as she entered Dr. Greg Phillips's office and paused in front of his big oak desk. He was on his feet, holding out his right hand. She breathed in deeply and then relaxed. Though her flawed body had failed her on numerous occasions, her brain never had. "Philly Cream" they called the man behind his back. Well, there were worse names.

Yes, he'd just gotten back from lunch, he said, so sure he had time to talk. She knew he would. He prided himself on his availability to his department, so he kept himself on call from nine to four.

She had purposely worn a sensible tweed skirt and her good silk blouse for this "impromptu" interview with the Head of the Biology Department. Of course, she didn't know him as well as she had the Head of Biology at the U of T in Toronto, but Dr. Phillips had a good reputation. She was finishing her doctorate at McGill University here in Montreal after all—a world class university that even attracted Americans!

She looked around. Just as she had anticipated, Phillips's office was full of books and memorabilia, a record of his life. A family portrait dominated his huge shiny desk: the husband, the wife and two adult sons. A real *Leave it to Beaver* family, tall and handsome, with huge toothy smiles and lots of hair. They were New Englanders, originally from Maine. Noting the similarity between her clothes and the wife's, Kathleen mirrored the older woman's smile.

And talked. In all her academic career, Kathleen had never groveled so hard, but it worked. Though it irked her to think she could have gotten away with just a smile and a toss of her hair in her undergraduate years, she didn't show it. Time moved on and here in university with its annual influx of fresh faced eighteen and nineteen-year-olds, a woman aged fast. She was a fair-skinned blonde too. By her own reckoning, her looks would be finished in about three years. Yes, time was running out. She had to wrap up her PhD, find the monarchs' wintering place and a real man fast—a sexual partner and a companion that is. She certainly didn't want to end up alone or married in name only.

"Do you mind if I enjoy my after lunch pipe?" Dr. Phillips inquired and of course she said no. She wasn't a smoker, but she liked the way his office smelled of pipe tobacco and leather and dusty old books. The smell reminded her of her stepfather, who really wasn't such a bad man.

After they exchanged a few more pleasantries, she gave the little speech she'd written and rehearsed. She was good at writing, especially if she stuck to the facts. She'd planned three minutes—sufficient to convince Dr. Phillips, but not enough to bore him—and that's exactly what it took. She held his attention the entire time, his bifocals riveted to her. In addition to her stellar academic successes, she highlighted the many adversities she'd overcome in life. Most of the men she'd known so far had been rather sentimental. Their sentiments didn't run that deep though, so they could often be mined.

She finished by saying, "So you see, sir, I fell in love with monarch butterflies when I was a child in the San. I almost found their wintering grounds in Mexico, but then I ran out of money and time. Maybe if I get a bursary next time..."

Dr. Phillips waved a well-manicured hand, a dismissive little gesture, though he might not have intended it that way. They'd been standing, but now he turned his back on her and sat down. He looked bored, so Kathleen closed her mouth with a snap and let him talk. He didn't know about the bursary—she'd have to make an application for that and get it approved—but he'd let her back into the Department, with the stipulation that she have a draft of her dissertation ready by June.

So he wasn't a total pushover. Well, fair enough. She could do it. She had fifty pages and all her citations. She had to tighten up her thesis, that's all.

Dr. Phillips was a courteous man, so he'd asked her to sit down in a shabby leather chair when she'd first come in, but she couldn't. Ever since she'd gotten back, she had trouble sitting in one place for too long. A part of her still wanted to be on the road, even if all that wide open space had scared the bejesus out of her. That little wild streak in her—where had that come from? Her father whom her mother had once called a "maverick man"? God knows, the woman hadn't told her much else, except that he was real smart. Like Kathleen was, usually. She shivered now, just thinking about all the stupid stuff she'd done. What a mess, if...

"Are you cold, Miss Aldous?" Dr. Phillips asked.

"I've had some emotional problems, but I'm all fixed now," Kathleen volunteered.

Phillips stopped sucking on his pipe and eyed her. Still standing there, Kathleen ground one of her high heels into the floor like a scolded little girl. *Careful*, she thought. She shouldn't have said that.

She had another request though, she said as she backed towards the door. She craved the privacy of her office where she could reflect and distill her brilliant research. The grad student who had "borrowed" her office in her absence would have to be removed.

Dr. Phillips looked relieved, no doubt because he could so easily fulfill this last request. "Uh, Miss, uh Aldous! Yes, yes, of course, you can have your old office back," he said. "You really haven't been gone that long and these things happen. Dr. Meadowvale will speak to that presumptuous grad student right away. I wonder who gave him a key? Surely he didn't pick the lock! Well, let's just say you took a well-deserved vacation. The pursuit of monarch butterflies is certainly a worthy cause."

You don't really think so, she thought. *You just think it's a frilly*

130

woman's project. But if you'd ever watched thousands upon thousands of monarch butterflies flying south, you'd be singing a different tune.

Maybe. Dr. Phillips didn't look at her again, so it was difficult to accurately read his face. He shuffled through some papers on his desk instead. What would a good academic do without a bunch of paper to paw? He probably wanted to say more, but it looked like he was having trouble spitting out the words. Did he have a speech impediment, was he getting absentminded, or was he just plain old? His cheek jowls waggled and for a moment, she almost felt sorry for him, another impotent old man, like Murphy, like Percy Meadowvale, though Percy hadn't been that old. Another little chill passed over Kathleen because someday she would be old too.

Philly Cream had a super clean desk, except for the photo, but perhaps his secretary kept it that way for him. What did he do with his time besides attend a bunch of faculty meetings? For the life of her, Kathleen couldn't recall the focus of his academic career. Most academics had an obsession, but he hadn't published anything for years. Well, he was an old man close to retirement, although much to the dismay of their subordinates, some of these guys sure hung on a long time. Of course he didn't want to hear anymore of her problems. *Yeah, yeah, fair enough.*

If only he didn't have such antiquated opinions, though. "I'm sure they're bright enough, but girls have so many personal issues," she'd heard him complain more than once. "Their love interests, their menses, their moods. From a biological viewpoint, it's obvious that such things can and do get in the way. I really wonder if women belong in the business or academic world. Especially in Biology or any of the Sciences. Maybe in the Arts or the soft sciences, they do okay. They can combine that sort of thing with a husband, with a family. My wife—God bless her— looked after the house and the children," he'd said. "She did a great job too and the kids turned out wonderful, just wonderful."

"Miss uh Aldous," he finally got out now, much to their mutual relief. "If I remember correctly, you had a fine record at the U of T—top of your class. Now lots of girls are smart, but they, uh, let's say, they want a life. A *real* life. They fall in love, get married, have babies and invest their intelligence in future generations perhaps."

"In their sons?" Kathleen asked.

"But you," Dr. Phillips ignored her, "You PhD girls choose to delay adulthood. And you came here—left a fine man like Dr. Sheridan, who's no doubt on some kind of breakthrough about monarch butterflies. I don't need to know why you left. It's just a lot harder now. You have a lot of hurdles to pass, but there are not a lot of rewards. Immediate ones, that is. Most of our male PhDs have their wives to help them, but a young gal! Well, she can't expect that now, can she? Females have other obligations, other needs. Of course, we have our quota system for young women, but it's still a tough climb."

"Excuse me, sir, I didn't get into the University of Toronto or McGill University on the quota system!" Kathleen said, raising her voice a little.

Dr. Phillips still acted like he hadn't heard her. "You've got to— uh, stay the course, stick to the straight and narrow and while I'm on the subject, Dr. Meadowvale does too. Umm—the university has an, uh, unwritten policy—though it's rarely enforced. Do you know what I mean? If you want... "

To get into the old boys' club. Yes, Kathleen thought. Yes, she really had to get her act together and stop screwing around with men. She didn't need one. At least not now. Maybe when she was forty or fifty. Real old. What the hell was wrong with her? What had she done? She'd almost gotten herself mixed up with an escaped convict, for crying out loud. And with Murphy, that yucky man.

She closed her eyes, but opened them again real fast. The last thing she wanted to think about was Dr. Murphy. Her academic reputation would be shot if their relationship was ever confirmed. Her reputation, not his.

Ditto if anybody ever heard about her and Dace Devereux. And they might, if he got into the news again. And he was bound to, a man like him. Whatever happened, she had no intention of visiting him in prison, like that cousin of his, who had probably dropped out of school and gotten herself mixed up with a bunch of bikers by now. Kathleen wasn't that kind of girl.

Oh, God, please keep him out of the news!

After she left Dr. Phillips's office, she felt a little wistful. Though she had anticipated a letdown after giving her little speech, the happy family photo on Phillips's desk definitely hadn't helped.

132

Or maybe it was his little talk about babies that had really done her in. Not that she wanted one of the noisy, messy, painful and time-sucking things. Besides, you never knew what the hell you were getting when you had a kid, what they'd inherit. She stumbled a little in her unaccustomed four-inch heels. No wonder. It was getting dark outside, but they hadn't turned on the corridor lights yet. Too cheap. She'd already eaten—just a ten ounce bag of Hostess barbecue potato chips, but so what? She'd get a coffee from that machine downstairs, double sugar, and burn some midnight oil.

Where had Dace gone? Part of her hoped he was making out alright; another part hoped he was back in jail. Especially if he'd gotten mad at her. No telling what a man like him might do—if he felt betrayed. What if he stalked her, killed her? She shivered again, almost as if his strong hands had tightened around her neck. She didn't mind pretending, but she sure as hell didn't want to get choked for real.

Dace hadn't seemed like a murderer, but you never knew. He was a criminal after all and she'd read horrible stories in the newspapers about perfectly ordinary, noncriminal men who'd butchered their wives on some pretext or other. Boredom, infidelity, who knew. Who cared. Especially if the wife had been a bitch. No doubt defense lawyers dreamed up the reasons, re-victimized the murdered wives. Well, why not? The women were already dead—nobody could hurt them anymore—and the lawyers had a job to do. She could see that, but sometimes the defendants had killed their own children too. How did that happen? From a strictly genetic point of view, not only did it make zero sense, it was just plain nuts. Especially for those purportedly middle class husbands and fathers with everything to lose.

Of course, she should have turned Dace Devereux in—for his own good and hers—but she'd felt so conflicted. To tell the truth, she'd gotten a little bit sentimental herself. The boy had looked so beautiful while he slept and from the sounds of it, he'd gotten a raw deal. And he was like her a little: he just wanted to go to Mexico, that's all. Maybe he could set up a little business down there, send for his cousin and start living. Rescue the girl from the bikers—rescue himself. The stupid cousin's name was Liza or Lizzie or something. Kathleen really hadn't given her much thought. It didn't sound like much of a life, but if that's all they wanted, let them have it. Some people sure as hell didn't want much.

The monarchs had mattered more in the end though. She'd worked so hard to find their wintering ground and for so long. Most of her twenties! All that tagging, all that research. She had to find them, she had to.

Yes, if it ever got out that she'd associated with an escaped convict, her credibility and her career would be shot.

Her office was in the basement of the Science building. When she finally reached it and her key still worked, she breathed a huge sigh of relief. She didn't knock. Why the hell should she? It was her office. *Ah,* she thought, *home again, home again, jiggety-jig. Safe at last.* She could cocoon here. If that grad student was still here, she'd kick out his fat ass, stat. For a moment, she almost hoped he was. She flicked the light switch inside the door. Ah, the light still worked too. Some grad students holed up in their offices and slept on the floor, but it didn't look like anybody was here. *Get a grip,* she told herself as she entered the small room and navigated through the waist high stacks of books she'd left on the floor. It looked like the nervy grad student had just left. She'd kill him if he'd touched any of her papers or her books! There were ashtrays and Coke cans all over the place and another smell she didn't like. Grass, probably. She didn't do stuff like that.

Thank God, she wasn't always this lonely. It was only in bed that she let herself remember lying in a convict's arms while he stroked her pretty blonde hair.

Chapter 16
Mexico, Circa 1973

Canadian professor seeks "research
Associates" to help track monarch
Butterflies. ~**Mexico City News,**
February 2, 1973

The Southern States, February 1973

Dace hitched the rest of the way down south, through Mississippi, Louisiana and Texas. Nobody knew where he was. Most of the time he wasn't too sure himself. Sometimes he felt lonely, but for a wanted man, he was having a helluva good time. He'd almost stopped worrying. He was a city boy at heart, but he figured he'd stick to small towns, places that didn't get much news.

Each state was different, a law unto itself, a town with its own sheriff, reminding him of the television Westerns he'd watched when he was six-years-old. *Gunsmoke* had been his favorite and his mother's too, with Marshall Matt Dillon, Miss Kitty and those clown cowboys, Chester and Festus.

He'd heard that spring came early in the south, but right now it was just a breath on the wind. The landscape was still brownish, like an old, worn-out photograph. Waiting for spring, he took stock of some small changes: the rise in temperature, the different birds songs, the roadkill.

He sent Liza a couple of notes. *The monarchs passed this way*, he'd write, but he couldn't write much. All the usual avenues of communication were closed to him, the phone lines, the federal mail. When he finally stopped worrying about the RCMP or the FBI catching up with him, it was time to look ahead. It seemed simple enough. The border between the States and Mexico was an invisible line he'd figured he'd just walk across. They couldn't guard the whole border.

He'd never left Canada before. Long before he reached Mexico, he felt like he'd stumbled into a foreign country. No wonder people loved the States, no wonder they acted like Canada was a poor country cousin — white bread and boring to boot.

He knew little about his own country, let alone the history of the States, but he'd heard stories from his father about the Great Depression and the jobless men who'd ridden the rails. He pictured himself a happy hobo, hopping from train to train.

The people he encountered were even less informed. Americans — at least Southerners — knew more about the Civil War than they did about what had happened at a big prison called Attica in upper New York state. As far he could tell, they'd never heard about the Maitland Penitentiary Riot way up in Ontario, Canada. Which suited him just fine.

Everything about his new life did. No walls, no bars. No fucking jailhouse Gestapo telling him what to do.

"You can be anybody you want," the prison psych used to say. *Yeah, sure, the self-satisfied son-of-a-bitch jerk.* As far as Dace was concerned, some other fucker had always called the shots, except when he was on his Harley.

The brotherhood, the Wolfhounds, his home, Canada. Hindsight was always 20/20. Okay, maybe he should have taken to the road years before, but he hadn't. The brotherhood and Liza had both held him back. Not that Liza would have agreed. "Ah, so now it's my fault," he heard say, but she was smiling too.

Dirt Beard, a little voice deep inside him sometimes keened, but he liked traveling light and alone. He especially liked not being accountable to anybody else. What the hell was wrong with him anyway — had he really wanted to belong to a gang that bad, to go along with the majority? If he'd stuck with the gang, he would have ended up a leader and he couldn't. Gang life was changing. A lot of the bros had gotten into some real bad stuff.

His spirits soared on every hilltop and at every welcoming sign into a new state. With every step he took, the temperature climbed too. It felt like nothing could possibly go wrong. If he'd grown up someplace warm like this, he might have flown straight.

He kept to the open road. *Hide in plain sight*, that was his new philosophy. He ate chips at truck stops, a sweetened coffee here and there, a ninety-nine-cent breakfast of bacon and eggs with enough fat and protein to get him through the day.

And for the most part, he fit right in. He was a chameleon, a scarlet king snake, a hawk moth, a viceroy butterfly. You couldn't tell him from most of the people he met—at least until he opened his mouth. It seemed like everybody was running from something, even if it was just for the day. Most of his rides paid for him at truck stops, but sometimes he went to the washroom and slipped out a back window. He tried not to let it bother him. Pride was a luxury.

He hadn't visited the Mammoth Caves in Kentucky and he didn't visit the Civil War sites in Tennessee. They were all out of his way, off the monarchs' migration path, the one Kathleen had shared with him. He had been a little nervous at first, half-expecting an FBI agent or an RCMP officer to give chase, but he soon got over that. Nobody would be expecting him to follow a butterfly path.

It was easy to hitchhike in early 1973. People drove fast, so he made good time. Officials still hadn't lowered speed limits in response to the oil crisis. Watergate hadn't happened.

Yes, the United States was still the greatest place on earth. Listening to an American trucker—a heavyset, salt-of-the-earth type—talk about how proud he was of his country was enough to make a grown man cry. The war driven economy thrived while Americans shared their good fortune and their passion for freedom abroad. A spate of assassinations had shaken American self-confidence during the sixties, but now trouble only happened in faraway Communist places like Vietnam. If they could just get rid of all the Commies at home and abroad. Where the hell was Vietnam anyway? The Vietnam War was almost over too. Americans were doing the right thing by adopting orphaned Vietnamese children and bringing surviving soldiers home.

Most Americans weren't on the outlook for serial killers or

escaped convicts in 1973. They weren't suspicious of fellow citizens, especially their vets. At some of the highway interchanges, returning veterans outnumbered other hitchhikers, but Dace always got a ride, usually with the brash, breezy American girl-type who liked his looks.

"Where you going, soldier?" she'd ask, while she fiddled with the knobs on her car radio and waited for him to climb inside. Real relaxed, no worries here. As long as he wasn't in Bible Belt country, "Tie a Yellow Ribbon Round the Old Oak Tree" came in loud and strong.

"Mexico," he'd reply laconically, although he'd heard from several fellow hitchhikers that Sedona, Arizona was a wonderful, magical place too. "My grandparents are spending the winter there," he'd lie.

Most of his drivers preferred talking about themselves, but he had a backstory ready for those who didn't. He played a shattered man, an army sergeant who'd accidentally killed a couple of his own men though of course he'd killed lots of Commie bastards too. And they fell for it. Some of them even felt sorry for him. Who would admit to such a thing except that he was so upset? The guys punched him playfully in the shoulder; the girls reached over and stroked his hand.

"Ah, man," they all said. "That's rough." He was twenty-four, a non-college-educated white boy, just about the right age to have been sent off to war. He always got a ride with a girl if he could. That's just the way he was. He had almost no money left, so the girls fed him and put him up for the night. In return, he checked under the hoods of their cars and tightened up this or that. Especially with American cars, he could always tell what was about to go wrong.

"You'll need a new fan belt soon," he'd say or "Get an oil change once in a while," he'd remind them. "It will add years to your car."

A fellow biker or a long-distance trucker was a pretty good bet too. They all had the same idea: to get someplace warm.

He began to feel safe, even a little cocky. He felt like he was on drugs, stoned on hot American air. Maybe the fearlessness and self-confidence of his drivers had infected him. If they happened to be Bible thumpers, he just ignored that. America was a free country, they could believe anything they wanted. And he could believe anything he wanted, do anything he wanted too.

After two or three days on the road, he noticed that his prison-wasted leg muscles had tightened, just from running to catch a ride. And his thick dark hair had nearly all grown back in too. He had to stop shaving for a while, though. Too much bother, too much time. No need to worry about a disguise. He was such a long way from home. The authorities or Savage would never find him here. He had a hard time believing he was that important. Come on, he was just a cog in some huge cosmic wheel. In roadside bars, the jukeboxes played Joni Mitchell's "The Circle Game" all the time. *We can't return we can only look behind from where we came…*

"That's a Canadian song," he told the drinkers he met in the bars, but they looked at him blankly. Though the Americans complained about no-good shirkers — draft dodgers — who had gone to Canada, most of them couldn't point it out on a map.

Dace brought watered-down beer and cigarettes in the bars. Cigarettes were cheap in the States, cheaper than even the contraband ones on the reserve had been. He wrote messages on the insides of Lucky Strike cigarette packages and scrubbed off his finger prints with his fist. He gave the notes to truck drivers and relaxed.

Even if most of his messages got lost among the coffee cups and beer cans in their truck cabs, he figured it would be like the other kites he'd sent Liza from jail. The more he sent the better. A few of his notes would find their way home. He missed writing to Liza; he missed her too, especially on the nights he slept alone under the stars. The further south he went, the fewer public phones there were, but he couldn't use them anyway. If the RCMP hadn't tapped his dad's phone, they were stupider than he thought.

His sister Rosie and her husband also had a phone. He wondered about calling Rosie, but he couldn't involve her. She'd lost her mother at an early age, she'd had enough trouble in her life and some of it had come from him. Well, let's face it. Most of it had come from him. All that stuff in the newspapers. She'd probably had her baby by now — a girl he prayed, who'd guarantee her the trouble-free life she deserved.

Even when he crossed the border into Mexico, his luck held. It was real easy for him to get in, not so easy for Mexicans to get out. Expatriates loved hearing his English-speaking voice in the bars with their little barbed-wired yards. In the very first cantina he visited, he gambled his last twenty bucks and got enough money to buy an old bike. A family of four skinny little Mexicans had traveled on the bike, all at the same time. Well, why not, if two fat bikers could. The bike was a little Jap scrap Honda, but it would have to do. At least it hadn't rusted too badly. Gas prices were creeping up. The family who'd owned the bike could no longer afford it. He tooled around on it, whenever he scrounged up a little gas. He picked up a little work here and there, mostly just for his room and board.

Several months passed.

It was in Mexico that he started calling himself René Gagnon, which was pretty close to the name of his great-great grandfather or something. With Liza's help, he might even be able to track down a corresponding Social Security number someday, of a deceased octoroon born in Louisiana in the mid-1940s, let's say. Something to tie in with his almost black eyes, the ones he might have inherited from a distant native Indian ancestor. A little octoroon blood, a little Indian blood—to most people, it was probably more or less the same thing. He'd just introduced himself as "D'Arcy" before. Though he'd been careless when he drank, dropping details about his birthplace and his schooling or lack of schooling, telling stories about crimes. Without even trying, he picked up a little Spanish too.

Everybody was talking about monarch butterflies. All the Anglos anyway. He couldn't believe it. Butterflies were in the English news all the time. Better that than a bunch of crap about the Mafia and the drug cartels, he supposed. Or escaped cons like him.

It was the same story Kathleen Aldous had told. For decades, some lone Canadian professor and later an American one had studied the life cycle of monarch butterflies. Well, they had fellow enthusiasts and associates, of course, a whole clubhouse of scientists. Like Kathleen. The American professor was still in his forties, but the Canadian professor was in his sixties and running out of time. They were fighting about who had done what first. These Ivy League types weren't too different from the men he'd met in jail.

The Canadian guy had tagged a lot of butterflies; some of the tags had shown up northwest of Mexico City. Unlikely as it seemed, people thought that monarch butterflies headed to the province of Michoacán. No English-speaking person could pronounce Michoacán. Most of them had never even heard of the place. The state capital was Morelia, so they just called it that.

Dace had a hard time locating Michoacán, in the center west of Mexico. He asked questions, but he didn't always get the right answers. Also, although Michoacán had one hundred and thirty-five miles of coastline on the Pacific Ocean, it wasn't the most popular tourist destination, not then.

And his new bike was useless. It broke down near Morelia. He knew what was wrong, but he couldn't get the parts. The bike wasn't much use in this part of the country anyway, so when it rolled down a hill, he let it go. The mountainous roads were too bumpy and steep. If the bike had kept working, he could have traded for a burro and let the animal pick its way through the rocks.

He didn't even have a map anymore. Kathleen's verbal map had stopped at the Mexican border. She'd been to a Cancun resort with her mother on a reconnecting visit when she was twenty-one, but she knew nothing else about Mexico's interior. He drew little maps of the area and walked, but he still didn't know exactly where to go. Everywhere he went, he carried Kathleen's pictures of monarchs with him and asked the locals if they'd seen these kinds of butterflies—"mariposa monarca."

They took his money when they could but, no, they hadn't seen them, the shifty-eyed little devils lied. Not that he blamed them. They didn't trust Americans and they didn't trust anyone who talked like one either.

A Spanish speaking interpreter, a girlfriend, would have helped, but he avoided them at first. Besides, he was flat broke. He still got lots of offers, though. Everywhere he went, little Mexican girls smiled winsomely at him, while their menfolk sat back with folded arms and glared. Were they pimping the girls or protecting them? He couldn't tell. Some of the girls didn't look much more than ten. *Get me out of here*, their eyes said. As if he needed a kid holding onto his shirttail or some Mexican papá breathing down his neck.

He wasn't looking for butterflies for Kathleen; he was doing it for Liza. He never thought about Kathleen if he could help it. He'd misjudged her and it bothered him that his instincts had been so poor. If she'd told him she had to leave, he would have understood, but, no, she'd just run off and left him wondering what she'd do next.

On a bad day, he still felt like wringing her scrawny little neck. If she hadn't gone back to that Jesus Murphy guy, she'd probably gone back to McGill University, back to her other professor, but who the hell knew? At least she hadn't betrayed him to the authorities or they'd have been after him, damn quick. No, she hadn't done that. Not yet. He wondered why.

He wasn't the only one looking for butterflies. Other Americans and Canadians wintered in Mexico and read the local newspapers too. The monarchs' long distance migration fascinated people who'd also travelled over two, three, four thousand miles just to get someplace warm. The plucky little insects had their own super highway for sure.

Most of the locals in Michoacán were woodcutters or ranchers. A few fished. There weren't a lot of young men. They worked up north and sent their money home. Well, most of it. Butterfly enthusiasts questioned the older men in the cantinas in Morelia, but they didn't talk. The men and some of the women slept in hammocks in more razor-wired topped yards. They were suspicious of outsiders and rightly so. Sure, white men came and promised riches, but they spent most of their American dollars back home. And they drove the illegal drug trade.

When Dace showed people his pictures of the monarchs, they looked cagey or maybe just a little protective. The men's mustaches and the women's eyes twitched. It made him uneasy. He hadn't grown up around these people, so he had trouble reading their faces. Though few admitted to seeing monarchs, they liked telling tales. Whether these were true stories or just tall tales, he couldn't tell, but the Mexicans' ancestors, the ancient Aztecs, had revered the monarchs. Modern-day Mexicans revered American dollars more, but they also doubted outsiders had the butterflies' best interests at heart.

It didn't help that the monarch migration had been smaller than usual this year, perhaps due to a freak snowstorm in the southern states. This had happened before and nature had her own way of compensating, so the next crop of butterflies might increase by a thousand fold, but you never knew. Something bad had happened, that's for sure, and Americans were behind most of the trouble that Mexicans got. If this year's monarch butterfly decline was the fault of the Americans, the local Mexicans weren't surprised.

Lots of Mexicans believed the butterflies were the reborn spirits of fallen warriors, dressed in battle colors. Which made a kind of desolate sense. The monarchs always arrived in Mexico on November 1, the Day of the Dead. People heard from travelers that the butterflies were somnolent through November and December. In the mountains, they covered the coniferous trees like dead leaves. In this state of torpor, they didn't make much noise. It was said that you had to be a local to find them.

Maybe the monarchs were waking up now, getting ready for their long trek back north. He sure as hell hoped so.

The further Dace walked into Michoacán, the more he hoped to see them in action, but nobody could or would tell him exactly where to find them. People just seemed to like telling stories, that's all. The heat slowed him down, but when he finally met a certain young Mexican woman, his luck changed. Her name was Thalia Elenas-Gomez. She had been born on a ranch in the mountains at El Salto, in the Mexican state of Michoacán in 1943, but her father owned a cantina in Angangueo now. She worked for him. Sometimes one of her married sisters worked there too, with a little child strapped to her back and another one in tow. "Come meet my sister," one of them said the first time Dace came into their bar.

Thalia did what people often do when they sell alcohol: she smiled and listened to stories. Her customers drank and talked about Life. Even life in Mexico was awfully darn good, especially when they drank. They shared their wildest dreams with complete strangers in a lovely, drunken euphoria. If they didn't become silent and morose, that is.

Luckily, Thalia was not morose. If her sister had fetched him a pubescent child, Dace wouldn't have been surprised, but Thalia turned out to be about the same age as him, with a flat, rather plain-looking face until she smiled. She looked like she had more Indian than Spanish blood in her. Years ago, her great-grandfather, her "Biabuelo" had said she did too. Mexican girls like her were usually married with a family of five or six children by now, but she had bigger dreams. Besides, her sisters had done all that and they lived nearby. Once she'd saved enough money, she wanted to see the world, like the little hippie girls with the long straight hair who'd traveled through this out-of-the-way part of Mexico when she was in her teens. She'd learned English working for an American family one summer in Austin, Texas, so she'd left Mexico once.

Every man who came into her father's cantina hit on Thalia, with or without her sister's help. The poorest American was richer than most

Mexicans. Americans were all potential tickets out of there, but so far she'd never taken one, even though she'd had her pick. If Dace knew girls, she was probably waiting for true love or the real deal—or maybe she just couldn't stand to leave her mother. Thalia was the youngest in a big family and her mother was quite old. According to local legend, the woman had been fifty when her fourteenth child was born.

Dace moved in with Thalia, slipping in at night after her parents went to bed, so they could look the other way. For several days, he followed her into work at the bar too. He didn't ask her about the butterflies right away, though. He couldn't. He needed her trust and not just in bed.

If only he'd had some money, something he could give her in exchange for whatever clues she had about the monarchs' wintering grounds. Or if he could help her get out of this place, but he couldn't. He couldn't do anything for anybody. He never had. Wanting to do something didn't count. But mostly, he just wanted to do something special, to be part of something bigger than himself.

Christ, he figured, even the Parole Board would approve of an enterprise like that.

When he finally talked to Thalia about the monarch butterflies' wintering grounds, he could have kicked himself for waiting so long.

"I know that place. I can take you there," she said so fast that he almost fell off his bar stool.

Dace stared at her, wondering if she was just pulling his leg. "What—to the monarchs' wintering grounds? Are you sure? I'm not looking for any old butterflies, you know. These are Canadian butterflies, they're orange and black and…"

"Si, you want to find the butterflies that the Canadian scientist has been advertising about in the paper. You're not the only person who's looking for them, you know. Some Americanos came into the cantina the other day and they asked me the same thing."

Dace reached across the bar counter and grabbed both her hands. "Some Americans?" he asked, staring into her eyes.

"Well, maybe," Thalia hesitated. "there were two people, an older man and a girl, well, a woman, a blonde. They both spoke English. The man was a doctor. That's what the girl called him. It was 'Dr. This' and

144

'Dr. That.' The man called the girl 'doctor' too, but it sounded like he was making fun of her or something. I didn't like him. His name was Murray Francis, no, Dr. Francis Murphy he said to call him. My sister was working too and he said, 'If you'd like a threesome, it's alright with me. My colleague here, she's not putting out.'

For a moment, Dace was stunned, though certainly not by Dr. Murphy's boorishness or his sexual tastes. Let the old bastard dream — it would have surprised Dace if Murphy could get it up for one girl, let alone two. *So Kathleen and her friend are back*, he thought. *But if they think I'm going to let an American and her find those butterflies first, they're wrong. The monarchs belong to Canada. Wherever they are, they're our claim to fame and if my name's attached to the discovery, well, why not? This is my chance to do something important. It's a win-win situation. Liza will turn cartwheels and my Dad won't know what to make of it all.*

Thalia was still talking, though. He'd almost stopped listening, but then he heard one word: "Feds."

He reached across the bar again, tipped her chin up with one hand and looked into her eyes. "What did you say?" he asked.

She smiled and rubbed her chin into his hand. "Just that last Friday was a busy day for Americans. Some Feds came in right after Dr. Murphy and the girl and then you came in too."

"I'm not an American," Dace said mechanically. "Do you think maybe, just maybe, you could have mentioned this last Friday?" Though they probably couldn't understand a word of English, three old men in the bar looked around. They were the only other people there. "What did they look like? The feds?" he asked in a lower voice.

Thalia scrubbed furiously at the wooden bar with a damp cloth. Water was hard to come by; she used it sparingly. Sweat glistened on her forehead and she looked close to tears. Dace put his hand over hers to still the motion. What the hell was wrong with him? At least he hadn't called her bad names. The only air conditioning offered in the bar — a small overhead fan — was broken and the sun hadn't gone down yet, so there was no air.

"I don't know — except they were white guys like you. Tall, big, kind of scary. They talked like you too. English, but not American. There were two of them. They wore suits and they dressed better than they tipped. Real Americanos usually tip well. They had one oddball with them — a fat, nasty man. 'Hey, Savage,' they called him. I thought it was a funny name for a man. He didn't say anything."

"Yes, it's a funny name," Dace agreed, "but it suits him well. Where the hell do you think they went?" *Damn,* he thought, if only he'd asked her about the monarchs earlier. But he'd been too busy playing his fucking cards just right. Oh, yeah. Planning and conniving, he reminded himself — it had never been his strongest suit. "Did you tell them where the butterflies live?" he asked.

Thalia poured a beer for another customer to the right of him, but then she back turned to Dace and smiled. "Sure I did. But I didn't like the doctor or Savage or the girl or the bad guys, so I told them all the same thing. I sent them where the drug lords live. That should keep them busy for a while. Especially the Feds. I don't know about the girl. She was pushing thirty, so she was more woman than girl and she acted like she was sixty-five. She hardly noticed me, just called me 'Chiquita' when she wanted a G & T. She wanted quinine in the tonic, but we didn't have any. I hope she gets malaria, I really do."

Dace grinned. "She won't get malaria. That girl knows exactly what to pump into her veins. She'll have come prepared this time, with an arsenal of pills and money from the university. I don't think those guys were Feds either," he said. "You say they sounded like me?"

"Si, but they swore a lot more."

"American, Canadian, they probably all sound the same to you. It sounds like they were Canadians though." *So Savage is down here for sure,* he thought, *and maybe some RCMP guys too or some of Silverton's personal flunkies.* Would the Canadian police look for him this far south? He wasn't sure. "So what about me — will you give me the right directions to the butterfly wintering grounds? Maybe even show me the way?"

"Me?" Thalia asked doubtfully, but she looked a little wistful too and he knew he had her again. "My father…well, okay, but we'll have to borrow some burros when we get nearer. Or we could just walk. I haven't been up there since I was a little girl, but it took a long, long time. My abuelo…"

"Your grandfather?"

"Si, my abuelo, his ranch is near there. He took me. Mother of God, it was an incredible experience. Like going to the big cathedral in Morelia. I dream about it still. And the sound those butterflies made — I didn't know what it was at first. There were millions of them, René, millions! I had two long braids—braids that hung down past my waist. The mariposa—the butterflies— landed on my hair and tickled my face. It was a long way up the mountain, though. My abuelo carried me part way."

"Ah, you were just a little girl. Your legs were much shorter then. I'll carry you too if I have to…you'll see," Dace said. "I'm strong too."

Thalia passed him a beer, his second that day. His heart felt like it was expanding in his chest. His mind stayed perfectly clear, even after he had downed the warm beer. Mexican beer wasn't as light as the American stuff.

For the first time in a long time, anything seemed possible—that he would find the monarch butterflies and that he would outwit three or four men and that somehow in the process, he would clear his name. And then he could go home to Liza—a clean man, a redeemed man, maybe even a hero. Yes, somehow everything would work out right.

He looked at Thalia, wiping down the counter between them again. She really was a sweetheart. *What the hell am I going to do with you?* he thought.

Chapter 17
Right Place, Wrong Time

Transverse Neo-Volcanic Mountains, Mexico, March 28, 1973

He was going to be such a big man, even if Thalia was the one who knew the way. He'd imagined carrying her up the path like a bride, but the little showoff was way ahead of him right now, climbing the mountainside like a surefooted deer. He lost sight of her a couple of times, he was so busy watching his own feet. If there were any signs of butterflies, he'd miss them for sure.

It was all he could do just to breathe. Every ten feet or so, he stopped and sucked great gulps of air into his punished lungs. At this rate, they were never going to get anywhere. When Thalia finally noticed him over her shoulder, she stopped too.

"Go, just go," he felt like saying—somebody had to—but he couldn't.

Thalia didn't seem too concerned. She stared down at him while he rested in the shade of a bush and tried to avoid a particularly vicious looking prickly pear cactus threatened his ass.

"It's the air," she said, "it's thinner up here. Some of the gringos can't take it." She smiled and put her hand on her chest. "But you can— you'll be alright."

Sure, he thought, *if I don't pass out and roll down the mountainside.*

"Breathe—breathe like this," she said, drawing air down into her own lungs. "And walk slower," she ordered, coming back towards him, taking his hand and slowing down her own pace too. "Your breathing's too shallow and you're climbing way too fast."

Christ, he thought, if he went any slower, he'd be crawling on his hands and knees and now here he was again letting another girl tell him what to do. Nothing was going the way he'd anticipated, nothing. Thalia wasn't Kathleen, though. She wasn't going to run out on him. She wouldn't turn him into the police either. And she had already seen the monarchs when she was a child. She loved them just for themselves. She didn't care if they made her career, if they made her a big shot in the eyes of the world.

He slowed his pace and took the deep breaths she'd recommended. Almost immediately, his lungs started to ease. A couple of minutes later, he took his eyes off his feet and looked around him at a green panorama set off by a brilliant blue sky.

So this is paradise, he thought. He'd never been up in an airplane and he'd never climbed so high. He sucked in more air. Nothing could hurt them up here. If there really was a butterfly roosting area, someday this place might be a preserve, with cigarette butts on the forest floor and skinny children hawking souvenirs, but right now it was completely unspoiled, a visionary's dream. He'd never seen anything like it before. If he was in the right place, nobody had, except the Mexicans, of course.

Why the hell wasn't there a bunch of yahoo tourists beating the path to this place? His line of vision stretched up the mountain path, strained up into the sky. He'd give anything to have some artistic talent, but he didn't. At least he'd brought along a camera. And some topographical maps from Mexico City to determine the altitude, weather, and contour of the ravines. Not that he really needed them with Thalia along. Her childhood memory was phenomenal.

They tread lightly, aiming to leave no mark on the forest floor and no trail for his enemies to follow. When they got a little higher, balsamic-looking fir trees lined the switchback mountain path. Thalia thought that English-speaking people called them "oxaymel," but she wasn't sure. They saw an armadillo and heard a coyote's call. He'd never seen an armadillo before. Thalia pointed out hummingbirds and mockingbirds, but she didn't recognize the rest of the birds flying along the way. Most of the vegetation was foreign too.

150

"Flora and fauna," Kathleen had called plants and animals. Yeah, well maybe someday when he was old and grey, he'd have time to dip into biology and look up stuff like that too.

He let go of Thalia's hand and she skipped ahead of him, an easy girl to please. When she first told him about the monarch butterflies flying through the air, up from a ditch, down the mountain and out to the sea, a stream of black and orange, her dark eyes had glowed. Let her see them again first. If the overwintering monarchs belonged to anybody, they belonged to Thalia and her people. At least he'd be first the white man to see them. Too bad Liza wouldn't be the first white girl.

Now that he was breathing better, he could focus on more practical things and Thalia's backside too. His backpack was filled with their supplies, with the camera he'd gone to Morelia to purchase dangling from one side. He'd liked Morelia with its seventeenth century architectural lines, but he liked Thalia's construction more. He trained his eyes on her, his focal point, enjoying the lovely lines of her small working shoulders and back, the muscles in her rear and thighs.

Halfway up the mountain, she slowed down and started walking even more carefully. So did he. So many lethal-looking cacti grew low to the cracked ground. *Self-impalement,* he thought, *what a way to go.* All he knew about cacti was that they were desert plants and that if you sliced one open, you could suck out the moisture. Where had he found that out—an old cowboys and Indians movie?

Christ, it was hot. He pulled a flask out of a side pocket on the backpack, drank a little water and wiped his mouth. Thalia grabbed the flask from him and took a swig too. She had her own flask, but she wanted his. He followed the water down her taut throat. She looked ravishing, her dark skin sleek and unmarred, her hair bundled up on her head, away from her neck. He would have taken her on the ground, but there were a lot of woodcutters around. So far, they had passed a woodcutter with a burro every twenty minutes or so, mostly on their way down.

His own skin was glistening. He wanted to suck his water bottle dry, but he didn't know how long it had to last.

"Gringo," every woodcutter said, pointing to the sweat dripping from his brow, pooling under his arms and staining the front of his T-shirt. Yeah, yeah, so what? he thought. He eyeballed them, towering over them, so they didn't say anything else. Mexico was just like most places—his size got him lots of respect. Most of the Mexican men he'd met so far were less than five feet four and the women even smaller. But Thalia was tall for a Mexican woman, as tall as the men. She took the heat like they did too. As far as she knew, her Purépecha ancestors had lived in desert-like conditions for millennia. He didn't know much about his ancestors, except that they had probably inhabited colder places.

They passed more woodcutters with loaded burros. Thalia said that the kind of wood they cut — the oxaymel — only grew way up here and that they were good for wood. When they found the monarchs, they would be perched on these trees. What would happen when these trees were all gone? Dace felt like he'd gone back in time. The woodcutters looked like something from a Bible story or a wood cutout. More time passed and two hours and ten miles later, he wished he'd brought a burro too.

And a gun — just in case Savage found his way here. If they ambushed him, he'd have nowhere to go.

He had nothing to worry about, though. Nothing. That's what he kept telling himself anyway. He was the first white man up here and until he told somebody, he'd be the last. Maybe he'd just keep this place to himself. He remembered his dream in prison: They lived on a mountain with only one way up, and D'Arcy Devereux was at the top, a young man still. Liza wore a yellow dress. There were two motorcycles in the garage and always a party going on —

"Look!" Thalia exclaimed when a couple of butterfly ambassadors finally fluttered by them. The sight elated him like nothing had for a long time and filled him with a deep sense of peace too. These butterflies had translucent orange-gold wings and black bodies, so maybe they really were from Canada, unless they had come from some other place in the States. What else could they be? Viceroys? He'd never heard about the little copycats coming this far.

Whenever they spotted another butterfly, Thalia looked back at him and made a "V" with her two forefingers, the peace symbol she picked up somewhere. It was cute when she did it, a little Mexican skirt. Yes, if there was even one butterfly, there was bound to be more. Monarch butterflies weren't loners any more than he was.

Miraculously, Dace could still breathe at a height of nearly ninety-five hundred feet, so they kept climbing. He was okay as long as they took it easy, as long as they took it real slow. By now, they had been climbing for almost half a day, searching for the heart or the nucleus of the butterfly colony. The same "nucleus" that Kathleen had so much wanted to find too. Thalia thought that maybe the colony moved around the mountain, hanging out on mostly south-facing fir trees.

Thalia wasn't the least bit shy. Whenever they encountered another woodcutter, she'd stop and chat with them for a while about their work and ask about the monarchs too. Dace heard "mariposa monarca" a lot, but even way up here, the Mexicans were a suspicious lot. A good thing they talked to Thalia because they sure as hell wouldn't talk to him. He felt like a cowboy in a movie, except in a movie, they'd be outsiders, not him.

By high noon, they still hadn't found the nucleus, just some more strays. What the hell had happened to the rest of the monarchs' gang? Thalia asked another woodcutter again. For some reason, this man was a little more forthcoming. Maybe he didn't believe all that guff about the mariposas being the souls of dead children or something. Or maybe he just liked to blab, plus it was getting late in the day. *What the heck*, he probably figured, as he gesticulated and pointed up into the air, *I've got nothing to lose. I'll be home with my wife and kiddies real soon.* The woodcutter probably hadn't expected Thalia's reaction though. When her face fell, he took one look at Dace and his big hands and rushed off.

Then Thalia started that goddamn talking-crying thing that women do and within seconds, she was going pretty good. Not that it mattered because Dace couldn't understand a word she said. She sounded more like a Spanish speaking auctioneer than a girl.

He listened a moment longer before he dropped their backpack and grabbed her flying hands. He knew he had to be careful. Forcing himself to speak in slow English, he said. "Look at me—what's wrong?" He knew, though. Shit, shit, he thought. Right place, wrong time.

"It's too late," Thalia bawled. She didn't know anything about monarchs, she didn't! She had only been to their mountain retreat once, in February, she suddenly recalled.

Great, Dace thought, *just great.*

Thalia had heard they left around the end of March, but she was off by a week. Oh, Mary, mother of Jesus, a week, a week, that's all! Dace itched to strangle somebody, but he managed to keep his hands at his sides. How could they have missed the big migration by just days? he argued, reluctant to accept the obvious, even with that dumb lyric playing in his head. Right place, wrong time. He couldn't be that stupid or unlucky, he couldn't. Nobody could.

Surely to Christ, he hadn't been drinking in some bar, while the monarchs winged their fucking way home.

Eventually Thalia stopped crying. She had to. Nobody could keep that level of emotional intensity up and live. She smiled through her tears, an optimist at heart. "Maybe part of the colony's still here," she said.

"Yeah, right," he replied, but what the hell. Sunset was still a couple of hours off.

They pressed on a little further, just in case.

Eventually they found one of the places where the colony must have stayed. The butterflies were all gone, but a mouse cache alerted them. "Ratón," Thalia shuddered when a little grey mouse darted from a hole at the bottom of a tree, but it was just a mouse for God's sake. When Dace poked the cache with the toe of his new hiking boot, it broke apart and scattered like leaves.

They weren't leaves, though. They were wings, hundreds of them. Dace was puzzled until he realized that the mice, the greedy little bastards, must have dined on the monarchs' protein-packed bodies and left their colorful wings behind.

That was it for Thalia. She insisted on going home. They retraced their steps down the mountain, sorting out things on the way. It was March 28, several days past the vernal equinox and the six-month-old butterflies were obviously on their way north—to Canada, to Liza. Well, the egg carrying females anyway. Scientists thought that the male monarchs, after enjoying a seventy-two hour mating season, all died.

Bully for them, Dace thought. There were worse ways to go. And bully for him too. He had learned more from Kathleen than he thought. He was still mad at her, but valuable little bits and pieces about the life cycle of monarch butterflies kept coming back to him, almost everything that Kathleen knew. God, what a motor mouth the woman had. She'd talked all the time and if even part of what she'd told him was true, the departing butterflies would mate on the Gulf coast of Texas and Florida and then die.

The monarchs Liza saw in Canada would be their children or maybe their grandchildren, he wasn't sure. When Kathleen had first told him, he'd felt like he was in a classroom listening to a teacher drone, but this close to the monarchs' wintering grounds, it blew his mind.

It was faster going down. At the bottom of the mountain, they practically fell into the nearest bar. There were so many cantinas around. Dace swore it was the last time. He absolutely had to stay sharp. Look what had happened! He still couldn't believe it. It was the story of his life — getting so close to the monarch butterflies in their wintering grounds, missing them by days. Christ, what a loser, he berated himself, though he didn't say this aloud. Instead, he scowled at the beer in his hand, while Thalia fussed at his side, worried that he was still mad at her. And he was, goddamn it. He knew he should take her hand to make her feel better, but he couldn't.

Yes, alcohol was definitely part of his problem. In the relative cool of the cantina, he got a pen and paper from Thalia and started making notes. If he didn't start drinking less, he'd end up a shaky old man. He was really thirsty, though, after that long hike, so they shared a second beer. Well, it was a start, so he felt better. He took Thalia's hand and kissed the hollow of her throat. She shrank back a little, as if he'd hit her or something, but then she smiled and pressed up against him. She felt real good. That's it, he thought, I'll start drinking less tomorrow.
Thalia made some contributions too, all about the color and the light on the mountain and the connection she felt with the monarch butterflies, what they'd done to her insides.

He wondered if the researcher who'd advertised in the newspaper would be interested in what they'd "found" so far — if they alerted the Anglo world to what the Mexicans around here had always known. Suppose he lied about his academic credentials, used his fake name. Said he had what, a PhD? That would never work though. He'd just listened to those smarty-pants, those university girls, Liza and Kathleen talk. He really should have asked more questions though. Or gone to school when he had the chance. It was ridiculous. When it came right down to it, he didn't know enough about an academic's life to fabricate one. He hadn't even finished high school for God's sake.

How many chances did one man get? He didn't know what he'd expected, or what he'd have done if he'd actually found a whole mess of butterflies before they flew home. Other than take a lot of pictures. For the most part, he just wanted to show off to Liza, to surprise her, to delight her.

Okay—and if he was really honest—he'd wanted to be a big man for a while. To see his name in the newspaper associated with something good. Even a fake name. You couldn't beat that.

Oh, sure, and how would that have worked? He'd definitely been drinking too much. All this self-pity, all this goddamned circular thought. If his name got into any newspaper again, he was royally screwed.

No fucking way he wanted to end up in a Mexican jail—a place that would undoubtedly make Maitland Pen look like the Ritz.

Too late, Thalia tried to stop him. He jerked his hand out of her reach and crushed his notes into a ball.

He was stuffing the crumpled paper into his pocket, when a man who looked a lot like Savage walked through the door. Dace almost choked on his beer. *It can't be*, he thought, but he sure as hell wasn't taking any chances. He pulled his hat down over his face. He still couldn't swallow, though. Beer dribbled from the corner of his mouth. He wiped it off his chin with the heel of his hand and studied the three newcomers.

Savage had lost some weight, but it was him alright, flanked by a couple of narcs or feds or RCMP officers, he couldn't tell, wouldn't be able to tell until they talked and he heard their accents. The officers—whatever the hell kind they were—had on pale-colored suits and porkpie hats. Savage had stuffed his sweaty hulk into a suit too, the Lord knew how. He sported a light polyester jacket with white pants and a Hawaiian shirt. He'd lost some weight, but not nearly enough. The second last button on his shirt had popped, so his hairy navel showed.

The men were arguing about something, so they didn't see Dace, but everybody saw them or heard them. Maybe the heat had gotten to them. They acted like they were on a movie set and nothing was real. They plopped down at a table in the corner and shouted over to the bartender at the counter that they wanted a jug of beer, pronto, stat, right now!

"Sure enough, Americanos," a couple of drunks slurred, but the lone bartender couldn't say "Si" fast enough. Not that Dace blamed him. On the down side, Americans brought a lot of trouble; on the upside, they always spent lots of money.

Dace looked straight ahead, but his beer glass shot sideways down the counter. It travelled past two customers who were watching the newcomers and landed in the lap of a rather fat Mexican female, the only other woman besides Thalia in the bar. The woman had been sitting beside her husband, trying to coax him to come home and hold on to the last of his wages. She didn't know what had happened, so she did just what Dace wanted. She jumped up and started berating the bartender, who had so far thwarted her efforts to remove her husband and worse, had just finished topping up his beer.

"My dress, my dress!" she shouted in Spanish, pointing to the apron sized stain on her front.

While everybody else in the bar watched this drama unfold, Dace grabbed Thalia's hand and pulled her out the door. She had no idea what was happening, but she went along. She'd recognized Savage too and that was enough for her.

When they left, Savage was laughing and pointing at the woman's dress, so he hadn't changed much. But just as the door closed, Dace heard some more English and then one of the narcs said: "Whoa—who the hell was that?"

Chapter 18
Airplanes

Gomez-Kallestad residences, Morelia, Mexico, March 29, 1973

Thalia woke up with an idea. Her idea was so good that Dace wondered why she hadn't thought of it before, but then she hadn't known she was sleeping with a wanted man. Yesterday must have scared the bejesus out of her. First Savage and his friends and then him. She had been very quiet last evening, as if she was afraid he might explode. She didn't ask what he'd done, but she must have wanted to know.

"The stuff that happened back in Canada," he'd tried to reassure her, "it really wasn't such a big deal."

"Sure," she'd said, closing her eyes and retreating into sleep.

"Let's visit my abuelo," she said now, "nobody'll find you there."

They were still in bed. "Ah, Thalia, my darling," he said, rolling over and squeezing her a little too tightly, "I can't believe you want to get rid of me this soon."

Her grandfather's ranch was only a few miles out of town, in the hills. They hitchhiked there, in the back of another rancher's cart.

"I just met him," she swore to the old man when they arrived, "at the cantina. He needs a job, that's all."

Mr. Gomez was burning rubbish in a small fire in his front yard. Before replying, he raked some soup cans into the fire and flattened them with the edge of his metal rake. Dace watched as the labels on the cans went up in ash. "Does your papá know that you brought a gringo home?" he asked Thalia. Dace stood well back from the fire, trying his best to look respectable while he checked out the old man's property. Mr. Gomez's red roofed stone house sat squarely on fifty acres. The rancher was well over eighty, but he still insisted on living on his own. No doubt he could have lived with one of his daughters. Though he didn't have anybody else staying with him right now, he took in a couple of boarders from time to time, that's all.

Practically the minute they arrived at the Gomez place and while Thalia's grandfather was still giving him the hairy eyeball, Dace heard an airplane engine revving up.

"What's that?" he asked as casually as he could, which had the added bonus of getting Mr. Gomez off the topic of him and onto his noisy neighbor, the man with all the planes.

In the end, the old guy let Dace stay—maybe just to humor his granddaughter, but Thalia took off pretty quick.

Mr. Gomez gave him a room in a whitewashed shack behind the main house and told him he could cut some firewood. All that day and evening, Dace listened to more planes taking off and landing, alert to the kind of stimulus that had always made him feel alive. In prison, he used to crave peace and quiet, but now he longed for stimuli and noise. He wasn't sure when it had happened, but somewhere along the line, he'd gotten used to bustle and activity, emotional outbursts, the daily tolling of a bell.

Maybe even too used to it, he thought.

Whatever—it was way too quiet for him at Thalia's grandfather's place, but not quiet enough for the old man. A couple of weeks ago, some men had come down from the hills and raided the ranch. The old guy had repeated the story so many times in the past twenty-four hours—almost every time he saw Dace—that Dace could have probably given the police a description of the perpetrators himself.

In his youth, Mr. Gomez could have handled the bandits, but at eighty-five, he was just starting to get a little frail. The looters sounded like a kind of Mexican Mafia who exacted their due from vulnerable locals from time to time. On their last visit, they had left the old man's house alone, but they had taken a couple of his prize horses, which really made him mad. He couldn't stop talking about the horses.

160

This was probably the real reason he'd agreed to take Dace in, the strapping young gringo sleeping with his granddaughter Thalia with no money and butterflies on his brain.

To make the old rancher feel better, Dace started calling him "Abuelo" right away.

What a bonus about the planes next door, though. He had always enjoyed the noise they made, the way they moved, the way they did things humans couldn't do. And he'd wanted to know what made them tick. As a kid, his father had bought him one of the very first toy remote-control planes, but then motorcycles had taken over his life. He had been fourteen years old, so his life could have gone either way, but he'd wanted the company and excitement of other boys and piloting a plane was such a solo thing to do. Even so, if his best friend had taken up flying lessons, he probably would have too. What was it that everybody said to their kid? "If your friend jumped off a cliff, would you too?"

He really wished he had now though. Taken flying lessons, that is or gone to work in a hangar instead of his father's auto shop. But once he found out how an airplane engine worked, how hard could it be to fly one? If he flew a plane, he could lurch up over the soft, rounded mauve mountaintops and be guaranteed anonymity. In a private plane, he could be anybody and take refuge in the sky.

Dace lasted less than forty-eight hours on the ranch before he started to go a bit nuts. An artist might have savored the landscape and withdrawn into himself, but he couldn't. There was too much stuff inside himself that he didn't want to know. And he'd spent too much time in jail to just sit around. He wanted to go places, to set the world on fire and not get caught this time. And he kept hearing those little planes, taking off and landing, from sunup to sundown.

On the third morning, Dace hiked up into the trees behind Abuelo Gomez's house, before it got too hot. At the top of a hill, he had an aerial view of the neighbor's property—a man named Jon Kallestad, Abuelo had said. Kallestad had four or five planes. Judging by the size of his hangar, it was too small to hold more. There was something wrong with the oldest looking plane though. It never moved. The man might be a drug runner, but Dace doubted it. No, it looked like Kallestad ran a legit business, flying Americans, mostly surveyors, around to inspect the local mines. Or so a big sign at the side of the road leading into his property claimed.

Dace sat down on the hill and watched the planes for a while. Suits came and went. They drove up in dusty cars, handed over a wad of cash to Kallestad, showed him a license or borrowed his pilot and then climbed into the pit of a plane, sometimes with a pretty girl or a nervous looking friend in tow. No wonder they were nervous. The planes were small, supersized toys, that's all. Dace liked the noise the aircraft engines made when they took off though. They reminded him of his Harley, safe back home in his father's garage. *Look at me, look at me.*

He was pretty sure he could figure a plane out. How hard could it be? He just needed a bit of time. Figuring Kallestad out might be tougher though. The guy looked like a hard sell, the way he barked orders at his Mexican employees.

Thalia's grandfather and Kallestad bore a certain resemblance, though one was of Spanish extraction and judging by his name, the other man's ancestors had come from Norway. Maybe it was just because of their advanced age that they looked so much alike. People came by to rent planes, but nobody stayed. The Kallestad house was smaller than Gomez's, so the staff probably just hiked in for the day.

Thalia's grandfather didn't see any similarities between himself and his neighbor. "He's a gringo," he'd said when Dace mentioned the man in the morning, as if that explained everything.

"That's okay," Dace said, "I am too."

Dace waited a couple of hours until the rush died down and every plane but the disabled one had gone. By then, he'd smoked half a pack of cigarettes, digging a little hole with his fingers and burying the butts in the ground. He'd check out Kallestad's place tomorrow. He got up to go, but he didn't get far. He was halfway down the hill when a couple of Mexican thugs came out of nowhere, some of Kallestad's men for sure. They grabbed him by the arms, but he shook them off. He couldn't ignore the gun prodding his back, though, so he let them steer him down.

Kallestad was still outside his house, swishing his mouth out with coffee and spitting it on the ground. "What the hell are you doing hiding up on my hill? You've been there since first light. You aren't as crafty as you think. My boys spotted you first thing. Did the policia send you here?" he demanded.

"No," Dace said. "I was just checking out your place. I'm looking for a job."

Kallestad snorted and emptied the rest of his coffee on the ground. It was so hot out that the dirt dried instantly. "What kind of job? Do I look like a rich man? These Mexican kids here are cheap, cheap and I've got two ex-wives up north. This stuff gives me acid reflux. I don't know why I drink it. I never seen you in these parts," he said, "or anywhere else."

"It doesn't matter," Dace said. "I noticed one of your planes isn't working and that can't be good for business. Mind if I take a look?"

By now, two more young Mexicans had arrived, bringing the total number of men flanking Dace to four. The men were black-haired, lithe and tan and all dressed the same, in sombreros, cowboy boots and jeans. In a lineup, Dace knew he would have had a hard time telling them apart, so they probably got away with a lot. Well, as long as there weren't any bodies buried anywhere. He started to sweat a little. They were small guys, but there were more of them and they looked kind of lethal.

Kallestad looked like he was about to say something else, but he changed his mind. "It's okay, boys," he said. "It'll take me a week to get a mechanic from Morelia or Mexico City, the lazy fuckers. Let's give this kid a chance. But keep an eye on him, hey. My heart's acting up—too much excitement for the old ticker this morning. I'm going to take a little nap."

Kallestad went back into his house while the young Mexicans watched Dace open the door to the disabled plane's engine. First he looked, then he touched, then he talked, to the airplane that is. The boys sat down in the shade of a tree and pulled their sombreros down over their faces, but Dace wasn't fooled. They looked pretty sneaky, especially the youngest one in the lot. He let them think he was just some stupid American dude while he tightened up some screws.

"So which one of you is stashing stuff here?" he asked, holding up his right index finger which was covered in white dust. He was tempted to taste his finger, but he didn't. Cocaine had never been his drug of choice, but he had tried it like almost everybody else who'd spent time in jail and he'd liked it a bit too much. He couldn't take another chance.

All four boys stood up and started doing a little jiggling dance on the balls of their feet. "No hablo inglés, no hablo inglés," they said, shaking the tassels on their hats up and down.

Dace didn't care if they understood English or not. Kallestad was coming back out of his house. "Well, I understand you," he said to the boys who were watching him like the enemy he was. "And this stuff on my finger isn't any old dust. Is that why you loosened this here cylinder? So you could store some of your bricks here for a while? There's nothing in here right now, but somebody's been using this little plane like it's their own private treasure chest."

None of the boys said anything, but they sure jumped when Kallestad suddenly boomed: "Is that right? Has one of you little buggers been messing with my plane? I told you I didn't want any drugs here. The fucking Mexican policia will be all over me and the feds too for all I know. I'm too old for all this drama. That's why I'm not married anymore. Get out, you little fuckers. Get the hell out of here!"

Shit, Dace thought, realizing what he'd just done. He didn't know these kids, but still. It went against his grain to rat somebody out. He'd never have made it out of prison alive if he'd been a stool pigeon. And what if these guys were supporting an old mother or something? He'd been so pumped to find out what was wrong with the plane, that's all. He still had no idea how a plane engine worked. Also, there was only one of him. He couldn't protect the old man by himself.

"Uh, sir," he said, "I'm not sure that's such a good idea. You don't need no enemies and you need lots of help..."

But the old man had already turned around and started walking back to his house, his former employees scattering like grasshoppers from his path. He muttered to himself, complaining that he had no friends and why did everybody always try to do him in? Sure, he'd inherited some money, but he'd worked his ass off, building his business up from the ground. He planned to give his business to his nephew up north when he was gone. His ex-wives weren't getting it, that's for sure. And he certainly wasn't going to give it to some Spic, if that's what they thought.

"No, you can do everything," he yelled back at Dace. "You wanted a job, you got one. But stay the hell next door. I don't want your face around here all the time."

But he must have thought better of his decision. How he communicated this, Dace didn't know. All four boys were there the next day, though, oiling up the planes.

Chapter 19
Fear of Flying

Dace climbed into the little Cessna. "Buenas días," he said to the instructor, a dazzling brown skinned, white suited man. Dace wore a long-sleeved shirt and blue jeans, a mistake, because he was already sweating up a storm, just from nerves. The outside temperature was only about seventy degrees Fahrenheit.

He sat down, strapped himself in and looked around the tiny cockpit. How safe was this goddamn little tin box anyway? Bits and pieces were jiggling and they weren't even up in the air. He hated putting his life in a stranger's hands. If only Kallestad could have taught him how to fly, but the old guy had a problem with his balance now. His balance and a couple of other things. Well, Dace could do this. He'd survived prison and worse. How the hell hard could it be?

"Buenos días, señor," the man replied, pointing out a tiny front view window to the rising sun. "Es un dia hermoso."

And it was a beautiful day, except Liza wasn't there. Dace thought about her all the time, even when the instructor started showing him the controls in the plane, which worked just like he thought they would. *Yeah, yeah,* he thought, *let's go.* One good shove and he could push the instructor out the door, but the guy was just being thorough, that's all. *Just give me the controls,* he nearly said. He had to go back to Canada for Liza, he had to. He felt like she was in trouble, but there was no way she could tell him. His gut kept cramping and for days now, he'd had the kind of headache that just wouldn't go away.

Lucky us, he thought, *to be so connected, to find your soulmate in your own family, to feel the other person's pain.* This was what everybody wanted, well, most women anyway. He stared out of the rattling cockpit window at his slice of blue sky, with the instructor babbling away in his ear. *Yeah, lucky us, except she can't tell me anything and here I am, way down in Morelia and there's nothing I can do.*

Eventually the instructor stopped talking and smiled at Dace. "Presten atención, por favor," he said.

What the hell did the guy think he was doing? Dace nodded just to be polite. If only he'd had half as much patience when he was teaching Liza to ride a motorbike. Determinedly, he took in what the instructor was saying and filed it in his head, right along with Liza. His memory had always served him well and his reasoning too. Okay, so he hadn't always acted on the information he had. Some of the reasons might have had to do with drink and drugs and the fact that he wanted everything instantly, the same way he'd wanted Liza. The only thing that stopped him the first time was that she had been just fourteen. If only he hadn't screwed up so badly, they would have still been together, sorted out all that cousin stuff and made it okay. Because it was okay. They could have lived freely and openly in this Mexican paradise, or gone back to Canada and set a lot of stuff straight. Without anybody getting killed. God help him, an old man like Judge Silverton had to die of his own accord sometime. As for Silverton's priest nephew and the police and even the guards at Maitland Pen, they would be nothing when the old bastard was no longer around. Silverton was running the show, if only they knew and when he died, all their secrets were bound to come oozing out.

Well, there was one thing he could do right now—he could learn how to fly and the minute he got his license, he'd fetch Liza. He knew exactly where he'd land a plane on his father's farm—in the field where he'd taught her to ride a motorbike. Never mind that he'd almost killed her and now he'd have to take her out of school too, yeah, right. If only he could figure something out so they both could go home.

He was learning stuff too, picking up some Spanish and such. "Estás casado?" he made the mistake of asking the instructor, the next time the guy paused for breath. For ten minutes, the instructor stopped teaching him anything and they just sat on the ground, while he waxed on and on in Spanish, presumably about his lovely "epousa" because he repeated the same word over and over.

Dace smiled. *What a bunch of romantics Mexicans are*, he thought. Most of the guys he knew just called their wives "the old lady." Not that Liza would put up with anything like that.

"Okay," the instructor finally said in heavily accented English, "let's try again."

And Dace went through the steps with him several more times while the plane sat on the ground. He sure wasn't nervous anymore, just bored stiff.

"Christ," he said in English, after the third walk through, "enough's enough. Let's get this baby up in the air."

The instructor sat back and folded his arms over his chest. "Okay," he said, "You take baby up, up and away. You fly, my friend."

Chapter 20
A Seed about to Break

*I miss you even more than I could have believed;
and I was prepared to miss you a good deal.
~Vita Sackville-West

Devereux Farm, near Maitland, April 22, 1973

By mid-April, most people thought Liza was due, but she still had seven weeks to go. "Oh, my," they said ominously. "That's a big one." She'd finished all classes and a good thing too, for she had difficulty walking and she was so exhausted, she could read nothing. Not even the *Maitland Spectator* or Millie's stupid Harlequin romances. She despaired of both her body and her mind. Maybe if Dace had been around to remind her she was beautiful, but he wasn't—her cousin, that wanderer, that escaped convict, oh, what the hell. As for the people she lived with, Millie had helped set up a crib but her uncle hadn't even acknowledged a child was on the way. It didn't matter. He had done her a huge favor, just by taking her in. It bothered her that she needed so much help, but she did.

Last year at this time, she'd been running around Maitland and Toronto with Dace and then in June she'd started her summer job. What an amazing amount of energy she'd had! This year she just sat in the family room and stared at the fire in the potbellied stove while outside a cold wind roared.

"How about watching the *Six Million Dollar Man*?" Millie always asked before going into the formal living room to catch her favorite television program.

It hadn't been this cold in April last year. Liza had gone walking with Dace in the bush. She'd worn a summer dress! And he—well, she was old and tired now, all passion spent. She couldn't imagine ever wanting to make love again, but she'd do it—for him, fit him in. Well, maybe. Yes, though spring had come early the past two years, it looked like it might never come again. People talked about another Ice Age, but spring could be brutal in southern Ontario, the early spring at least. Toronto—the city where she'd lived until she turned fourteen—sat on the shores of Lake Ontario. On a clear day, you could see the States on the other side, but the lake was large. She remembered several cold springs due to lake effects.

"Why don't you learn to knit or something?" Millie nagged constantly. "It's not good for you or the baby to sit around and brood. That kid's going to need all the help it can get."

In her worst moments, Liza knew this pregnancy had drained her completely, that this was the price women paid. For love, for children, to do what they were born to do. For the first time, she felt a grudging respect for her own mother. How had she done it? Through two pregnancies at least; the second time with twins. When people suggested Liza might be having twins, she panicked, though the midwife kept reassuring her that it was only one baby—a large singleton with the low heartbeat of a boy.

Bringing life into the world was nothing for a man, Liza thought. No wonder some guys refused to get involved. According to her mother, her own father had been totally useless, and look at Tony Harper, that would-be actor, that jerk. He couldn't acknowledge his own flesh and blood. Tony's memory had faded, though. She had been only sixteen. It was a long time ago and in the intervening years, so much else had happened. She didn't even think about Tony that often anymore. He was just a bit player on a distant stage. It was only when she got really tired that her thoughts darkened and she cursed him. It reflected badly on her, she supposed, but she didn't care. *May you be a bit player on every stage,* she thought when she remembered him. *Forever and always.*

Sometimes she even wondered if Tony was part of the reason she'd been in such a hurry to get pregnant again. She'd been nipped in the bud and she had been bound and determined to flower again.

Oh, God, she wasn't going to give him that much credence. No, she'd gotten pregnant again because she couldn't have Dace. He'd had to flee — way down to Mexico, she hoped — or they'd have killed him. It was simple. She couldn't have him, so she'd wanted his child, that's all. This baby was no mistake. She had access to birth control this time and nobody had forced her. She'd let people think it was an accident, but she had made a rational, if impassioned choice — hadn't she? She had a brain! She couldn't let herself be ruled by her emotions. She was crazy about Dace, she had always been crazy about him, but she'd let him go, for the sake of both of them, for the sake of their child. Yes, for the sake of their unborn child, she'd used her head.

For the most part, she'd stayed calm and focused in school, but after she'd written her last exam in mid-April, her mind scattered. She had to start thinking about her future, but if she did, she'd go insane. What the hell had she been thinking? What had she done? Getting pregnant deliberately — what the hell did she have to offer a child? My God, she must have been bewitched.

On Sundays, she went to Mass with Millie and lit a candle to St. Jude, the patron saint of lost causes. She wasn't Catholic, but maybe it would still work. *Please, God*, she prayed, *keep my lover, keep my baby's father, keep my cousin Dace Devereux safe.*

She thought about the baby — for surely she would be ecstatic when her perfect child arrived — as long as nothing bad happened to Dace and they weren't all struck deaf, dumb, dead with grief.

Oh, she was probably just being melodramatic. Where the hell was Dace though? He really was in a terrible bind. He had the prison authorities and all sorts of police after him. That fiendish jail guard Savage was probably in the lead. Savage would kill him if he caught him. If the guy was that smart. But what if Savage had teamed up with somebody else? Like Judge Silverton? If she found out he was in cahoots with him, she wouldn't be surprised.

Could she help Dace get home? Not for herself, of course. She didn't want him, not if he didn't want her, not if he couldn't behave. Why the hell was everything so complicated? The bikers — why had he allowed himself to get so ensnared by them? When he'd had her…ah, sweet Jesus. Such a terrible, fucking, aching waste. *My life, my love*, she thought. He made her furious and he wasn't even here.

She'd have to find some way to exonerate him, to prove he shouldn't have been in jail in the first place, at least not this time. *You're daydreaming,* a snappish little voice inside her said. Her old roommate Janice was engaged to a boy who was a law student; she'd pump him about what to do. Or get in touch with Hugh Gold, Dace's lawyer. Would that work? In his own way, Gold had tried. She didn't want Dace the way he was, she kept telling herself, she just wanted him home. For Uncle Norm.

What if she'd had an older child or a paying job demanding her energy and her time? She'd had all sorts of energy in the middle months of pregnancy, but not now. For one thing, she wasn't sleeping. At night, she rolled with great effort from side to side in her bed. She had to use both hands. Lodged deep inside her, the baby's head had already spread her hips. She felt like a giant wishbone waiting to be snapped. Like Sylvia Plath had said in a poem, "A seed about to break." Thank God, she didn't have to share a bed. The baby moved around a lot, but that wasn't the problem. She just couldn't get comfortable.

Norm and Millie Devereux slept on the other side of the house in the master bedroom with an en suite that buffered all sorts of nocturnal noises, but Millie still heard every movement Liza made. Man-like, Norm slept through anything; he always had. Millie concocted milk remedies — a little spiked milk wouldn't hurt her. Under her watchful eye, Liza always took a tiny sip but tossed the rest of the milk and rum down the toilet on her next bathroom run. She didn't like the taste and she'd already put on more than thirty pounds, almost a third of her pre-pregnancy weight.

Dr. Shaw, the obstetrician they'd made her see in Maitland, had been aghast, though her blood pressure, her sugar levels and her heartrate were fine. His wife-nurse had tested those things, while he clucked at another patient in the next room. A fiftyish man in a three-piece suit with a roomful of maternity patients, Dr. Shaw had spent three minutes tops with Liza.

"How much did you weigh when you were born?" he'd asked. "And the baby's father...hmm, I see you're not married...I guess you don't know how much he weighed either?" The obstetrician didn't know she'd been practically anorexic before, or how much weight she'd lost keeping up with Dace and he didn't ask. When she dutifully revealed that the baby's father was a cousin, he'd raised an eyebrow, but no matter. Liza liked him slightly more after that. Although he hadn't kept up with the latest medical news that mothers who put on more weight had healthier babies, at least he knew about cousins.

"There's a very slight increase in fetal abnormalities when the parents are first cousins, but not nearly as much as people think," he'd said. "Especially if your family doesn't have any known inherited diseases. I'm much more concerned about the risk you're taking in planning a homebirth. It's definitely not wise. This baby is large for its due date and your pelvis is small. Also, you're four centimeters dilated which is odd in a primipara. You could go anytime at all. If you feel anything — anything at all — you must seek medical attention at once."

Scaremonger, Liza had thought. *You just want me in your thrall and I'm tired of being in some man's thrall. I want to sit up in that proverbial ivory tower in my own little office and write: poetry, short stories, novels, whatever, I don't know. I'll keep the baby in a little cradle by the desk and feed him under a shawl while I discuss with students whether or not Tess of the d'Ubervilles was raped or seduced. When the baby's a little older, he can play with his blocks on the rug and then he'll go to school. I'll get my PhD and teach and Dace will…oh, God, what will Dace do?* One thing was certain. She couldn't be on her own her whole life. She wasn't that kind of girl, that kind of woman. She'd never last on her own. She couldn't. She wanted, needed a man.

"You have to see the OB," the midwife had insisted, "just in case you end up in the hospital. They won't treat you right if you don't have a doctor."

Well, it didn't matter. She wasn't going to any hospital and she wasn't having any more kids either. This one, this one perfect boy would have to do. The baby's head pressed down on her right side, causing an almost continuous pain in her hip. Except for that, she glowed or so lots of people said.

On April 22, Liza left the house and made her way down the long laneway to the mailbox. It was just past Easter. Millie had baked a big ham on the weekend. Her son and his brood had come to dinner. Uncle Norm had hidden Easter eggs all over the house for the little girls and while the kids had hunted eggs, Liza had wondered who was still hunting Dace. Much to Millie's annoyance, Norm had mentioned him when he said Grace. "Keep D'Arcy safe and bring him home to Maitland in one piece. Clear his name." Dear Uncle Norm had such a deep faith that his son was alright. In her current condition, Liza envied him both his faith and his lack of imagination.

The air was finally warming, but the trees were still whited out with snow. Liza felt small, like a tiny plastic figurine in a giant white bowl. As she walked, nothing broke the monotony of the snow-covered landscape until a brown jackrabbit cut across the front lawn and streaked for the bush. *Ah, country life,* she thought, suddenly yearning for Toronto, a city of more than two million people now.

She went for days here without speaking to anybody, especially when the newly created Mrs. Millie Devereux was in a cleaning mood and Uncle Norm was out fixing a car. Spring had made a brief appearance in early April, but it had snowed again, trapping Liza in the house. She hadn't stepped outside for nearly two days. She didn't mind the cold, but it bothered her that all her uncle's newly emerged crocuses, the early blooming tulips and the brave bright daffodils lay under snow.

Liza looked back at the house once. A curtain fluttered. Of course. From a window in the master bedroom, Millie was watching her progress down the slushy road.

She brushed melting snow away from the lettering on the mailbox—*Devereux Auto*—and stuck her gloveless hand inside. Her baby was a little fire burning inside of her. She never got cold. She pulled out two envelopes, hardly worth the trip. Norm and Millie got mostly bills, but there were none today. Both letters were for her— one with no return address and just her name on the front and the other from the Office of the Registrar. She knew it: her marks had come! She tore the envelope open and studied her marks on the road by her uncle's mailbox. A damp wind nearly whipped the transcript from her hands, but except for the bathroom (where Millie got nervous if she locked the door) it was the only place she had any privacy.

Millie had warmed to her since the wedding, hence the milk, but she wanted to know everything. And worse, she acted like she knew everything— about pregnancy and delivery too. Never mind that her only known pregnancy had ended in a Caesarean section when she was barely seventeen. If Liza hadn't visited the midwife regularly, Millie's constant talk of lost babies, botched deliveries and children with something "not right" would have driven her insane.

It doesn't matter, Liza kept telling herself. She trusted her midwife

Mary Bergen implicitly. Mary had caught hundreds of babies and never lost one. Everything was going to be alright.

Liza read her marks a second time, just in case. She had gotten As in everything except the Communications course where Joe Armitage was the Teaching Assistant. He—the asshole!—had given her an overall grade of C minus. She stomped the snowy laneway, wishing to hell it was his head. She'd done all her assignments and Prof. Diamond had loved her essay on how the media shaped public opinion, but he'd left it to his assistant to compile the class's final marks. He was much too busy writing his third book.

"Well," Joe had said about her A plus essay. "Of course he likes your paper. You're a girl. He likes your ass."

This poor mark in the Communications course would affect her GPA, but right now she didn't care, or at least not as much as Joe probably hoped. She'd just have to make sure she never took another course with him. At least the Communications course was an elective and not part of her major. It was the principle of the thing, that's all. Too bad she had neither the energy nor the time to appeal. If she ever found a way to screw Joe, she'd do it, that's all. Here she was not yet twenty-one and she had two men she wanted to see dead, three if she counted her father. *Revenge is a dish best served cold.*

She put her back to the wind and walked to the house, still under Millie's watchful gaze. Well, she was always watching, wasn't she? Given Joe's little present in the mail, Liza had forgotten all about the pain in her hip. She walked so quickly that she almost ran, holding her belly with both hands. Millie meant well, but she bugged her. She really did. If only the woman would mind her own business. *What the hell*, she thought, did Millie expect her to pull a Plath or worse—to tumble into a ditch and suffocate herself and her unborn child in the snow?

As she entered the house by the backdoor, she almost collided with Millie who had come downstairs and started sweeping the floor. Liza jumped out the way of Millie's broom and crashed into the door frame. Now that Millie was married, she had taken to dressing like the chatelaine of Norm's house, well, of her house too. Instead of her customary stretch pants, she had on a knee-length skirt, nude hosiery and two-inch high pumps. Her hair was pulled back into a loose chignon at the nape of her neck.

The house cat, a youthful tabby, hissed at Millie's broom while she swept the tiled floor. The cat hated both Millie and her broom. He had only gained full access to the house after an unusual infestation of field mice in the fall. In the laundry room behind the porch, the washing machine and the dryer rumbled and shook. With only three people in the house, Millie still managed to do two loads of laundry a day.

Millie stopped sweeping for a moment and leaned on her broom. *A regular old witch*, Liza thought unkindly. Tired as she was, she would have taken over the sweeping for Millie, but the woman wouldn't let her.

"Mind your feet," Millie said. "I see you got your marks. Who's that other letter for?"

One good thing about Millie, Liza reminded herself as she righted herself and inched through the back porch and into the vestibule adjoining the laundry room. *She doesn't expect me to fail, mainly because she has no notion of what goes on in the academic world.* For just a moment, she wished she had somebody she could really talk to about school.

Millie picked up the snow-clotted boots Liza had pulled off with great effort and shook them distastefully outside the backdoor. Liza wished she wouldn't pick up after her, but nothing made her stop.

"The other letter, Liza," she repeated, after she'd double locked the door. You never knew who might show up, one of those bikers maybe out looking for bailout or a loan. "Is it a cheque? A lot of people owe Norm...I know it looks like we're made of money around here, but we've got lots of bills to pay. The electricity alone—and you, your bedroom light is on half the night."

Liza took off her coat and hung it up on the closest hook, just inside the laundry room door, and entered the family room on the right. She had completely forgotten about the other letter. She must be losing her mind or else it was those pregnancy hormones again. What had she done with the other letter? Was it in her pocket or had she dropped it in the snow?

"There was only one letter," she lied reflexively, not caring that Millie had followed her into the family room and looked quite skeptical.

Whatever she'd done with the second letter, it was probably just another anonymous note. Millie would go on and on if she found out, fussing about RCMP stings or the possibility that Uncle Norm was the real target and somebody wanted to extort money from him. As if. The police or Savage or Judge Silverton or whoever was writing the anonymous notes wanted only one thing: Dace Devereux back in the clink.

Though it was quite a leap, this in turn would lead to Millie's favourite topic of conversation as Liza's pregnancy had progressed: how Liza should do everybody a favour and give the kid up for adoption, although she'd have to tell the adopted parents who the baby's father really was, just in case something was wrong — wrong with the baby, that is.

Liza usually picked up the mail on the way back from school, so she had intercepted three similar hand-delivered letters before. She'd hidden them and then come down in the dead of night and destroyed them all in the potbellied stove, but it was unlit at this time of day. Just the memory of the other letters made her skin crawl. It troubled her that a stranger snuck past the farmhouse late at night and stuck threatening notes in their mailbox — probably from the passenger side of a car or the cab of a truck. She knew it would trouble her uncle even more, so she hadn't told him either. She wouldn't put it past him to sit up all night with his shotgun and just wait.

The letters all said basically the same thing: "If you don't tell where Dace is, the police ain't ever going to let you keep that baby because you ain't fit."

By now, Liza felt even more exhausted than she had earlier in the day. The little trip to get the mail and this business with Millie hadn't helped. There were two very comfortable couches in the family room. The tabby cat had taken up residence on one, leaving the other one free. Liza desperately wanted to lie down on it, but she couldn't. Not with Millie around. The staircase leading to the upper story was just through the next door, but it looked a long way up and Millie was still standing there, evidently waiting for her to produce more mail.

Give me a moment, Liza felt like saying as she turned her back on Millie. *I'll give you a letter — I'll write one myself. Leave me alone,* it would say. "I'm going upstairs to take a nap," she flung over her shoulder. Mom and Gran would have been just as nosy, she reminded herself as she grasped the handrail and slowly hauled herself up the stairs. Her calves and the backs of her thighs ached. If Millie hadn't been looking, she would have crawled up the winding staircase hand over hand.

Millie clicked her tongue. "Must be nice," she observed, "To nap whenever you please. When I was pregnant, I worked in a variety store. We opened before seven a.m. I was on my feet all day and my husband was never around. Ronnie was a truck driver, you see, and he never did a thing in the house. I did good, though; I only gained fourteen pounds..."

When Liza finally made it upstairs, she could still hear Millie, who had launched into a long story about the variety store, a Chinaman and what she'd had to put up with there.

The cat had leapt up the stairs behind Liza, anything to get away from the sound of Millie's voice. He headed straight into her room for the quilt on the bed, while his mistress detoured into the bathroom and double-locked the door. She sank to the floor with her back against the door, but she could still hear Millie, so she got up and turned on the cold water tap in the sink.

When she sat back down, the missing letter poked up through the top of her bra. She pulled it out. She had every intention of tearing it into tiny pieces and flushing it down the toilet, but when she read it, she just couldn't. This letter was different from the others. It was from Dace; it had to be. Who else would write to her about butterflies? It might be from somebody who was trying to trick her, like the person who had purposely used the word "ain't" in the anonymous notes, but she doubted it. She had never talked about monarch butterflies to anybody except Dace. The printing in this note was different too.

"Butterflies make a perilous journey," the hand-lettered note said, "but arrive safe."

Liza buried her face in the letter before she put it back in her bra. She was sure she could smell him. If only she hadn't started crying. It felt like she'd unstopped something inside. She leaned against the side of the cold bathtub and sobbed until Millie came upstairs and hammered on the door.

"What's happening?" she yelled. "Are you bleeding? Are you getting pains?"

Liza wiped her face and clumsily hauled herself to her feet, by reaching up and pulling on the brass handled door. She unlocked the door, but kept her reddened eyes lowered to the floor. Millie stood right there, this time with an old cloth rag and a can of Ajax in her hands.

"Nothing's happening," she mumbled. "It's too soon."

Millie eyed her suspiciously. "Don't lock the bathroom door," she said, "it's not safe."

My God, Liza thought as she went into her bedroom and slammed the door, *how old is this letter? The monarchs shouldn't be arriving down south; they should be on the return journey to Canada. Look at all this goddamn snow! If they get here too early, they'll die.*

Chapter 21
Time's Up

Devereux Farm, near Maitland, June 21, 1973

The baby was not early. He was late and in trouble. He was so late that somebody from the obstetrician's office even called to see what was happening. Liza was impressed, or she would have been if she wasn't so damned scared.

It was nine o'clock at night. She was in the kitchen when Millie took the call. The avocado colored wall phone was turned up so loud that she could hear both sides of the conversation, especially when Millie held the receiver away from her ear as usual.

"Dr. Shaw asked me to call. Miss Devereux should have had that baby by now," the doctor's secretary said. "She's almost two weeks overdue. Dr. Shaw will have the midwife charged if anything happens. Homebirths aren't really legal in Ontario. If nothing goes wrong, the authorities will probably look the other way, but if it does, the midwife and Liza will both be in trouble—not to mention anybody's who helped her and that likely means you…"

Liza, who was sitting at the kitchen table, almost choked on a prune. She hadn't told Millie or Norm that she was planning a homebirth. If she could help it, she never spoke about anything important. She couldn't. *Here be dragons*, she thought, imagining what they would say. It was summer now and when the pains came, she thought she'd just walk down the road to the midwife's. How hard could that be? Women had babies all the time.

If she had to, she could probably deliver this baby by herself. For he was a real baby now, perfect and complete. He stretched and kicked inside her, pulling her overstretched abdomen even tauter. "Let me out," he said, "there's no more room in here." Liza's self-confidence was only skin deep though. Deep in her heart, she feared something had gone wrong, that her baby couldn't find his way out and that they were both doomed.

Gagging a little, Liza removed the pitted prune from her mouth. She waved a tired hand at Millie as if to say—*she doesn't know what she's talking about, it's okay*—but there was no need. Millie never took any guff from anybody. Liza doubted she wanted a dead baby either, but she really, really hated being told what to do.

"Now listen here," Millie interrupted the secretary, "I don't know about any homebirth, but one thing I do know—a baby comes when he's ready! Dr. Shaw pulled my son out of me with a couple of salad forks and he was only four pounds and you know the rest of the story—his lungs weren't developed and he almost died! I had to feed him milk with an eye dropper, the little guy couldn't even suck!"

When Millie got off the phone, Liza just looked at her. Words failed her. She felt like such a willful brat. *It's not my fault*, she wanted to say. *The baby's just in no hurry to be born*. She had no idea why. She was eating prunes and climbing stairs and doing everything in her power to bring him on. If she could have, she would have pushed the baby right out on the clean kitchen floor. The only thing she couldn't do was have sex, which the midwife had also said might help. Apparently orgasm released oxytocin, a love hormone that might trigger birth. In her current condition, Liza didn't feel much like having sex and there wasn't anybody available anyway, but she was beyond desperate to have the baby now, so anxious that she would have gone under the knife without drugs if somebody had insisted.

Millie slammed some pots in the sink. "My God!," she yelled, "Are you crazy? Were you actually planning to have a baby here? Maybe on the kitchen table or on one of my clean beds? Never mind what I told that snippy secretary. You're going to the hospital—someplace super antiseptic. This is your first birth, girl, and you're just a little thing.

182

Homebirth's not safe."

"I'm not having the baby here," Liza said defensively. "I'm having it at Mary's — at the midwife's. She's got everything ready and she's just down the road."

Millie's face blew up. "What — that Mennonite woman? What does she know?" she shrieked. She tossed her dishcloth after the pots into the sink. "She doesn't even have electricity, for God's sake. And all those kids — the germs in her place! I have a good mind to go talk to her. What the hell is she waiting for? You can't carry that kid forever."

My God, Liza thought, *Millie's so scared.* "It's okay," she tried to reassure her. "I'm going to take some castor oil tonight. She gave me some."

"Castor oil? Yuck! That's an old wife's tale. It'll never work. What are you trying to do, grease him out? Just look at yourself, he's stuck the wrong way! What if he's upside down? Or crossways? Your shape's a little funny…I always said…"

"Oh, God, Millie. Mary Bergen checked. She knows what she's doing. She's delivered nearly a thousand babies and she's never lost one. The baby's head is engaged, so that means it's down…"

"Up, down, it doesn't matter! Norm doesn't say much, but he's beside himself — a nut bar. You're making him crazy! Do you hear me? Why do you think he spends so much time in the garage? It's because of you! He can't even look at you now, for God's sake. You're as big as a beached whale, as a house! Come on — let's take a ride on a bumpy road. We'll shake the kid loose…"

Liza pushed the rest of her prunes aside and got up slowly from the table. Lately the urge to urinate never left her and last night she'd seen a little blood on her underclothes. She had to use the bathroom right now. Well, what else was new? She smiled grimly. "I'm ready. The baby is too. It'll work," she said. It had to. She couldn't hold onto him another night. He had to get out. He was just getting bigger and if he wasn't, that was even worse. It meant the placenta — the thing that nourished him — was drying up, calcifying or whatever the hell a tired one did.

"Oh, you're a stubborn one, aren't you?" Millie said as she watched her exiting the kitchen sideways through the door.

As if any mother has control over what her child does, Liza thought. Maybe she could still walk through the door facing forward, but she'd gotten so big, she'd lost all faith. A strong smell of bleach drifted after her. *Damn*. If Millie had decided to disinfect the kitchen sink, she'd do the rest of the house too.

"Come and get me if you feel anything—anything at all," Millie called, unwittingly echoing the obstetrician's caution. "They left me alone in the hospital—I was only seventeen—but I wouldn't leave a dog to labor alone. You'll see. You're going to need help wherever you go. Everybody will tell you, walk, walk and you think you'll be able to walk, but you won't. It will take two people to drag you around by your arms once that kid starts to drop. It sure did with me. You're not, I repeat, you're not having it here!"

No, Liza thought, *I'm not having him here. Definitely not.* Once out of Millie's line of vision, she clutched her belly. *My God,* she chided herself, *what do you think this is, a movie? That you'll have a couple of pains and just drop the baby out here on the hall floor? You? Girl, you should be so lucky. Get real.* Something had tightened, though. There it was again! Would it turn into a real pain? *I want my midwife,* she thought, *I want Mary right now.* She was probably getting her children ready for bed. No point in bothering her with a false alarm.

Liza went upstairs and got into bed. Several hours passed, but she didn't feel anything more. She might have slept a little, but she wasn't sure. She was worried sick and there was no one to help her. By all counts, the baby was at least two weeks overdue, maybe more. She'd have to do something herself. At two a.m. on June 22, she got out of bed for the third time that night, gagged down the first dose of castor oil and wiped the nasty film off her mouth.

"That's it," she said to the baby in her belly with more bravado than she felt, "Time's up." *My darling, my life.*

Chapter 22
May He Keep So

Who is he, this blue, furious boy,
Shiny and strange, as if he had hurtled from a star?
He is looking so angrily!
He flew into the room, a shriek at his heel.
The blue color pales. He is human after all.
A red lotus opens in its bowl of blood;
They are stitching me up with silk, as if I were a material.

What did my fingers do before they held him?
What did my heart do, with its love?
I have never seen a thing so clear.
His lids are like the lilac-flower
And soft as a moth, his breath.
I shall not let go.
There is no guile or warp in him. May he keep so.
~"Three Women," by Sylvia Plath

Devereux Farm, near Maitland, June 22, 1973

L iza refused to leave the house. She couldn't anyway. Seriously, how the hell did they expect her to get to the hospital in this shape? How did anybody whose body had been invaded by such gigantic life? She gritted her teeth, determined not to scream. Even Mary's house, the midwife's, was too far down the road. When the first tentative pain had come, low down, a flirtatious little grab in her groin—*ha, can you take this, it's time and if you think this is bad, well, just wait*—she'd felt almost giddy with relief.

It was three a.m. now and she was alone in her room, rousted from a fitful sleep. Something was happening at last! She watched the alarm clock on the bedside table and waited a good ten minutes before the second pain came and it wasn't too bad. *Whew*, she thought. She could do this, she really could! She could do what she was made to do. She sat up and studied the sheet underneath her. There was a little blood on the bed, but the midwife had said that was okay. The mucus plug, she'd call it.

Yes, she thought, as she climbed out of bed and counted, *I can do this*. She breathed and rested, breathed and rested. Millie and Norm (in their terrible, painful innocence) were still both fast asleep, spared all this. Looking out of her doorway and checking both ways, she crept across the hall to the bathroom, a cuckoo bird, a stranger in their little love nest. Or an albatross around their necks, take your pick.

Mummy, she thought. *You lucked out. You got rid of me a long time ago.*

She shut the bathroom door, but she didn't lock it this time. Just in case. She knew she had a long way to go—twelve hours if she was a textbook case— so she drew a bath, scattered rose-scented bath salts into the water and climbed into the tub, so quietly that even Millie slept on. Her stomach heaved out of the water, a stretched and shiny knoll, but that was okay. Her breasts floated too, milky-white with blue veins. She doubted they would ever be the same again, not that she cared. Who the hell was going to look at them? Dace could come waltzing back with a carton full of live monarch butterflies, a handful of two-carat canary diamonds and all the yellow roses in the world. She'd had enough of love. Especially his kind of love, the dangerous kind. She was through, absolutely through with men.

She splashed some water on her sweating face and lie back with a folded towel tucked under her neck. Some raccoons were having a riot on the roof. They knew something was up too. There was no curtain on the bathroom window, but there was no house close enough for anybody to see her either. Outside it was completely dark, a cloudy, starless night and hot, though she didn't know it. She needed to be inside. It was safe in her uncle's house, safe for her and her baby. Who the hell knew what lurked outside. She relaxed a little in the bath and kept adding hot water while loosening the rubber plug a little with her big toe, but within two hours she'd completely drained the hot water tank. She was all body, no mind. Where had time gone? She might have slept a little; she wasn't sure.

The pains were about five minutes apart now, but bearable as long as she stayed in the water. The water rippled a little each time her belly tightened. Then slowly, inexorably, the contractions stopped having identities of their own. She felt intense pain all over her body instead. She even felt a little pressure low down in her back. Somewhere she'd read that getting on her hands and knees might help, and she wanted to, but she couldn't. Not here, not now. It made her too nervous and she knew she shouldn't be alone. She'd have to get somebody soon, whether she wanted to or not.

Oh, God, she thought. Another thing she couldn't do herself. *And it's just going to get worse,* something warned her. Especially if she couldn't stop thinking about the next pain.

She didn't want Millie to find her in the tub though, so she climbed out of the bath and made it back to her room, before anybody heard her—the low growl ripped from her throat— and all hell broke loose. Listening to herself, she thought, *This isn't me.*

Wild-eyed and wild-haired, Millie came running down the hall, the shiny bottoms of her furry pink slippers almost catapulting her into the room. "You're not having that baby here," she said from the doorway. At first, she looked afraid to enter, but then she came right inside and grabbed Liza's robe from the floor. She even managed to stuff Liza's arms into the robe before she started shrieking for Norm.

"Norm!" she called, "Norm! We've got to get her to the hospital."

No, no, Liza thought, but she didn't have time to think more. The next two pains robbed her of all thought.

Millie had gotten her completely robed and pulled some cotton socks onto her feet before Norm even stumbled into the room.

He glanced at Liza writhing on the bed and then away. "Jesus, Millie..." he said, backing up and grabbing the doorway. "Get her out of here...no, wait, I'll go..."

Millie's eyes had gotten so wide that all Liza could see were the whites. "What do you mean, you'll go?!" she asked Norm.

"Can't..." Liza said, rolling over onto her side and hugging a pillow. Did they really think she was going to move? Jesus, she couldn't even talk. Besides, it hurt a tiny bit less if she didn't move. Maybe if she just stayed on her side. And bit into the pillow, so she wouldn't scream. Like a coward. *Oh, God, it isn't supposed to hurt this much,* she thought as another powerful contraction ripped through her and her face contorted. She'd hate them if she had time. The midwife, the natural childbirth people – all those people who had lied and lied and lied! "In sorrow thou shalt bring forth children." What was she doing wrong? What had she done wrong? And Dace, who just because he was a man, had gotten off scot-free! Why did her mother have to be right, about this of all things? Though it wasn't just her mother who had been right, it was the Bible.

"What do you mean, you can't?" Millie said. "It's a little late for that now. You're having that baby whether you want to or not."

"Go. Can't...go."

"Oh, I see, yes, you can, my girl, yes you can. You can get to the hospital. Millions of women do. They don't loll around their uncle's houses and grunt out babies like gypsies on a filthy, germy floor. Not in this country anyway. I'll get dressed. We'll just roll you out to the car, the two of us..." Millie said, flouncing out of the room. She re-appeared just two contractions later, dressed in a T-shirt and some jeans.

"Where'd Norm go?" she demanded.

Liza let out another tremendous groan. Millie would just have to wait.

"Don't know," she said when the contraction finished. By now, even her forearms were sweating, she noted with interest from somewhere up on the ceiling where she had retreated to observe the scene on the bed. *God,* she thought, *I don't care if we both die. Me and this baby.*

"Damn, damn," Millie said, pacing around the room in small circles and striking her own forehead with the heel of her hand. She must have heard something besides Liza, though. She dashed to the window, opened it from the bottom and yelled down in the general direction of the garage, "Get that woman – that midwife – get Mary Bergen! Maybe she can talk some sense into her! The stupid girl's in so much pain! If you don't do something, she'll bring half the countryside here with her screams."

She came back to Liza who was still lying on her side, facing the wall and pushed the knuckles of both her hands into the small of Liza's back.

"Does that help?" she asked. "Norm was just standing there," she volunteered next, "throwing up beside the car. He's dressed, but his shirt is only half on. Honestly—at a time like this! Maybe if Mary sees you, she can talk some sense into you…get you to the hospital."

"No time," Liza said, pulling on the lower part of the bed's headboard with both her hands.

"Oh, honey," Millie said, gently prying Liza's left hand from the headboard so she could grip her instead, "Your pains are real close together, but you'd be surprised how long these things can take. There's always some little wrinkle. Look what happened with my son! Children—kids—it's like they have their own ideas long before they're born. And some of them are in no hurry to get here. Maybe they know what's in store for them—maybe they know and they forget after they're born."

Well, I'm not, Liza thought, *I'm not going to ever forget this. No way.* Dear God, where was Mary? And why was Uncle Norm taking so long to fetch her? The pains were now about a minute apart. Mary was supposed to be here. *Please don't be out on another call,* she prayed and screamed through another ten contractions. *Me, me, I need you right now!*

When Mary finally arrived, Liza thought she'd feel better, but she didn't. If anything, she felt worse. The contractions still hurt and they hurt like hell. And when the woman inserted two gloved fingers into her vagina to check the dilation and progress of her cervix, it didn't help at all. Liza had to know how much she was dilated though. "How much?" she begged, managing to string two words together. "How high?"

It was the first day of summer and the sun was just starting to come up when Mary announced that Liza's cervix was nearly seven centimeters dilated, but the baby was still very high.

Liza had almost lost her ability to speak now, but she was also hypersensitive to everything else happening in the sun-filled room. She saw the concern the midwife tried to mask and the glances she exchanged with Millie. She read their minds. The midwife was hungry and wanted to go down to the kitchen to grab a bite to eat, but her client's pains were too close. Millie just wanted the hell out of the room. Liza calculated quickly, her mind in overdrive, desperate to get this child born. Almost seven centimeters—that meant she was in the active phase of labor, but might still have hours to go, depending on how long she snagged at each stage and what surprises came her way.

Where on earth was the beauty in so much pain and why did a woman still have to suffer so much in this day and age? Even with Liza's heightened sense of awareness, it made no sense at all. "What—only six centimeters?" she cried while Mary sponged her brow with a damp cloth. "I can't go on like this, I can't...I'll never reach ten."

It bothered her that Mary didn't look too concerned. She placed her cool hands on Liza's abdomen, feeling for the exact position of the baby's head. "Almost seven centimeters is good! You only have another three to go..."

"The worst three!"

"The contractions hurt like this because the baby's posterior," she went on. "The biggest part of his head is presenting. If the baby delivers head first, they usually come out facing down towards the bed, the floor. Few women are big enough to deliver a baby sunny-side up. Remember we talked about this kind of presentation? It will take longer because he's going to try and rotate his head..."

"You mean he can't find his way out?" both Liza and Millie gasped.

"He can and he will," Mary said while she massaged the back of Liza's neck and swept her hands down over her shoulders and arms as if to push the pain away or the baby out. "Your baby knows what to do and so do you. He just needs some more time. It's like when you try to pull a sweater over your head the wrong way..."

Millie started crying. Liza had never seen a woman wring her hands before, but she did now. "So let's take her to the hospital then," Millie pleaded. "They'll give her something for the pain...or use those forceps things...or do a section...I can't stand to see somebody in so much pain. I don't care and she doesn't care anymore either...you can't do anything here. What do you have in your black bag anyway?"

"Oxygen," Mary said after a slight pause, "And ergot to stop any bleeding..."

But nothing else, Liza thought. *Nada.* Of course she'd known that, read a midwifery textbook in fact. *Labor with a posterior birth may border on the abnormal...*

She'd also read *Spiritual Midwifery*, Ina May Gaskin's book, all that stuff about "rushes," what a load of crap. Why didn't they call a pain a pain? Because she'd take anything now. Yes, anything—alcohol, poison! Why hadn't she wanted a needle in her back, an epidural, the cold steel of the hospital, the indifference of strangers who'd seen it all before? What the hell was wrong with that? And she'd go anywhere too. With anybody. Back to her mother's even. *Call me an ambulance,* she thought. Get somebody strong enough to carry me out of here. *I can't do this, I can't and I won't!*

"Mummy," she was astounded to hear herself say. But she knew she couldn't move. She didn't have enough time between the pains. How had this happened? She'd read there would be time—that she might even be able to rest and that she should definitely try—but ever since Mary had checked her, there had been no intervals between the contractions at all. The contractions were holding her whole body in a vise-like grip.

Millie stopped crying and started tidying up the room instead, but she was scowling at Mary who said placidly, "It's not safe to move her now. Liza has already done a lot of good work by herself. It's just too late. If the baby does turn, she might deliver him in the car or the hospital parking lot...C'mon, Liza, let's try sitting up. You can't open up enough just laying on your back. If he was smaller or you were bigger, you'd have a lot less work. And it's your first baby..."

"And last!" Liza shouted.

Mary smiled. "We'll get him angled better...put some more pressure on your cervix...but don't start pushing yet, okay? You'll know when it's time. The baby will get things started. As soon as your cervix opens up to ten centimeters, he'll find the best fit."

Fat chance, Liza thought, as Mary and a dubious Millie heaved her into a sitting position on the edge of the bed. Christ, she was a whale and she didn't have any clothes on, but she didn't care. *I'm not going to do anything to make these contractions hurt anymore and besides he'll never get out, never!* Oh, Goddamn Mary to hell, the contractions hurt even more now. She wanted to lie back down again and curl into a ball and die, but she was stuck. She couldn't lie back down, not without a lot of help.

"Are you listening to me?" Mary asked, taking Liza's face between her hands and staring into her eyes. "You've got to think positive thoughts. Out, baby, out. You're doing a great job. In a few hours, you'll hold your little baby..."

In a few hours, Liza thought, once again abandoning herself to the pain. *A few hours! Nobody can do this for me. There's only one way out of this. Me. I'm going to have to turn myself completely inside out, leave me, give up... Dace,* she wailed in her head.

"Shut...door," she said out loud. "The noise..."

"Don't worry," Mary said. "You're just making some lovely birthing noises."

Millie had calmed down little. She folded her arms over her chest and glared at Mary and Liza. "Yeah, don't worry," she said, "everybody screams. The ones who don't are liars or cats. And don't worry about Norm either," she added. "He's gone into town. He's not like some of those hippie father types, agitating to get into the delivery room and see stuff he shouldn't."

Yeah, like Dace, Liza thought, *who should be here to call his kid out, to tell him to stop corkscrewing down my birth canal, to tell him to get the hell out.*

The next few hours passed in a blur, with Mary patiently sitting on the floor in front of Liza waiting to catch the baby and a frantic Millie pacing the perimeter of the shrinking room. Liza observed all this from her vantage point as a spectator way up on the ceiling.

And then it happened. She forgot Dace, she forgot everybody, she forgot herself and Micah James Devereux was finally born. Born in summer. Though Liza had no idea how much time had passed, or even if it was night or day, the sun was high in the sky. Noontime. Millie and Mary saw the baby's hair when they finally let her out of the sitting position to kneel against the bed, but it was only when Liza stood up and slung herself between the two women with her hands on their shoulders that the baby finished his descent.

No doubt the world still looked very dark to the baby, but up ahead was a hint of brilliance. He had to be exhausted and desperate for just one good breath. He had already done everything in his power to get out, squeezing the fontanel bones in his head as tightly as he could and now with just a little more room, he accomplished the rest, he did it all by himself. He navigated the last inch of his mother's tight birth canal, slipped under her pubic bone and slid into the midwife's waiting hands.

And they were no longer the same person.

Birth, death, it came to his mother. *It's all the same thing.*

Liza fell back down onto the bed and Mary put the almost limp baby beside her. At first, nobody was too worried, least of all Liza. *Ah,* she thought, *the pain – it's stopped.* That's all she cared about right now. She felt blissful, rather than ecstatic, maybe even a little detached. The baby was a little blue and his elongated head looked strange, but he was moving and he was all there, even longer and bigger than she'd imagined. Mary started to examine him, working her fingers down his little body, from his head to his toes.

Birth, death, Liza thought again as her son finally gave a choked wail in the midwife's practiced hands. *I understand now. It really is all the same thing.*

But she didn't understand for long. In the next instance, she forgot everything about life while the midwife suctioned her baby and tried to clear one blocked lung.

Forgot life and understood only death.

Forgot pain and felt only loss.

All this for nothing, she thought as Millie took her hand and started weeping again. *It can't, it just can't be.*

And it wasn't.

After a long while, Mary picked up the baby and held him out to Liza. "Look, his color's getting better," she said. "His first Apgar score was only four, but don't worry, it's the five-minute one that really counts and now he's a seven. In a couple of minutes, he'll be a ten. You did a great job, Liza. You're a mother and he's a fine, healthy son, ten pounds at least."

No, Liza thought, *no,* as a smiling Mary placed the baby in her arms, but she took him anyway because that's what both women expected her to do.

"Be the mother you want to be," Mary whispered in her ear. And it worked. Just one touch, just one sniff of her firstborn son and that was enough.

I'm yours for life, she thought as he worked his way down her chest onto her right breast. *I'll never let you go. No other woman is ever getting you after all I've been through.*

Chapter 23
Micah James Devereux

How long can I be a wall around my green property?
How long can my hands
Be a bandage to his hurt, and my words
Bright birds in the sky, consoling, consoling?
It is a terrible thing
To be so open: it is as if my heart
Put on a face and walked into the world.
~"Three Women," by Sylvia Plath

Maitland University, September 10, 1973

When Liza began her third and perhaps final year at Maitland University, she had two additional courses under her belt. She'd taken the courses at summer school while Millie watched baby Micah for an hour or two, twice a week. Uncle Norm liked sending Liza to school. She was such a smarty pants, he said. A real little mother, but a smart girl too. He wondered what some of his sisters would have done if they'd ever gotten the chance. Or his own daughter Rosie. Maybe he should have made her finish high school and sent her to college instead of letting the little tomboy work in the shop.

Liza hadn't even liked leaving the baby while he slept, but it had been worth it just to pull ahead. What had she been thinking? She couldn't possibly have worked fulltime at a summer job. For the first six to eight weeks, Micah had nursed practically all the time.

By September, Micah James Devereux was two and a half months old, a lovely, placid baby who was already sleeping through the night. Just like the midwife promised, his pharaoh-like head had returned to normal. He looked such a model baby with his headful of soft black curls. Liza had been a little worried after he was born, but now he was a ten for sure.

She signed up for mostly English courses in her third year and people kept asking about him, this whopping ten pounder she'd given birth to at home. Thank God, they didn't want to talk about his birth. If they didn't have a child—and most of her fellow students didn't—they were too scared. And if they'd already had a baby, they wanted to talk about their own labors.

It was still hot in early September, so Liza dressed Micah in a little jumpsuit and sun hat. Most of his sweet flesh was still on display. She rubbed her face against his dimpled cheeks and kissed them.

When she first came into the Humanities building, the boys stood off to the side, but the girls descended on Liza and her son. They delighted in Micah's pudgy cheeks, his delectable, sausage fingers, his perfect little toes.

"Ah," they said when he smiled at them with his lovely, gummy baby's smile. "Can I hold him?" The little angel had been smiling since he was three weeks old.

After she'd gotten him out of his car seat, Liza had put him in the baby carrier. He liked the carrier, so for the most part, he slept against her chest. She hoped to do some research in the library before class. It was a Tuesday and she had only one lecture, her Canadian Literature class at 11:30. She'd already read all the Margarets: Atwood, Avison, Laurence, but except for Leonard Cohen, she hadn't read any Canadian male authors, so she wanted to concentrate on them. *Please, God*, she thought, *don't let them go on and on about war and shooting and all that stuff men love.* Her classes were spread all over the week, so she could study in the library, she supposed. That's what she had done the last few years. But the staff wouldn't let her take the baby into the library, no matter how adorable he was and even if he wasn't making a sound. They had a rule. They pointed to a sign on the wall: "No children under twelve."

Liza had gotten to know most of the English majors last year. It had taken her a while, but she was starting to feel part of university life. When she went to her Can-Lit class, several girls gave her congratulatory cards. They didn't know how she did it—went to school and had a baby too. They certainly couldn't have. Liza was very touched. Uncle Norm had given her the car seat and baby carrier and Millie was trying to knit him a sweater, but most people didn't even know she'd had a baby. Autumn was coming on; she'd love a bunch of little hand-knit sweaters and hats.

She hadn't gone back to Toronto where both her parents and her brothers still lived. Her Gran and her mother were good knitters, but she couldn't tell them, she just couldn't.

"What—again?" her Gran would write all the way from Dublin, if she wrote at all.

As for her mother, she would be worse than Millie even.

"If there isn't something wrong with him now, I bet there is later. One of my cousins looked normal, but he wasn't, not by a long shot," she'd say.

Yes, her classmates wanted to see him, but once was enough. They started worrying about him crying and disrupting lectures. She took him with her several more times, but people talked when she fed him under a receiving blanket in class. She had lost most of her pregnancy weight, but her milk laden breasts were still bigger than the baby's head. Her fellow students—the boys and some of the girls—were both fascinated and repulsed.

"She can't do that here, can she?" one of the nicest girls said and the rest followed.

"I think we should take up a petition," Liza overheard another say. "Of course, she can't do that here! It's such a private thing—I'm surprised. She's so smart and it's such an ignorant, hillbilly thing to do. I just don't understand it. Why doesn't she use the washroom or fill up some bottles at home?"

My God, Liza thought, *they must think my breasts are taps, that all I have to do is turn them on and fill up bottles to go.* It bothered her, but after she heard that, she couldn't feed the baby in front of them. Her letdown reflex didn't work. Her milk stopped while Micah wailed in frustration.

On the last day she brought him to school, she left class early and finished feeding him in the parking lot, in the backseat of the station wagon. She changed him too. Micah still wasn't content, though. Perhaps he sensed he wasn't wanted, that his mother had done a terrible thing in having him alone. *This is one of the reasons people shouldn't have babies out of wedlock*, a censorious little voice said in her head.

Liza was suddenly desperate to get off campus. She had made it back to the Humanities parking lot, but what if Mel or Joe showed up for some reason? Walking some new girl back to her car? Or one of her professors? Dr. Jack Diamond, perhaps? They liked girls; they didn't like women. They'd laugh at her, they'd... Well, she wasn't sure what they'd do. She felt fat and her breasts tingled in anticipation of another feed. She didn't want them to see her this way — an incompetent mother who'd gotten just what she deserved.

She strapped Micah into his car seat and started the car. His little feet drummed the back of her seat. What a brat. The car was low on gas, a minor problem that upset her no end. She didn't have time to gas up the car. She didn't! She stared at the dusty dashboard. Goddammit, another little red light had come on too. What the hell did it mean? Uncle Norm would have to check out the car. If it stopped working, she didn't know what she'd do.

Both she and the baby cried all the way back to the farm. His cries still sounded like a newborn's, but they made her frantic. In her rearview mirror, she could see his little face. She pounded the wheel of the car until she hurt her hand. For a moment he wasn't her beloved baby, he was just some horrible noise. What had she expected? Well, not this. Dimly, she sensed what was happening. Her hormones were crashing. The euphoria of his birth had started to wear off. Soon the memory of the terrible pain would replace it, just in case she got the notion to impregnate herself again. Well, she wouldn't. She was never going to have another child again, never. Not for anyone. And certainly not to replace Dace! Where the hell was he anyway? Off gallivanting around and having a good time, while she coped with everything else. She drove past the highway exit. She took the back roads and let the tears run down her face. Thank God nobody could see her.

It didn't have to be this way, though. She had to keep going to school and at least finish one degree. She had to. Why? Well, just because. Who the hell else was going to support her and Micah in the long years to come? She just wasn't sure how. She couldn't go on welfare, or stay with her uncle forever.

Damn, this wasn't getting her anywhere. With one hand still on

198

the wheel, she wiped her face with her left sleeve. Millie was desperate to get her hands on Micah and feed him some formula, the same smelly stuff she'd fed her own son. That would be Millie's price, that and perhaps more. Yes, Liza could leave the baby with her, especially if she took shorter, more frequent runs into the university. She'd done it during the summer for very brief periods after all.

And maybe she could pump some milk, slowly over time. She'd get the midwife to show her how. She could save it in ice cube trays. She knew that much. She'd kill Millie if she resorted to formula with Micah still so young, just kill her. But she had to accept Millie and Uncle Norm's help if she wanted to keep going to university, she just had to. And what about Dace? Even if he was having fun now, he wouldn't be for long. She had to find some way to exonerate him, so he could come back home. She should be in the university library doing some research right now.

At least Uncle Norm had come around and Liza felt slightly less alone. "My boy," he'd whispered the first time he held the baby, no doubt thinking of his lost Dace.

Last night, he and Millie had argued over who would hold the baby while Liza ate dinner. If it was possible, Millie was even more enamored of Micah than Norm. The last few weeks, it had gotten harder and harder for Liza to prise the baby, her own child, from Millie's arms.

"Let me bathe him," she'd beg Liza. "He's getting cradle cap. You're not washing his head right and look at all that fluff between his toes."

Liza didn't say too much. She should have, but she hated discord while she was nursing and Millie had held her hand while she labored with Micah and cried with her when he was born.

Okay and she felt bad for the older woman too. Millie wanted another child of her own, but Norm didn't.

"We both have grandkids," he'd said, never mind that Millie's grandchildren had started to arrive before she was thirty-five.

When Liza finally got back to the farm from the campus, Norm was in the driveway, inspecting something under the hood of his car. He came over to the station wagon and unstrapped Micah from his car seat. Somewhat to Liza's annoyance, the baby immediately stopped howling and cooed.

Liza started talking, a litany of problems about the car. Just like a helpless old woman, she thought.

The news about the red light on the dashboard didn't faze her uncle at all though. Norm just shrugged. "I'll take care of it," he said. He lifted the baby high in the air. Liza's stomach flipped, but Micah smiled. He had a little drool on his chin, but it didn't matter, not to her or the baby's grandfather anyway.

"How's my boy?" Uncle Norm asked, wiping away the baby's drool with his thumb.

Oh, God, Liza thought. *I've got to get away before they get too attached.* At night, she still dreamed of following monarch butterflies down south and finding Dace.

She'd thought she could live without him — that maybe it was even best for the baby to never know his renegade dad — but she couldn't. Live without Dace, that is. If it wasn't for the baby, she'd have been better off dead. The autumnal equinox was almost here. The monarchs would begin their journey soon. If only she could go too.

It was impossible though. She couldn't travel alone with her boy. They'd be so vulnerable. Helpless, helpless! Monsters probably lurked in the States. Driving into Maitland and braving her classmates took everything she had.

What about during Reading Week, though? Micah would be almost eight months old in February 1974. He'd be sitting up and eating other food. He'd be able to hold a toy in his fat little hands and entertain himself. He might even be crawling. Dace... Ah, Dace if he ever saw his son, he'd be thrilled. Thrilled and reformed. Yes, Micah would do what she couldn't.

Millie came outside and took the baby from Norm. The smell of a chicken roasting in the oven wafted after her. Liza's stomach rumbled.

"You're getting grease on his jumpsuit," Millie complained to Norm. She kissed the baby on his fat cheeks and his nose. Liza really wished she wouldn't.

"He's almost grown out of that suit anyway," Liza said.

"The police called..." Millie added, looking a bit smug. She expected trouble and she often got it. She chattered on a bit more, oblivious to Norm and Liza's aghast looks. At least the police had the decency to let Liza recover from the birth. Actually, the young guy who called didn't sound so bad. Turned out he was Millie's old friend's nephew, a McGregor or something. "They want to talk to Liza," she finally confessed. "They said be there tomorrow at the police station at ten or they'll go get her in class. I wouldn't put it past them, I wouldn't! Remember what happened on our wedding day. I had been baking for days…"

"For God's sake, Millie, what do they want?" Norm shouted.

"I told them Liza was feeding the baby — insisted on doing it on her own, though her milk is thin and it looks like he's not getting enough — but they don't listen, do they…no, of course, they didn't say what it was about," she said, finally noticing their stricken faces.

"I'll take you into the police station, Liza," Norm said, "but leave the baby at home."

Liza turned pale. She wrapped her arms around herself. "Why — you don't think they'll try to take Micah from me, do you?" she cried.

"Over my dead body," Millie said as she kissed the top of Micah's warm head and squeezed him so hard he let out a little squawk. "This kid has a good home. Norm and I can take custody…"

"No," Liza said, coming over and grabbing Micah from Millie's arms, so fast and high that his little heels swung up into the air. "He's my son. Mine and Dace's."

Millie and Norm looked at each other. They both drew in sharp breaths. "Don't tell people that, Liza," they said in unison. "The cousin stuff, it's not right."

Liza buried her face in Micah's little chest while she walked into the house and upstairs. He smelled of baby powder and something else. She loved her uncle and she was grateful to have a place to stay, but Millie had her nerve. She was never going to get her mitts on Micah, never. He was Liza's, every ounce of him, his sweet-smelling flesh, his heart-stopping smile, his bones. She still didn't know where she began and he ended.

Chapter 24
Maitland's Finest

Maitland Police Station, September 11, 1973

The Maitland police wouldn't let Norm stay with Liza. At the age of twenty-one, she wasn't a minor. She was on their turf and they sure as hell could question her alone. Not that they said so. They didn't have to. No, they just shook their heads at Norm when he came into the police station with Liza and the older cop grunted something like, "Not you." When he spoke, crumbs of something fell out of his mouth.

Liza had just finished feeding Micah thirty minutes ago at home, but her breasts tingled and ached. She had a lot of milk in the morning. She was so scared that it started to leak. She held out her hand to Norm behind her back, then pulled her sweater tight against her chest and followed the two officers down a narrow hall. They walked in single file. To her doom. She felt terrible, sloppy and fat.

The younger constable pretended not to notice. He was the same pimpled young man who'd given her a hard time at the farm. He must have been in training. The older man opened a door and led the way into a small room with two chairs. Everything in Liza screamed, *Don't go,* but she knew better than to argue. Innocent people cooperated with the police.

It was just them and two chairs in a grey room, nothing else. Liza felt like she had gone colorblind. She hesitated in the doorway, but when the older man yelled, "Sit down!" her knees buckled and she sat down in the corner, like a good little girl. At least she could see the reinforced door and a small barred window, high on the wall. She was already breaking inside. A part of her wanted to spill everything she knew, even stuff she didn't know, but she couldn't. Wouldn't. The police, at least the Maitland police couldn't be trusted. *Uncle Norm's outside waiting for me*, she kept telling herself. *And I haven't done anything wrong.*

The young cop said his name, but she didn't catch it. Something Gaelic maybe. He even looked a bit like the skinny Irish garda with his pale, freckled skin. He didn't sound much like them though with their lovely lilting voices. Why had she ever wanted to leave Dublin anyway? For the life of her, she couldn't remember. And she was having trouble recalling why she was in the police station too. These cops scared her. She didn't look directly at them. She was too busy watching a fly walk across the window. She knew what was going on, though. In her peripheral vision, she noticed the balding older man examining some wax he'd just removed from ear. He didn't fool her though. He was old, but he still looked strong enough to snap her wrist with just one hand.

The boy cop — a year or two her junior — clutched some papers and sat down too. When he started reading, he sounded like a grade three student who was just becoming fluent. She was reminded of herself, nervously presenting a paper in class.

"Thank you, Miss Devereux," he started off innocently enough, "for coming in. I understand you've just had a baby and that this is kind of a tough time for you..."

"Especially since you don't have no husband," the older cop said.

"And don't need one," Liza replied. He probably wasn't married himself. He wasn't wearing a ring. Well, no wonder. No woman with half a brain would marry him. He looked like a wife beater for sure.

The younger man ignored both her and his mentor. "We want you to look at this..." He pulled something out of his sheaf of papers and passed her a glossy photo, a black and white eight by ten.

Liza didn't want to take anything from him, but she took it. If she hadn't, he would have shoved it right under her nose, while the other cop pried open her eyes. *Whatever it is, don't react,* she thought.

Because that's what they must want, she figured. To spook her, to surprise her into revealing Dace's whereabouts. Like those cops had done with poor, dumb, blind Blanche Barrow in *Bonnie and Clyde*. As if Liza knew anything or cared to speculate with them.

Before she had even taken the item from the young officer's gnawed, moist looking hands, she knew it was the picture of a dead person — what else? Once it was in her hands, she stared at the sticky picture as dispassionately as she could. She had gone to the other side to give birth to Micah — lived, died and then been reborn. She could do a simple little thing like this. Look at a picture of a dead person. Yes, she could. She'd pretend it was something on television, that's all.

Lots of people had handled the photo. There were fingerprints all over it. Then she saw what the fingerprints had tried to smudge, to hide. Though his eyes were wide open, the bearded, dark headed man in the photo was indisputably dead. There was so much blood, a black spread, a shroud — on the body and in the parking lot. Nobody could possibly lose that much blood and live.

It was Dirt Beard, she realized instantly, still trying to keep her facial expression as neutral as possible. The Wolfhounds' lady charmer and Dace's best biker friend. Her heart broke a little and she couldn't help it. A single tear leaked from her right eye. And she let it. Who the hell cared what these guys thought? She hadn't loved Dirt Beard, but she'd known him, a young man in his early to mid-twenties, Dace's age. It could have been Dace, for God's sake. A lot of people would say that Dirt Beard never had a chance — that his father had mob connections and that he'd knocked him flat out of high school with his fists. *I didn't get no diploma — why should you?* Others would say he'd had the same chances as anyone else. Had he been able to help Dace? Was that why the police wanted to talk to her?

Dirt Beard had been wounded on the left side of his chest, probably in the heart. Shot through the heart. It sounded kind of romantic. Oh, for God's sake, there was nothing romantic about getting shot. At least they hadn't shot him in the head. The thought of somebody with his brains splattered all over the ground almost made her gag.

Now that she'd taken the picture, she didn't want to let it go. She could feel it, Dace had been there in…where was this place? She focused on the rest of the picture — the bleak, almost empty parking lot with a dump truck in the background. It looked like wintertime. There was still snow on the ground, white death all around. *Would spring ever come?*

Why had they waited so long to show her this photo? What was the date today? For God's sake, she couldn't even remember the month! Her mind had gone completely blank. Panicked, she counted off the seasons since she'd come to live with Millie and Uncle Norm. Late winter, spring, summer. That's right, it was almost autumn now, the time of year when the monarch butterflies flew south. Dace had been gone so long. Had he really met up with Dirt Beard? He couldn't have. Because Dace was safe. He had to be. She'd just gotten his note.

Oh, God, how old was his note?

"The poor bugger in the photo has been dead awhile, Liza," the young cop confirmed. "except his prints aren't in the system, so we're asking you. You could be a real help and the more help you and your family are, the better it will go for lover boy Dace…and your baby too."

"My baby isn't even three months old," Liza said. "What's he got to do with this?"

The other cop stopped cleaning his ear and stared at her. "Micah, isn't it?" he asked. "What kind of name is that?"

"Biblical," Liza said, which for some reason made both men laugh.

"You want to raise him, don't you?" the younger man went on.

"Yeah, we heard you went to a lot of trouble to have that kid," the older cop interrupted again. His eyes dropped to his shoes, but the sneaky bastard was still looking at her. "It's a funny thing about trouble," he said. "It makes some people give up real quick, but other people just hang on and on. And something tells me you're a hanger-on."

The younger cop looked a little puzzled, like his boss might have gone off script and he didn't know what to do. "The shooting happened in Cornwall," he said. "Something bad is going down there now, so the OPP is looking into a bunch of cases. They think maybe the diocese here in Maitland is involved… "

The older cop drew a finger across his own throat and shook his head, but it wasn't enough. He lumbered over. When he was almost on top of them, he pointed to the script in the younger cop's hand. "Better stick to that, Laddie," he said. "The young lady doesn't have to know everything. It's her civic duty to help the police. And the more she helps us, the more we help her."

So Dirt Beard didn't have a record! He hadn't even been "known to the police." Liza didn't know what possessed her, but if she didn't want to talk, if she wanted to get their minds off Micah, she had to deflect them. She stood up and waved her arms, a "right lunatic" her Irish grandmother would have said. The younger cop stood up too and tried to grab her arms.

She brushed him off, her hair flying around her face. Her upper arms burned where he had touched her. "Who shot him?" she demanded, conscious of how self-righteous she sounded. "Surely to God you guys didn't just shoot an unarmed man? What a bunch of big, brave men!"

"He wasn't unarmed…" the older cop started to say, but then he leaned over and stuck his face in Liza's. "You," he said, as he backed her up against the wall and she clutched her sweater even tighter to her throat, "Don't come in here and tell us how to do our job, Missy or I'll…"

Liza swallowed, her eyes wide. *Or you'll what*, she felt like saying, as if she didn't know. He'd suffocate her or rip out her throat and he had that goddamn gun too.

"Look, sir, I wouldn't dream of doing that," she said, almost gagging on her own submissiveness. She wasn't crying, but she was damn close. She steeled herself by clenching her teeth. "I just had a baby. I don't know anything," she stammered, "And I want to go home…now. To my family, to my Uncle Norm. Do I need a lawyer? I haven't done anything."

"You haven't done anything that we know about. But we got the right to talk to you for a while. So who's in the photo?"

They were both bigger than she was. If she screamed, nobody in the outer office would come running or care. When she'd first come in with her uncle, the woman at the desk had looked at her like she was a mess of garbage she'd had to sidestep in the street. And she'd ignored Norm. "You're a university student?" she'd clucked and shook her head, like she knew all about careless young girls and more. "I can't believe it. You should have known better."

If she didn't say something, they would never let her go. Her breasts would grow hard and lumpy with milk while her infant son starved and she went stark raving mad. Even if she held out for a few hours, what was the point? And if they kept her in this closet long enough, God knows what else she'd say. She was practically babbling now, for Christ's sake. What if she knew more than she thought?

Let me out, she thought. *I'm a person and I'm a mother. You can't do this to me!*

Still clutching her sweater, Liza slid around the cinderblock wall towards the door. She didn't know what the hell else to do. Both men watched their prey. The younger one was smiling as if he'd like to help her, but he couldn't because his boss was kind of sick, don't you know. She tried to reach the door handle, but she wasn't close enough yet. She took another step. They didn't stop her, so she touched the handle. *So it's the usual*, she thought. They were just playing with her. *Cat and mouse*. They'd never let her go. Yes, if she didn't give them something soon, they'd tackle her to the floor. What did it matter? Dirt Beard was dead and Dace was gone too.

Dace—who never would have told—Dace and his goddamn stupid biker's code.

"I knew him as Sal 'Dirt Beard' Perazzi," she said, trying the door handle just in case.

She couldn't believe it. Oh, God, what had she done? She shouldn't have broken the stupid biker code and told. The door wasn't even locked. No point in taking any chances, though. Before the police had time to change their minds, she had flung the door wide open and started running. Who the hell knew what they'd think of next? The nasty lady at the desk was waving some kind of paper, something she wanted her to sign, a release form maybe. As if.

"Hey," she called, but Liza ignored her. *You don't care about me*, she thought *and why should you? I'm nothing, nothing to you. You'll go home and gossip about me to your children. If you have any, that is.*

With her heart pounding in her chest, she ran straight out of the building, practically into traffic. The world exploded into color outside: the cars, the people, the yellow-bricked buildings and the canopy provided by waxy green maple leaves. It was noontime and busy in Maitland.

And then she saw him, her kinsman and her ally. Her uncle was sitting in his car, just at the curb. *I love you*, she thought, *more than you'll ever know*. When he saw her, he got out and came around to open the passenger door for her. She got into his smoky car and buried her face in her hands. The minute he was back in the car, she told him what the younger cop had said.

At first, Norm didn't say anything. He started driving, an automaton. They were both so rattled that they forgot to put on their seatbelts, not that Norm usually bothered with his. He made a legal left at the next intersection. It took a long time. The truck behind them honked at him to go.

Uncle Norm continued driving a little jerkily, but he had both hands on the wheel. He was doing okay. It bothered Liza that she'd upset him, that she couldn't hold everything inside.

He waited until they were out in the country and then he stopped on a dirt road. During the ride, Liza's heart had slowed down a little, but it started racing again. What was he going to say? A ginger cat ran out of the ditch beside them, across the road and into some trees. From a distance of a hundred yards, the windows of a yellow brick farmhouse watched them but there was nothing else in sight. Most of the houses in the vicinity sat on a hundred acres or more. Norm could talk here alright, but he was still going to take his time. His car was bug-free; he checked it frequently. He got out of the car and checked under the hood again just in case, but then he got right back into the car. He didn't trust the police, that's all. He never had. He kept watch in his rearview mirror, though. He complained about a Crown Vic following him sometimes, probably the same one that used to follow Liza and Dace. Or maybe Norm was just delaying. Whatever he wanted to say, it looked like it was hard for him to get it out.

Liza didn't care at first. She was relieved to have left the police station, that's all. But the longer she sat there, the more she felt like shaking him, anything to make him talk. As if she could have—him with his huge hands. She was running out of time, though. She had to get home to Micah, she had to. Any moment now, he'd wake up from his morning nap.

Besides, Norm was scaring her. "What is it?" she demanded, although she was deathly afraid of what he might say.

Norm was still watching his rear view mirror. "I heard something about that mess," he said finally, though he was speaking so low that it was hard to hear him. "It was kids."

"What do you mean?" Liza asked, imagining all sorts of things.

"Yes, kids," Norm repeated. "They were doing stuff with kids— just some of them, I guess, but it doesn't look too good. Well, some of the priests and the police, they're all cut from the same cloth. You know that and I know that, so I don't know why some people act so goddamned surprised. I didn't hear if it was Canadians or Americans or which diocese or police force it was. Maybe more than one, some people thought. It was just hints and stuff, though. But some of the priests and the police — they're the bad guys, Liza. It's a ring or something…"

Liza didn't know what he meant by a ring and she didn't ask. It didn't matter right now. She just knew it was something bad. "Who told you this?" she asked, mentally kicking herself for not keeping up with current events. What a fool she'd been to almost stop reading the paper after Micah was born. Still, if Joe Armitage had written some kind of exposé, she'd know. He'd have bragged about it for sure. And if someone else had written such an exposé, he would have disparaged it, said it was a lie.

Norm shrugged and started driving again. "Some of the guys at the shop got talking — I don't know how they know. Lenny's brother is on the Maitland police force though."

Chapter 25
Joe Armitage and Dr. Jack Diamond

Maitland University Library, September 27, 1973

Eventually Liza did what she had sworn she'd never do. She talked to Joe Armitage. Again. Micah had just turned three months old and Liza could fit back into her jeans. She had a few pounds to go, most of it in her breasts, so her cotton university T-shirt strained across her chest. Her hair had grown down to the middle of her back. She needed to cut it. She couldn't look after it. Most of the time, she either hauled it back into a ponytail or tied a scarf babushka style around her face.

She ran into Joe at the library, but then she was always running into him. It was hard not to. They frequented different faculties, but they were on the same campus, still a spread of undulating green. If she had any advance warning, she pretended she didn't see him and walked away, her stomach churning. Whenever Joe had a young girl on his arm, he acted like he didn't see Liza either. Whatever was the most convenient for him.

Joe was still working for the Communications professor, Dr. Jack Diamond as a research and teaching assistant. Perhaps he helped research Diamond's books. The last time Liza had seen Joe was in the university bookstore where he was promoting Diamond's latest book, the one with the sexy cover. The book — *Sex Sells: Subliminal Suggestion in Advertising* — was selling wildly. She'd picked one up, but she didn't buy it. She couldn't spare the cash. Besides, the book looked kind of stupid. *Imagine,* she'd felt like blurting out, *sex sells!* Also, the book's cover was a bit of a cheat. The other professors couldn't imbed sex into the illustrations of their textbooks, although perhaps they should. *Publish or perish.* She wondered if people were jealous of Diamond's success. Ah, but she was a novice in the Ivory Tower or maybe just a minion. She had no idea of the sacrifices professors made to get and keep their tenures, no idea of what they probably thought of as their desperate lives.

On this occasion, she was standing at a tall table in the university library, flipping through three months' worth of newspapers, searching for some reference to the police officer's and her uncle's allegations when Joe strolled through the double entrance doors.

The psychology and social science sections were right behind the newspapers. She stiffened, watching his progress out of the corner of her eye. He was headed her way, but maybe it wasn't intentional. He looked so preoccupied. He stopped in the stacks to look at some books, so for a moment she thought she was safe. Just a little jittery. She had just found a small news article on July 2 about a couple of police officers in Cornwall and a parole officer in Maitland who'd been charged with some kind of misconduct, but there was no follow-up.

She had newsprint all over her fingers and some on her nose, but she had no choice except to keep searching this way. Maybe someday there would be an index to the big Canadian dailies, but there was nothing now. She'd checked and the university library had a copy of the *Maitland Spectator* index she'd found in her hometown library when she was fourteen, but it stopped in 1969. Four years ago. Just her luck. The index had been a grad student's pet project perhaps.

How ridiculous, she fumed to herself now. *How did a real investigator research the past?* The *Maitland Spectator* and the *Globe and Mail* were the only two newspapers the university had microfilmed and they were both six months behind. If she was a reporter, she'd probably hang around the courthouse a lot and maybe the jail. That's what Joe had done when he worked for the *Maitland Spectator.*

Dr. Jack Diamond was in the library too. Strange. When she'd first come in, she'd waved at him in the Psychology section, chatting up a giggly first-year girl. He was hard to miss. What was he doing here, though? It was rare to see faculty in the library. They had all sorts of help — research assistants and students who were thrilled to work pro bono just for a leg up. Surely a suck up like Joe Armitage did all his research.

Dr. Diamond said something and the girl giggled again. Liza tried to ignore it, but the girl was getting on her nerves. Joe called such girls "sweet young things." From what she'd observed this year and already knew about Joe, both he and Diamond liked their girls young. Diamond's girlfriend didn't look eighteen, but she probably was if she was in university and nineteen was legal here in Ontario, so close enough.

Liza had gotten to know Diamond a little in class. All his students had. He had coffee with them on a regular basis down in the Social Sciences cafeteria or took them for martinis in the Faculty Lounge, a real treat. He wanted to be different, but he wanted everybody to like him too, so he was always trying to charm someone. Girl-women especially, but he'd made friends with his male colleagues and some of his younger male students too. As long as they weren't any competition, Liza supposed. Or maybe his young male students served another purpose—reeling in more girls.

Diamond always kept one special young man, a sidekick, a protégé hanging around. For the past term or two, it had been Joe.

Whenever Dr. Diamond spoke to Liza, he looked right at her with an intense, blue-eyed gaze. She didn't find him especially attractive, but he was compelling. It was hard to look away. A part of her wanted to please him. She enjoyed hearing him talk. She was drawn to his immense intelligence, his quirky mind. He leapt from idea to idea and made all sorts of associations when he talked.

She didn't trust him though. He wasn't from around here, so there was an air of mystery about him, of matters best left unsaid. A Rhett Butler kind of guy, though no way as handsome. He made the best of what he had, that's all. How many women had he married anyway? Hopefully they were all divorcées and not dead. He wasn't Bluebeard, for God's sake.

Like so many of her more charismatic professors and some who were just plain bores, he'd talked a lot about himself when he lectured his Communications class. He claimed a background in the military and advertising and he had a PhD in Psychology, but from where? Well, there was one clue. He called all his female students, "Darling" with a Texan drawl.

From where Liza stood at age twenty-one, Diamond's life seemed over, even though he was an established author and an enthusiastic contributor to faculty gossip. He was a tall, athletic American in his forties or fifties. Old, older than her anyway. As old as her father and Uncle Norm maybe. Like Telly Savalas, he'd completely shaved his head, so it was hard to tell his age.

From the moment she saw him in the library, Liza knew he would come over. Her hesitant little wave would have been insufficient. His larger-than-life presence commanded more of a response, always had. He was the head honcho, the dominant personality in any room. It pleased her that he dwarfed Joe.

During Joe's approach, Dr. Diamond glanced from Liza to his protégé. Liza thought it odd that both men were in library at the same time, but perhaps Diamond was meeting Joe here before they headed off to the Faculty Lounge. He really should have been home with his wife. Diamond had recently married, for possibly the third time, a very young and exquisitely tiny woman from the Philippines.

Oh, Liza thought, *the egos of some men.*

And Joe, just look at him. In the past year, he'd changed his style, striving for a more collegiate look, or perhaps he was just aping his mentor. Joe's blue oxford shirt was carefully pressed. He'd left it unbuttoned at the neck. Both his brown belt and his matching loafers were polished. When he came up to Liza, first he looked blank, but then he did a double-take. He flipped his straight hair off his forehead. He was carrying a library copy of Vance Packard's, *The Hidden Persuaders.*

Of course, Liza thought, recalling the reading list for the Communications course Joe had almost failed her in last year. *The Hidden Persuaders* was Dr. Diamond's Bible. Well, one of them anyway. It surprised her that Joe didn't have his own copy. Surely he had read it before this. She had certainly read everything on Diamond's reading list, from Freud and Jung to Marshall McLuhan. His reading list had helped keep her sane. She'd loved it. She'd almost done another degree.   *Ah,* she could almost hear Joe saying, *aren't you the little bookworm, though.*

"Ah, Liza, Liza, I almost didn't recognize you!" he said now. "I guess you've had the baby, but you still look the same—how's that? Well, maybe, you're a little bigger in the bust..." Joe brushed very lightly against her breasts, as if she belonged to him.

Never mind, Liza thought, stepping back. Even if she had wanted to, she couldn't feel a thing through the thick cotton and wire armor of her nursing bra. She gave him a disgusted look, though—*I know what you did, you creep.* She had zero interest in sex now that she was nursing Micah and even less interest in Joe. She was desperate, though and nobody could say he wasn't knowledgeable. He might know something. He knew all the dirt in Maitland and a few other places besides. Yes, she might as well talk to him. Maybe he had some information about this pedo-police-priest thing.

She started talking and once she started, she almost couldn't stop. It felt so good to share her concerns, even with Joe. For once, he stepped back to give her some physical space. She felt a bit better then. He really was such a good listener—when he wanted to be, especially if there was something in it for him. He had that reporter's nose for a good story, she supposed. *Be careful*, she reminded herself. She was too embarrassed to mention her command appearance at the police station, but she told him what she'd heard. He didn't ask how she knew, not then. She had connections to the underworld, through that cousin, that escaped convict's friends and that was good enough for him.

For the most part, Joe smiled and nodded, the way any good listener does. "Excuse me—may I?" he interrupted just once to wipe the newsprint from her nose with his forefinger, while she did her best not to cringe. From time to time, he also glanced over at his mentor-professor as if for approval. There was nobody else in the library, just Diamond's girl and a couple of librarians at the Reference Desk. The librarians kept staring. They bugged Liza. Didn't they have anything else to do? What the hell did they do anyway besides pick up books? They definitely recognized Dr. Diamond who had been in the news lately with his commercially successful book, something that was probably just a little suspect in the academic world.

Liza and Joe kept standing. When she finally stopped talking, he loomed over her lover-like and moved his mouth closer to her ear. He'd eat me, Liza thought. He'd eat me up if he could. "Well, there's an ongoing investigation here in eastern Ontario," he confirmed. His voice kept dropping so she almost couldn't hear the words at the end of his sentences. "About a pedophile ring that involves quite a few higher-ups. It stretches from Maitland all the way to Cornwall and then down into the States. Sort of like your biker friends."

Liza's stomach heaved. In her mind's eye, she saw Dirt Beard shot dead on the ground. *They're not my friends, they're what…my acquaintances?*

Oh, never mind, she thought. "Surely to God you're not implying that the Wolfhounds are part of something nasty like this too?" she blurted.

"Well, no, it's mostly white, male professional people who…"

Oh, God, Liza thought. *Was he a sociologist too?* Besides, she bet he was wrong—about white male professionals anyway. "Never mind!" she said. "A pedophile ring—what's that?"

"It's where, and I hate to say this because it reflects so poorly on my sex—it's where a bunch of men share children for uh, sexual purposes. They usually document everything in photos too. Sometimes they even make movies. God knows why."

Liza blanched. She remembered Dace talking about his school, the one where he and his sister Rosie had been sent. St. Matthew's. Not that he'd really told her much. He'd just said that his old teacher, Father Danby, had tried and his sister was really the target. Dace's lawyer, Hubert Gold had told her a different tale though.

But surely what happened to Dace and Rosie had been an anomaly, a random event, the practice of one sick mind—Father Danby's. Not a whole bunch of sick minds! Powerful, professional people didn't use small children for deviant sexual purposes and then share what they had found—what, with letters, pictures, home movies, in a clandestine club? Evil, drunken people maybe. But everybody wasn't an evil drunk. No, Joe was wrong. She didn't believe him. Somebody would have stopped them—the school administrators, the Bishop, someone.

But Judge Silverton didn't, she thought darkly. Father Danby was his nephew and it sounded like the good judge would have done anything to protect him. Like sacrifice a school full of children for his own flesh and blood. Was blood thicker than water or was it something worse? What if Judge Silverton shared his nephew's proclivities? *Oh, he couldn't, he couldn't.* She didn't believe it. Silverton was an old, old man.

She put her hand on Joe's wrist. "How do you know this?" she asked. "Has it made the news yet? Or has somebody written a book?"

"No—nobody's published anything, but there are a couple of manuscripts making the rounds. Mark my words—somebody's going to make a lot of money from this sick stuff. These stories are an untapped source of wealth, a library of stories…"

"But they're not verified?"

Joe shook his head. "We need some primary sources — some letters or something. Court transcripts. Internal reviews. Some people have implicated the staff at a Catholic boarding school, though. A local one, I'm afraid. Uh, Saint…"

"St. Matthew's?" Liza asked, sick at heart.

Joe looked at her sharply, but he pressed on, too caught up in his own rhetoric to stop now. Thank God he didn't know Dace's whole life story, about the two or three years he and his sister Rosie had spent at St. Matthew's after their mother's death. None of that had come out in court. Dace's lawyer had spoken to Liza in private. Dace probably would have killed him if he heard him.

"Yes, St. Matthew's! That's it!' he said. "You're not Catholic, so presumably your family's not. I'm surprised you know somebody who went there, though. Who, I'm wondering? Well, never mind right now. The place has been a regular goldmine — or should I say cesspool — of these allegations. They're pouring out from kids who went there in the thirties and early forties. Lots of investigations too, but they dead end and go nowhere. Maybe somebody's paid off, but it can take years for stuff like this to come to light. It looks like most of the 'victims' (and I use this term very lightly, mind) didn't make it — either killed themselves or drank themselves into the ground. And the ones left aren't educated enough to write and tell their stories. Most of those kids weren't too smart, but, yeah, the school authorities made sure of that. No point in educating people if you want to keep them down. Look at those third world women overseas — nothing like you, little Liza. You Canadian girls are so privileged these days. Oh, there have been rumours for years about this or that priest, even a cop or two, but nobody does anything. At most, the bad guys get moved someplace else. You know what it's like…"

Liza felt numb, but she made her lips move. "Yes, a priest gets sent to a northern residential school…" At least that's what had happened to Father Danby, the Judge's nephew.

Joe raised an eyebrow and shrugged. "Ah, Liza, why do I always get the feeling you know so much more than you're telling? You really shouldn't keep stuff from me, you know. I always find out. So tell me, is this all about Dace Devereux? Is he involved?"

"Of course not!" she said, more loudly than she intended.

"Well, nothing's ever black or white. Most of the so called

victims—the ones who survived— aren't exactly innocent and a lot of good people could get hurt...Powerful, professional people too. That's why the press wants to keep everything under wraps..." Joe smiled and shook his head. "I know it's hard to believe, but we've got ethics, I guess."

Liza lowered her voice almost to a whisper: "You mean a powerful, professional person like Judge Silverton? What would it take to get him off the bench?"

Joe shook his head again. "Whoa now—that's sure as hell is not going to happen! I haven't heard anything about him, anyway. Besides he's done a lot of good in this town. He cleared out the bikers for one..."

And put my cousin back in jail, Liza thought. Who would have made good. Why the hell was that?

She refolded a newspaper from August 22 and added it to the stack on her left. There had been nothing in it. What had happened in Silverton's court still made her feel sick. He'd really had it in for Dace.

She didn't have any more time to talk right now. She looked over at Dr. Diamond and his girl. The older man was still watching her and Joe. He looked a little wistful to Liza.

Well, she had to go home and feed Micah. She picked up her canvas bag, looping the strap over her shoulder.

Joe was still talking and strutting a little too. Once on a roll, he rarely stopped. "It's the fixers who are talking," he mused. "Maybe they feel guilty about all the bad guys getting away... I don't think they should, but you know what Catholics are like—guilt's what they do..."

Liza stopped moving and looked at him, her face frozen. Oh, he was masterful. He had her again. If they weren't in the library and the staff and Dr. Diamond weren't watching, she would have kicked him in the shins.

"The fixers?" she played on.

"Yes, monks who were dispatched to tidy up messy sexual problems of priests and laymen at troubled parishes and schools. They literally wiped down crime scenes that involved children—boys mostly, but that's changing now the Church has begun to welcome female altar servers. Some of the fixers have already worked on cases where priests impregnated girls and then procured abortions for them..."

Liza shook her head. She didn't believe him this time. What a bunch of crazy talk! Joe was really getting carried away. "A Catholic priest arranging an abortion? If that's a mortal sin for his parishioner, what's it for him?"

Joe smirked. "It's hard to believe—because you and I don't feel this way—but maybe the evidence that he had sex is worse—I don't know. My family's agnostic. Except for the fact that a girl's really, really careless to get caught and we don't want her and her brat on the city welfare rolls, we don't give a horse's ass about stuff like that."

Liza looked at him sharply. Was he talking about her? *Micah wasn't an accident,* she almost blurted through her clenched teeth, *I had him on purpose…And we're not on welfare either.*

Her stomach was still churning when Dr. Diamond came over, the young girl trailing a couple of steps behind. Except that she was on the plump side and had cat hair on her pea jacket, Liza couldn't have described her. Her long blonde hair fell over face as she looked down at the floor.

"We're just on our way to the Faculty Lounge," Diamond said. "Melanie's never had a martini—can you imagine? A good thing the drinking age here in Ontario has been lowered to nineteen." He put his arm around the girl's rounded shoulders and squeezed them. When she smiled shyly up at him, Liza saw her appeal. "May we request the pleasure of your company?" the professor asked. "Perhaps you could continue your no doubt delightful academic conversation there. Liza, Joe showed me the draft of his thesis and it's brilliant, just brilliant, all about how newspapers shape public opinion…"

Wait a minute, Liza thought—wasn't that the subject of her Communications paper last year? Well, never mind, she hadn't had time for Joe's crap then and she didn't now. "No, I can't," she said aloud, though she felt conflicted. What if Joe knew something more? What if he could write a book about the pedophile ring instead of the bikers? He must be good for something and she couldn't do it. It wasn't her thing. Just reading about stuff like that made her sick to her stomach. No, if she ever got a chance to write, she'd write fiction. Women's fiction, fairy tales. Yes, she'd write about butterflies and people who lived happily ever after. She'd write about exonerating Dace and flying him home. She'd write about their son Micah, chortling happily in Millie's arms back at the farm.

She felt outnumbered. The three of them, the two men and the girl, were waiting for her answer. The men were eager, the girl was indifferent.

Liza didn't look at Joe. She smiled at Dr. Diamond instead and he looked right back at her. Oh, God, he was so much like Joe. *He can see through me too*, she thought. But she didn't have anything against him and she hated to hurt his feelings. Yes, although she couldn't exactly put her finger on it, he certainly had some charm. Well, so what?

"Thank you so much for asking me," she said, unnerved again. *How stupid*, she thought, *to feel like I'm being impolite.* "Perhaps another time."

"Now that's a cute little girl," she heard Professor Diamond say as she walked away.

Chapter 26
Considering Liza

Joe Armitage wanted Liza Devereux. Mostly because she played hard to get. Lots of girls were like that, but get one into bed and watch out. Especially a 'good' girl. Assuage her guilt by offering her a diamond solitaire and she'd agree to marry Jack the Ripper just to prove she didn't sleep around and hadn't made another mistake. He'd proposed to several girls, so he knew. He just hadn't followed through. He liked playing with sweet young things, that's all. He always had.

And so did his mentor, Dr. Diamond. Right now, the older man was staring into the little blonde's eyes like he found her the most intelligent and/or the most attractive thing in the world. And she really wasn't—attractive at least. Her hair was bleached, she had a weak chin, crooked teeth and a bit of acne to boot. Her youth was her chief appeal. Both Diamond and the girl had ordered drinks (although she'd needed some help) but not Joe. He'd ordered a large Coke instead, no ice. It was cold enough outside. It warmed his heart that Diamond had found Liza attractive too. Mostly because it validated his own choice.

Not that Liza was perfect. Her nose was a little long and she could have used a few pounds, but she'd look okay in a skirt or a dress at a faculty function with him. As long as she kept her mouth shut, that is. She didn't say much, but when she did, she usually spoke her mind. Once he got her in bed, he'd soon fix that. Show her what was what, if he had to tie a rope around her neck.

Sure she was crazy and always had been, ever since he'd met her outside the prison at the Maitland Penitentiary Riot in 1971, but he didn't care. Because he was crazy too. Maybe crazier. In his adolescence, some quack had diagnosed him with antisocial disorder, but screw that. He might be a little schizophrenic — lots of smart people were — but as long as he took his meds and got enough sleep, he was okay. Except for that little manic episode last year after he'd worked too hard, even his own family wouldn't have known.

Liza's family was something else, though. He had absolutely no doubt she was in cahoots with that cousin of hers who was on the lam. None whatsoever. And she had slept with the low-browed bastard, too. Well, well, well. Their degenerative little brat was the living proof. Micah — a Biblical name. Fancy that. Joe wasn't sure what he'd do about the kid, but he'd figure out something. He had lots of connections, his own sister Shelly was a social worker for God's sake. He'd never had much in common with old Shel, but she'd know what to do. *What*, he'd ask her, *can I do about a kid who's at risk?*

Dr. Diamond was ordering his little blonde friend a second martini. The girl looked a bit dubious, but she took the drink just like he knew she would. They all did. She'd made a face when she tasted the first drink, but she fed Dr. Diamond the olives out of this one and downed it real fast. *Sip it,* Joe almost urged her, but she wasn't his problem. Within minutes, she was giggling and gibbering even more than she had before. Going on about her parents or something — about how upset she was that they no longer slept in the same room. It sure took some people a long time to grow up.

"Would you like to go for a little drive with me?" Dr. Diamond said, standing up and holding out his big hand. In her place, Diamond's smile would have scared Joe, but the girl didn't seem fazed at all. Two unaccustomed martinis had definitely helped. For a plump girl, she rose gracefully enough and took Diamond's hand.

Joe stood up too as they left the table, wiping his mouth with a napkin to hide his smile. He even bowed a little. *Don't mind me,* he thought. *I've got more important things to do.*

Chapter 27
Mariposa

Westmount, Montreal, Thanksgiving 1973

Caught completely off guard, Kathleen called her baby Mariposa, which as any fool knew, was Spanish for butterfly.

"What kind of name is that?" her mother had asked. Kathleen rarely entertained flights of fancy, but it suited the child, who looked a bit Spanish. She'd let her mother decide everything else.

Her mother had wanted a grandchild badly and would have dragged Kathleen to the Pope to prevent a therapeutic abortion. If they'd known in time and Kathleen had taken such a notion, that is. So Kathleen had absolutely no qualms about giving her the kid. She wanted her, she could have her. As for how the baby got fed, formula had been good enough for her.

Kathleen couldn't even think about the baby without getting queasy and in the end, she didn't have to. Her mother hadn't let go of her prize since she'd picked it up off the clean bathroom floor. Though Kathleen wasn't that conniving, the surprise of the baby's birth had worked in her favour. Her mother would have brokered a grandchild at any price, although when her only child reached the age of twenty-five and still hadn't married, she'd almost resigned herself to never having any.

No, Kathleen wasn't conniving. Nobody had ever accused her of that. Festering and fussing about something took too much time away from really important projects. But she was focused, yes—focused on discovering the wintering grounds of the monarch butterfly and focused on ignoring her body, which had betrayed her so spectacularly in the past.

She'd sickened with tuberculosis as a child, came home from summer camp infected with the bacteria (God knows how, although the camp cook, one those "displaced persons," a DP, was a prime suspect) and ended up at the Children's Sanatorium in Toronto. Yes, everybody had a story and for years, that was hers. She was tired of it, that's all.

"My daughter," her mother always told anybody who would listen, "spent almost three years in the San! They cured her of TB and when she came out, she had to learn to walk all over again."

Ever since then, Kathleen had gotten good at ignoring signals from her body. Because if she paid attention to every little twinge, she'd end up crazy or a hypochondriac. Just like her mother. She couldn't have that. For the first five months of the pregnancy, she hadn't acknowledged her dilemma. She just couldn't. Even when the baby started kicking and it was too late to do anything, she'd hid her condition so well that nobody at the university where she lived and worked had noticed either.

Well, no wonder. Most of her colleagues were too busy navel-gazing, trying to get published, pursuing an academic life. Maybe if Kathleen had been in a relationship at the time, but she wasn't. First she had the Professor and then Dace Devereux, an escaped con... Except the latter was just a fling. Both her choices spoke volumes, especially Dace. Even her therapist's composure had slipped a little when Kathleen told her about him. Clearly, she wasn't good at picking men. Mating was a waste of time really. So she'd funneled everything into her dissertation. Stayed late at the library every night, skipped staff meetings and slept in her office, which was out of the way in the basement. When she first transferred to McGill, she'd complained bitterly about the windowless office the university had allocated her, but she'd sure appreciated it that summer.

The University and the Social Sciences Building had shut down at Thanksgiving though, so she'd gone home to her mother's in Westmount for the holiday, ended up with a bout of indigestion and popped the kid out in the bathroom. Just like that. Well, almost. For a long time afterwards, Kathleen and her mother couldn't stand the smell of turkey or blood, but it really hadn't been that bad.

Why did some women make such a fuss about childbirth anyway? Counting back, she'd figured out that Mariposa had been a little early, but she'd weighed in at a healthy seven and a half pounds. Well, okay, Kathleen had freaked out a little when she saw the huge head coming out between her legs and felt a final ripping tear. It was well worth the look on her mother's face though.

"What's the matter with you?" her mother had cried, flinging the bathroom door open and bursting in like she always did. And stopping, with her hand to her mouth, perfectly attired, though not for long. She'd dressed up for Thanksgiving dinner, in her high heels and her genuine pearls with an apron over her dark, slimming dress.

Earlier that day, she'd carped about the Mexican peasant blouse and blue jeans Kathleen had on. In retrospect, a skirt might have been more practical because the jeans were down around Kathleen's ankles now, her feet bound in a tangle of unyielding denim. For a moment, they'd both stared at what else was between Kathleen's legs like it was an inkblot test that they couldn't quite figure out.

Her mother was the first to speak. "It's a baby!" she accused her. Later on she'd bragged to everybody: "So there was Kathleen sliding almost soundlessly to the bathroom floor and holding a mess between her shaking legs. For one terrifying moment, I thought she was dead or dying." But at the time, she'd just sounded aggrieved.

"Your father said 'What's that grunting noise?' but you haven't been home since God knows when, so how would I know? Now that I think about it, you looked like you were putting on a little weight, but I thought maybe it was just middle age spread. I was thirty-six when I had you and it was all downhill after that."

In her head, Kathleen had responded, *I've just turned thirty for God's sake*, but she couldn't answer. Pure instinct had taken over. She was too busy supporting the newborn's head and wondering what the hell to do next.

For a while, her mother had just stood there, one hand over her mouth, the other hanging onto to the door frame for support.

"Oh my, the bathroom looks like a bloodbath, " she said while she took in the whole mess, but then she did just what she always did. She jumped right in and started cleaning up everything—the clear amniotic fluid, the blood, Kathleen's streaked thighs—while her daughter sat on the tiled floor with her legs scissored out in front of her, like an overgrown child playing with a life-size doll.

Kathleen's stepfather had been downstairs in the living room watching the football game. At some point, her mother must have closed the bathroom door, but he heard the commotion anyway — Kathleen's little cries now that her mother was there, the baby's wails, the older woman's exclamations. Thank God, he said later, that they'd had no guests.

"What's going on?" he hollered up from the bottom of the stairs after he'd turned down the television volume a bit. It was halftime anyway.

"Kathleen's just had a baby, dear," her mother shouted back. "I can't really talk right now."

"Kathleen who?"

"Our Kathleen."

There was a longish pause. The women held their breaths while he started upstairs, but then he turned around and clumped back down again.

For the first time in her life, Kathleen was almost inarticulate. Her mind was empty. She was barely a human being, just a life force in danger of flowing down the drain in the tiled bathroom floor. She tried, but whole phrases didn't come.

"Oh — should I ring for a doctor, then?" her stepfather called up.

"No men, no men," both Kathleen and her mother said over the baby's cries.

Her mother also stilled her hand, which was creeping down towards the child's mouth. "No," she'd said again, this time to her daughter. Not that Kathleen would have done anything to the baby. She just wasn't thinking. She'd wanted to stifle the noise, that long, thin wail, the unmistakable sound of a newborn, of exposure and betrayal, that's all.

Because once her faculty found out she'd really had a baby, they'd be embarrassed, horrified, titillated, take your pick, and old Philly would ask her to leave. Not that the Head could force her out in this day and age, but he'd sure as hell try.

"For your sake and the baby's," he'd say.

And then Kathleen would never, ever be able to do what she had been born to do. She'd be just like her former thesis advisor in Toronto who had studied monarch butterflies for fifty years and still didn't know where the hell they went. The poor man was well into his sixties now.

226

Chapter 28
Larry Savage's Break

Larry Savage should have been glad to be out in the almost unpolluted Texas air, but he wasn't. No sirree. For one thing, he was never going to get the jail stink out of his hair.

"I've been holed up waiting for you fellas for months," he yelled, even though the driver and his partner were right up in front of him, with no divider, nothing in the way. There had been so much noise in the jail, such a din and racket that his hearing had started to go. "And let me tell you this, Dallas isn't my kind of town."

The FBI guy, the one driving the car, did a poor job of smothering a laugh. He was also a pretty bad driver, screeching around corners and racing up to intersections and slamming on his brakes. Who did he think he was, Jackie Stewart?

"Well, maybe you should have chosen better accommodations," the other FBI guy sniggered or at least that's how it sounded to Larry, who hated people laughing at him. "What the hell were you thinking?" the FBI guy went on. "The Dallas County Jail isn't exactly the Ritz. Look buddy, if you hadn't picked that fight in the bar, you wouldn't have ended up there. And you had no ID, not even a birth certificate. Turns out you're registered under your father's name, a name you've never used. What some folks call a bastard child. It took the Maitland police up in Canada months to locate you and when they told us, we headed straight here."

"Well, what about the guy who was with me?" Larry protested. "The RCMP officer they sent to meet me in Massena and 'help out'?! Why didn't Howie tell them what had happened?"

The FBI driver took his hands off the wheel for a minute and raised them in the air.

"Hey, there," his front seat companion said. "I don't want to fucking die down here."

"Howie's dead," the driver said, looking somber for a moment. "Traffic accident."

"No, shit," Larry replied. "So I'm the lucky one now, right? I spent months in the clinker with a bunch of effing niggers and I'm the lucky one?"

"Jesus," the companion said, shaking his head. "Don't the Canucks have any other resources except him? This Dace Devereux fellow has been on the lam for months. He can't be that hard to find. He's hardly more than a kid, he's got no education and he's never been anyplace."

Chapter 29
Fact Gathering at Joe's

February 1974

It was almost Reading Week. Liza could stretch it into two weeks, if she left a little early and came back a little late. She'd miss a class or two, that's all.

Yes, it was crazy, but what the hell. She had to get out of Maitland, especially now. She had to. She just wasn't sure how.

She'd gone to Student Services and got a couple days' worth of Valium, but nothing helped. Nothing. She didn't like taking pills anyway. Micah had started eating solid food, but she was still breastfeeding. The counsellor had looked something up in a compendium and said it was okay, but what did he know, a childless man like him? Liza wasn't even sure if he had a PhD.

Best to just take Micah and go. He was seven-and-a-half months old and not crawling yet, though he could sit up and roll over. She'd take the baby sling along, a big poncho and a well-packed backpack with their clothes in tight little rolls. Micah had his two bottom front teeth, he could clap his hands, blow kisses and say "Mama" and "Hi." He was a good-natured, brilliant child. As long as he was with her, he'd love life on the road.

The only question was how to accomplish this amazing feat. The station wagon got Liza back and forth to Maitland University, but it wouldn't get her down to Mexico. Obviously. It already had clocked over

400,000 miles. And how far was Mexico anyway?

She went to the library to check a map. Her hands shook. They shook all the time now. Could she take a bus or a train with Micah across America? Like Jon Voight and Dustin Hoffman had in the movie *Midnight Cowboy*? Maybe.

Jon and Dustin had just been trying to go to Florida, though. Florida wasn't nearly as far as Mexico. She knew that much. And she had to get to Mexico. She just had to. Dace was waiting for her down there. Jon Voight's girlfriend in the movie—Crazy Annie, the girl who had been gang-raped in their hometown—had always said: "You're the only one." Well, Dace was that too. The only one for her. Even if he didn't or couldn't or wouldn't change. She could live with who he was. As long as he didn't end up back in jail.

The social worker from Children's Aid who'd come sniffing out to the farm just yesterday had been the last straw. The woman had visited Rosie and her undersized baby first. Rosie's premature son had tripled his birth weight, but he still wasn't the size of an average one-year-old yet. The woman had asked a lot of personal questions, picked the baby up and made him scream. Rosie had gone nuts and fled up north with little Daniel, after she'd yelled into the phone at her dad. At least she had a husband to look out for her, a badly shaken Uncle Norm had reported. Rosie's husband Vince McCaud had gone straight down to the Children's Aid office, roaring about how he'd fucking well lay charges and he would have too. He was lithe and strong, a bit like Dace and he had the family to back him. Nobody fooled with him.

The police had probably put Children's Aid up to the visits. Or Joe Armitage, that creep. Ever since September, the police had talked to Liza every two or three weeks at least.

And Joe, well, he had taken what wasn't his, plain and simple.

"It's not rape," he'd said, "if you don't close your legs." And she hadn't. Because she was a bad girl. And because of the information he'd promised her, she reminded herself, not to mention he was so much bigger than her that she didn't have much choice. Once she'd gone to his apartment, once she'd stepped into his lair.

A little monkey, a black marmoset, had watched from the corner of the bedroom in its cage. According to Maitland city bylaws, Joe wasn't supposed to have the marmoset, but he did. He'd 'borrowed' it from an international student who'd been called home to China or something. Joe was no good with animals though. The marmoset had a worried, wrinkled little face and it was piss-scared of him. It wouldn't even take food from his hand. Liza had tried to feed the little thing too, but it wouldn't come near her either, not with goddamn Joe in the room. What if the little guy starved? It wasn't a human baby, just a monkey, but still. It looked kind of skinny, but she really couldn't tell. How fat was a monkey supposed to be?

"Something bad happened here one night," Joe had explained nonchalantly. "He escaped from his cage and made me chase him all around the room. I spanked him, that's all." The size of Joe and the size of the animal. Did the marmoset even weigh five pounds? Liza had just shaken her head. The marmoset had been even more afraid afterwards.

It was all her fault. She shouldn't have visited. There must have been another way to get what she needed. She just hadn't thought of it yet.

Except for baby Micah, she would have got Uncle Norm's shotgun from its hiding place in the wall, stalked Joe and shot him in his bed.

Yes, add murder to my list of crimes, she thought. *Bad daughter, border-line incest offender, accessory after the fact, unwed mother, sponger.*

She'd gone to see the counsellor at Student Health Services instead. The counsellor was one of two. His name was Dr. Fred Cooper. He looked a bit like Jon Voight, but not as cute. She had a bunch of term papers to finish and she couldn't concentrate. After getting this far, she didn't want to blow her year. Her parents wouldn't know or care. But her maternal grandmother who had sacrificed her own principles to send her to university and her proud uncle Norm certainly would.

She also wanted to admit culpability to the counsellor—to someone—but it was difficult when she couldn't even talk about what had happened at Joe's. In the end, she'd dropped just a few hints, focusing mainly on the marmoset in the cage.

At first, the counsellor had just looked perplexed, so she tried again.

"He hurt me...I think maybe Joe's a sociopath," she'd said.

Hearing this, the counsellor had finally sat up a little straighter in his chair. She was talking his kind of language, not that she knew much. She'd taken one course in Psychology, that's all.

"How so?"

Liza looked down at her lap.

The counsellor had waited, but when she didn't say anything else, he nodded sagely and said, "You could charge him with assault, but I know his family quite well and he'll just lawyer up, get the best one in town. He said, she said. You've been around the block enough. You know how that goes." The counsellor was Joe's age, but he was already balding. He'd leaned back in his chair, put his hands behind his head and looked at Liza, like she was a colleague instead of a patient. When she saw the struggle in his face, she held her breath and waited. And it worked.

Even so, when he'd looked up at the ceiling instead of at her and said, "You're right," she couldn't believe her ears. "Joe Armitage *is* a sociopath. There's no telling what he'd do if you charged him. My family used to visit his when we were children, at their cottage in Grand Bend. I can't believe how Papa Hank Armitage treated that kid in his own living room."

Liza wasn't interested in Mr. Armitage's parenting skills, not then. Or meeting him and she wished to hell that she'd never met his son. "Why, what else has Joe done?" she'd asked immediately, but the counsellor must have realized he'd crossed a professional boundary, for he shut up and suddenly she was the enemy in the room.

"I'm not at liberty to discuss somebody else," he'd said. Of course not.

"Why—is he a patient here too?" she'd persisted anyway, which was unlike her. People were entitled to their own opinions, their own privacy, even a pseudo-psych. Oh, God, the secrets he must know.

"Besides," the counsellor scrambled on, smirking a little, "he has a new girlfriend, so if you charge him with anything, he'll just say you're a woman scorned."

But I don't want him, Liza thought, a sick feeling in the pit of her stomach. Did this man really think she was just a vengeful girlfriend?

"Anyway," the counsellor added, "You went to his place, didn't you? Of your own free will? When you knew, absolutely knew what he was like." He looked down at the floor. His jaw was working and Liza could hear him grinding his teeth. Then he'd said, as if it might excuse Joe, "You know, maybe he was just drunk."

Liza had stared into his dispassionate eyes. The man was useless.

232

A bit of her high school French came back to her—*no succor*. She didn't belong here either. Another mistake. She'd made a lot lately. She got up to leave.

"Yes, maybe he was drunk," she agreed, but not before the counsellor said that she was okay now, right, so there was no need for her to come back and see him anymore. Once was enough. Lots of other students were a lot worse off than her. He had quite a lineup, yes, he did and if you really need something, here's a little Valium for the next few days.

Yeah, right, Liza had thought as she walked out of Student Health Services and left the man sitting there, with his eyes darting side to side, anything so he didn't have to look at her. *Yeah, right, true enough, the only drunk person was me.*

******

It took weeks to wipe what had happened from her conscious mind, to move on.

Joe had called to say he had some important information— something that might help Dace. He'd just rented a one bedroom apartment in a high-rise on the outskirts of campus. His apartment was on the tenth floor. "So I can bring girlfriends home more often," he'd said. It had been hard for him in the student residence. He was several years older than most of the other students and there were so many nubile things in their teens. *Sweet young things, don't you know.* But people talked, oh how they loved to talk. And can you believe it—one stupid girl had even taken some pills. His pills. He had to take those pills, that's why he didn't drink. Why had she taken his pills? Because she was crazy of course. Manic-depressive or maybe schizoid. Hard to tell. How the hell was he supposed to know? He wasn't a psych. What? Oh, she was all right now, the manipulative little bitch. She'd gotten her stomach pumped. He didn't really want to talk about it though.

"And while I'm sharing this important info with you, I have a little monkey you might want to see too," he'd added.

When Liza had gotten there, the overstuffed living room with castoffs of his parents' furniture had looked okay, but the bedroom had been full of rape and bondage magazines, a hardcore kind she'd never seen. Stacks and stacks. Where were Joe's books? He was a PhD student for God's sake. What did he read besides trash? Even now, especially now, she couldn't remember any of the magazines' names.

He'd threatened to tie her up if she didn't cooperate.

No, that wasn't true. She still could have gotten away. Yes, she could have. She was—she still was—the mistress of her own fate. That's what Dace would say.

She had a beer—a Labatt's Blue—and Joe had a Coke. She hadn't had time to eat dinner, so the beer slid down her throat real fast. Joe kept some beer in his fridge for people like her, just in case. People who drank. He didn't drink, oh, no, not him. Drink interfered with his medication, he said. So what if he was sick in the head? He was also a bad man.

"So what about it, Joe? Can you show me what you've found?" she'd asked, sitting cross-legged in a beige armchair with a greasy headrest.

"It was bad," he'd said, "real bad."

He'd waited while she drank another beer or two to fortify herself. She couldn't remember how many. It didn't matter. She'd had to, that's all. She was starving and her breasts ached with unexpressed milk.

Millie was looking after Micah. O, baby. She'd closed her eyes briefly and thought about him, practically smelling his sweet baby flesh. Every instinct told her to keep Micah as far away from Joe as possible and to protect herself too, but she couldn't.

She had to find out what he knew.

Joe had introduced her to the monkey first, a tiny humanoid she'd very much regretted leaving behind. Oh, God, the marmoset's eyes. She'd done something about him though, the only way she could. A couple of days later, she'd sent an anonymous note to the Maitland Humane Society and somebody had come and taken the little creature away. So the marmoset was safe. Unlike her. Because Joe had…

Die, die, she thought. It was easier than thinking about what she'd let him do.

And if she got caught for shooting him, arrested for first-degree murder, it wouldn't matter. Ah, yes, it would be worth it just to watch him draw his last breath. She'd love it. He'd tasted her breasts and run his hand over her back when he had finished and that had been worse than anything else. Worse than… No, she couldn't even think about it. And she didn't have to. Except when he touched the cut on her lip, he'd looked so goddamned relaxed.

Liza hadn't cried. Not then. "I don't want your tenderness," she'd said, wishing to hell she'd had the strength to crawl back into his bed and jam her knee hard up between his legs. He'd reached up and grabbed at her crotch. "I never did and I don't now. I'm going home, " she'd said, backing away. And she had. If only she'd done that before, but she hadn't. No, she'd left his apartment at four in the morning and caught a cab down in the street, while he lie back on his bed, a toothy, triumphant, satisfied man whose teeth she wished she'd kicked in.

It was just sex, she'd thought when she got into the cab. *I'm not really hurt.*

Back at the farm, she'd showered and pretended nothing had happened, though she woke up with her heart pounding in her chest the next couple of nights.

It's all over, I'm dying, she thought. *What will become of my son?*

She took Micah into bed with her then. He slept in the crook of her arm and did what he was born to do. The sound of his heart beat slowed down hers. He made her want to live forever so he'd never have to be alone. *My sweet boy*, she thought. *I love you, I love you more than Dace. It's you, my darling – you're the only one.* She kissed her baby's warm head and the desperate need to murder Joe Armitage passed. *I have a child*, she reminded herself. *I can't go to jail.*

"It doesn't matter," she told herself over and over, although it did and she hated that she had been so weak. She'd die before she told anybody else what Joe had done to her. Die before she'd tell them what she'd let him do. In the end, she hadn't even really told the counsellor, that useless man.

"He wanted to, but he didn't really do anything," she'd lied to the counsellor, just before she left, though her inner thighs were still bruised. "I stopped him. I kicked him in the groin." And the counsellor had had the goddamn nerve to look at her as if she were the criminal and might be charged.

Joe had used a condom at least. And he hadn't taken off all her clothes, so she'd been able to re-dress real fast. She'd felt almost grateful at the time. People mightn't like what he'd done, but they'd despise her even more.

Because the counsellor was right. She'd gone willingly to Joe's apartment.

"I can't risk sharing information like this with you in public," Joe had said. "What if I'm seen? But I like you and I really want to help you, so…"

This is why children didn't tell on their abusers, she realized. Rightly or wrongly, they felt complicit.

She hadn't been a child though.

She hung onto one thing. Joe had told her what she needed to know. He had gotten hold of some letters. It really didn't matter how. Well, okay, so he'd 'borrowed' some letters from a file marked "Sweet Kids" when he was interviewing Judge Silverton one day. He couldn't help himself. He hadn't planned it. Really. It was just serendipity. When the judge slipped into his adjoining washroom for an old man's brief leak, Joe had slid open the nearest filing cabinet and took what he could get, anything that might be useful to him later. It didn't even have to pertain to the bikers or Dace Devereux. He was just looking, that's all. The old guy had been gone three minutes tops, but long enough. The hardest part for Joe had been getting the letters back in the folder after he'd made copies. This time, he'd had to break into the judge's office, but he'd done that too.

"Oh, God, he left a reporter alone in his office?" Liza had asked.

"Well, let's just say the guy's gotten a little cocky and that he and my father go back a long way," Joe had bragged.

Joe hadn't read all the letters—too sickening—but it looked like Judge Silverton was part of that ring, he'd said while she was dressing, forcing her sore limbs into the legs of her jeans. Silverton's nephew—some guy called Father Danby—was too. Danby had been moved by the diocese from a school in a northern Ontario town to Cornwall. Danby had once worked at St. Matthew's. Did Liza know that? She'd probably recognize some of the other letter writers too.

If Joe could have used the letters, he would have, but he couldn't, he didn't dare. Because in addition to Judge Silverton, Joe knew too many of the people involved. Not that he owed them anything, but some of them were practically family friends. If he revealed stuff about them, they might realize he'd turned them in. It was okay for Liza—whatever she said, people probably wouldn't believe her anyway—but he couldn't afford to be the chief whistleblower. He just couldn't. You had to be careful with sensitive stuff like this and she would be, right? She'd leave out the Armitages and their close friends or innocent people might get hurt too. What if he blew the whistle and his own father got caught up in the net? The Armitage name—his name—would be fucking ruined. Six generations in Maitland, all down the drain.

Then he'd said, "I know you have to get back to your baby, but you'll come back again soon, won't you? You're in my blood. I can see we're into the same things and now that we've had this dry run, it will be much, much better next time," he'd promised.

"Yes," she'd agreed, wanting nothing more than to get out of his apartment, take the elevator downstairs and run.

"Well, then, this stuff is yours—a little reward for being such a good, almost cooperative girl."

Though she was still half-expecting him to renege, he'd pulled the manila envelope from under his bed with the air of such a big man. Gingerly accepting it and standing just out of his long reach, she'd taken a quick look at the contents. She spotted Father Danby's name right away. Joe really had given her something, he had!

For a moment, she felt almost grateful, no matter what he'd just done. Dry-eyed, she'd lifted her chin and crushed the envelope into her bag. Her upper legs quivered, but she'd forced herself to look unaffected, so he'd let her go. Joe worried about his neighbors and what they thought. He never would have let her go if she'd made a scene. She'd even managed a small smile.

"You're all right," he'd said, almost admiringly and then with a little sneer, a curl of his lip: "You sure can take a lot."

Her eyes slid to the bed, half-expecting to see the outline of her body where he'd pounded her into the mattress forever it had seemed. "I'll come back," she'd promised. *And stab you in the chest,* she'd thought. If the letters panned out, the police—somebody—would have to throw Silverton off the bench and when they did, they'd throw out his other cases too.

Well, maybe. Just a couple of weeks later, after she'd taken a closer look at the documents Joe had given her, she wasn't so sure. Some of the felons Silverton had convicted actually were guilty. They couldn't just toss him and all his stupid criminal cases out into the street.

What can I do, she thought. *Send an anonymous letter to the national newspaper, the Globe and Mail?* She doubted they would print it though.

They probably got letters from nuts all the time. What about the RCMP? Would they be interested in what had happened to a bunch of delinquents, orphans, other unwanted children and such?

She doubted that too.

Chapter 30
Message in a Car Seat

A week later when she got out of class, she found some money in Micah's car seat. A lot of money, so it definitely hadn't been there before. Her uncle paid for everything. He spotted her a twenty now and then, but she'd only seen such a wad of money a couple of times in her life. When she was with Dace two summers ago.

There was note from Dace too. It had to be. Who else talked like this? *I know where the monarchs go.*

Hastily, she dropped her book bag into the backseat and then she just stood in the parking lot with the baby on one hip and looked around. A chill passed over her, though it was an unusually mild February day, a recent snowfall already forgotten. Had Dace been here? Oh, surely not. A friend had probably left the money, but who? She had only been in the Arts building for three hours and it was still light outside. An outlaw biker or a long distance trucker would have stuck out on campus. Not that they were anymore unkempt than most of the male students, just a little older. Unless people were talking about such an unusual sighting in the cafeteria right now.

But what if the police had planted the money, in the foolish, pigheaded hope that she would be equally stupid and lead them straight to Dace? Yeah, take the money and run. The idea had a certain appeal, though she didn't see how the hell she could.

Nah, the police weren't that smart—at least she hoped they weren't—nor were they likely to risk the public's money on the likes of her.

Thoughtfully, she counted the paper money—twenty-four

unmarked American twenties plus a twenty-fifth bill with 'Cuitzeo' marked in ink along the edge. Five hundred dollars was a lot of money, even in American cash. Enough for a return trip to Cuitzeo, Mexico for sure, with a bit to spare. If Cuitzeo was in Mexico, that is. She'd have to look it up and see.

Briefly she wondered if the money had come from legitimate sources, not that she really cared. She needed it too much. The bills felt greasy, like they'd passed through many hands. She sniffed them, but they were odorless, scoured scent-free by the brisk wind. She double-checked each note for another message while the wind tried to tear them from her hand and Micah lunged for one of the greenbacks too, but there was none.

A couple of passing students looked curiously at her. "Is anything wrong?" one of them asked.

"No," Liza said, quickly composing her face. "I thought I lost my rent money, but I just found it." *My God*, she thought, *I'm living a lie. I lie all the time.* Micah was still trying to grab the money, but she managed to stuff it into her coat pocket. Shakily, she strapped the baby into his car seat. Car seats weren't mandatory, but after reading what happened to an unrestrained infant in even a minor crash, she'd wanted one. The baby protested at his confinement, so she gave him a clean sheet of paper to crumple in his fat little hands and then buckled herself into the driver's seat and started the car.

The car didn't blow up. More good fortune. Oh, God, she was really doing well today.

Seated in her car, she wondered how the person had gotten in and stashed the money in the baby's seat. How he'd even known it was her car. He must have followed her from the farm. She shivered a little. She was pretty sure she'd locked the doors. She always did. Oh, Christ, it had to be one of the bikers then — perhaps a biker who'd come by in a nondescript car. Somebody real loyal to Dace, but somebody who could pick a lock in seconds flat. Had some of the Wolfhounds come back to Maitland — fuck Judge Silverton — or were they just passing through?

Tears pricked her eyelids, but she didn't let them trickle onto her cheeks. She had to be able to see. *I can't go*, Dace, she thought as she drove with both hands clenching the wheel, headed for the highway at a great speed. *I just can't. Micah's much too young...or is he?* She looked back at the baby in her rear view mirror, completely absorbed in his papier-mâché. He was going to be an artist, for sure. Unlike her and Dace, he'd have all the time in the world. Yes, he'd have everything, the safe, secure childhood denied them. Yeah, sure. At the rate she was driving, maybe not. She braked a little and slowed down. Even a car seat wouldn't help the baby if she wrapped the car around a tree. *Maybe this is the best time*, she thought, *while Micah's still relatively immobile. Five hundred dollars is a lot of money. I could probably get to Mexico on that, find Dace and see where the monarchs over-winter.*

"Liza," a little voice cautioned her, "do you really want to start all this again?"

"Ah," she countered, "but maybe he's changed," though she knew, absolutely knew what a psychiatrist would say if she could afford a real one: "He was forged in prison."

And maybe, just maybe, you're crazy, little lady — a manic-depressive or something — so here, take some pills.

Just like the counsellor at Student Services. Yeah, just like him.

Chapter 31
Dream On, Little Dreamer

February 1974

At first she thought she was dreaming, just like all the other times. Until he came to her that night, they'd almost never done it in a bed before. She'd left the window slightly open and the blind up, but he wasn't Peter Pan, so he didn't come in through the window.

He didn't have to — he knew where his father kept an extra key out in the shed. He entered through the backdoor and took the stairs to the second floor in the usual way, a man this time, not a boy. She heard a click and then the light from the hall spilled in, the light she kept on so she could quickly find her way to Micah's crib. Luckily, she slept in the first guest bedroom at the top of the stairs, so Dace didn't have to try every door.

The last time anybody had come into her room (while she was there anyway), she'd been giving birth. She rolled over and looked up and suddenly he was just there, tanned and fit, his hair trimmed, while she must have looked a wild thing with her hair in a huge, matted clump. He was wearing jeans and a T-shirt. All she had on was an oversized man's shirt. Her breasts were spilling out.

She still wasn't convinced, though. He was man on the run, so he should have been the one who was a mess. *I must be seeing things*, she thought. She didn't care though. She'd take him. A dream was better than nothing, it always was. She sat up, pushed his mother's quilt from her body and threw herself at him. She breathed in his scent, felt the muscles in his arms and ran her hands down his strong back. And it was him, it was him, it really was. Oh, God, she wasn't dreaming. Her throat seized up. *Great*, now she couldn't even talk.

"Liza, Liza," he said over and over, or at least that's what it sounded like. Outside the bedroom window, the country night was quiet, but there was a roaring in her ears, the sound of her own blood, rushing to meet his.

She couldn't hear very well. And when she did make out a few words, they didn't make much sense. He had a plane, he said and it was the first time he'd flown this far. He wanted to get a license, even if it wasn't in his own name. In the four hours he spent there, he told her lots of other incredible stuff too. They raced through a hasty recital of the time they'd spent apart—the long, lonely nights. Well, for her anyway.

And quickly, quickly, his hands slid down to her breasts.

"I can't," she lied automatically, shying away. *I'm so slack*, she thought. Besides, what if he felt the baby—or even worse—Joe on her skin?

He withdrew his hands, but she knew the look he gave her. He was just biding his time. If he had to woo her, well, fine. He'd do it. This time.

He was Dace Devereux, for God's sake, and he always did what he wanted, except when he was in jail. She pulled him down to her and put her head on his chest.

My cousin, my lover, she thought. Who the hell cared? She'd given birth, but she still fit into him just right. And their son had turned out fine too, whatever the hell doomsayers like her mother and Millie might have thought. She nestled into him.

"Wait—did you find the monarchs?" she finally asked.

"Almost," he said, "but at least I know where they go. I've been waiting to take you."

They whispered together while he stroked her hair. He had a new stepmother, she finally informed him, who slept lightly down the hall, in another wing actually, a woman with the keen hearing of a dog.

"Who?" he frowned, tugging a bit on her hair. His father hadn't even been seeing anybody when he left, or at least he didn't think he had.

"Ouch," Liza said, "Millie O'Connor."

"What, the housekeeper!" he exploded, holding her at arm's length and staring into her eyes. "Are you kidding me? He never went with women after — after my mother died…"

Liza sat up on her knees on the bed and smiled. "Not that you could tell, but you weren't always here…"

"Yeah, I was in jail, right. Well, if you think I'm sticking around to congratulate them, I'm not," he said, getting up and tossing the nearest pillow at the window. "I don't have time for this kind of crap."

"Poor Uncle Norm!" Liza said, starting to laugh a little. Dace didn't scare her. But he was kind of funny about his mother. "He's happy, you know, for the first time in years. Even with you on the lam."

"Well, that certainly hasn't changed," he said, coming back to the bed and taking her in his arms. "The authorities are still after me. I don't know who he's working for, but I saw Savage in Mexico and I bet he's still there. Just because he found his way down to Mexico doesn't mean he'll be able to figure out his way back."

She didn't know what else he was leaving out, but then she was leaving Micah — the most important part of her life — out too.

Mentally, she had already started packing her clothes. "Oh, God," she said, "Please take me with you. I can help keep the bastards off your back," while his hands stroked lower and lower, but he couldn't. Not this time. The plane had only two seats, he explained and he had somebody else with him.

"Who?" she demanded sharply. "I thought you flew the plane here by yourself."

"I did, but I haven't put in enough flying hours yet to fly solo, even under my assumed name. We landed the plane in Maitland and I hitched a ride out here. The guy who owns the plane, Jon Kallestad, came with me…he had some stuff to deliver, anyway. What's that look mean? Do you think I'm lying or something?"

Liza didn't have time for this stuff. She wrapped her legs around him and pulled him into her. He was ready and so was she. The walls of her vagina clamped down tight. A low moan escaped her throat, so she let him cover her mouth with one of his hands. He was silent, the way he always was. If she was imagining things, she didn't care. *This is like married sex*, she thought, but she didn't mind. It sure beat sleeping in a bed alone. Except for that bad stuff with Joe, she hadn't made love to anybody else for over a year. Forget all that fancy stuff, everything else she and Dace had done, exulted and tried.

It didn't matter how it had happened, just that he was there. She hadn't wanted sex, she'd just wanted him in her arms. At first she wasn't going to, but here they were making love and nothing else mattered anymore. She loved the full length of his taut body over hers.

The baby—his son—slept on silently in the very next room. *Please, please, don't cry*, she begged between thrusts that went on and on. Not now. *There isn't enough time for me to love your father and take care of you too. And don't let me cry either. Or leak, oh, my God.*

"My, but you have grown," Dace said, echoing Van Morrison's song while he held her breasts with both hands. Well, of course she had. She smiled a little to herself. Dace probably thought she had big breasts because she was a woman now, twenty-one plus.

She couldn't give him up, she just couldn't. It was only with her, only through their union that he'd change. *Dream on, little dreamer*, her annoying inner voice said.

In the next room, the baby stirred a couple of times, but Dace still didn't cotton on.

"What," he said, the first time they were through and they were just lying there on the bed, "is that squeaky sound?"

She'd take him in to see the baby later, she thought and so she did, around six in the morning, after they had made love four more times.

****

When she woke up the next morning with just the baby in her arms, he was gone. She'd tried so hard not to fall asleep, but in the end she had. For one bereft moment, she even wondered if she'd dreamed him: *Dace, the Highwayman who came riding, riding up to the old inn door.* But she couldn't have.

He'd left a ring under her pillow, a simple gold band.

She couldn't marry him, though, she just couldn't.

Chapter 32
Savage Dream

Apatzingan, Mexico, January 1974

L arry Savage put down his beer. It was just after six p.m., bright and sunny as usual. He had no special plans for the evening, but he had just spied a tasty little snack. A dark-skinned chiquita was strolling the green square and peddling her wares. Ah, Mexico. Chits like her were everywhere. Some skinny, oily-looking homos were also advertising in the shade of the stunted trees, but he didn't need them. If he'd wanted boys, he could have had his pick back in Maitland Pen, no matter what those cons said.

He crooked a finger at the girl. She smiled and started drifting his way, real slow, like she was retarded, but they all acted that way. Maybe the heat fried their brains. She was cute for a Spic, but the last one had been cuter and a virgin to boot. Well, maybe not — he wasn't a complete idiot — but she sure had been tight. Her eyes had watered when he entered her and she had cried when he stuck his unlit cigar up her rear. It took him awhile to get it up sometimes — his stressed out life and all — but a constant turnover in girls helped. Yeah, lots of girls in Apatzingan were interested in an "Americano." He picked up a new one most nights.

When he didn't have to take care of drug-carrying, gun-slinging bad boys, that is. Luckily he still had his pistol, the one he'd bought up in Buffalo. The other guys in his group of vigilantes were equipped with hunting rifles, old pistols and small-bore shotguns, that's all. What a bunch of losers, but as long as they were on the right side of the law like him, he didn't much care.

As she approached him, the little Spic girl smiled like crazy. *Take me, take me, I'll make you crazy too!* She was loaded down, but it didn't seem to bother her. He liked that—a female who did something besides lie on her back. When push came to shove, she could take care of him. He wouldn't even have to marry her. No sirree. In addition to some men's shirts she carried on some cheap wire hangers, she had a baby tied onto her back and a toddler pulling at her skirt. So what if she was a little mother, she was still sweet enough to give him an ache in his groin. She looked about fourteen, but some of the boys had a saying back in Maitland: *If they're old enough to bleed, they're old enough to fuck.* When she finally reached him, he took hold of her free hand without getting up and shook it hard.

"How much?" he asked, smiling benevolently over the shelf of his gut which had started to expand again.

"How much you pay?" she asked, rubbing her cheek against a blue checked shirt. No way she just selling those shirts though. He could tell from her smile and her old eyes, which were far from guileless.

"As much as you're worth," he said, holding up his beer to her lips so she could take a sip.

He was still in Mexico all right, living it up, which was why he'd just about given up on Dace Devereux and the fucking snow up Canada way. Why the hell had he been born there?—it wasn't fair. The guys from the RCMP had gone back home, at least for now, leaving him to pursue ring-a-ding Devereux, though how they expected him to find the bastard when they couldn't, he really didn't know. As it turned out, Devereux had been way down on their list, especially after he crossed the border and they had to worry about interfering with the drug trade and such.

And here's the thing. It made Larry feel like such a fat useless fuck—the way they'd given up and left him on his lonesome to find the goddamn punk—and he didn't much like feeling this way. If the law was losing interest in Devereux and he wasn't going to get his old job back, why the hell should he bother? He didn't want his old job back anyway. Maybe if he hadn't ended up down in Mexico—"Mayheeco" as the natives said — but he had. He knew how to do other stuff now, like relax for Christ's sake, which was why he was sitting here in this sunny cantina on the square. He never wanted to see fucking Canada or his old lady mother again. Never, never — or "nunca, nunca" like they said here in Mexico. He'd even toyed with the idea of changing his name, not that anybody was looking for him. He just wanted to start over, to be a winner, instead of a loser. And he'd surprised himself too. Because he was doing all right. For somebody who'd never even dreamed of spending winters in a tropical climate, he'd taken to Mexican life — or at least a foreigner's idea of Mexican life — right away.

He liked everything about his new digs — the sun, the food, the girls, even his gut. His big belly signaled to the little chiquitas that he ate well and so would they. No doubt the one dollar American bills he padded their little busts with helped too. For two bucks — and so far, he'd never wasted a dime on food or drink for a Mexican chit much less on a condom — he could do what he wanted. "I bet this is what you're after," he said, waving a couple of dirty bills under the girl's nose before he stuffed them down the front of her cheap cotton dress.

But there was trouble in paradise, there always was. Take now. Some bugger was hiding under a tree and eyeballing him from across the square. It might be the girl's father, but he didn't think so. If the girl hadn't been so tiny and he wasn't so careful, he might have missed the fellow. The guy had on a white shirt like one of the good guys in the vigilante, but if he didn't want to blow paradise sky high and send all the Spics here running, he'd better wait a minute and make sure.

Irritated, he shoved at the girl's chest. She got the point and turned around and left right away, but no worries, she'd be back. The little guy toddled after her, still clutching her skirt, but he looked back at Larry and the baby did too, both of them whining for a treat or maybe just a pet. Like a couple of puppies for fuck's sake. Larry felt like getting up and smacking the older brat, but there wasn't time. The white shirted fellow was definitely headed his way. He was fast moving for a Spic and yeah, he was pretty sure he recognized him (though most of them looked the same). Any who! If it was somebody from the vigilante, he had work to do.

"Buenos noches," the guy said the minute he reached him, all smarmy-faced and mealy-mouthed like most of his type.

His evening ruined along with his fledgling erection, Larry sighed.

Up close, his visitor certainly looked like that Julio fellow from the vigilante group, but he still wasn't one hundred percent sure. There were so many guys in the group and they changed all the time.

"Buenos noches," Larry replied, reluctantly shaking the guy's greasy hand. He'd have to help this guy, take care of whatever he asked. From what Larry had seen and heard so far, drug gangs had wormed themselves deep into the fabric of Michoacán society and if there was one thing he hated even worse than Dace Devereux, it was drugs, especially marijuana. Since 1914, Canadians and Americans had known that marijuana was a "corrupting menace," that it made its users comatose and led to even worse drugs, but they had tolerated its growth in various Mexican provinces, even encouraged it under certain circumstances. Like after the vets started coming back from that Asian hellhole, Vietnam, all turned on from the crap they'd smoked over there. Christ, even Canadian doctors had been able to prescribe it until 1932. It boggled the mind.

Back home, there were rogue guards who still smuggled the stuff into jails. Marijuana — reefers — pot, whatever the hell they called it now. Larry didn't smoke the stuff, that's all he knew. Worse stuff got smuggled in too, but pot — that's where it all started. He'd had a shitload of trouble with some of those guys and he couldn't do much about them, Canadian law and all. Still, when he was head guard at Maitland Pen, he'd managed to keep the place clean — at least as far as the guards went. There had been a couple of bad apples in the guard ranks like the one who'd smuggled in heroin in his ass, but he'd gotten rid of him too. The colleges and universities were another cesspool. He couldn't do much about the prisoners' visitors, like Dace's smart-mouthed college cousin. But he sure as hell knew her type. If Devereux hadn't been locked down most of the time and she'd visited him a bit more, little Miss Florence Nightingale would have brought in all sorts of illegal remedies to "help" her con cousin.

So of course Larry had joined the first vigilante self-defense group who asked him. They did business two or three nights a week. It was the right thing to do and it really wasn't such a bad job. There was usually enough time left over to come back and pick up a girl. Of course, Larry really liked the work, but in Apatzingan, you didn't have much choice. Life was black and white. If you were a man, you joined the vigilante group or else the drug gang. It was that simple.

He was feeling a bit tired tonight, that's all, plus he'd already had several beers. Well, maybe Julio would like a beer too before he started work. It was odd, but at least the guy was alone. El Cheapo Larry (as the guys sometimes called him) would only have to buy one beer. But when he patted the wooden seat beside him, the fellow just shook his head. He didn't want to sit down. Well, goody-goody for him. Larry sure wasn't going to argue—especially with somebody from the vigilante. He'd seen plenty of times what they did to guys they didn't trust, to somebody they thought might be playing both sides. Well, that definitely wasn't him. Cheapness was Larry's greatest sin. He was a real standup guy. At a jerk from Julio's head, he got up and followed him, lumbering a little through the fragrant night air.

****

Fifty-eight bodies believed to be victims of a drug gang have been found in mass graves in the western Mexican state of Jalisco.

A total of 27 graves contained the bodies, some of which showed signs of torture, an official at the attorney general's office said Monday. Authorities also said that some of the bodies had been bound by the hands and feet.

The search in the area bordering the drug-plagued state of Michoacán stemmed from a probe into the disappearance of an unidentified Canadian officer and several other suspected police killings. The Canadian, who was either a policeman or a correctional officer, may have been working undercover. He has not been identified, pending notification of next of kin.

One civilian and 20 Mexican police officers were arrested in the case. The detainees, who led police to the many mass graves, allegedly confessed to capturing the Canadian officer and turning him over to a local drug gang.

Police have also questioned a vigilante group in Apatzingan, Michoacán about the Canadian, but there have been no arrests. Some of the bodies had been dead for months, others for two or three years, a spokesman for the attorney general's office said.
~ **Mexico City News**, March 3, 1974

Chapter 33
Kathleen's Return

Kathleen never thought about her daughter Mariposa if she could help it. She had no problem leaving the child and no problem going down to Mexico again, none at all. The baby was three months old and except for some gummy smiles—which sent the child's grandmother into raptures—not very engaging. And dark—God she was dark—with masses of black hair. Nothing like pretty little Kathleen had been with her wispy blonde curls. Kathleen never looked at her if she could help it and she was afraid to hold her. The kid wiggled too much. She didn't visit her mother's house much either. A single monarch butterfly was more entrancing than her newborn daughter and, with any luck, she'd see millions of monarchs before they left their Mexican home.

She put it off for a while, but then she filled out all the paperwork, got a grant and called up her old acquaintance Murphy. It didn't take very long. Murphy was kind of creepy, but she'd do what she had to do. She always had. At heart, she was a good girl and she worked hard. It was one of the reasons she'd been cured of tuberculosis—well, that and the development of the antibiotic streptomycin—and it was the reason she was going to find those monarch butterflies, that's for sure.

Chapter 34
Border Crossing

February 1974

The police sergeant was furious, but that didn't scare his pimple faced constable at all. The sergeant would have a heart attack before he fired him. The constable knew this because his father had looked the same way—sweating and red-faced—just before he up and had a coronary and died.

"You were supposed to be watching her!" the sergeant shouted. The whole police station heard him. "That's your only job. A special job, so you could strut your stuff. Do you even know what that means? How the hell did she get across the border?"

The young constable pulled at his collar and cleared his throat. Okay, so maybe he was just a bit scared. "It's Reading Week at Maitland University, sir and at the college too."

The police sergeant turned his back on the constable, shoved his shirt back into his pants and looked at the calendar on the wall. He looked like he was calming down a little, thank God. "Yeah, yeah, Slack Week, you mean. That's what the students call it."

"Yeah, well, every spoiled brat in Maitland is flocking down south. I'm guessing Liza Devereux is no exception."

The sergeant reared around and roared in the constable's face again, "You're guessing?! We don't have time for this shit. You goddamn fool, she's on her way to him! Whatever--she's got a line on him for sure!"

"Who—the cousin?" The younger cop shrank back against the wall a little, but he held his ground.

"Who the hell else?"

"Oh, yeah, well, I see what you mean. But I have a theory —"

"Oh, so now you have a theory?! You're not paid to have theories, but go ahead, let's hear it."

"Well," the constable faltered, but then he carried on, "she might have just wanted a vacation—you know, to fit in with the rest of the college kids. And to get away from Henry Armitage's son, Joe. You know—Joe, that mall owner's kid, he did something to her, I think. It was her own fault, going to his place at that time of night, but..."

At the mention of the Armitages, the sergeant's face went from red to purple. "Listen, Hank Armitage's son didn't do nothing to nobody, you got that? Or have you forgotten that Hank's a good friend of mine? He's had enough trouble with that boy of his. Kids! I can't get my own to go to school and that Armitage kid was in the loony bin back a year or two."

"Okay, well, I don't think she'll go near him for a while. I didn't know he was crazy, though, sir, or I might have..."

The sergeant made an odd sound, a bit like a laugh. "What, gone and rescued her? She don't need no rescuing, that one. You seen her. She's a tough little broad. So what if something happened to her, she got just what she deserves. Where the hell is she now?"

"She hitched a ride with some bigwig Jew's daughter, Esther Cohen, sir." The constable shook his head. If the sergeant thought he had an easy job, he didn't. "I had a hard time keeping an eye on the Devereux girl while she was on campus. She was always darting here and there, feeding the kid in a washroom stall or running out to her car and when she was inside a classroom or the library, well, what kind of trouble could she get up to there?"

"Plenty, you fool. Haven't you heard of Kent State and the trouble them radical types caused? I know most of you young fellows can't read too well, but don't they teach you anything at the Police Academy these days?" The sergeant sat down at his desk, wiped his sweating forehead with his sleeve and sighed. "Okay, get on with it, get on with it!"

"Well, this is what I've pieced together so far. The Cohen girl—the driver— had advertised on a bulletin board for some riders to help pay her way south. Not that she needed the money, but she's greedy, I guess. The

Devereux girl must have seen the ad. The little bitch read everything and I mean everything! She'd stand in front of those bulletin boards patting and rocking her baby in that contraption she wore. She could've passed for a squaw or something in that poncho with her long black hair. She left the kid at home for a while, but then damn near every time I saw her, she had the baby in one hand and a book in the other…"

"Yeah, yeah!"

"Esther Cohen wanted to go to Fort Lauderdale—she's twenty-two years old and she's already been everywhere else. And man, oh, man, she's real stacked. Like, a lot of the university girls are. Um, the van's registered to Esther's daddy. There was a bunch of other kids in the van too. A big van like that with a bunch of hippie students, they checked it out, sir. I talked to the border police myself. They said there were no drugs, not even the stink of grass or hash. One of the boys is on the SDS list—uh, that *Students for a Democrat Society* crap— so they strip-searched him, but he was clean. They did their job, sir, they really did. There was a lot of traffic at the border, that's all. The other girls in the van were clean and polite— student types—so nobody even asked for their ID. It's hands-off with the Cohen girl anyway. Her dad's on the Board of Directors at the U…"

"And nobody thought it odd that one of the girls was toting a baby?"

"They didn't see no baby, Sir."

"Well, what did the Devereux girl do with the kid then? Leave it on the farm with her folks?"

"We already checked that out too. No baby." The officer flipped open his notes. "Mr. and Mrs. Norm Devereux…"

"Mister and Missus? Give me a fucking break!"

"Yeah, well, Norm and Millie Devereux said their niece ran off with the baby after an argument, that she's a headstrong girl…"

"Yeah, tell me about it…"

"That she wanted a vacation, that she deserved one, in fact. That she'd been working so-o-o hard. Can you believe it? What does it take to sit around reading books and feeding a baby? They thought Liza might have gone to Toronto. Her mother still lives there. They were worried about the baby, that's all. Oh, yeah, and I guess her too."

The sergeant bounced his own hand off the side of his head. "Well, maybe they have good reason to be worried about the baby! Did you ever think about that? What if the girl got tired of the kid and planted it in a cornfield or buried it in the Devereux sugar bush? The stuff some of these unwed mothers do! Let's see if she's ditched the brat for Devereux. I bet she has. And for your sake, I hope to hell somebody's tracking that van."

"Somebody's definitely tracking the van, sir. Can I be the one to go to Florida, can I? I've never been..."

"Don't be stupid. We'll intercept the van long before then. She's one little bitch that won't get far."

There was a knock on the door and one of the female dispatchers strutted into the room like she owned the place, so both officers knew she had some juicy news. She didn't open her mouth until they gave her the say-so though.

"What is it?" they growled in unison.

"Sir," she addressed the sergeant, "it's the Armitage boy, sir. We just got a call from a 'concerned' neighbor. Joe's been hurt real bad. The neighbor had already called the ambulance, but he said it was some bikers who came to rob the place. I don't know why he thinks that though — they just dumped Joe on the front lawn, so they probably didn't assault him there."

"Hey, hey, you let us do the police work here."

"I think the neighbor probably just wants to get some extra protection for himself and his little girl."

"Well, tell him we don't have the resources and then phone the hospital and find out what kind of shape my friend Hank's kid is in."

The constable rubbed his temple. "You think it was bikers who attacked Joe Armitage?" he asked. "I can see why they might have a beef with him — all those articles he wrote — but I thought we ran them all out of town."

Chapter 35
Fixing Joe

From inside his high hospital bed with the metal rails, Joe Armitage drifted.

"He looks like death warmed over," a female voice said. "His eyes are open—do you think he's seeing anything? Can he hear us? Does he even know we're here?"

"No," another voice said.

There were cameras everywhere and people spying, but they couldn't keep a good man down. A good man like him, that is. In Joe's mind, he kept walking to his car in the parking lot near the university gates. A little snow had fallen and was still falling and settling on the ground.

"Go home and get some rest," the second voice said. "We'll let you know if there's any change."

He had left the Social Sciences Building at dusk, eager to get back to his apartment and open up a fresh tin of Heinz Baked Beans. He loved beans doused in corn syrup, a much healthier alternative to all the pizza and mac and cheese the kids ate nowadays.

The female wasn't leaving. Something cold touched his hand. "Wake up and say something," she said. "I'll make you some of those beans."

He'd stocked the little kitchenette in his apartment with lots of beans and syrup, but he was all out of Coke. The tuck shop would still be open though. Maybe he'd pop in and pick up some Coke and the February edition of *Penthouse* magazine, if they weren't all out. He much preferred *Penthouse* to *Playboy* because he liked his sex down and dirty. Real. The bunnies were beautiful, but all that *Playboy* shit was just a little too air-brushed for him. If it hadn't been for Liza, he would have bought a copy already. Now she was a real girl. Milk had dripped from her breasts and she still had such a little snatch... He'd really liked it when she almost cried, though he hadn't really hurt her that much.

Maybe he should give her a call? Nah, she'd looked so prune-faced when she left. Funny, he'd expected a lot more gratitude from her. He'd risked his ass getting that file and she hadn't wanted to put out. But then she'd always been so volatile, ever since he'd met her outside Maitland Pen during the riot three years ago. She must have gone over to Student Services because when he went there to renew his prescription, that doctor dude had looked at him kind of funny. God knows what the lying little bitch had said.

"Your apartment is chockful of beans," the voice beside him yammering. "Really, dear, is that all you eat? And those magazines...I don't know what your father's going to say. They make me queasy."

Joe ignored the voice. When he got home, he'd wash the beans down with a sixteen- ounce bottle of Coca-Cola while he thumbed through his magazines and watched a little television. A good evening. He had to stop eating in the university cafeterias anyway. Much as he liked the ditzy little girls who hung out in the Arts Café, he couldn't afford to eat out every day.

He heard more voices in the distance, but he couldn't see anybody else on campus. He looked around him just in case, walking tall. Some of the lights on the path were out—why was that? Well, maybe they'd all burned out at the same time. It made sense. In three or four long strides, he made it to the arterial campus road. He knew the route by heart. He'd caroused the campus for years, even got lucky and caught the odd bit of tail down in the ravines. More lights were burnt out here too. What the hell was wrong with the custodial staff? A bunch of immigrants and foreigners. If you asked him, they got paid way too much. They sure as heck weren't doing their jobs. And what was that? For days, he'd heard a crunch here, a creak there, the wheezy intake of a smoker, but when he'd looked around, he couldn't see anything. He didn't have to. His body knew when somebody was stalking him. His hair stood up on the back of his neck and he got a small, damp spot on his crotch.

Here's the thing—you had to expect trouble when you worked for the press, even a little paper like the *Maitland Spectator*. Last summer, when he'd been writing his series of articles on the bikers, he'd gotten a slew of nasty, misspelled letters from the bikers' mothers and girlfriends. Funny, ha, ha. He used to lie in bed at night and read them and laugh. *Women's letters. You had to love them. All bark, no bite.*

And it was safe enough here on campus, in spite of the burnt out lights and the dips and valleys leading to the river through a thicket of dark trees. Safe even for a sweet young thing, strutting around campus in blue jeans or a calf-length skirt molded to her thighs and boots up to her ass. Especially now that it was winter and the trees were leafless. A low-life, criminal biker would sure stand out.

"Fuck off, punks!" he yelled down the road, just in case.

Not that he was worried. Nobody was going to bother him here in Maitland, the city where his family had lived for six generations. How many people could say that?

Although he'd bothered them. Because he'd had to. How the hell else was he supposed to pay for his antipsychotic drugs? No way he could have asked his parents. He knew what his father would say. "Pull up your socks, son."

He wasn't a real criminal, though. Because he'd stopped. Besides, he'd just done that B and B stuff for a little while. A part of him still missed it, though, that awesome adrenaline rush. That and poking around other people's houses, including his childhood home which was crammed full of old papers and unexpected treasures. He went back as often as he could.

Lucky him. His parents and his schoolmates' parents were always going somewhere: the cottage, the Bahamas, the Caribbean or France or Spain. Pretty tempting. Really, it was their own damn fault. What the hell did they expect when they took off and left a couple of teenagers in charge? He and his friends had broken into their houses and blamed it on strangers, until a bunch of them had moved away, to school, to a job and, at least in one case, to the Army.

If the boys couldn't find any booze or cigarettes or cash, they had spirited away all sorts of little family treasures—great-grandma's engagement ring, a sterling silver cigarette case, a monogrammed pen, a gleaming string of real pearls. Nothing too valuable. Just little things that would be sorely missed when the owner finally realized they were gone. So what? They'd sold them or trashed them, it didn't matter. Joe had no interest in mementos, which was another reason he wasn't a criminal. His private school friends didn't either. From what he'd heard, only a real kept souvenirs of his crimes.

At last he reached the parking lot. Most of the time, he didn't mind the walk, but it was a damn cold hike tonight and he was tired. Extreme cold affected him that way. In the unlikely event that somebody jumped at him out of the dark, he prayed for strength. The parking lot lights were out too, but he found his Malibu, right where he always left it, in the front row.

He stumbled a little when he unlocked the car, stubbed his right toes and cursed. His toes hurt like hell for about thirty seconds, but then, ah, the pain stopped. He still felt like slamming something in retaliation, the car or whatever had tripped him. Well, maybe not the car. He needed it too much, for interviews and such.

Hanging onto his door, he looked down at the ground and saw something black. What the hell was it—a rock? *Oh, no*, he thought, *it's a truncheon and it's moving*. Some legs appeared next, followed by the rest of a body from underneath his car.

The body slithered up beside him, on two legs and not four, so it was probably human, but it was too dark to tell and the son-of-a-bitch snow wasn't helping. The body held up something, about the size and shape of a small flashlight.

"Hey, watch where you're going! That's my foot," a voice snapped, though Joe still wasn't too worried. The speaker—a male, of course—was a lot smaller than him and the way he was glaring at him was kind of funny. He looked like an enraged girl.

The fellow had no business under his car, but so what? Joe was hungry and he just wanted to get home. Besides, the jerk was probably just a homeless person trying to keep warm. Yeah, a homeless person with a flashlight, something for his own protection. Joe's mind raced. No point in being foolhardy, but this probably wasn't one of the guys who was after him. Not here, not on campus where he—big Joe Armitage, investigative reporter—had always been in charge. Of little freshmen girls down in the ravine anyway. And of Liza, if she let him, if she came back, because she was a real woman and a real woman liked it that way.

Yeah, this was just some homeless guy for sure. His enemies might try to rattle him—witness the noises he'd heard this week—but that's all. Shit, Maitland was getting worse than Toronto, where homeless people—mostly drunks—slept down at the new City Hall all the time. This little perp was lucky he didn't stick out his foot and trip him to the ground.

"Fuck off," he repeated, swooping some parking tickets off his window shield and almost, but not quite, making it into his car.

The first whack hit him in the small of the back. The second one knocked him to his knees. The third one felled him to the ground.

He caught a glimpse of the rest of his attackers—four big, black-clad bruisers—just before he rolled over to protect his face. They had started hitting him with their unlit black flashlights, in the back and in the head, but they stopped when he was on the ground.

They used their boots instead.

I'll be alright, he thought, *if they kick low*. They didn't, though.

They went straight for his head.

Chapter 36
Liza on the Lam

February 1974

Liza thought she'd feel great once she crossed the border, but she didn't. "Professor almost killed by bikers in an unprovoked attack," she'd heard on the car radio just as they pulled up to the border, but she hadn't caught the name and they wouldn't be getting much Canadian news now. They were in the States and as far as the Americans were concerned, little happened in the Great White North, except snow.

Still she wondered, *What professor? What bikers?* The Wolfhounds were all gone—some of them down to Cornwall, Dace had said. And why would they attack a professor? Now if some of the bikers had gone after a teaching assistant like Joe Armitage—that she could understand. Joe had really done a number on them. As for her—well, she was hard-pressed to care what happened to Joe. She'd probably kill him herself if she ever got her hands on him again. In the overheated van, she shivered a little. Let Joe find out what it felt like to be powerless and alone.

It was cold and drizzling in upper New York State. No snow. Well, that was good. My God, how many miles did they still have to go? She stared at the back of the driver's head. The girl kept looking back over her shoulder to talk. It got on Liza's nerves. Esther Cohen was a smart girl, but did she really know the way? The sky hung over the van like a grey construction cover. There were four other people in the van, in addition to Esther, two boys and two girls, but they were all sleeping or pretending to.

When she first got into the van, the girl in the front passenger seat had glared at her and said, "I hope your baby doesn't cry all day."

It was just past seven a.m. The moment they got over the border, the rest of the passengers had fallen asleep, pasty-faced and, at least in the case of the boy from the SDS, the *Students for a Democratic Society*, a little hung over from the night before. He'd been raving mad when the border cops strip-searched him and rightly so, but fortunately the cop-types had just been amused.

"Man," the boy (his name was Alex) had said when he came out of a little room, "I've been fucking raped."

At the first golden-arched Mcdonald's, Esther stopped to get a coffee at the drive-in window. Liza wanted one too, but she had to conserve her cash. She inhaled the aroma of fresh brewed coffee instead. She was sitting behind Esther, with the baby still strapped into the cloth carrier on her chest and his car seat beside her. The baby was sleeping again, lulled by his early rising and the motion of the van. Not to mention she'd held him and breastfed him for the past two hours so he wouldn't cry and bother the stupid girl in the front seat, Sandi something or other. Liza sniffed his sweet-smelling head. She really should put him into the car seat, but they would have to stop the van and unpack the car seat, which was piled high with some girl's junk and though she didn't know it then, the SDS boy's weed.

Plus, she was totally exhausted. *So shift the kid, anyway*, a maternal voice inside of her nagged. *You're a mother now, not some heedless girl, no matter what Uncle Norm and Millie think.* The way they'd talked to her, Liza had felt kind of hurt, but she didn't have time for hurt feelings now. They had just been trying to help her anyway. What would she have done without them? Not that she owed them her son.

With one free hand, Liza knocked the stuff from the car seat down to the floor of the van. Somehow, over the next twenty minutes or so, she also managed to extract the baby from his carrier and slide him, still sleeping, under the straps in the car seat. Alex, the SDS boy on the other side of the seat, woke up and helped her, bending down at the same time to pick up a small, grassy-smelling pouch from the floor. Liza took a liking to him then. He was nicer than the three other passengers who hadn't said a word to her since she got into the car.

266

They had passed their biggest obstacle, but they were just getting under way and who knew what lay up ahead. Liza stared at the back of Esther's frizzy head, willing her to keep on going. At least she didn't have to drag the baby all the way to Mexico by herself, though that had been the original plan.

Dace had promised to pick them up at the Albany airport the day after tomorrow. He was picking up a package there for his boss or something, plus he was putting in his solo hours, so there would be room for her with the baby on her knee. She felt totally embarrassed about being so emotional now, though she sure hadn't at the time. As soon as he had put in a few more flying hours, he had planned to come back anyway, but he hadn't wanted to take her out of school.

"It's Reading Week," she'd sworn. As if she'd just abandon school, but she'd never cried that much around him before. He probably couldn't believe she had so many tears and she didn't either. What the hell was wrong with her? She'd lived on her own for years. But when she'd finally taken him into the room next door to see the baby, he'd understood why. He'd seen enough crying mothers in his day, mostly in a prison visiting room. His own mother had died when he was nine. It was still dark outside, four o'clock in the morning. The baby had been sleeping for eight hours and with any luck, he'd sleep for at least two more.

"Oh, so you're a mother," Dace had said a little foolishly, grabbing her forearms so hard that he left fingerprints while he stared into her eyes. "How did this happen?" he'd asked.

"He's yours, you fool," she'd replied a little edgily, which was definitely not the hearts-and-flowers way she'd imagined telling him, "Do the math. He's seven-and-a-half months old."

Slowly he'd sunk down to the floor beside the baby's crib. He'd looked like he might cry, but he didn't. Oh, no, not him. Liza had hovered over the end of the crib too. They both watched the baby. *My lover, our son,* she'd thought. *He's perfect,* her eyes had said. *Because we made him that way.*

The baby hadn't stirred. He was so sweet and dear. He'd been lying on his stomach, with his tiny thumb plugged into his mouth, but he wasn't sucking. Liza's breath had caught. Was he even breathing? Maybe not. Dace must have wondered too because he'd done exactly what she always did. He'd reached between the bars of the crib and held one of his thick fingers in front of the baby's miniscule nose.

"He's breathing," he'd said like he'd just witnessed a miracle.

And then a little later: "Mine?" he'd asked, "is he really mine?" while she repeated, "Yours, yours," over and over and said, "Look at his hair."

"And he's okay?"

"What do you mean, because we're cousins? Of course he's okay!"

"Oh, God," he'd finally said, though he was smiling for now, "little darling, what have you done?" As if it was all her doing!

******

Drive, girl, just drive, she thought in the hippie van with Esther Cohen and her crew. *If you keep stopping for coffee, we'll never get anyplace. And for God's sake, keep your eyes on the road.* If Esther got stopped for some driving infraction or they got into an accident, she didn't know what she'd do. Run, run, with the baby strapped to her chest? She couldn't bear to think about that, so she leaned her head back, put her hand into the baby's car seat, held onto the closest little foot and closed her eyes. *And I have miles to go before I sleep,* she thought.

Esther wanted to talk some more though. "What were you doing back there?" she asked as she drove back onto the highway with one hand on the wheel of the big van and the other hand clutching her coffee cup. "Feeding the kid under that thing? I don't think those border guys even noticed you had a baby. That poncho thing sure is great. If I ever have a kid, I'm going to get one too. I don't think I will though. Have kids, I mean. In the unlikely event that I get married and my husband wants a baby, I'm going to have just one. I'm not Orthodox or anything. Nobody's going to make me have a huge brood. I mean it's alright for the guy, isn't it? It's not their body—gosh, kids sure are a lot of trouble. I'm going to do something with my life, I'm...well, I'm not sure what, but there are a lot of things I want to do."

Esther had several more coffees before she started drinking Coca-Cola in the afternoon. Caffeine fueled her. She was doing most of the driving. She let the boys take over a couple of times, but not Liza, which was just as well. They kept getting lost. That was okay though. The border police knew they were driving to Fort Lauderdale, Florida, so if anybody was following them, Liza and the baby or the SDS boy, it would throw them off-track. They had lots of time to get to Albany anyway. Besides,

Dace would never leave without her or Micah, his only son.

Ah, the price of a cheap ride. Esther talked and talked, but Liza stopped hearing her after a while. She opened her shoulder bag and checked for the stolen letters Joe had given her. The manila envelope was still there. Just in case, she'd made photocopies and stuck them in between the pages of "The Collected Works of Shakespeare" back home. Who the hell would look for them there? Maybe Dace would know what to do with the letters, especially the one Judge Silverton had been stupid enough to write his nephew Father Danby. It worried her though. What if they didn't get the letters into the right hands?

Don't worry, son, Judge Silverton had written. *The Devereux kid played right into our hands. I put him away.*

In the dead of the night, something else had occurred to her too. What if Dace wasn't the only one? What if the judge and his people were still hurting other kids? She knew she had to finish reading the letters, but she couldn't. Whenever she tried, she got sick.

Alex must have been made of tougher stuff though. Or maybe he didn't know the people in the letters, couldn't conceptualize the horror they'd endured, their loss of innocence, their faith in mankind. "What the hell is this?" he demanded a couple of hours later, waving the stolen letters in his hand. While Liza had slept, he must have ransacked her bag. So much for dozing and letting down her guard.

Dammit, she thought. *So you're not so nice after all.*

"Give me those," she said, snatching the letters back after a couple tries and tearing one in the process.

"Listen, guys," Esther said, laying on her horn and narrowly avoiding a motorcyclist who must have been going a bit too slow, "I'm not driving a carload of kids anywhere. I'll have an accident if you keep up this commotion."

"Okay, okay," Alex said. "I've read them all anyway."

Which is more than I've done, Liza thought.

"And so?"

"I don't know where you got this shit. But you can't sit on something like this. I know some people…"

"Like what shit?" Esther asked, cranking her head around to look at Alex. "What's in those letters?"

"Really?" Liza asked sharply. "Who do you know?"

"You need to get them into the hands of a couple of investigative reporters or a radical-type columnist down Toronto way...Like that guy who's been writing those books, ah, fuck, you know the one I mean!"

Although he wasn't from Toronto, Joe immediately came to Liza's mind. "You're not thinking of Joe Armitage, are you?"

"Armitage? Armi*toad*? Are you mixed up with that psych case? I'd think a hell of lot less of you if you were."

Liza stopped looking at Alex and looked out the window instead.

"I'm really not interested in your opinion of me," she said primly adding defensively, "He was in one of my classes, that's all."

"If you're talking about that guy in the Journalism department, I met Joe Armitage once," Esther volunteered. "He's some kind of weird dude."

For God's sake, shut up, Liza thought.

Alex shook his head and pulled his woolen hat so far down over his face that it must have been hard for him to see. He slumped down a bit more and hooked his feet under the front seat. "I know Joe and his family too. A bit too well. My older brother and him got up to some bad stuff when they were in their teens. I was only ten, so I never told anybody. Well, never mind. If you'd grown up in Maitland, you'd know all about Joe too. The guy's nuts and a real suck-up too. For a job like this, you're going to need somebody with a lot more balls, girl. Somebody who doesn't give a fuck about the status quo."

Much you know, Liza thought. She looked over at Alex and reached across the baby's seat to touch his shoulder. Alex was slight, acned and already starting to bald, though he was still under twenty-one. His Adam's apple was the biggest part of him, but he might be more appealing someday and some girl would love him anyway. He was a male. It wouldn't take much. "Like who?" she asked as casually as she could.

Alex looked down at her hand and smiled. "Well, what about that investigative reporter who works for the *Telegram*? Or maybe he's moved up to the *Globe and Mail*. I think his name's Herbert Yonge. 'Yonge' like in the street name. He's always got something contentious to say. You must have read some of his columns, you know his views. His position would be a little to the right of the John Birch Society, but he's not a bad newspaperman."

"The John Birch Society?" Esther asked. "What's that?"

Liza stared at Alex, who just rolled his eyes at Esther's back. In that moment, she would have done anything for him, a skinny boy she didn't even know. It amazed her. Often the stupidest people were smarter than she was. And this boy was probably on drugs too.

She could've kicked herself. Really. What in hell was wrong with her anyway? She should have thought about Herbert Yonge long before this. She had been so focused on Dace's role on the Inmate Police Force during the 1971 Maitland Penitentiary Riot, but the prisoners had formed other committees too.

She knew this because she had attended the trial and researched the riot for months. She had so wanted to convince everybody that Dace wasn't a murderer, that he had protected his six guard hostages and that he had been nowhere near the two prisoners who were tortured and killed.

All for naught, but everything came flooding back to her now, hard and fast. She remembered Herbert Yonge. He had attended the trial, once or twice, but then it all blew up and there was no story, except the one about Judge Silverton that nobody knew enough to tell.

Yes, Herbert Yonge—a prize-winning reporter from a big Toronto daily—had had an inside track to the riot, lucky him. He knew Dace's friend Rick Lowery, so he had gotten on the Citizen's Committee. Imagine that. At the time, Liza would have given anything to get inside the jail and spirit Dace away. Along with some other street people, some lawyers, Yonge had spent three tense days inside Maitland Pen, mediating an end to the prison uprising. He was credited with playing a key role in averting a major bloodbath, another Attica. And like the gentleman he was, he had shared some of this credit with Rick Lowery.

If only Dace had had a special friend, someone to look out for him.

Well, maybe Yonge could still help. Why not? The man had won a prize for his coverage of the riot, so his journalism career was still in full swing. Too bad he hadn't received a commendation for bravery, Liza thought a little sourly. The letters she had would interest him very much, though. He was a smart man and a well-connected man, but best of all, he wasn't Joe Armitage with family ties to Maitland. Yes, Herbert Yonge would know what to do.

The minute she hit Albany and the local YWCA where she holed up for a night, she put the letters into the mail. There was a blue letterbox right there, just outside the YWCA doors. *Don't, don't*, a little voice inside her said. The over analytical part of her worried that she might do more harm than good. She wasn't sure how, but she might.

Chapter 37
Airborne

February 1974

*C*hrist, Dace thought, looking out the cockpit window. *What's happening? Give me solid ground.* He'd done good yesterday, but the weather hadn't cooperated and he'd had to leave a little later today, due to clouds. If he'd had half a brain, he wouldn't have started out at all. He didn't have a flying fuck of a chance in Kallestad's little old Cessna at night. It was hardly bigger than a cat carrier anyway. When he'd first gotten into the cockpit in midmorning, he'd put on his headset as usual, checked the wings, the gauges and other equipment and revved the engine to make sure it was running properly. He'd had a visibility of six or seven miles, not bad, not good, but now all he saw was nothingness. Or eternity, take your pick. Once he loved the darkness, but he had no use for it now. He was a father, or so Liza said. And must be, because she'd never lied to him before or at least not outright. When he'd slowed down a little during some turbulence, night had come rushing in, a black one with absolutely no stars.

Okay and now he'd gone off-course just a bit. It was the first time he'd really flown alone.

He really didn't like the Cessna much. Too small. Somehow it was different without a companion. He'd felt less claustrophobic in the Hole.

He checked the lit gauges on the control panel again, but he was having a hard time believing them. Because his brain kept telling him one thing, while the gauges said something else. *Careful*, he thought, remembering the last thing his instructor had said. "Whatever happens, it's counterintuitive. Trust the needles on the dials, not your head. Your instincts might be lying to you, your mind's eye might be blind." Jesus, what the hell could go wrong, way up here in the sky? There was no traffic, that's for sure.

Except he really wasn't supposed to be flying at night. Not without his full license. Kallestad didn't fly by himself anymore either. Too old. He'd been forced to depend on other people for the last couple of years, to make them come to his place to borrow a plane, so he wanted Dace up to speed fast.

So did Dace. It was now or never. If he didn't fetch Liza and the baby, they'd never get to the monarchs' wintering grounds before the little devils flew back home. No, it would just be a rerun of last year. Only worse. What a balls-up that had been! He didn't know exactly what Savage and his cronies were doing, but he knew this much. Guys like that didn't just disappear. Slime never did. They stuck to things, they really did. And if they couldn't find him because he was way up here in a plane, there was still plenty of illegal activity in Mexico for them to inspect, plenty of criminal law careers to be made, plenty of notoriety to be gained.

Especially if they went over to the dark side and took up drug trafficking themselves. It happened. Cops and criminals, two sides of the same coin. It depended which way the coin flipped, that's all. It always had. The lawmen pursuing him were probably holed up with a couple of Mexican cuties, drinking tequila right now. He sure as hell hoped so.

And what about Kathleen, if she came back? Well, she could take all the fucking credit, if she wanted it so much. He couldn't afford to blow his cover anyway.

He just wanted to show Liza the monarch butterflies, that's all. He remembered them following her on the farm when she had been what — fourteen? Sure, it mattered to scientists like Kathleen — lepidopterists who had been tracking the monarchs' wintering grounds for years — but it didn't matter to him who made the first "official" discovery or how it was recorded in the annals of time.

Or Liza. She wanted to see some butterflies, that's all. So let her.

He had to get her the fuck out of Maitland anyway. She was trapped and dying there. Anybody could see that. The police were hounding her (instead of him!) and her eyes had darkened when she mentioned that reporter guy, Joe Armitage. In sorrow or rage, he couldn't tell. What the hell had the bastard done to her? He really didn't want to know. Because he'd have to do something about it then. She'd said something about Joe almost failing her in a course, but it was more than that. A smart girl like her. They hadn't had much time to talk. Christ, and whose fault was that?

Still, if he had his druthers, he'd have lined up Joe and Savage and Judge Silverton and a couple of others and shot them all dead. Well, maybe that could still be arranged. He could just see the headlines now: *Six bodies found in the river, shot through the head…*

He was just dreaming, though. He wasn't a murderer, no matter what the fucking authorities and the sicko Maitland press said.

So he'd settled — with pleasure — for siicking some of his buddies on Joe instead. The Wolfhounds all knew Joe. He'd sought interviews with several of them for his articles on outlaw bikers and if that didn't pan out, why, he'd just made his "facts" up. Some of the guys were still effing freaking mad. It was something of a miracle that they'd left him alone this long, but they'd been too busy, Dace guessed, drifting back to Maitland at Christmastime if they had family ties and trying to keep out of Judge Silverton's way. Joe would have been labelled a heat-score in prison, a weasel at best. Someone would have stuck a shiv in his back sooner or later. He certainly wouldn't have lasted long. So when Dace said: "Rough him up a little," he knew his friends would be only too happy to oblige. *Whatever happens to the bastard, it's on me,* Dace thought — not that he gave a fuck.

Shit, shit, shit. He was losing altitude. Instinct told him to drop down, but the dials said, go up. He pulled on the hand control a little too sharply and the plane bounced. A warning. *Shut up,* he said to the scream in his head. For a moment, he even thought he heard a slight buzzing on his headset, but he couldn't make out any words.

Ground control to Major Tom… Christ, what was he thinking? He had a plane to fly. He didn't have time for David Bowie now. Besides, his mind had frozen. He couldn't remember another line. He straightened up and widened his eyes. He peered through the window of the aircraft, tempted to pull his headset off and toss it on the cockpit floor. It was bothering him.

He still couldn't see a damn thing. Instinct told him the runway was straight up ahead, but the dials sure as hell didn't. He checked the time again. He'd certainly been flying long enough and if he didn't land soon, he'd run out of gas.

Down, down, the cacophony in his head said.

"Albany," he shouted, as if shouting would help, "do you read me?"

Don't go down and don't overcompensate, the dials all read.

"Albany?" he repeated over and over until his throat got hoarse. When he still heard nothing except the voices in his head, he double-checked his audio. The light indicator was definitely on, but he couldn't hear a thing.

Well, enough of this. *Do or die.* He was going down. Yeah, yeah, as if he had a fucking choice.

But just as he started to ease the throttle, his headphones decided to come to life. "Mexico," a real human voice sputtered. "No clearance, we don't have you on our radar. You can't land. Bring your nose up, right up."

"Jesus, Albany, I gotta get out of here. Let me down."

"Pull up, Mexico, or you'll fry yourself and us on the ground."

Dace thought for less than ten agonizing seconds—if the frantic buzzing in his head could be called thinking—and for the first time in his life, he bowed to another in authority and pulled the little bitch plane up.

And that was that, except for the shaking in his hands and thighs. He'd saved his own life and kept Kallestad's little Cessna intact too. Air control talked him through another twenty minutes or so, then he levelled the plane and flew straight, straight to Albany where the night fog cleared just in time and the lights on the little runway gleamed.

He had to drop the plane more slowly than he liked too. So far, everything he'd done that day had gone against his grain.

"Our father who art in heaven," he prayed, the only prayer he knew, but there wasn't any need. The wheels came out just in time and bumped along the ground.

Dace unbuckled his seatbelt and rubbed his eyes. It was dark inside the cockpit, though the dials were still lit. He looked around. He touched his upper arms and his face, unstrapped his seatbelt and got to his feet. *I'm alive,* he thought. *I'm alive.* A part of him still wasn't entirely convinced — that the plane was in one piece and so was he. But the air traffic controller had said so. He must be right. He'd done it, he'd done it, he really had.

Everything else was going to be okay too. He staggered out of the plane, blinded by the runway lights, fully expecting to find Liza on the tarmac.

Except she wasn't there.

He stood there like a fool, a returning hero, with nobody to welcome him home. He didn't care about getting his license anymore. All he wanted was Liza. *All this for nothing,* he thought, both his heart and stomach plummeting again. He'd delivered Kallestad's package, that's all. The damn box was still in the passenger seat. Okay and he'd gotten in some solo flight hours, but what the hell did it matter if Liza wasn't here? There were a couple of controllers to his left, but not her, not her, not her!

And then he heard his name. Somebody — Liza! — was standing by an aluminum- sided building, alone, with a dark bulge strapped to her chest. Well, no wonder he hadn't recognized her. Who the hell would? She looked huge, an immoveable part of the landscape, the kind of woman who didn't care about monarch butterflies , who would never crave anything except the comforts of home. He'd take her anyway. As long as she still wanted him, after the mess he'd made of things. She had the baby in one of those carrier things, he supposed. Of course. He'd almost forgotten about the kid. She was part of a package now.

"Dace," she called, jumping up and down and finally starting to wave her arms, "Over here!"

He started walking toward the building. Briefly, it occurred to him that the police might be holding his woman and his baby like bait, but he didn't care. He had to get to Liza and the baby. The baby… Yeah, Micah, Micah, that was his name. Micah James Devereux. Well, maybe. For the kid's sake, he'd have to call him Mike or something less girly.

Time enough to sort out his name, he was only a baby. The three of them would rest a little in the hangar while the plane got refueled and then get the hell out.

The man came out of the building, just as Dace reached Liza. She'd been holding out her arms to him, but she dropped them and wrapped them around the baby instead. Her smile faltered and she took a step backwards.

Dace tensed his fists, fully prepared to knock the guy out of his way.

"We need to see your license," the man said, but he had an obsequious smile on his face, so maybe it was okay.

"It's in the cockpit," Dace said, relaxing his hands a little. "Just get the hell out of my way."

He must have looked alarming because the man practically leapt away. He didn't argue either. "Well, son, it's been a while since you saw her, I guess," he said.

Dace and the man both moved in the same direction, almost colliding. They tried again. "Yeah," Dace said, finally circumventing the man, the bulging baby and burying his face in Liza's hair while she grabbed his with both hands.

She lifted his head and stared at him with her hands still in his hair. She wouldn't or couldn't let go. She must have been travelling for a couple of days with a seven-month-old baby, but she looked radiant. She had cried a lot the last time he saw her, but there wasn't a single tear on her face today. Dace saw that she was a woman now, not a girl and something in him grieved because he hadn't been there to witness her transformation. So many lost years and it was his own damn fault. Well, he'd changed too. They'd both lost something, but they'd made a family too. Or she had. The family she'd always wanted, he realized, when he'd thought she just wanted butterflies and books and him.

God help him, what if she wanted the kid more than him? He looked at the baby still strapped to her. His son, he kept reminding himself. It was okay. The kid was just hanging on her, a large, sleeping doll, no trouble at all.

The man had made it into the cockpit. After witnessing his reception, the rest of the grounds crew hung back too. "Mexico," the air traffic controller came over just long enough to say, "that landing was a little rough, but for a newbie, you did swell."

Liza's eyes swept the small airport, giving the other people there the smallest glance. She was always on the lookout, just like him. She couldn't afford to stop now. She rocked a little and patted the back of the baby. "I think the guys here are okay," she whispered, jutting her face out over the baby's head to brush her warm lips against Dace's ear. "But let's go to Mexico before the real bad guys get here—the ones who are after you and the Maitland police—the ones who always want me." And Joe Armitage, she thought ruefully, though she didn't say this out loud or Dace would kill the bastard for sure. "I want to go someplace warm. Oh, Dace, I've been so scared, but I'm not now. Nobody knows where we are, right? We're safe. They can't get us now."

Dace leaned in a little and kissed the top of his sleeping son's head, though he would have preferred to kiss her, but he didn't say anything. He couldn't. *Maybe, little darling*, he thought, still high on her presence and adrenaline and the fact that he had just finished his first solo flight. *Maybe. All I know for sure is that we gotta get the hell out of here.*

They'd have to spend the night in Albany though. Even if they let him, no way he'd get back in that little hellhole of a plane right now.

Chapter 38
Mexican Matrimony

Near Cuitzeo, Mexico, February 1974

The heavy scent of dew soaked flowers, wafting from the rear garden woke Liza up, an hour later than the sun. She could smell the burritos the housekeeper was cooking for breakfast. It was already hot, but she thrived in the heat. She had come alive down here in Mexico, or maybe it was just that the old anxious, information hunting student part of her was hibernating. Naked and ready under the thin cotton sheet, she opened her eyes and quickly closed them again. Something buzzed in the corner of the high ceiling bedroom, but there was also an iguana on the little rattan bedside table, watching her and her sleeping son. She shivered. The prehistoric looking creature had the most dispassionate eyes.

Baby Micah lie curled up beside her with a heavy, block-like cushion and her arms to prevent him from slipping away and hitting the sloping, hardwood floor. She had been too lazy to put him back into the antique cradle Dace had found. On her right side, the space was empty.

Of course. Where the hell is Dace, she wondered, *off on a flight again? Not with Jon Kallestad, that's for sure.* Through the billowing lace curtains on the open casement window, she could hear the old man bellowing at one of his employees. She liked him, even if he was a bit curmudgeonly, with his two missing front teeth and the veiny, bulbous nose of a drinking man. Kallestad's red-tile roofed adobe house practically sat on a small airstrip, part of the business. It almost made her feel like she was back in Toronto with her father in one of his moods or with her Gran in Dublin giving the dustmen their dues.

Please don't wake up Micah, she thought. The baby had heat rash all over his little chest and arms and had fussed half the night. She had eventually got him to sleep after giving him a sponge bath in a ceramic washbasin. She reveled in the sultry Mexican heat, but it didn't suit her son at all. She felt like getting up, putting on a thin silken wrap and running down to the lake, giving Kallestad's Mexican workers a good show. She'd plunge into the aqua water, her skin would glisten, her heavy breasts would float. She'd dive deeper into the water, with her hair streaming out behind her, her only anchor to the past. Dace could join her. They'd forget everything and everybody. They'd stay on the shore all day.

The housekeeper could speak English when she wanted to. "Senorita," she called from the kitchen, "coma—eat!"

Right. She was going to have to keep Micah in the shade, preferably under one of Kallestad's big wooden ceiling fans. Who the hell did she think she was anyway—Ava Gardner in *Night of the Iguana,* dancing in the waves? When she opened her eyes again, the iguana was gone. She stared at a little wall calendar instead.

Time was running out, both for the monarch butterflies programmed to start flying back to Canada in mid-March and Liza who should have been back in class yesterday. "Mariposa monarca," the Mexicans said. The monarchs were still dozing and Liza hadn't really missed much school yet, but she was afraid she'd never get back. Or maybe that she'd never want to go back, which would be a real shame after all the time she'd put into her degree. Never want to because it was so warm way down here in Mexico and Dace was here too, safe from the penitentiary and the police and whoever or whatever was after him.

And safe from the bikers too, come to think of it. As far as Liza was concerned, they had been the real problem, the reason he'd ended up back in jail. Because he couldn't quit the Life. Strange that the Wolfhounds hadn't found him yet, but then they were such creatures of habit. They never strayed far from their hometowns. Well, the bikers she'd known didn't anyway. In one of his newspaper articles, Joe Armitage had hinted that the gang had ties to the Mafia, but maybe they didn't and they were nervous about getting mixed in the drug cartels. Or maybe they were just a bunch of somnolent insects, stunned by the crazy Canadian cold.

She still had a couple of worries though. Because Dace was never around and she wondered if this was a harbinger of things to come. In a matter of days, they had become like an old married couple for God's sake. Sure, she wanted to grow old with him, but not like this. He had taken to slipping into her bed for a few hours, that's all. Deep down, though she didn't even admit it to herself, she was afraid he had stopped loving her.

Doing her best not to shake the bed, she got up and looked in a tarnished old mirror on the whitewashed wall, checking for lines in her face. There were none, but she still looked a fright. She lifted her hair with her hands and then her milk-filled breasts. It didn't help. My God, she felt and looked like some kind of hausfrau, a concubine, or worse.

Because Dace had all these other relationships. Because he was a man, a real man, yeah, yeah, right. She never thought about them when she was with him—his other women—but when she was alone, she sure did. It drove her crazy. She felt kind of bruised, like he had beaten her with his bare hands. How could he? Although she had been previously convinced she would never play second fiddle, she wasn't so sure now. She loved him too much. And she was so far from home, trapped with a child—no, that wasn't right. She'd had Micah by herself and if she had to, she could figure out to raise him by herself too. She didn't want to, that's all.

Dace hadn't dared take her to Grandpa Gomez's place—because of Thalia—so he'd taken her and baby Micah to his employer Kallestad's place instead. When it came right down to it, he didn't have that much nerve, he'd said with just the smallest hint of a smirk.

Yeah, right, Liza thought.

The Gomez family had already done a lot for him, he'd added. Thalia had shown him where the butterflies roosted and her grandfather had taken him in.

As if I haven't done a lot for you too, Liza thought.

"So get rid of Thalia," she'd said, taken aback by her own ruthlessness and irritated to find herself feeling even slightly sorry for a stranger—a disadvantaged Mexican woman who'd never had half her chances. Ah, but she'd probably had a loving family though. This Thalia woman didn't need Dace and he didn't need her. "Tell her you have a child with me. She obviously doesn't really want to have a husband or a family or she'd have one by now." *God, just listen to me*, she'd thought. *I could have married Mel, had the same problems and been safe at home.*

Dace had taken her in his arms and stroked her hair, but he'd looked a little discomfited too. Not about his relationship with Thalia, that's for sure. It was about the baby. It always was. Sometimes it seemed to Liza that he wasn't real anxious to claim his son. Dace of all people, with his strong arms and his wild heart. She couldn't believe it.

Surely he didn't care what people thought about him having a relationship with a cousin or having a child with her too. Who cared who knew, especially down here in Mexico where it seemed like anything went? If you were a white person, that is. Americans and Canadians came here and did exactly what they pleased.

As for the Mexicans, they probably married their cousins all the time. Lots of people used to marry their cousins, even in the States. Opinions had changed about first cousin relationships in the past fifty years, but it hadn't always been this way.

My God, it wasn't even like Dace was a conservative person, one who lived on the right side of the law. After all that had happened, it was silly, bourgeois, to be bound by blind, stupid convention. And all that stuff about heredity. "You're reckless just like him," she remembered Mel saying. Still, if you inherited double the bad things from your parents just because they were cousins, you could inherit double the good things too. Besides, the risk was far from double. The obstetrician back in Maitland had said so.

She'd tried to talk to Dace about the baby, but he wouldn't. Or couldn't. Not even when he drank. "Let's talk about Micah," she'd tried just last night while they were outside in the yard, dancing in the moonlight. "Look how he smiles at you." Whatever happened, she'd never let him get away with denying his own child.

"Liza," he'd begged off, swirling her away with one hand, "the kid's only seven months old. I don't have to worry about my relationship with him yet." There had always been a lot he couldn't talk about—what had happened to him in school and later in prison—and he wasn't about to start now. Talking had never done him any good and truthfully, it hadn't done her much good either.

He'd had to talk about Thalia though. She was practically right there, over on the next ranch, visiting her Abuelo Gomez all the time. *More than usual*, Liza thought whenever she caught sight of Thalia's dark hair, the flash of her black eyes and heard her laughter too.

"Maybe," Dace had shrugged with regard to Thalia's marital status. "She's a beautiful woman. She's had plenty of chances."

Liza had seen red and probably would have said something more, but then Kallestad had started shouting again, at his housekeeper this time. Kallestad had a Mexican housekeeper with whom Liza suspected he slept (at his age!), but he had been surprisingly pleased to have another young woman, even an encumbered one around.

"You sure know how to pick them," the old chauvinist had said to Dace when he'd arrived at the ranch with Liza. "May I?" he'd asked, reaching out and twisting a dark lock of Liza's hair around his finger. "You really have quite the head of hair, Miss—for a white girl, anyway. So you're what—Dace's family, his wife…?"

"I'm his family—his cousin actually," Liza had said, embarrassed that Dace hadn't prepared the man for her arrival at all. "And we're…the baby and I don't have to stay here, we could…" *Yeah, what,* she had thought, stopping in mid speech. Christ, this was embarrassing. And when Dace still didn't say anything—which was just like him!—and baby Micah twisted his head out of the carrier on her chest to see who was talking, she'd added lamely, "And this is baby Micah."

"Ah, c'mon," Kallestad had said to Dace who was already headed for the kitchen. "This must be your kid. He's the spitting image of you."

"Yeah, well," Dace had said, "Liza and I are first cousins. People always said we looked alike. Maybe he takes after her."

For Kallestad, Baby Micah was pure entertainment. To hear the baby giggling in the old man's face, life was just one big joke, a long butterfly hunt.

"My grandchildren are all up north. They never come around. The kids all went over to their mother's side," Kallestad had said while making faces at the baby and plying him with crackers. He'd tried popping chocolates into the child's mouth too, but Liza had intervened. Kallestad's housekeeper wasn't much better. Left to her own devices, the woman would have nourished Micah on pure nectar, like a fat little honey bee.

At night in bed at Kallestad's ranch, while the baby slept and Dace was flying a plane to God knows where and she couldn't do anything else but fret, Liza thought about these things:

How nobody would ever find Dace here as long as he did everything right.

How the past might really be the past.

How their own child turned out perfect no matter what a bunch of doomsayers said.

How Dace would surely come around and see that too.

How he'd never need another woman again.

How lucky they were.

How monarchs didn't really migrate en masse but flitted off singly over the Great Lakes on their epic journey.

How a creature who was the weight of a postage stamp could possibly fly all the way from Canada to Mexico.

How monarch butterflies tasted with their feet.

Sometimes she thought she could even hear them, the whirring of their wings, the sound their soft bodies made as they fluttered to the forest ground.

In the cool of the night, even with the man she loved beside her, she hardly slept. She hadn't for years. She wondered if she ever would again. *There's something wrong with me*, she thought. *Here I am in Mexico with Dace, but I want more. I always want more.* She wanted, she had to see the monarch butterflies' wintering grounds soon. Thank God Dace did too.

Chapter 39
Mariposa Monarca

Two more days passed. Dace had been gone all night, again, but then she heard him on the stairs. She heard everything in the house, the crickets in the walls, Kallestad's snores from his leather living room couch, one of his Mexican boys or the little woman he kept in the kitchen firing up a huge woodstove. It worried her. Everything did. *I'm getting just like Millie*, she thought. Dace came into the room, but he didn't take off his clothes. It was just before dawn.

"Liza," he said, a dark shape looming over the bed.

You used to call me "Little Darling," she thought, *but now it's just Liza, if that.* She stayed in the center of the bed, clutching a pillow to her chest instead of him, reluctant for once. The baby was in his cradle. She had taken over the whole damn "matrimonial bed." Well, why not? Dace slept so little in the bed and she loved the name.

"Do you want two rooms or do you want the matrimonial bed?" Kallestad's puzzled housekeeper had asked when they first came into the kitchen, her head swiveling from Dace to Liza. She'd had to ask. Dace hadn't told her anything either. He hadn't prepared anybody at the ranch—just left them to figure out exactly what his real relationship with Liza was.

"For God's sake, it's none of their business," he'd snapped at Liza in private. Liza had still felt embarrassed. She should have spoken up herself, but she hadn't.

Please don't ask me, she'd thought instead, feeling like a simpering little fool. Kallestad's staff had soon figured things out, but for a day or so, they weren't sure if she was Dace's sister, his cousin or his wife, just that she had the same last name as him and needed a place to stay.

Like I'm a slut he's dragged home and it doesn't matter, Liza had thought, a little irritated.

Dace stripped the sheet from her body now. The muscles in his upper arms rippled. Liza brought her knees up to her chest. Out of the corner of her eye, she saw the front of his jeans swelling. Her own groin stirred too. She felt like reaching up to him, but she didn't.

Dace had something else in mind anyway, something more pressing than making love to her. "Let's go," he said. "God, little darling, all you do is sleep and feed Micah. Kallestad doesn't need me today. If we get a head start, we can be up on the mountaintop by noon. We can take the jeep over to the base. The housekeeper has already packed up some supplies."

Liza smiled. She was in Mexico! She still couldn't believe she was here. *Ah*, she thought, *that's better*. Her heart speeded up too, though she still felt disoriented and confused. Maybe if she'd had more than four hours' sleep, but everything always happened so fast with Dace. She couldn't keep up with him. She just couldn't. He was way more spontaneous than her. Always had been. "And always will be, if he lives that long," a yapping little voice inside her nagged. What if that horrid guard Savage was still looking for him? Or God help him, the American feds or the Royal Canadian Mounted Police?

She uncoiled her legs and rolled away from him, burying her face in the closest feather pillow. He must be talking about the monarchs' wintering ground. Could they really get there in just one day? She doubted it. Especially with the baby. Now that she had the opportunity, a part of her just wanted to stay here and make wild, passionate love instead (or even the ordinary kind.)

"Get up," Dace said, reaching over and smacking her several times on her exposed rear.

"Stop it," Liza said, moving quickly out of his reach, "Those aren't exactly love pats, you know."

He leaned further over the bed and raised his hand again.

"I'm moving," she said, sitting up and swinging her legs over the edge of the bed, but not before he left his handprint on her thigh. Involuntarily, she opened her legs and her mouth. Oh, God, she wanted him. She always did.

He tried to kiss her but she moved her mouth away.

She didn't want to be disappointed, that's all. She and Dace were just amateurs—amateur butterfly enthusiasts, or at least she was. He knew way more about monarchs than she did right now. But the sight of a monarch butterfly had always lifted her heart and the more she'd found out about them, the more she'd wanted to know. Wanting wasn't the same as getting though. They might not be able to find the wintering grounds. A real butterfly scientist, a lepidopterist (she forgot his name) had searched for their southern sanctuary, their winter roosting grounds for years.

So far, Dace only had Thalia's word about where the monarchs wintered. Thalia was probably just a better storyteller than her. A Scheherazade, a liar, spinning tales to keep Dace enthralled. Liza wished to hell she'd never heard of her, but Dace had told her about Thalia while they were flying from Albany to the ranch. Spoiled things a bit, although he'd had to, she supposed. God knows he usually didn't volunteer much, even to her. A little more reluctantly and with just a bit of prodding, he'd told her about Summer and Kathleen too.

"You and me—I don't want us to have any more secrets," he'd said, the only time he'd ever reproached her. "You should have told me about Micah when I left. You must have known you were pregnant. It makes it kind of hard to feel like he's really mine. You can see that, can't you?"

They'd had a fight about that too. They kept stopping to refuel the plane and Liza had thought the flight would never end. "I couldn't tell you," she'd said, "or you might have stayed behind." *And got sent back to jail.*

Liza lowered her feet until she felt the cool floor. *Get moving*, she told herself now. *This is what you wanted, the reason you came here—well, that and Dace of course.*

Besides, she had been dying up in Canada with all the snow and Joe, especially that sick Joe hanging around. No time to dither. If the scientists were right about the Mexican monarchs, they were due to fly back to Canada real soon. And if they didn't get moving soon, Kallestad might change his mind. The old man was always after Dace to fix this or that on one of his ancient planes.

Dace tried again. He brushed her hair out of her eyes, took her face in his hands and kissed her mouth.

She almost kissed him back, but just then the baby stirred, like he knew something was going on and didn't want them to have any fun. "Stop touching me or we'll never get anyplace," she said crossly. "And please, please don't wake up Micah or you'll have to look after him."

Dace dropped his hands to his sides, his fists clenched. If they hadn't been going on this expedition, he would have taken her anyway and she would have let him. "Let me in," he always said.

"Yeah, right," he said. "The only person that kid wants is you."

****

When Dace and Liza went down to the kitchen to grab a burrito and drink some strong Mexican coffee, Kallestad's housekeeper immediately offered to look after Micah while they went on their outing.

"You don't take bebé in jeep," she said in English for Liza's sake. The woman was in her fifties, warmhearted and perfectly capable. What was with these housekeepers anyway? Uncle Norm and Kallestad were lucky to have somebody to clean up and cook for them, that's for sure.

Liza's skin crawled and her stomach churned as she watched the housekeeper fuss around the practically stone age kitchen. For one thing, she hardly knew the woman. She might run off with her son. Well, she might. Micah was a healthy white baby boy and, even with his dark Devereux eyes and hair, probably worth a fortune. And the housekeeper was childless too. She might try to keep him. Micah was beyond adorable.

But the woman was right. They really shouldn't take Micah out in the jeep, especially on such a long ride.

Incredibly, it was Dace who objected. "Liza's still feeding the kid," he pointed out. "He needs her milk."

On a day like this, Liza and Dace went back upstairs to argue, as if they had the time. She couldn't believe it.

"What do you know about babies?" she asked, crosser still that he'd question her judgment when so far she'd made every decision about Micah alone. "He's seven months old. He can get by without my milk for

290

one day—the housekeeper can boil some goat's milk! Anyway, he can't take the heat."

"I know almost as much as you," Dace said, looking down at his sleeping son in the cradle and reluctantly allowing the baby to grab his finger, "You've only had him for seven months, plus I told you about living with Summer and her son…"

"Yeah, sure, that's some kind of firsthand experience," Liza said sarcastically, snapping her bra into place before she pulled a soft cotton T-shirt over her head and began the five minute struggle into her jeans.

Dace laughed. "Do you want some help pulling those up?" he asked, delivering another smart slap on her rump. "Are you planning to lose some more weight or what?"

"I've already lost ninety-nine percent of my pregnancy weight, you jerk."

Dace kissed the back of her neck. "Little darling, I'd love you even if you weighed a ton."

******

Oh, sure, she thought. It really bugged her that he could have a child without having to sacrifice his whole body. Not that Micah wasn't wonderful and that if she got the chance, she'd do the same thing all over again. Christ, she was a masochist through and through. It just bugged her, that's all, that Dace was getting off scot-free as usual—which was really ridiculous when his reputation was in shreds, he had a gang of Canadians chasing him and complete strangers would turn him in for a dime.

In the end, they took Micah with them, securing him behind Dace so Liza could put her hand between the front seats and hold onto his fat little foot. *Goddamn it*, Liza thought, *you always get your own way. There's no point in arguing with you at all.*

Having failed to appeal to Liza's maternal instincts, the housekeeper had expostulated and pulled on her rosary instead.

"What was she saying back there?" Liza asked Dace who seemed to have become amazingly proficient in Spanish in just over a year.

"Ah, just that you're—I mean, that we're—we're reckless or something. And 'estúpido.' C'mon, you know that that means."

It was cool enough while they were driving, Liza supposed and Dace had found an old infant car seat, God knows where. In the end, the fact that Dace wanted the baby along was what really sold her. Grumbling just a little for effect, she'd packed some diapers and grabbed the baby carrier too.

"Okay, smartass," Liza asked him now, "so how are we going to climb a mountain with a baby and some supplies—we *do* have some supplies, right?"

Dace looked at her like she was crazy. What? Him go someplace unprepared? "It's all taken care of," he promised after a moment or so.

They drove for just over two hours, arguing most of the way, she couldn't have said about what, though there was plenty of talk about the poor choices somebody had made.

"If you let me love you this morning, we wouldn't be arguing this way," Dace shouted over the wind.

"For God's sake, I can't spend all my time on my back servicing you…"

"How about on your front, then?" he asked. "You'll do what I tell you tonight."

"Or what?"

They never used to argue before. What was wrong with them? They were worse than an old married couple. It was the tension, Liza supposed, finally settling back in the front passenger seat and letting the hot wind tear through her hair. She loved, loved the climate. Her whole life had been leading up to this. Screw school. She was never going home. She had more important things to do. What if they didn't find a Canadian colony of monarchs, though? Or what if somebody had ratted out Dace and this was just some kind of trap? What if…

She slept for the last twenty minutes of the drive. In his car seat, the baby slept too, his head wobbling helplessly on his chest. When she woke up, her own head was against Dace's strong shoulder and he was holding her hand. She had a hard time lifting up her head, but he helped her.

"My God, you're so sweet," he said, caressing her cheek.

In her sleep, she'd let go of Micah's soft foot.

******

They parked at the bottom of a hill, or maybe it was a mountain. They had passed a bunch of dilapidated, tin-roofed shacks and now there were so many coniferous trees around that Liza couldn't tell. She couldn't see any butterflies either. From what Dace had said, she'd expected to see some monarch messengers the minute she got here. She looked around, while she sat in the jeep feeding the baby. She felt drained. She had absolutely no energy left for this adventure, not a speck. How the heck had Dace even recognized the place? He hadn't been here for almost a year, plus he was the kind of person who was always getting lost. They both were.

There were no other cars, just an open truck dropping off some woodworkers, or at least that's what they looked like. There were lots of burros too or donkeys or whatever and most of the woodcutters had their own hatchets. Well, this wasn't a holiday spot, so it made sense.

After laying a freshly changed Micah down on the driver's seat and watching him gurgle, Liza strapped on the cloth carrier and maneuvered him into it as slowly as she could. It galled her. Here she was about to embark on a wonderful adventure and she was dragging her feet. Dace wasn't having any of it though. While she had been nursing and changing the baby, he'd walked miles around the jeep. Now he grabbed their backpack out of the backseat with one arm and pulled her and Micah out with the other. When they started off, it was just after nine a.m.

"For God's sake, just leave us in the car," she almost said. It felt strange not to lock up a car, but there wasn't any point.

Just before they all disappeared up the mountain, a man separated himself from the other workers and came back towards them. He was leading a saddled burro. He passed the animal's lead to Dace, took one look at Liza's face and hurried away.

First Liza looked at the burro and then she looked at Dace, who was smiling from ear to ear like he'd just accomplished a miracle. He reached out, patted the burro's head and raised his eyebrows at her.

"No way, José," she said, backing up and tightening her arms around Micah in his carrier, "I'm not getting up on that thing with *our* baby. It's not safe."

"Just try it," Dace coaxed. "There's no other way up. You can't carry him all the way up the mountain…"

Imitating him, Liza raised her eyebrows too. "So what's wrong with *you*? You're the one who wanted to bring him!"

Still holding the reins, Dace patted the burro's saddle with his free hand. "Try it," he said again, a little irritably. "I'm not gonna carry the kid in that thing, like some kind of squaw."

Liza looked back longingly towards the jeep. "You never hold him," she complained.

"Are you trying to spoil this or what? There's no road up the mountain, little darling, just a couple of ancient paths," he said.

Liza's stomach turned over. Dace was speaking to her calmly, but she knew she was trying his patience and that he'd get his own way in the end. He always did. She felt sick with anxiety, just sick, a helpless, browbeaten wife. If she'd had the car keys, she would have left him and let him find his own way back to the ranch. She didn't though.

"I hate you," she said, finally allowing him to ease her and the baby up onto the saddle. It hurt a bit between her legs. In spite of Dace's frequent absences, they'd had a lot of sex in the last few days. *If you swat my rear again*, I'll kill you, she thought.

"Well, I love you," Dace said but she ignored him and his annoying grin too.

From her precarious perch, she looked down dubiously at the animal's pointed ears and thought fleetingly about the first time Dace had put her on a motorcycle alone. He had pushed her that time too, really pushed her. Sure, he'd taught her how to ride the Honda, but not before he'd almost killed her.

She'd lived, though. She loved riding that bike, in fact, but this— this was ridiculous.

The burro started moving, a slow amble, with Dace walking alongside them. She had to let go of the baby so she could hold onto the saddle. Micah was perfectly safe in the baby carrier—as long as she was, that is, as long as she could keep her seat on this burro. She hoped the animal had a mind of its own and knew what to do because she sure as hell didn't.

She tried to steel herself, but the minute the burro picked up a little speed, her legs started to shake. She gripped the saddle even tighter. "What if this thing stumbles and we both go flying?" she asked.

"He won't," Dace said, reaching and stroking her trembling left leg, "I bet he's been up this trail a thousand times before and besides, I'll catch you if you fall."

Sure, just like you did all those other times before, Liza thought. "Yeah, right," she said aloud, stretching out a tentative hand and scratching her ride's ears. "Can you tie us on or something? This is crazy, crazy, you know me, I won't even take the baby in a car without a car seat."

"Okay, so you're a bit obsessed, so what?" Dace said, taking hold of the rope that was tied to the burro's lead and pulling them along, "Everything's going to be alright."

You used to say that to me all the time, Liza thought mutinously, *and it sure as hell wasn't*. "You're going way too fast," she said, but Dace wasn't listening. He was too busy looking up ahead. The burro slipped a little, so she looked down. *Oh, no*, she thought, almost vomiting. It couldn't be, but it was.

"Dace," she stuttered, while the burro tried to sidestep what looked like thousands of butterflies, thick on the ground. Dead monarchs, not just sleeping ones. What on earth had happened to them and why were there so many? At first, Dace just kept pulling her along on the lead, but when she repeated his name with a sob in her throat, he finally heard her and stopped.

"Look," she said, pointing to a branch on the path. Two inches in diameter, it had broken off a tree under the weight of so many butterflies. "They're all dead."

From the look on his face, Liza knew that even Dace was taken aback, but he didn't let on. "Oh, Liza, little darling, it's okay," he said, "they don't all make it. But have a little faith. With this many dead ones, there's bound to be lots of live ones up ahead. We have to find their colony, that's all. Or maybe there's several colonies — who knows?"

Liza took a deep breath and shut her mouth with a snap. *Yeah, sure, Mr. Know-it-All*, she thought. And that was it. She stopped thinking. For the next little while, she didn't do anything except hang onto to her seat. It took all her strength just to keep going. She was afraid for both her baby and herself, afraid for their lives.

But forty-five minutes later when they spotted the first live monarch butterfly, then two more, then tens, then hundreds, all that changed. In a matter of just a few minutes, the air became so thick with butterflies that they could hardly see. Was this the nucleus of a colony? It must be. There couldn't be anymore monarchs in one spot than this. They didn't say much because they couldn't.

Eventually, they stopped on a plateau just to watch and listen to the monarchs and filled their lungs with more of the good, clean mountain air. Liza took Micah out of the carrier to change and feed him again. He wasn't acting hungry, but almost three hours had passed since they'd started up the trail. She still felt a bit worried about him, but he was feeding and breathing at the same time, so he must be doing okay.

Dace didn't look like he was doing so good though, which was really strange because he'd always been so strong. She shivered a little, in spite of the heat. She'd liked the fact that they were alone at first, but she didn't now. She hadn't even seen a woodcutter since they were down at the base. They must have taken another path, not that they were likely to be of much use. When Dace had first told her about visiting the mountain with Thalia, he had talked about seeing lots of animals, but they hadn't seen any today. It was so hot—maybe they had gone into hiding. She looked at Dace who was sweating profusely and her heart dropped. She and Micah were fine, but they weren't really exerting themselves. The poor burro was doing all the work, though he was used to it, she supposed.

Don't you dare die on me, Dace Devereux she thought, which was just ridiculous. A strong young man wouldn't drop dead on a simple mountain climb. He was strong, way stronger than her. He had to be.

"It's better to take it slow," Dace said when he finally sucked in enough air to speak. "That's what Thalia—what I did last time and it worked."

It enraged Liza just to hear Thalia's name, but she didn't let on. Dace could drop all the girlfriends' names he wanted to, Thalia was gone. Gone like Summer—though it was kind of a pretty name. Maybe Dace and her would have a daughter someday and call her Summer too. Liza couldn't believe her luck. Yes, it was all very convenient, but that's how things happened sometimes. Thalia had just up and left to go north with another man, God bless her. She'd gone to Texas or something.

"In a bit of a snit," Kallestad had come home just yesterday and announced this news, though it wasn't the first time. She hadn't even seen Liza and the baby, just heard they were there.

It didn't matter anyway. Because Dace loved her and only her. Sure, he might have a lapse if Liza wasn't around, but he was loyal to a fault. Look at his loyalty to the Wolfhounds and those guys in prison, for Jesus's sake.

Liza got back on the burro with the baby still in the carrier. It was easier this time. Her groin felt good against the saddle, kind of sexy, the way it did on a bike. They left the little plateau and went up even higher. Dace shifted his backpack and slid his hand between her legs. His fingertips brushed her clitoris. He said something about Thalia again, about her childhood experience.

"Thalia, Thalia," Liza muttered, pushing his hand away.

"She helped me find the butterflies," he reminded her gently, putting his hand right back.

She, Liza thought, sitting up a little straighter, she and that scientist girl Kathleen. Any moment and he'd invoke her name too. If only he'd stop talking about them.

Liza took another deep breath and sucked it right down into her lungs. It felt so good and Dace's hand felt so good, that she took two more. She liked it up here on the burro, looking down at him. He was a head taller than her, so she didn't get much chance. "It doesn't matter," she said and it didn't. She was in paradise with him, she had him to herself and they had the rest of the day. She felt like Eve must have, opening her eyes in a newly created world. And once she started smiling, she couldn't stop. Her cheeks hurt a little. Maybe she was getting high on the thin mountain air. They kept on going, struggling up the mountainside, with Dace still doing most of the struggling, not her.

He was smiling too, almost relaxed and even a bit reverent for once, looking up at the brilliant sky. She had never seen him this way before. He looked like he was in the Sistine Chapel, at peace with the world, a man who had never spent time in prison, a man with no challenges and nothing to atone. There were no demons here. It made her love him even more, it made her love the whole world. Dace was right. Everything was going to be alright.

She closed her eyes for an instance and almost fell asleep on the burro.

They were definitely on the right track, she thought when she opened her eyes again. There were just too many monarch butterflies around for this to be the wrong place. *Forgive those who trespass against us. Forget the children and the little boy Dace was, all those children who were done wrong.* Nothing evil existed up here.

They stopped again. This time, the butterflies came to them and settled down, resting lightly on their heads, their arms, their backs, their knees, the top of Micah's sweet covered head. At first the baby had seemed a little dazed, but he perked up now. These butterflies were monarchs for sure—a little tattered in some cases, but still large and magnificently orange and black. Micah grabbed at the butterflies and missed, but Liza and Dace kept their hands loose at their sides, the unspoken assumption that they would do no harm. Up here, they didn't even touch each other. For now, nothing else mattered, except these beautiful creatures.

Incredibly, it got even better. Even with all the butterflies they had seen coming up the trail, nothing prepared them for what happened next. At a sudden high summit that spilled into a dry streambed, more monarchs cascaded through the air.

The sight took Liza's breath away. The baby, who had begun to fuss a little on this last leg of their trip, went quiet and stared. *It was the nucleus of the colony for sure and this streambed was their superhighway*, Liza thought. *What else could it be?*

Gazing around at the greatest art in the world, Liza thought that Michelangelo himself could never have painted such a picture. Within seconds, hundreds, then thousands of butterflies had become millions.

Yes, millions, way more than she could count anyway. She looked around her, determined not to forget a single thing. *Remember forever*, she thought. Up ahead, the piney trees and the ground were all covered in orange. Sunrays penetrated the forest canopy and the mountain glowed in a brilliant orange light. Liza gave up even trying to speak. She was awestruck, tongue-tied and it looked like Dace was too.

"Holy," Dace started to say, but even when he caught his breath, he couldn't finish his sentence. "Holy," he tried again and it was.

And then something else happened. They heard a noise, the kind of sound that only millions of butterflies could make with their wings. They only heard it after they stopped talking though—a constant whir, the way they sounded like falling leaves as they fluttered to the ground.

Neither one of them noticed the sun sinking in the sky.

******

"Dace," Liza said a little later when the monarchs got too cold to fly and clung to the trees, "it's getting dark. It took us hours just to get up here."

"Yeah, I know, it took a lot longer than I thought it would."

Leaning over and putting her hand on his shoulder, she slid down from the burro. She wanted to fall into his arms, but she couldn't. The baby had started fussing again, eager to get out of his carrier, now that they had stopped moving. She undid the snaps of the carrier at her shoulders and started to ease Micah off her chest. "It's spectacular, but we never should have brought the baby," she said.

"Liza, Liza," Dace said, sounding a hell of lot more annoyed than concerned. "Just listen to yourself—one minute, you're overjoyed and the next you're fussing like a mother hen!"

"But Micah's too young—he won't remember any of this! It was crazy, just crazy to drag him all the way up here! And how are we going to find our way down the mountain in the dark?"

Dace smiled and grasped the nape of her neck. She let him massage the muscles with one of his large hands, even though she suspected he had come perilously close to snapping it once or twice that day. *I should be rubbing your muscles*, she thought a little ruefully, but by now, she was so exhausted that she could hardly stand.

"We don't have to go back down tonight—if I can just figure out where that kid put the tent and the rest of our supplies. Stop looking at me like that, I'm not crazy—I wanted to surprise you, that's all, so I sent one of Kallestad's guys on ahead."

Liza was almost past caring. My God, she wasn't going to guard the look on her face, not with Dace. Maybe when he found the tent...She slid out of his grasp and sat down with the baby on the ground, just off the path. A little hillock provided some support for her lower back. She felt tired enough to just keel over and fall asleep under the stars. Except she was hungry. Starving, in fact. On the walk up, they'd drunk a little water and crammed bits of tortillas into their mouths, that's all. She'd fed Dace while he walked beside her. *So that's what he's been doing for the last few nights*, she thought. *Organizing this expedition.*

"Well, go find it then," she said. "I hope your Mexican friend set it up someplace where it doesn't disturb the monarchs and he better have left us some food too." She stopped, thinking of all the other things they needed with the baby along.

"Of course he did...what do you think I am, stupid? I didn't expect the trek up here to take so long, that's all, but what with you and the kid on that burro—"

"Well, what if some animals got at the food or something? I'm absolutely famished."

"Yeah, yeah, " Dace muttered, heading off to the side into some trees. "I've never seen a girl eat as much as you."

"It's because I'm nursing, dummy."

He turned around, almost started back to her and then stopped. "Watch it, Liza, or you'll make me—well, never mind. You're tired and I don't want you to fall off the mountain with the baby in the dark. Just stay here and wait. I'll take the burro with me and tie him up near the tent."

Liza never thought she would miss the burro, but she did. For as long as she could, she watched and listened for Dace and the animal, but in the evening dusk, her sight dimmed and even with her precious son still bundled in his cloth carrier and sleeping in her arms, she felt old and alone, not to mention irked at her own helplessness. She heard a couple of animals call, but she didn't recognize them. Something crashed in the brush beside her or maybe mated. She held onto Micah even tighter.

"Dace," she whispered under her breath, while all around her life much bigger than the sleeping monarch butterflies stirred, "Don't leave us. Please don't leave us here all alone."

*****

Micah's cries woke her, but they must have alerted Dace too because when she opened her eyes, he was standing there like he'd never left.

He hauled her to her feet and shook her a little. "Jesus, Liza," he said, "Didn't you hear me calling you? I thought I was lost up there for good. C'mon, I finally found the effing tent, I was walking in circles for a while, but it's just thirty feet up to the left."

It was just an old canvas tent, a relic of Kallestad's, a pale phantom that looked like an ark in the dark, but it was home. Well, not exactly home. For one thing, except for the sleeping butterflies, there were almost no insects here. If they were camping back home in Canada, they would have been eaten alive by mosquitoes and black flies.

Let's stay up here forever, Liza thought. She entered the tent first, with Dace watching her progress, the movement of her behind. He was holding Micah, so he didn't touch her. He handed the baby to her before coming in himself. They had to crawl through the front flap on their hands

300

and knees, but once inside, they were both able to stand.

Liza checked their supplies—not that she didn't trust him. There were two sleeping bags on a plastic sheet on the ground, a blanket-padded cardboard box for the baby, a Coleman lantern and a cooler full of roast chicken, cheese, olives, crusty bread and wine, all of her favorite foods.

She no longer felt quite so tired, but the baby had clearly had enough for one day. He woke up long enough to make sure she was really there and then closed his eyes. Sinking to her knees on one of the sleeping bags, she changed him and made a nest for him in the cardboard box. He stirred a little in his unaccustomed bed when she first laid him down, but he slept on.

Dace has thought of everything, she thought, a little surprised. She stuffed one of the baby's diapers into a plastic bag and wiped her fingers on a damp washcloth that had been stored inside another little bag.

He was so dear, so handsome, she couldn't wait to get into bed with him.

On the other sleeping bag, Dace lie on his side with his dark head propped on his hand and watched her for a moment, but he didn't watch for long. The next thing she knew, he had covered her body with his, fit himself into all those places where he figured he belonged. He'd left the Coleman lantern on in the furthest corner of the tent. Their combined bodies cast a great, looming shadow on the tent wall. She couldn't have moved if she wanted to and she didn't. Her acquiescence turned him on and she knew it, but she didn't care. There was power in submission—especially when it was her own choice. He could crush the life out of her for all she cared.

She'd seen a miracle today and it was because of him—it was him, he'd brought her here. *Before that lady scientist.* Dace smelled sweaty and she probably did too, but she didn't care about that either. There must be a stream around somewhere. She'd look for it at first light, but right now she hoped morning never came.

She still felt just a bit contrary, though. It had been a really long day.

"Dace," she protested weakly as he turned her over and entered her, almost without any preliminaries. "Can't we eat first?"

"You want me and only me," he said with his face buried in her neck and his hands grasping her milk-soaked breasts. "And the baby is sleeping, thank God."

Just the reminder that the baby slept was enough to make Liza completely relax. She reached back with both her hands and dug her fingers into Dace's taut buttocks. She might be under him, but she still felt powerful and strong.

"Yes," she said.

"This place is just like a cathedral," he said, his hands still full of her breasts.

"Um, yes," she agreed, momentarily indifferent to the beauty she could no longer see.

"Marry me, Liza," it sounded like he said then, but she wasn't sure, so she didn't reply. She doubted she could have spoken right then anyway. She arched her backside up to receive him even deeper. Two more strokes and he'd tap her cervix. He had already found the best spot, just inside her labia, towards the front, which was partly why she loved this position so much.

Ah, she thought, *the amazing ability of a man to fit himself into a tight little place.*

"Marry me," he said again and this time she didn't doubt what she heard.

There was only one problem. Whatever she had dreamed, they weren't the marrying kind, not really. She hadn't thought so before — when she was pregnant and vulnerable — but she sure as hell did now.

Something like dread flooded her veins, instead of the pure, unadulterated happiness she wanted. Or maybe craving, she wasn't sure. It was hard to tell the difference sometimes.

Especially when she wanted him so much, wanted his pulsing penis, wanted the full length of him, wanted his hands. And always had, since she was fourteen.

And he wanted her too.

Please, she thought, *don't come yet. Don't stop.*

It didn't matter what they wanted though. They couldn't get married, they just couldn't. Sure, they could get hitched in a park or Las Vegas or City Hall like Uncle Norm and Millie had, but not in a church. And if they couldn't get married in a church, why bother? Dace was Catholic, so even if it didn't matter to him or Liza, it was bound to matter to everybody else—the Church, the Pope and for all she knew, her mother and Uncle Norm too. It always had, they just didn't say anything, that's all. The Devereux and the Magill families had always let their grown kids do their own thing. But if Liza and Dace really got married, advertised what they'd gone and done—advertised their intimacy—all sorts of other people would come out the woodwork, just to disapprove.

They'd need some kind of special dispensation from the Church for sure, not to mention Dace was still on the lam.

It can't work, it can't, she thought. She started to cry.

And still she came in an explosion that probably would have woken the butterflies if they'd been making love outside.

Dace didn't notice her tears. He was so far gone, maybe he thought she'd said yes, just like she always did.

May morning never come, she thought when he rolled her over and entered her missionary-style with her knees drawn so far up, she thought her legs would break.

"Open your eyes and look at me, Liza," he said.

"I don't want anymore," she lied.

"Sure you do, little darling, " he said and she did.

Chapter 40
Downhill

They started back early the next morning while it was still relatively cool. Dace had an easier time going down than he had coming up, but it was much worse for Liza. Petrifying, really. She had to watch her step or she'd stumble down the slope. With her arms wrapped around the baby, she wouldn't be able to break her fall. Within minutes, she was dripping in sweat and almost crying in frustration. She swore several times, off-balance with an eighteen pound baby strapped to her chest. She hadn't got back on the burro because her legs were still too sore from riding. The burro was carrying their camping gear anyway. Dace was walking in front of her leading the animal, his body a bulwark in case she tripped and rolled, she supposed, though much good he'd do. Maybe he'd catch her, maybe not.

Much help he's ever been, she fumed. From time to time, he cast an amused glance over his shoulder. It made her even madder.

"Quit looking at me!" she yelled, finally catching up to where he was waiting for her by a bend in the path.

He was still grinning in that irritating way, but when he held out his canteen of water to her, she forced herself to take a small sip. "Look, Liza, maybe you'd better give me Micah…" he volunteered, kind of half-heartedly she thought.

"No," she said, clutching their son so tightly to his chest that he gave a small squawk. "I'm fine, I just need to rest for a minute," she continued as she started to bounce the baby.

Something was distracting Dace though. He stared off in the opposite direction. "What's that?" he asked.

"Oh, for Christ's sake, it's nothing, he isn't hurt, he's just surprised..." Liza started to say, but then she realized Dace wasn't talking about Micah because she could hear it too. Voices. Yes, English-speaking voices were caroling, yodeling up the mountainside. If the people approaching hoped to see any sort of wild life, they were out of luck. Well, good. She didn't feel like sharing the monarch butterflies with anybody except Dace right now. She listened, but she couldn't make out any words.

"Shhh--keep quiet," Dace said needlessly, coming back to her and gripping her by the arm. "Maybe it's just the woodcutters..."

Shut up yourself, Liza felt like saying. "English-speaking wood-cutters?" she asked instead.

"Shhh," Dace said again, giving her arm a little shake, while he tried see through the trees.

The voices—a woman's and a man's—got louder. A minute passed and then Liza and Dace recognized a few words, mostly expletives.

"Why, I'm sure—it must be—it's Dace Devereux!" a female voice finally crowed, evidently having spotted him first through some trick of the topography.

Reluctantly, Dace and Liza moved toward the voice just in time to see three people emerge from some foliage. The two men in the group were led by a slim, blonde, cool Cybill Shepherd of a woman.

Shit, Liza thought. *Shit, shit, shit. Look what Dace called up, just by invoking the nasty woman's name yesterday.* "I told you so," she nearly said. Based on Dace's earlier description, she figured the woman was Kathleen Aldous, but she didn't recognize either of the men with her: a short, older, professorial type and a young Mexican who was carrying some supplies.

But Dace did. "Kathleen," he said quite coolly, as he gave her a curt nod and then glanced briefly at the older man, "So you're back. And I see you brought the old guy from the bar too."

The older man mumbled that his name was Dr. Francis Murphy and wasn't Dace that loser from the bar, but Kathleen Aldous held up a smooth, freckled hand and cut him off. They all stared at her, waiting for her to speak, like she was queen of the mountain.

306

What the hell, Liza thought. She had the strongest urge to step forward and tumble her down the nearest incline, or at least rip off her wide-brimmed hat and expose her to the heartless sun.

Liza and Dace hadn't seen a single butterfly that morning, but the moment Kathleen Aldous put up her hand, a couple of monarchs landed on her sunburned arm, the traitors. It was midmorning by now and just the temperature the monarchs loved. Kathleen stood there, a pale statue in the dazzling sunlight, like she was the only person the monarchs had ever favored. Liza couldn't read the expression on her face, though. She wasn't smiling and she wasn't crying. Based on her own reaction, Liza realized that cool Kathleen was somehow internalizing and privatizing what could only be an intense joy. From what Dace had told her, Kathleen had been passionate about monarchs since she was nine years old.

The Murphy guy with her started babbling about the monarchs. "They don't seem to like me," he said. "Do you see that? They aren't landing on me."

"I wish it was just us," Kathleen said, ignoring everybody else on the path while she feasted on Dace's face, "because I really wanted to be the first to find this place."

"Except you aren't," Dace said bluntly. "We—"

"Kathy, Kathy," Professor Murphy interjected. "Much as I hate to admit it, your felonious friend here is probably right. As a matter of fact, we aren't even the second people. Dr. Sheridan—I'd really like an American to take the credit, but I'm not sure we can just push that old guy out of the way."

Without looking at her companion, Kathleen held up her hand in front of Murphy's face. She was still focused on Dace. "Ah, but you certainly can't take any credit," she said to him, "so you don't count either…unless you've got a pardon, I mean," she said.

"And how the hell would I do that?" Dace asked. "Every time I turn around, another Canadian pops up. I suppose I should be grateful you don't have somebody from the Pen or the police in tow."

"Maybe because the stupid fucks are holed up in some brothel," Professor Murphy said.

"Or because the Canadian authorities have all given up on him," Kathleen said coolly. "I told you before, Murph—Dace Devereux really isn't that important. But he's a man, so he likes to think he is."

"Ah, Kathy," Professor Murphy said. "You're a real little ballbreaker, exactly what I like."

Dace grinned. "I sure as hell hope you're right, Kathleen and that your friend here keeps his mouth shut or I'll have to—well, I'll have to leave Mexico and I kind of like it here. So the fact that my cousin and myself found a monarch colony doesn't count?" he asked. "What—because we've got no degrees? Never mind that the Mexicans have always known the monarchs were here."

"Dace, Dace, they're just Mexicans," Kathleen said, staring intently at the largest butterfly on her arm. "Who's going to listen to them? They don't even know that monarchs come all the way from Canada—they don't know what they've got. What use is it to them?"

Having read about the great treasures of Egypt in the British Museum, Liza asked, "Isn't that what every looter says?" Nobody was listening to her, though. *I might as well be invisible*, she thought crossly.

"Well," Dace said, "Here's what I'm going to do: I'm going to say that Elizabeth 'Liza' Lavinia Devereux of Maitland University, Canada found them first because that's basically what happened..."

"Dace," Liza said, sick and irritated that she was having such a hard time getting a word in edgewise, but Kathleen sure was a talker and once he started, Dace was too. "I really don't think that's such a good idea."

"Listen to the little woman," Kathleen said, "that really wouldn't be such a good idea because—and please correct me if I'm wrong—I think you're still a wanted man and she's your cousin! A relative who's aiding and abetting you, I might add. Not to mention some little Mexican chiquita—does the name Gomez ring a bell?—went and tipped off Dr. Gene Sheridan and that's how he got here so darn fast. Do you know anything about her, Dace?" At this point, Kathleen finally flicked Liza the merest glance. "Because she sure sounds like your type—starry-eyed or maybe just plain stupid and kind of swarthy with bunches of dark hair. Somebody as ignorant as the indigents, the Mexicans here. Somebody who doesn't know enough about monarchs to really care about them at all. 'Oh, they're so pretty!' she'll say, ignorant about just how amazing these creatures are. I realize Professor Sheridan from the University of Toronto has been advertising in the Mexican newspapers, but I'm still a bit surprised to hear that some Mexican chit's heard about him and his research, all the way up in Canada! From what I've heard, most girls here can't even read!"

"Mexicans educate their daughters for something else," Professor Murphy said snidely, from the ground where he had sat down and sprawled out to watch the butterflies — *his* monarch butterflies, the look on his face said.

Liza was a bit surprised that Dace didn't kick Murphy in the shins, but she was relieved too. Too many witnesses. "So where the hell is Sheridan now?" he asked instead.

"Back a ways," Kathleen said, holding out a rolled sheet of paper and gesturing to the Mexican boy who'd accompanied her to come and fan her face. "The last I saw him, he was struggling up the hill with his wife, his groupies and a bunch of cameras..."

Dace stared at her, a thoughtful look on his face. "Really?" he said. "So if good old Murphy — your so-called friend here — if what 'Professor Murphy' says is true, Dr. Sheridan got here before you did. I don't think you can claim first sighting either."

"Yeah, he's probably taken lots of documentary photos by now in a real careful way..." Liza chimed in, thrilled to note how Kathleen's glowing face suddenly blanched and her freckles stood out.

"C'mon, now, Kathleen," Professor Murphy said, evidently feeling they were both above all approach, "tell them what we did. They'll understand. Tell them how we snuck around the old bugger and beat him up the mountainside."

"Okay, so it's a real bummer," Kathleen admitted, slowly sinking down to a sitting position on the ground and putting her head in her hands. "But I don't think we did anything wrong. Still, if I — if we don't let Sheridan claim the first sighting, he'll probably have a heart attack just to get back at us. He is pretty old."

They all stared over her lowered head like they expected Sheridan to materialize instantly.

"I thought you were working for him and maybe McGill U..." Dace started to say when they didn't see anybody right away.

"No, no, not now. I used to," Kathleen said a little defensively. "But I agree more with Professor Murphy's theories and Princeton has a good reputation, so...I thought I might finish my PhD down here."

Professor Murphy regarded her fondly. "So, let him have a heart attack," he said mildly. "And since he's not here right now, maybe we can work out something so everybody benefits. Well, you and me anyway. We can still claim we saw these gorgeous creatures first, can't we? Who's to say we didn't? Unless you count some local-yokels like the Mexicans and these guys," he added with a little dismissive shrug in the direction of Liza and Dace.

"The Mexicans, the people who live here..." Liza started to say.

Professor Murphy glanced at her, licking his lips. "Well now, you're a pretty little thing, but I doubt you have the academic background for this, uh, expedition. Maybe we could tack your name onto the end of our research paper though, say you were part of our little team. But I don't think a bunch of uneducated locals are going to count—not in the eyes of Princeton, anyway," he said. "Or maybe you could peddle a human interest piece to one of the Canadian newspapers..."

"I don't think so," Liza said. "Dr. Sheridan..."

"Oh, that's right, you don't want to blow your cousin's cover," Professor Murphy said.

Liza had stopped listening to him, but her stomach was churning because Murphy couldn't keep his hands to himself and he kept trying to cup some of the monarchs. If it were up to him, he'd probably have them mounted in a wall cabinet in no time.

"Wait, I remember now, " she said. "That professor you mentioned—Sheridan—he's the one who's done all the real research, right? He's been looking for the monarchs' wintering grounds for forty years—that's what a recent article said."

"Ah, yes," Kathleen said coldly, not elaborating, although her tone spoke volumes, "let's listen to the cousin...Dace's...she knows so much."

Liza ignored this last comment, but inwardly she sighed. So Dace had blabbed to Kathleen Aldous about her, so what? It wasn't the worst betrayal. She never talked to anybody about their relationship if she could help it though. Not because she thought it was wrong exactly, just that people were bound to disapprove. "Besides, there's certainly lots of monarch butterflies here, but what proof do we have that they come all the way from Canada and that this is their wintering ground? Dace and I saw millions of monarchs yesterday, but we didn't find any of those tag

310

things," she pressed on.

Kathleen still wouldn't look Liza in the eyes, but she couldn't ignore her anymore either. "*Tag things?*" she repeated incredulously, adding , "Look, Miss, I know you're doing something artsy at university, but whatever your background," she said coolly, "you're not from the scientific community, or you wouldn't dream of asking such a stupid, uninformed question."

"Says you," Liza said. "With your limited vocabulary. You just used the word 'stupid' three times in a row…"

"Now just a minute, " Dace said.

"Yes, just a minute," a new voice boomed, Dr. Sheridan's as it turned out. Liza, Kathleen and the three men in their group all riveted their heads to look at him and his party, a group of six. The path was so crowded that some of Sheridan's men fell off into the trees. The woman with him, his wife, never let go of his arm, though, not for a minute. It looked like she was holding him up.

Liza was the first to smile, but it was Kathleen who introduced everybody because she had known Sheridan for years and even met his wife. Sheridan was her former thesis adviser after all. She said as much. Sheridan was old, but it looked like he had weathered the climb up the mountain a bit better than Dace had the day before. His wife certainly had.

"What the hell are you people doing here?" Sheridan demanded, pulling on his mustache in a worried fashion. "You're probably contaminating…"

From his front facing carrier, Micah took one look at these latest arrivals on the mountain and screamed. Everybody glared at Liza like she had pinched him on purpose. She backed off the path a bit and spent the next twenty minutes trying to pacify the shrieking baby to no avail. She was frantic, but she couldn't do anything to quiet her son.

And the monarchs, the ones that had been landing on Kathleen, vanished.

"They were just here," Kathleen said, looking a bit smug.

"That's okay," Dr. Sheridan said, "They'll be back and the colony will be a bit further up. Edith and I have seen lots of strays along the way."

"That's right, the colony…" Liza tried to say, but nobody was listening to her except Dace and it didn't matter anyway.

She watched the great man Dr. Sheridan instead who had sat

down on the ground with his wife, while his cameramen angled for better pictures. Plainly, he had waited so long to see the monarchs in their wintering grounds, he could wait a bit more. *If these butterflies were Canadian monarchs...* Liza, bouncing Micah in the baby carrier, could almost see what he was thinking.

Dr. Sheridan's wife patted his shoulder. "Never mind," she said, "There's always tomorrow and we're not even sure..."

Liza's eyes followed Dr. Sheridan's bespectacled ones to a tiny piece of white paper on the ground.

"Well, I am," Dr. Sheridan said, picking a dead butterfly up from the ground. "Look at this, Edith! This poor little beauty is wearing one of our tags."

Nothing went right after that—until they departed anyway. Both Kathleen Aldous and Professor Murphy were flipping furious while Liza was preoccupied and Dace was mostly just amused—but when they left, there was only one group left on the mountain: Dr. Gene Sheridan's.

Liza who had cheerfully handed Micah over to a Mexican to carry the rest of the way down the mountain, smiled.

"Listen, folks," she heard Sheridan booming out to his group: "The timing isn't right for photographing this discovery. We can't let this get out yet. Let's try again tomorrow."

Chapter 41
Nobody's Fault But His

And still he let her go. As if he had a choice. Something told him she would never let go of him—not without a good strong push. She'd sacrificed everything for him and he'd let her—a big mistake. Deep down, he knew she'd used up all her inner resources coming down to Mexico and that she'd been pretty depleted before. No wonder she acted like a person on heroin. She still looked perfect to him, but she had lost so much weight in the past few days. Almost as much as she'd lost when he was locked down in Maitland Pen and it looked like he'd never get out.

The spectacle of so many monarchs in their wintering grounds had also unleashed something primitive in her. She had become pure instinct, stopped using her brains. And he couldn't get enough of her either. It would be so easy to let her throw everything away, all those gains she'd made in school. It's what she wanted. Or did she? Sometimes in the middle of the night, he caught her looking out the window like she longed for something more.

He wished he didn't have to let her go though. Or the kid, who had gotten kind of cute. But down here near Cuitzeo, living under an alias with a bunch of assholes after him, he had nothing to offer a family. And never had. Worse, they might get caught in some crossfire if they stayed—both her and the kid. It would be nobody's fault but his.

He'd already booked a return flight for her—booked it the

moment they'd left Kathleen. Kathleen bugged the hell out of him. Because she'd walked out on him and because Liza was just as smart as she was, maybe smarter.

He was a bit scared of telling Liza, the way she was now. But on the third morning after they'd finished making love and he was running his fingers through her hair, he confessed that he'd booked an afternoon flight for her and the kid out of Mexico City the same day.

He had no idea she could scream so loud. Her body went rigid, then she jumped out of bed and started waving her hands and stomping around the room. It took him completely by surprise. She'd never acted this way before. She was so small that it looked kind of cute at first, but the shouting got to him. It might have been comical, except no Mexican woman would ever dare mouth off to a man like this. Not that he cared what Kallestad or his help thought, he reminded himself, but still. *Shut up, shut up,* he thought. Feeling his hands inching towards her throat, he balled them at his sides.

He smiled at her instead, partly out of embarrassment, but with the mood she was in, this didn't help his case either.

"You condescending jerk—how dare you make decisions for me when you've made such stupid decisions yourself!" she yelled, and as it turned out, that was the least offensive thing she said.

But it's me and you love me, little darling, he thought. *How can you talk to me like this?*

Dace figured everybody could hear the ruckus, maybe even Thalia's deaf old Abuelo at the Gomez ranch. Kallestad and his help probably thought he was crazy or that he'd tired of Liza, though he hadn't left her bed for the past two days. And why was he trying to convince her to go back to school? A pretty girl like Liza didn't need that much education, they'd think. But she had put way too much time into university to drop out now.

"It's too late!" she kept yelling and by now she was crying too. "I've missed too much time."

"You'll just have to go back and talk your way back in then," Dace said implacably. "You can do it." Oh, Christ, he really should have sent her packing before this, but he hadn't. He had wanted her too much, wanted her legs wrapped around his. And if he was really honest, it had pleased him to think that she'd give up everything for him. Then they'd found the butterflies and there was all their personal drama with the baby.

That she'd gotten as far as she had in university was a real miracle. She took it for granted, but it made him feel proud. It was a hell of a lot more than he'd ever done. Nobody else in their family had gone to university either. Liza had always wanted to do something academic though, God knows why. All that reading, he supposed. If she ever thought about her lonesome girlhood in Dublin, her unavailable parents, she didn't say. Typical childhood baggage, but she hadn't let it pull her down. The baby—yeah, yeah, okay, so it was *his* baby—might have derailed her though. And probably had. She should have known better, he thought, even if that was rich coming from him. He wanted her to be happy and problem-free, that's all. God knows he had enough problems of his own.

He wondered how much reading she did now. Down here with him and on the trip to find the butterflies, it was hard to tell. A few scattered paperbacks accessorized Kallestad's living room, but how could she read anything here? And up north she was too busy being a student and a Mom. Okay and too busy worrying and wanting him. Technically, she was only in her third year, but she'd taken a couple of extra courses last summer and with just a little more work, she could wrap up her degree by this fall. She'd explained all that to him, bit by bit.

So he drove her to the airport in Mexico City, put her and baby Micah on a commercial Air Canada flight and that was that.

Well, not quite. She had her pride, so she put on a bit of a face when they came downstairs and said goodbye to Kallestad and his help, even though they must have heard almost everything and concluded worse. He could tell just by looking at them and she must have been able to tell too. Liza was pretty good at reading faces, his anyway.

He got her and the baby into the jeep, no sweat, but once they were out of sight of both ranches, she went crazy. She fought him all the way, striking at him while he was driving for Christ's sake. She was oblivious to the almost empty road, the mauve colored mountains, the brilliant sunshine. When he finally got a word in edgewise, he tried reminiscing about the monarchs, but she was indifferent to them too. He couldn't believe it, so he pressed on.

"The monarchs just flew home too," he said, a comment that made her even angrier.

"I'm not a monarch! If I was, I'd have to die on the flight back and send Micah on alone. And I don't want to fly into all that shit up north — my God, there's probably still snow!" she cried while whacking him in the side. And she was right, of course. There was probably still snow in the fields and at least one more winter storm to come.

In the end, he had to pull over, restrain her hands in his and implore her to behave for Micah's sake. "Liza, my darling, my life," he said. "I love you. I really, really do—"

"You wouldn't give up the bikers for me, you wouldn't stop!" she cried.

"—but we can't stay together down here. Even if you didn't have a shitload of stuff to do up north."

"I don't give a fuck about school anymore! It's just too damn hard. I can't be a mother and a student too!"

Dace shook his head. "Ah, but you have been," he said, "and now you have to live with *your* choices too. Because Micah was a choice, wasn't he? And Mexico is beautiful, but there's stuff going on in Cuitzeo that you don't want to know. And the authorities are still after me. You know that! Any moment and it could all blow up in my face and that means yours and Micah's too. Even if you don't feel any responsibility to yourself, you must to him."

"My God, you're one to talk! What about *your* responsibility?" she cried, still trying to wrest her wrists free and strike him in the face. "To yourself, to me, to your kid!"

He felt like putting her over his knee and walloping the life out of her and he nearly did. Gripping her wrists even more tightly, he knew he was going to leave bruises, but he didn't care. It took all his strength not to hurt her even more. And that did it. That, or maybe what he'd just said about Micah. She collapsed against him for a moment, but then she sat right up. She just cried during the car ride after that—both her and the kid. For the first part of the journey, Micah had watched his parents like they were entertaining him, but then he started screaming too. He drummed his little heels against the back of Dace's seat the rest the way to the airport, like he was trying to tell him to stop upsetting his mother. Micah and Liza were still one and the same, alright. It made Dace feel a bit left out.

She stopped crying when they reached the airport. Waiting for her flight to be called, she was just sullen, all the fight gone from her while they sat down on some plastic chairs and waited for her gate to open. She had put the baby into his cloth carrier contraption so that he faced out. She wouldn't hold Dace's hand though. She let him slip her backpack over her shoulders, but then she wrapped her arms back around the kid. Sat there, hunched over him, protecting the kid, doing what Dace couldn't or wouldn't do even for his own son.

Dace didn't know what else to do, so he just kept on talking. He didn't do it often, but it had worked before. "Liza, I love you," he persisted, "and I'm coming back, but not to Maitland. I want to live somewhere bigger. I want to live with you. Finish up your courses and get that Diamond guy to jump you into a Master's at the U of T. That's what you want to do, right? He's a big shot at the U and a published author, so I bet he has some pull." Ever since she'd shared her plans, Dace had been thinking about this, trying to figure out what she could do.

"No," Liza said. "I'd have to sleep with him if I did and Joe Armitage too…They're a regular team. "

Well, not Armitage, Dace thought. *If the guys took care of him properly, he's a real gentleman now.*

"So don't," he said aloud, as if life at university was that simple, while she stared at him incredulously. "It will be better if we settle down in Toronto. How about in the west end, near Christie Pits, where our families used to live? Your Mom still lives on Clinton, doesn't she? I'll be able to come and go. I'll take on a new name, so I won't be as recognizable — the same one I used to fly into Canada before. We don't have to live with your mother, but you'll be able to see her whenever you want."

He knew instantly that he shouldn't have mentioned her mother because more tears flooded her eyes.

"I suppose you want to stay here with Kathleen," she said dully, not even bothering to wipe her eyes. "She's probably figured out how to finish her fucking PhD down here. She wasn't stupid enough to go and have a baby and try to raise him too! And she's still running around talking to the newspapers, toadying up to Sheridan from the looks of it."

Dace smiled. Kathleen might well have been fucking her way through her PhD, but at least Liza wasn't ranting at him anymore. Maybe he could calm her down enough for the flight home. He was on dangerous ground, though, so he tried to speak more carefully. He really did. "Actually, I think Kathleen's looking into ways to conserve the monarchs," he said. "That's what I took from those newspaper stories that came out the last few days. She knows she wasn't the first white person to find the monarch wintering grounds and that she's not going to get any credit. When the hell is Sheridan or somebody going to announce that they've found the monarchs' wintering grounds anyway? He found one of his tags, so he's proven they come all the way from Canada. "

His last comments elicited a shrug from Liza, but that was all, so Dace pressed his advantage. "You know, I feel kind of sorry for Kathleen. She grew up in a sanatorium. Imagine how you'd feel if you spent your whole life wanting something just to have it snatched from your grasp." In retrospect, he knew the look on Liza's face should have stopped him, but he went blithely on. "You might want to take a page from her and stop acting like a crazy woman the minute you don't get your own way."

Liza stood up with her arms still wrapped around Micah and looked down at him. She didn't have enough energy left to argue with him and he knew it. He felt like even more of a jerk. The airport intercom was blaring something, but he couldn't make out the words.

Liza had heard it though. She looked down at the ticket he'd thrust into her hand. "That's my plane," she said as she stood up and started to walk away backwards, with the baby staring out of his carrier at him like he didn't care either. She smiled then, but it wasn't the kind of smile he liked. "Have a nice life. Oh, yeah and try to stay out of jail."

For a moment, Dace just sat there, sucker-punched. But he got to his feet pretty fast. Burdened with the baby, she hadn't got very far. He reached her in two strides, knocking one man aside so he could grab her upper arms. "Sorry," he managed to say to the man. Luggage laden people rushed and flowed to both sides of them as he took hold of Liza's chin and forced her to look into his eyes. "I'm coming back for you for sure this time," he said. "And we'll get married no matter what I have to do. Everything's going to be alright."

Liza sagged against him with his son, all the strength gone from her legs.

But when the airport intercom said, "Last call," it was Dace who heard it this time. He let go of Liza and pushed her and his son away.

She looked backwards over her shoulder at him, just once. There was a smile on her face, a small smile, but it was a smile just the same.

I believe you, her eyes said.

Chapter 42
Monarch Watch

K athleen couldn't stand to have people feel sorry her. She'd gotten enough pity from outsiders when she was in the tuberculosis sanatorium, thank you. Pity, mixed with a kind of shameful fear that she might just look at a person and infect them with TB.

Her mother had visited her infrequently in the San. Their few relatives and friends hadn't come at all. When her mother finally married and moved with her new groom to Montreal, she sometimes forgot to mention she had a daughter. It was easier, really—easier than explaining how her only child had caught a filthy disease like tuberculosis, which enlightened people had begun to suspect was primarily a disease of refugees, the imprisoned and the poor. The Aldouses, Kathleen's mother's family, belonged to none of those groups.

But her own disrupted mothering didn't stop Ms. Aldous from wishing Kathleen was a better mother to little Mariposa than she had been. Wasn't that what every parent hoped—that their child would do better than them? Kathleen had a choice; she hadn't. And she still had lots of time! It didn't matter if Kathleen had missed out on the newborn period. Ms. Aldous didn't put too much stock in breastfeeding anyway—it was too restrictive and not really necessary in an industrialized culture—and little Mariposa was still only five months old.

Kathleen, however, had always wanted to be a biologist, or more accurately, a lepidopterist. Maybe she had inherited her scientific mind from her chemist grandfather, Ms. Aldous thought. Or her father, the one--oh, never mind him.

Sure, Kathleen had tried to tell her about witnessing a monarch butterfly migration at the San in Weston when she was nine years old, but Ms. Aldous hadn't been too interested. To her, butterflies were just colorful insects and they scared her a bit.

And now Kathleen was insisting on staying down in Morelia, Mexico, setting up a kind of butterfly watch or a sanctuary, she wasn't sure which. It was insane.

"Listen, Kathleen," Ms. Aldous said to her daughter over the crackling and no doubt hideously expensive telephone line, "Nobody is going to look down on you if you don't finish your PhD—or pity you or laugh at you because you didn't find the butterfly wintering grounds like you said you would! You really don't need that much education, you know. And nobody thinks less of a woman for having an out-of-wedlock child anymore, either. You don't have to go into hiding down there."

"I really don't care about all that stuff anymore, Mother," Kathleen said hastily, "and I've really got to go now, this call will be costing you a fortune. "Besides, it doesn't matter who 'found' them—I worked for Dr. Sheridan at the U of T, so I was still part of the team even if my name's not on anything! They can't take that away from me, they just can't. Oh, Mother, if you'd just seen all those monarch butterflies!" And just to needle her mother who once had artistic pretensions, she added, "They were way better than a Michelangelo—"

"That's impossible, dear," Ms. Aldous interrupted right on cue.

"And I don't care about my PhD anymore, I just want to be the best field researcher in the world and I can…"

"But what about our little Posie Pumpkin? Surely you miss her…"

Yes, Kathleen thought, *like you missed me.*

"Posie's so smart," her mother said, identifying the single attribute she thought might appeal to her daughter, "she's already crawling and pulling herself up and she's only five months old…"

Well, of course, the kid's smart, Kathleen thought. *I am and Dace Devereux isn't exactly stupid, just uneducated and misguided.*

Her mother was still bragging about Mariposa's intelligence, claiming that the five-month-old baby had uttered her first word, which was physiologically impossible, but Kathleen didn't set her straight. Let the woman dote. Her mother's nickname for the baby bothered a bit, but she didn't let on. There was always a price for her mother's help — in this case, the butchering of her baby's lovely, unusual name.

"The monarchs need me more, Ma," she almost interrupted but she knew how that would sound. "Listen," she said instead, stressing the baby's real name, "why don't you bring *Mariposa* down here next Christmas and we'll visit the mountain and see what all the woodcutters are doing to the monarchs' habitat. It's a crime against nature and once everybody starts coming here to see them…Oh, God, sometimes I wonder what we've done. Listen, Mother, if I don't do something to help them, millions of monarch butterflies will be wiped out in fifty years."

"Oh, but Christmas is so far away!" her mother wailed. "And your father and I aren't getting younger. I really don't know how long we can keep this up."

"Looking after the baby, you mean? But Mother I told you how important my work is — I've been saying this for years — and you're the one who wanted her…"

"Who's the father, Kathleen dear? Maybe he or his mother can help us. If your father and I could just get a little break…"

"There is no father!" Kathleen shouted. "What's wrong with that? I don't remember any father either, not until I was five or six years old. Maybe that's the only way the women in our family can procreate — Mother, Mother, are you still there?"

The line crackled with some more static and her mother's voice faded, but it sounded like she was saying, "You're sounding a little hysterical, dear and you know you have to watch your health. You really shouldn't stay down there. There's a lot of disease in those hot countries and there was a weakness on your father's side. Your real father's side, I mean." The usual, anything to pull her down. Kathleen closed her eyes and mentally cursed herself for breathing so hard. *I had TB,* she thought. *Maybe something made me more prone to the infection, but that doesn't mean I'm weak. I was just unlucky.*

Oh, God, her mother. She really was a piece of work. She'd better not answer the phone next time. But if she didn't answer the phone, her mother would send her a ten page letter detailing and repeating everything she had to say. She'd done it before. Never mind that all this emotional upheaval was bad for them both, Kathleen especially. In the old days, the nurses at the San had done anything to keep their charges calm.

"I can't hear you," Kathleen said, just before she hung up the phone and took several deep breaths. Her mother wouldn't phone again for a few days—too costly—and if a letter came, she just wouldn't open it. Outside the little house she'd rented, she could hear one of her lazy Mexican helpers strumming a banjo. She'd have to find him something else to do or she'd never get anyplace. At least Murphy had left this morning, to get back to his students.

Chapter 43
Alas, Poor Romeo

It was well below freezing outside and the snow had reached the tops of the fence posts, but Liza was boiling. It didn't help that Micah had decided to marathon nurse. Millie was sitting on the couch beside her, toying with the baby's feet. Liza listened in horror while Millie babbled about all the bad stuff that happened in Maitland during the past few weeks while she'd been gallivanting around with a helpless infant—in Mexico, did she say? Millie wasn't even too sure where Mexico was, except it was a long ways down south.

"You look so whey-faced," Millie finally interrupted herself. From somewhere in her small-town past, she had accumulated a host of old English expressions—gallivanting, lollygagging, shenanigans—that Liza rather liked. They reminded her of her mother. "Your vacation doesn't seem to have done you much good," Millie remarked with a self-satisfied air. "You really should have left Micah with me. I certainly wouldn't have dragged a baby down there, like a cat with a mouse. The heat! Micah could have died from heat prostration or gotten them Mexican runs. Well, he could have!" she insisted, responding to Liza's face.

"I'm breastfeeding him," Liza pointed out. "It makes him more immune to stuff like that."

Millie made a noise like pshaw and shook her head. "Why'd you go so far? Mexico's way further than Florida, isn't it and Florida's no hop, skip and jump from here. I don't know why so many of them students and snowbirds bother! The police came out to the farm, you know, but they thought you'd gone down to Fort Lauderdale—that's in Florida, right?—to look for your, um, cousin Dace. As if that boy would be caught dead with a bunch of university students I told them — bikers, maybe. They're more his type. You didn't see him, did you? By the way, where did you get the money for a trip like that?"

Liza hadn't said a word while she listened to Millie's ten-minute litany of disasters and she didn't now. Her head reeled. It was the first morning she was back from Mexico. She had done the impossible, left Dace. Again. Well, okay, he had made her. A fragment of a sad song played in her head, just the tune. She couldn't remember the lyric. Oh, Jesus, she had to pull herself together and fast. Uncle Norm's living room reeked of lemon furniture polish instead of fragrant Mexican flowers and the house was as quiet as a funeral parlor. She really didn't want to be here. The memory of Kallestad's bustling household flashed through her mind.

She looked down at the baby she was nursing and tried to concentrate on him instead. Micah looked back at her with his huge trusting eyes. He was so big now. She felt sick, even sicker than she had when she got off the plane yesterday.

Uncle Norm had been there to pick her up in Toronto and drive her back to Maitland, God bless him. When Liza saw him outside the gate, tears had welled in her eyes, much to his dismay. Both the Devereux and the Magill families loathed public displays of emotion and affection, the older generation anyway.

Somebody had called the house with her flight number, Norm said. A Spanish sounding woman, but she wouldn't give her name. Kallestad's housekeeper, Liza figured. During the nearly three-hour drive back to Maitland (they hit a blizzard near Belleville), Liza longed to tell Norm that she'd just spent three weeks with his prodigal son, but she hadn't dared. The questions he would have asked her, plus his car might be bugged. She felt even more paranoid, now that she really had something to hide. She had closed her eyes and pretended to sleep, anything so she wouldn't have to watch the falling snow and wonder what would happen to baby Micah if the car skidded off the road.

Sometimes it seemed like nothing ever happened, that winter just dragged on and on. But, oh God, a lot could happen in three weeks, especially in Maitland.

Both the Judge and Joe were dead or almost. And it was all her fault about Judge Silverton. It must be. He was an old man—seventy or so—but he had lived and thrived in sin for years until she came along. She didn't know what else to think. She hated Silverton—and by God, she certainly wasn't alone, but death was so final and to be responsible… She moaned a little when her stomach heaved and Millie looked at her sharply. She couldn't even kill somebody in self-defense. Well, maybe she could have killed Joe, if somebody else hadn't gotten to him first.

Who knew those terrible letters would work so fast, flying straight to their mark? Or that the Judge would try to kill himself? It had never crossed her mind. She'd just wanted Silverton strung up in a tree and exposed—figuratively. Oh, come on, her conscience nagged her. Obviously a prominent man like him would attempt suicide as the press closed in. Even Hitler had. It was just a matter of time. Yeah, well, hindsight was always 20/20. She could see that now.

But he's not dead yet, another little voice inside her wailed.

Micah nipped her slightly with his new front teeth, stopping when she yelped.

"One more time, little man," she said, shaking him slightly, but taking care to hold his head steady in the crook of her arm, "and this feeding is over."

"He's getting a bit big for breastfeeding, isn't he?" Millie said.

Liza sighed, but she didn't respond to this either. If she did, she'd scream. Now that Micah was no longer a newborn, the pressure on her to wean him was enormous. It came from all quarters, even an observant airline stewardess who said her own son had done just fine on formula, thank you very much, as if the sight of a breastfeeding mother was an indictment of her. Liza squirmed, trying to find a comfortable spot for her back on the oversized chintz couch.

Oh, God, she was practically a murderer for sure. She hadn't planned it that way, hadn't given a thought about what a guilty, exposed old man might do. The kind of man—who despite the terrible things he'd done and documented for his own pleasure—valued his sterling reputation more than he did his life. She had just cared about Dace and the other boys, that's all. And wanted Silverton off the bench, wanted him in jail, wanted him sealed off from boys in his care. And now Joe Armitage was dead—like some kind of crazy bonus and they said Judge Silverton had shot himself too. And bungled it, though he wasn't expected to live. He was under police protection in University Hospital, just in case somebody else had it in for him too.

Well, if Millie was right, they sure did. Millie the Queen of Clean hadn't kept the newspapers from the past few weeks, so Liza didn't know what the press had reported. Why in God's name did the woman clean so much?

The *Maitland Spectator* -which was reportedly controlled by the town's ultraconservative Mayor who had been in power for ten years, longer than Dace had been in trouble —was pretty much useless, but Uncle Norm also subscribed to the *Toronto Star*. No doubt the *Star* had reported Silverton's suicide attempt, given his prominence. The *Globe and Mail* would have too, but she didn't have such easy access to it.

Uncle Norm walked past them through the living room towards the backdoor. "I told her about Silverton," Millie said, while gently palming Micah's nursing head, "but she wants to know more. Have you heard anything else? Is he dead yet?"

Liza shrugged and rolled her eyes in her uncle's direction. *Damn it,* she thought, *Millie is always putting words in my mouth.*

"Who—Silverton? Who cares? Did you tell her about that fellow at the university? She might know him. Leave it alone, Liza," Uncle Norm said, heading outside and slamming the door behind him, but she just couldn't. She sank back further into the couch. She thought again about what she'd just heard. Though she hadn't planned it, she was somehow implicated in the demise of both men. She had driven Judge Silverton to suicide and she had history with Joe. Nice.

Not that she really gave a flying fuck about the old man who had caused Dace so much grief, she reminded herself—good riddance to bad rubbish!—but her relationship with Joe had been more complicated. If he hadn't hurt her so badly, she would have been even more upset. Also, Joe was young, less than thirty, and the Judge was real old, seventy or more, all possibility of redemption and all hope gone. Joe still would have had hope though and he'd certainly had dreams—nasty dreams in his case, but he'd wanted to make something of himself, just like she did. And he might have, years and years from now. Liza looked down at the child in her arms who was finally drifting off to sleep. Oh, God, he was so sweet. Yes, Joe could still have made his parents proud, gotten his PhD, written a shit-load of true crime books and lured a healthy, strong woman into his bed. Somebody who knew how to handle him and his proclivities. It was just so hard to imagine him dead.

What the hell had happened to Joe? She had to find out. At least she wasn't directly responsible for what had happened to him, she or anybody else she knew. That biker stuff was just a bunch of baloney.

Wishing somebody dead wasn't the same thing.

Millie had shared both news stories with her or at least her recollection of what she'd read or heard. Millie was especially interested in Judge Silverton's secret life and the fact that somebody wanted to blow the whistle on him, mostly because of the allegations about the boys.

Though Liza didn't blame her, she really wished she'd shut up.

"Norm was hopping mad when he read what Silverton did," Millie confided as soon as she heard her husband's car start up out in the back yard. "The judge was somehow related to Father Danby—you know, the one who was up to 'no good' at St. Matthew's—that awful school where Dace and his sister stayed. Poor Norm—you can't imagine how guilty he feels! Sending his kids there! 'I should have been able to manage them by myself after May died,' he says. And the stuff he tells me when he's had a few—phew! It sounds like Silverton and Danby had more than family in common. You know your uncle—most of the time, he wouldn't hurt a fly, but he's been hoping and praying old Silverton gets to suffer a bit more and I'm kind of hoping he does too," she said.

"Yeah, sure," Liza muttered uncomfortably.

"Imagine—he was supposed to be helping all those boys! The *Star* wrote some little stories about the poor bastards—the dead ones, that is. You know what the *Star's* like, always digging up shit. Oh, it was so sad. Some of the boys died in car accidents or from overdoses. The *Star* even named some of the boys who don't have folks in Maitland. The ones who lived—I guess they couldn't identify them—but they said they had all sorts of problems, never finished school, couldn't hold down no job, couldn't get it up, beat up their wives instead—'sexual dysfunction' or something they called it, but that's what they meant. I know how I would have felt if it had been my son who came in contact with Silverton. I was a single mother most of the time, my first husband died so young. My boy always wanted a Daddy. A good thing he never got in no trouble with the law in this town."

Or in any other town down this way, Liza thought, recalling the ring that stretched from Maitland to Cornwall and, God help them all, maybe beyond.

Suddenly thrusting Micah into Millie's surprised but willing arms, she ran into the powder room just off the living room. She didn't quite make it to the toilet, vomiting into the sink instead.

"I'm not pregnant," she said when she came out of the bathroom after cleaning up the sink and disinfecting it.

But Millie wouldn't even look at her. She shook her head and pursed her mouth instead. "Oh, little baby," she said to Micah, "what's your silly Mama gone and done?"

****

The next day was a Monday, the start of the university week. Rushing along the corridor to Dr. Diamond's office, Liza was still trying to piece together what had really happened to Joe and Silverton—a hopeless task, based on what little she knew—but a healthy sense of self-preservation had kicked in too. She had to think about herself. Nobody else was going to, that's for sure, and she had missed more than two weeks of classes, on top of spring break. Oh, God, Dace, the monarchs, the sun...This time she really had gone bonkers. And now she felt sick with anxiety, about whether or not her plan would work, but she had to do something. What the hell else could she do—hang out at Uncle Norm's and just vegetate?

On the plane ride home and for the next couple of days, she had considered various alternatives, between bouts of rage at Dace. She couldn't believe how angry she was at him. He had broken her goddamn heart. The phrase "personal problems" had worked pretty well when she was a pregnant student attending a murder trial. And now she was a mother and a student who had just spent spring break with a wanted man down in Mexico. That should count for something, it really should.

Except she couldn't tell anybody, not without betraying Dace and she was just like him, loyal to the bone. She could just imagine people's reactions too. Oh, they'd imply, you wicked, stupid girl. Even if people had forgotten she had a cousin on the run, they'd sure as hell recollect it now. She'd have to say—well, she'd have to tell more lies, she supposed. What a surprise.

Yes, she'd have to say the same thing again, "I'm having some personal problems."

And if her English lit professors or Dr. Diamond looked at her and waited for further clarification, or even if they were just idly curious:

"Yes, my mother's sick again. It's her nerves. They sent her back to the mental hospital, the one at 999 Queen…"

Yeah, right.

Oh, God, please let this plan work.

She stopped just down the hall from Dr. Diamond's office and rehearsed for a moment or two, her arms bereft of Micah. She had left him at home with Millie. She would take him to her classes if she had to, but nobody would believe she was capable of catching up on her coursework if she pleaded her case with a baby in tow.

****

In the end, she didn't have to use her mother. The minute she saw Dr. Diamond, she knew just what to say. Diamond had been with Joe Armitage the last time she saw him. It stunned her that she hadn't thought of something so obvious before. She really wasn't thinking straight. Of course he was going to be real upset about his protégé Joe. The creep hadn't been a total monster. He had people in his court too. Diamond had liked him.

"Ah, Liza Devereux," Dr. Diamond said, rising to greet her with a big smile on his face, "such a pretty name, such a pretty girl and Joe's special friend. I was tempted to call you." He walked around his desk and stood in front of her, a little too close. "You weren't at the funeral, so I knew you must be taking it pretty hard. We all are, my dear, I can hardly…"

"I went away on spring break and uh, got delayed, so I just heard about Joe, " Liza said, which was true enough. *Alas, poor Romeo, he is already dead!* "I feel so sick about him that I can hardly function…" she lied.

There was a leather couch in front of Dr. Diamond's desk, something the university psych didn't even have. Diamond sat on it and pulled Liza down to his side. He shut his eyes and took a deep breath.

Please, please don't cry, she thought.

"It made me pretty sick too, darling," he said, finally opening his eyes. "The entire Social Sciences faculty has been in a fog for the past three weeks. And the weather here! I'm from Texas, you know. You're the first ray of sunshine I've seen in ages—when does the snow here go away?"

"Oh, God, it's just terrible, " Liza said, wishing she had blonde hair so she could look more sunshiny for him. "I feel so awful. And I've missed so much time that I'm afraid I'll lose my year. The thing is I really don't care—about school, I mean. It's so hard to concentrate." She shook her head and tears came to her eyes with absolutely no effort at all. *God, I'm a such fool*, she thought, but she really didn't care.

When Dr. Diamond took her by the shoulders, it made her nervous, but she let him. He stared into her eyes. She could smell his cologne. Something flickered deep inside her. *Please don't call me 'darling' again*, she thought, *or I just might....*She looked away from him and focused on the rain slashing the window behind his desk instead. There was a tree outside the window, still bare, but it was early March.

"Oh, but you must," he said. "Life goes on, darling! How much time have you really missed?"

Oh, darling, she thought. "Weeks!" she wailed, looking at him like he was her lifeline and it worked. He puffed right up.

"But you're a smart girl, you'll catch up soon. Look, I'll put in a good word for you with your profs. I know most of them in Humanities— or they know me! That paper you wrote for me last year was one of the best I've ever seen..."

"Yeah, " Liza said, "and Joe gave me a C plus in that course."

Dr. Diamond winced. "And he cribbed your paper for his thesis proposal. I just realized that when I was going through his office here last week, but well, he probably would have credited you. He wasn't finished...Let me make up for his carelessness, Liza," he said, suddenly grabbing her hair and pulling her head back so he could kiss her mouth. "What are you in—third year or fourth year now?"

Liza was tempted to kiss him back, but she didn't. If she started a physical relationship with this man, all would be lost. Luckily for her, Diamond wasn't a rapist like Joe. He was forty-eight-years old, not a randy twenty-eight-old. She sat very still, determined not to encourage him. Instinct told her that an older man like him needed more stimulation than a limp, desperate girl. "Um, technically I'm in third year," she said, willing herself not to pull away too fast. "I've taken some extra courses and I was going to take a couple more this summer so I could finish up in the fall, but I..."

Dr. Diamond tried to kiss her again, but she managed to back her head up just far enough, so he missed. She noticed that his teeth were a bit crooked and yellowed too. "So you're going to grad school, right?" he asked.

Liza rested her palm on his shoulder, partly so she could push him back if necessary, ignoring the opportunity this gave him to brush the back of her tanned hand with his lips. "I was hoping to get into the U of T," she said with a rueful little smile. "My mother lives in Toronto and she'll help me with the baby — well, maybe..."

"Ah, right, the baby." Dr. Diamond shook his head and looked amused. "I'd almost forgotten about him — or is it a her? You know, I have a couple of daughters down in the States myself. Give me girls any day. I could never understand why Joe didn't do the right thing by you and marry you, but I guess it's all turned out for the best! I really can't picture you a widow."

Liza blinked, a bit confused about what Joe's mentor even meant. Was he saying what she thought he was saying? Did he really think that Micah's was Joe's? "He's not — I mean, he didn't, oh, God, I don't know!" she said, shuddering a little. *Speak up, stupid,* her inner voice said.

"Oh, dear, it doesn't matter now, he just said there were family problems, that yours wasn't good. Your family, he meant. Well, never mind. You're a fine girl. In my opinion, he could have just overlooked..."

Though he had also grabbed her free hand, Liza shoved a little at his shoulder and got to her feet. "There was nothing to overlook," she said crisply, her face and her resolve hardening. My God, she'd tell him the truth if she had to — that Micah was the son of Dace Devereux, an escaped convict and her cousin to boot. She had nothing to lose. Dr. Diamond was a maverick and an American, an outsider. He lived on the edge or at least fancied he did.

Diamond got up too, still holding onto her hand, which had started to sweat in his grasp. "Look, let me do this. I'll write you a recommendation so you can get into the Master's at the U of T. They might still have room this fall. Not everybody who's accepted a place is going to follow through..."

"Oh, I don't know," she said, trying not to sound too eager or too panicked, "Even if I get back into my courses, I won't be finished the summer ones until August." *Is this what I really want,* she thought, *all that reading, all those papers to write and Micah to raise?*

"So you'll get a conditional acceptance," Diamond said, swinging her captured hand high into the air above her head. "Hurrah! It's been done before. You're a real bright girl, you've got family in Toronto — what the hell else is a mother for? — and you're certainly going to need some help with Joe's baby. Kids don't raise themselves, you know."

"Really," Liza said drily.

Dr. Diamond looked at her and smiled. Obviously her sarcasm didn't bother him. He liked it, in fact. She smiled too. "You're a beautiful woman," he said, trailing his forefinger down the side of her cheek. "Are you sure? No?" he asked, accepting the regretful little shake of her head. "Well, I admire your spunk, I really do. And maybe Joe's family will help out too — it's their grandchild after all."

"No, no, I can't..."

"I don't know much about Canadian law, but they might even have some financial responsibility toward you and the baby. Joe would have gotten around to paying child support — when he could afford it. The university administration is so cheap these days. They scarcely pay their staff enough to eat! His family is well-off, though. I bet they could help you. Oh, Liza, I have a confession to make. I know Joe wasn't a saint, that he probably tried to weasel out of child support, claiming the baby was your cousin's — but that's a young man for you! He'll do anything to avoid responsibility and child-rearing is so arduous. A child can suck the life right out of a man. It's different for a woman. I'm ashamed to say I wasn't too different myself! Their mother raised my girls."

"But..."

Dr. Diamond stared at her intently, his large rather prominent blue eyes trying to burrow their way into her soul and make her like him, even love him if she dared. "Well, never mind about Joe's parents for now. I suppose you're too proud and there's always tomorrow. But let me try and do something for you. And Joe. I really want to. I'd be honored in fact. I know Joe played around, but you were his main girlfriend, weren't you? And I feel really bad about him. He had his problems — don't we all? — but he had a first-class brain and he was making up for lost time. No way he deserved to get killed like a dog in the street."

"Well, not exactly. Um, I mean I really wasn't his uh, girlfriend," Liza stuttered, trying desperately not to speak ill of the dead. *Maybe his plaything*, she thought.

Dr. Diamond smiled at her indulgently. "How so? Times are changing, darling. Young women don't have to hide their sex lives anymore," he lectured. "Even your relationship with your cousin—if it's true and I sure as heck don't care—that's not so bad. You're free to be as adventuresome as you want. I—well, I know Joe was into a little S and M too, a little spank and tickle—."

Is that really what he called it? 'A little spank and tickle'? Liza thought.

"—so I guess you might have—well, you know," Dr. Diamond continued. "Hey, it's almost noon," he said, looking at his watch. "Where are you going now? How about taking a little break and having a martini with me in the Faculty Lounge?"

Liza smiled brightly and stood up, fussing with her book bag. "I would love to, but I was just on my way to the library. The baby and all..." Oh, Christ she was jabbering. "I don't have much time," she rushed on. "And I was going to look up those articles at the library about Joe and the judge. It just seems kind of odd that something happened to both of them at the same time. The Armitages and the Silvertons were old family friends."

"I wondered about that too, but I can save you some work, darling. I don't have anything about Joe's, uh, accident—there really wasn't much in the *Maitland Spectator*—honestly, the journalism in this town!—just some palaver about bikers which I frankly find very hard to believe."

"Yeah, me too. The Wolfhounds couldn't be involved in his death, they just couldn't have been." *Or Dace would have said something to me about it*, Liza thought. *Wouldn't he? Besides, he doesn't have anything to do with bikers anymore.*

"I've got the clipping about the judge right here..."

Liza knew she should go, that she was in the lion's den, auditioning for the lead in his harem, but she sat back down on the couch. With her luck, the library copy might be missing too. Diamond sat down again and slipped his arm around her shoulders. Together they read the rather lengthy article that Herbert Yonge had just published in the *Globe and Mail*. From the very first paragraph, Liza realized that she and only she must have been responsible for much of Yonge's information. *Oh, God*, she thought, *it's really not your fault that the old pervert shot himself, it's not!* If the bastard had done it years ago, he might have spared some boys.

> *The Honorable Winston Silverton shot himself just hours before the Toronto Telegram released an article accusing him of abusing his power by sexually exploiting juvenile defendants who appeared before him, probably since the 1940s. He is in serious condition in Maitland University Hospital and not expected to survive.*

> *The scandal has raised many questions about the judicial system. A close relative of Judge Silverton's had been investigated in the 1950s, but the investigation was kept secret.*

> *In 1942, Silverton's first year as a judge, the Maitland Spectator received a tip about the judge's unusual relations with juvenile defendants. When the reporter investigated the matter, he found that Silverton's nephew Father Danby, had also been charged with sexual interference while he worked as a teacher at St. Matthew's in Maitland, Ontario. The charges were dismissed and Father Danby transferred to a northern residential school. The Maitland Spectator never published the story, but it sparked an investigation of similar schools as far east as Cornwall, Ontario. Many of these schools were visited by Judge Silverton. Rumors of a pedophile ring persist to this day.*

> *Reportedly, Silverton visited numerous male juvenile defendants in detention without their lawyers present. He also spent several nights with at least three boys outside of detention, claiming he was trying to help them and indeed, there is strong evidence suggesting that most, if not all the dark-haired youths who spent the night with Judge Silverton received reduced sentences. The investigators submitted a 56 page complaint to the Law Society of Upper Canada, which dismissed the case and ordered that the information remain confidential.*

> *Eventually, in 1968, Judge Silverton was removed from presiding over juvenile cases. Also that year, the first public mention of the subject was published in the Maitland Spectator. However, the reporter who wrote the article was soon pulled off the case, despite new evidence that came forth after its publication. At the same time, the Editor-in-Chief of the Maitland Spectator changed. The issue was once again swept under the rug, where it remained until today, when this reporter was finally able to resume the investigation.*

> *On the night of June 22, 1974, Winston Silverton was found lying in a pool of blood outside his chambers.*

> *The whereabouts of Father Danby are no longer known, but he reportedly left the*

336

By the time she finished reading the article, Liza was crying, though certainly not for Judge Silverton. The old pervert had gotten his just deserts. His reputation was in shreds and there was nothing he could do. No, she was crying for the boys, for all the lost boys and for Dace because she feared he was one too. She hadn't read all the letters Joe Armitage had stolen which she'd sent to Herbert Yonge in the full knowledge that he would expose Judge Silverton, but Yonge had summed them up in his article and she could read between the lines.

Out of nowhere, a purely selfish thought surfaced too: *I'm so lonesome I could die.*

"Ah, Liza," Dr. Diamond said, wiping the cold tears from her face with his warm fingers.

"I can't," she said, standing up to strengthen her resolve. She started for his office door, still holding onto the article.

"Can I borrow this, please?" she asked, waving the article a little, "I want to show it to somebody."

"Oh, keep it, keep it, my secretary can always get me another copy," Dr. Diamond said gallantly, rising to his feet as well and coming over to open the door for her.

He looked out into his hall and then kissed her a second time, but on the forehead.

Liza wavered just a little. She wanted to be in someone's arms, but she couldn't. And she desperately wanted somebody to rescue her too. God damn it, Dace was never around. "I'm sorry I just can't. Not right now," she said. "I've got to get home."

Dr. Diamond sighed, just enough to let her know that he regretted her decision and that he wasn't giving up. "Ah, well, darling," he drawled, "maybe another time. You can do something else for me though—go back to your classes. I'll make it alright."

Liza spent about five more minutes feeling guilty—for not sleeping with the older man and for the harm that had come to Silverton—but then she felt absolutely jubilant. Whatever had happened to Silverton, it was really good news for Dace.

She mailed a copy of the news article to the Kallestad residence that night.

******

And Diamond did make things right for her, though she never slept with him. Liza was forever indebted for the way he had rescued her, long after he and his fifth wife moved back to the States.

I don't know why, but I loved you, she sometimes thought, catching him in the controversial interviews he gave to the press or in an occasional appearance on her small black-and-white TV. *Loved all the wrong men maybe, so it made it real easy for me to love you too. Loved the way you came onto me with so much confidence, loved your mind. Or might have, if you'd been twenty years younger and I didn't have so much invested in Dace. Isn't life strange?*

One of her English professors held out, but in the end, she too relented, though Liza had to settle for a C+ in her course, Restoration and 18th Century Literature. The C+ disqualified her for a scholarship, but she still ended up with a teaching assistantship in the English department at the University of Toronto. Though she didn't know how he had done it, she gave Diamond credit for the teaching assistantship too.

Chapter 44
Dace

Across the Midwest, November 1974

D ace flew Kallestad's last plane from Cancun to Toronto, stopping to re-fuel along the way. That's all he had to do. And that's all he should do, he told himself every time he heard about another great deal going down or some twit sidled up to him to ask for help. "Please—you look like a tough guy, can you hold this for me? I can pay real good!" Yeah, right. He talked to people, but he didn't say much and he never told anybody his real name. "René Gagnon," he'd say if pressed.

For once, he had all the time in the world. Kallestad's business was finished and just as well. Dace was fed up living in Mexico with strangers and he missed his home. Ever since Liza had stayed with him at Kallestad's and they'd gone to the monarch wintering grounds, the whole Mexican scene had paled. He had been in hiding now for almost two years. He belonged in Canada with Liza and his son, but there were a couple of obstacles in his way.

For one thing, the Canadian police, the RCMP might still be waiting for him because they had nothing else to do.

And that asshole Larry Savage was another obstacle. Stupid people were so goddamn unpredictable. Not that Dace worried about Savage too much. He couldn't. He was alone in a small plane way up in the Jesus-air with almost idle hands, so worse people took up space in his head. Super demons like Father Danby and Judge Silverton, they were the devil's workshop alright. Christ, he hated their very names, but Liza had gone and dug up some dirt, so sooner or later, he was going to have to deal with it, he supposed. That's what happened when you stirred up muck. If only she had left well enough alone.

The flight took a week. Every time he stopped, he hiked to the nearest bar for a cool one, scanned the local headlines, reread Liza's postcards and did his damndest not to pick a fight. The usual. It was November, but warm enough in the Midwest. Ah, Liza. She was such a good girl and she'd always been so smart. She'd figured out what to do. She'd gotten her act together, sucked up to that Diamond guy and kept on writing Dace too.

First she'd mailed a copy of the article about Silverton's suicide attempt and every few weeks, she'd sent a postcard to Kallestad and his housekeeper, but she meant them for him.

"Oh, Christ," Kallestad said when he saw the article about Silverton. "There's been rumors about that old bugger for years."

Then on one card she'd written 207 Hallam Street, Toronto, that's all.

Where the fuck was Hallam?

Dace mailed her several little unsigned notes too, but never from the places he stopped. He wasn't that fucking stupid. He wasn't going to leave a trail. He told himself that over and over. *And get some balls,* he told himself too.

People thought he had balls though, too many for his own good. At the kinds of truck stops he favored, lone bikers and truckers came onto him in droves. People always had, so he took it for granted, especially now that he was a cool, bearded guy in a leather jacket who owned a plane. Well, that's the impression he tried to create, so that's what he said—that he owned the plane—not that he was selling it for his former employer.

The odd guy wanted to fight him—like he was some kind of fucking challenge, a labor of Hercules or something—but he knew better than to rise to the bait. He'd been in enough goddamn bar fights over the years and if he hadn't been in that last one, they never would have got him on a weapons charge. Goddamn it, he'd played right into Silverton's hands. He was going to be smart this time, Liza-smart, so he arm wrestled with some of the strangers, that's all.

For the price of a pint, a biker or a trucker was more than happy to post his love note from a random town in the Midwest, though he wondered how many of them actually did. Whatever, they rarely asked any questions. "Is she married or something?" a couple of them wondered. Their own lives were more interesting to them. They didn't give a fuck about somebody they would never see again and neither did he. They wanted a drinking buddy, not a friend. Once or twice, he slipped up and signed one of his notes.

Lucky for him that Liza hadn't changed her name and there weren't a lot of Devereux up in Toronto. She didn't have a Toronto phone listing for a while, but just before he left Mexico, he'd gotten her new number from Directory Assistance. He called her from each stopover just to hear her voice, though he never stayed on too long. Too risky. Whatever his cousin was up to in Toronto, whatever degree she was getting at the U of T, she was an escaped convict's girlfriend. Her phone might be tapped.

If the authorities could be bothered, if they had the time. Dace knew he was small potatoes in the great scheme of things, but that didn't matter. Most Canadian criminals were compared to American thugs, so he was no different than anybody else.

It was just that the Ontario police—the local forces and the RCMP—had long memories and lots of patience. Or nothing else to do, except take orders from creeps like Judge Silverton. Ah, that name again. Dace seethed and ground his teeth in his sleep. When he woke up in some sleazy motel or in the back of somebody's truck, his fists and his jaw were always aching. Drinking helped. It always had. Fighting would have helped too. Yes, if he could just take his fists to the old bastard, he'd feel a helluva lot better. Except he knew himself and he wouldn't be able to stop there. Once he got started—well, Silverton was an old man, but so what? Dace was no saint. He had done some bad things in his life, but he'd paid for them and okay, if he'd stayed away from the bikers and the booze, he would have been even better off.

But Silverton was behind damned near everything else that had happened to him—his latest incarceration for the weapons offence and the earlier attempts to blacken his name by labelling him a murderer. It must be in retaliation for what had happened to his nephew Father Danby, what the hell else?

You could almost admire Silverton's devotion to family, his only blood kin, Dace thought sourly. He'd have to check the family history, but the rest of the fucking Silverton/Danby line had probably died out and no wonder. Never mind that Dace had been nine years old and Danby, a man of the cloth had—ah, forget it. Danby had tried something and Dace had hurt him real bad. End of story. He wasn't going there, he wasn't. No way. He hated what it did to his head and nobody had to know. It was none of their fucking business anyway.

Except it wasn't just him. For some reason, Dace had always thought he was the only one, but he wasn't. From the looks of it, Silverton had ruined lots of other kids' lives too. There were names and places in those letters. As soon as Liza had told him about the letters, a couple of old memories had resurfaced, stuff he'd tried to forget, and these memories had bothered him even more. *I should have helped them,* he thought. Silverton had obviously used his power, used his position, whatever it took to betray the trust of many, many young boys. Risked everything, to satisfy a rampant, ravaging lust. And continued—if the dates in the letters were accurate—long after he'd gotten Dace out of the way.

Or maybe Mr. God hadn't thought he was risking anything. After all, he'd gotten away with it for years. As for there being two perverts in one family, why the hell not? The first time Dace got into trouble, a lot of people looked to his father and said, "The apple usually doesn't fall far from the tree."

In and out of the prison system, Dace knew this much: a person like Silverton and his goons—the police detectives—always set up their stings carefully, even if it took years. Especially in Canada, eh. Dace had heard this from other people in prison, so he knew. The stories he could tell from bits and pieces of reluctant confessions, the stuff he'd heard. People didn't talk much in jail, but when they did, they did—to the loose-lipped priest maybe, a so-called friend or the prison psych who was probably still writing that goddamn book. From what Dace had seen, Silverton and the police would never get away with those kinds of stings down in the States. Hard as it was to believe, certain types of marks—the stupid people the authorities targeted—would own up to a murder just to get into the mob or whatever. Maybe they'd even murder somebody. Not him, though.

No, he hadn't murdered anybody yet, he reminded himself as he dialed Liza's number just to hear her voice. Not yet. Sometimes in the background, he heard Micah too, squealing and prattling, though once he was hollering up a storm and he'd felt like shutting the kid up.

So things were working out, touch wood. As long as he laid low — and didn't mind giving up his name and living a fugitive's life — everything was going to be alright. How many times had he said this to Liza, just to keep her on his team? Lied to her, loved her, by turns. But things were working out now, they really were. Kallestad had closed up shop and made arrangements for him to sell this plane to a guy in St. Catharines down Niagara way.

Chapter 45
Hallam Street

The phone was ringing, but she ignored it while she washed the dishes. She had to. She really didn't have much time. It was a two-and-a-half mile walk to the campus. She couldn't afford to take the subway every day, though she would have to when it snowed. *Oh, God,* she thought. *I hope Val's not calling.* She had met her new friend at the park a couple of weeks ago.

Micah was sitting in his highchair, playing with a set of colorful nesting cups. She took a swipe at his mouth with a fresh cloth and made a goofy grin. He had a little oatmeal on his forehead, so she got that too. He laughed back at her. "I'll eat you up, I love you so!" she crooned and he laughed again. She made a note of every new word her little son learned, but their conversations were limited. Val had filled a spot in her life that she didn't even know was empty. She had long since lost track of her first year roommate, Janet. In her heart, she must have always wanted somebody she could really talk to, especially with Dace gone for so long.

The goddamn phone was still ringing. It probably wasn't Val though. She would be rushing downtown to her job at the magazine, all dressed up in a little blue suit. She didn't have time for casual chitchat: "My daughter drove me crazy today. She wouldn't eat her breakfast and cried over what to wear. I almost smacked the kid, I swear."

Liza rinsed the last cup under the running tap, stacking it in the plastic drainer beside the sink. She gritted her teeth and tried to calm down. But the damn phone wouldn't stop ringing. It wasn't Val, it wasn't!

Maybe it was her mother though. She called Liza nearly every day and sometimes came over to "help out," though she usually ended up clucking over the laundry because Micah would have nothing to do with her. "How's the baby?" she'd asked. Never "How are you, Liza dear?" No, her mother would be getting ready for work too. She was a cashier at Loblaws. Her mother didn't have a child to distract her, but she could only focus on one thing at a time. It was that stupid bastard for sure, the heavy breather who got his jollies pestering her all the time.

The window over the kitchen sink looked out into the backyard, just like it did at Uncle Norm's. There weren't many birds in the city, but it was still a pleasant view. Her black clad neighbor, Mrs. Campione, was already outside hanging up her husband's work clothes, jeans and shirts, trying to catch some of the weak autumn sun. Mrs. Campione waved at her. *Oh, dear, she can see me*, Liza thought. Distractedly, she waved back.

Liza yanked the plug out of the sink to muffle the ringing phone. The noise from the drain startled Micah. His face crumpled. *Please don't cry*, she thought, *I can't listen to that too*. She popped a piece of peanut buttered toast into his mouth to distract him.

"Eat," she muttered at him. "We've got to get out of here and I don't want daycare to think I'm starving you."

Sometimes she answered the phone and slammed the receiver down, but she refused to give the caller the satisfaction today. She'd had half a dozen calls from him just this week. Whoever he was, the man had a disconcerting way of calling just when Micah had woken up from his nap or the timer on the oven was dinging or she was hurrying out.

"What's the matter, are you a man hater?" a fellow student had asked when she mentioned the problem. "Women make crank calls too!"

Yeah, right, Liza thought. She really had to get moving. Dear God, where had she put her books and Micah's stuff? She stepped into the hall off the kitchen and Micah squealed in terror at her brief absence. She didn't care if he was just a baby, he was really starting to bug her. Oh, good, her backpack and the baby carrier were right by the front door where she'd left them.

She had a feeling somebody was watching her too. Like the man in the house behind hers, whose rear windows looked right into her yard. She didn't know his name and didn't want to, but the street he lived on was called Fernbank. Fernbank bordered Dovercourt Park on the north side, so from his front windows, he probably had a good view of the park too. He was real neighborly. Once every week or so, he hopped over the wire mesh fence he shared with Liza to cut her grass with his lawnmower. "Don't do that," she felt like saying, but then she'd have to talk to him. Thank God, it was almost November. She wondered what he was going to do when it snowed. Shovel her walk?

The man creeped her out. Whenever she took Micah out into the backyard to play, he masturbated while he watched them. What the hell else could he be doing? The rhythmic up-and-down motion of his hand was unmistakable. She figured he was interested in her and not Micah, but she wasn't sure. On these occasions, she kept to the upper end of the yard so she could bolt back into the house and lock the door if necessary. She refused to be kept out of her own yard.

The windows of the other houses overlooking the yard made her uneasy too. She had thought about this when she rented the house, but it was too good of a deal to pass up. She didn't know who or what was behind some of that glass though.

Her new home was idyllic otherwise. She had settled into it and was waiting for Dace to come home. He didn't have much choice. Kallestad's business was winding down. Dace couldn't afford to buy him out and there was nothing else for him in Mexico, nothing legal anyway. He needed an alias, though. The heat had died down, but he couldn't just come waltzing back here, using the Devereux name and looking the same.

Little darling, he'd written her, *you won't recognize me. I have no choice but to alter my charming good looks.*

My God, Liza had thought, *what did he do to himself—get fat?* Well, who cared? She'd take him anyway she could.

Judge Silverton had done wrong by him and tried to kill himself for that and other reasons, but Dace was still a wanted man, for the jailbreak at least.

Liza tugged Micah from the highchair and stuffed his fat little arms into the blue jacket she had laid out on the kitchen table. She had just changed him; his diaper should be good for a while. "Shush, shush," she said when he objected to getting dressed. "We'll walk to daycare and you'll have lots of fun with the other babies."

Oh, God, they said Silverton was so far gone that he had to wear diapers too. The Law Society of Upper Canada was reviewing some of his old court cases. Criminals were going to be thrown back out on the street, letters to the editors of the Toronto dailies whined. She read the papers at school during brief coffee breaks, eagerly combing them for more good news. Yeah, right. She'd believe it when she saw it. Was the man really a vegetable? She'd believe that when she saw it too. She didn't trust Silverton, she never had. She wouldn't put it past him to mastermind the search for Dace from his hospital bed, anything for a fucking distraction, anything to make himself look good.

Never mind that Dace had been gone almost two years now, she thought while she struggled to shut and lock the front door. It took her a minute or two. Her backpack kept getting caught in the door and Micah wanted to help. "Don't do that," she growled at him. "Or you'll crush your stupid little fingers and really howl." Silverton had collaborators anyway. Gruesome men who had the same bent as him and danced to his tune. Or maybe it was just his power over people in the legal system, who the hell knew? Or his power over boys — boys he still used. Boys who thought he loved them until he retired them for somebody younger. Silverton might use one of these boys or even one of his colleagues. Not all men were perverts though.

All this because Silverton hated Dace for something that had happened to his nephew Father Danby. Dace hadn't told her this, but she had deduced it from the little he had said. Besides, it was the only logical explanation.

In her mind's eye, she kept imagining Dace, walking down Hallam Street towards her, with his whole life in a duffel bag.

She was thin with waiting and stretched to the breaking point. Sometimes when Micah cried, she nearly snapped. Cigarette smoking tempted her — anything to calm her nerves, but she couldn't spare the cash.

Come home to me, she prayed, turning the corner on Hallam and walking down Salem to Bloor as fast as she could with Micah strapped to her chest in his cloth carrier and a pack of diapers and books on her back. There was a chill in the air, but fortunately she had put a hat on the baby. If she hadn't, some old lady would have come along and reminded her for sure.

Passing through the park, she stopped at the water fountain to

348

straighten her shoulders and readjust her backpack. She wondered if Dace would recognize her if she bumped headfirst into him. She was twenty-two and her looks were all gone, although her back and legs had gotten stronger. She wore her long hair in a single, messy braid over one shoulder and she'd lost so much weight once she started walking to and from school that her period still hadn't come back. She never thought about sex, well hardly ever, and she rarely relaxed except when she was talking to Val in the park. Most of the time, she looked like some poor woman working in a paddy field in a third-world country, for God's sake.

Chapter 46
Hide in Plain Sight

The guy who was going to collect the plane in Toronto did. He was right on time, a smooth, fast-talking salesman type about Dace's age, with a diamond stud in his left ear. Dace took the money, counted it, and everything went off like clockwork.

He caught the ferry from Toronto Island Airport and then a bus up Bay Street, marked for the subway. He slipped some cash into his pocket for his salary—the $500 he and his employer had agreed on—jumped off the bus briefly at the closest Canadian Imperial Bank of Commerce on Bay Street and deposited the rest of the money from the plane sale into Kallestad's account. The sale and the deposit had gone real smooth— nobody asked too many questions and Dace's new ID worked fine, but when he got back onto the bus, he still felt rushed and irritated. From a phone booth at the Toronto Island Airport, he had stopped to call Liza first thing, but she hadn't picked up. At 7:30 a.m.! Where the hell could she be? It made him want to stash her in a house in the country where he was the only one with a key, but it was just as well, he supposed. If she had answered, he wouldn't have been able to say anything.

There were even more old people on the bus and plump mamas with squalling brats in strollers. He had to stand, but he didn't mind. His ass had been squeezed into a pilot seat for days.

It had been ages since he'd been in Toronto with Liza and, man, had it changed. There were so many people. The bus passed between the new and old city halls until suddenly the Greyhound bus station was on the left. Ever since he'd gotten back on the bus, the driver had stopped more than he drove. The driver was probably new to the job or something. He waited for every runner to catch up to him before he cranked around the big wheel, a big patient smile on his face. It wore Dace out.

The Ford Hotel was just across the street from the bus station, with all the big silver buses wheeling in and out. By now, Dace felt so claustrophobic that his forehead was sweating and his heart was racing and he had only been in Toronto for two hours. He took another look at the grungy exterior of the Ford, but he didn't have to think twice. He leapt off the slow-moving bus, walked straight past a bunch of working girls in the hotel lobby and checked in.

The place smelled funny and somebody was yelling down the hall, but he'd stay here awhile, check out the scene. He couldn't afford to stay at the hotel forever, but if he went straight to Liza's place without checking things out and the police caught him there, the dirty devils might charge her with harboring a fugitive or some such crap. Or surround her place and draw guns.

There are hardly any guns in Canada, yeah, right.

Every night for the past week, he dreamed that he and Liza were trapped by gunmen, by a swat team who didn't care who the fuck they killed.

Maybe because he still had that bastard Savage to worry about, though come to think of it, he hadn't heard a peep out of the guy for a while. Well, maybe somebody had offed him. Yeah, sure. He should be so lucky. If Savage showed up, he'd take care of the cocksucker himself. Silverton was supposed to be in Toronto too. From a two-day-old headline in the *Globe and Mail* in the hotel lobby, Dace saw that Silverton's doctors had moved him to Sunnybrook Hospital, where they specialized in brain injuries.

The next day he hiked up to the subway station at Bay and Bloor and went six stops to Dufferin, the closest station to Hallam Street as far as he could tell. He'd bought a street map in the Greyhound bus station across from the hotel. He'd never been on the subway before. It looked like an underground city. A man could live in its cavernous tunnels for days. The subway had been built after his family moved from Toronto to

Maitland, such a bad move for him. Whenever he and Liza had come up to Toronto to listen to music in Yorkville, they'd gotten around on his bike.

He let a bunch of people out ahead of him and then got off the train, just before the doors sliced him in half. He took an escalator up from the platform. Just ahead of him, a woman with a shopping cart pulled a bus transfer out of a machine, so he did too. She looked back at him a little nervously like he was a fucking felon or something and hurried away, nearly tripping over the wheels of her cart. The people in the subway car had looked at him the same way, but maybe they were just put off by his size. The little paper transfer in his hand was stamped 4:20 p.m. Christ, I'm not Godzilla, lady, he thought, looking at the transfer and then tossing it into the nearest trash can. He looked perfectly respectable. Last night, he had trimmed his beard in a little mirror over the hotel room sink. Lots of guys had beards these days. The less he resembled his mug shot, the better. He hadn't had much facial hair when he was eighteen.

Following another stream of people — God, where did they all come from? — he chanced another escalator and found himself at the busy intersection of Bloor and Dufferin streets. He pulled out his map. He was standing on the east side of Dufferin, he figured, just where he wanted to be. Earlier in the day, he had traced the route he wanted to walk with a red pen. There was a little park behind Liza's house.

A familiar noise distracted him, a powerful roar, and he looked up. A cavalcade of bikers was whizzing by him, headed north on Dufferin Street in the same direction he wanted to go. The traffic light was with them, so they had sailed right through the intersection, their faces a blur to everybody watching them. If they had stopped, he might have hopped on the back of the closest bike. They pulled him, like nothing except maybe Liza had.

The hair on his head prickled and one of Granny's old sayings popped into his mind: "Somebody's walking on your grave." Standing still, almost blocking the sidewalk, he watched the bikes heading up the street. Fifteen or so bikes were flanked by a pair of armor-plated Caddies with six fat fucks in each car, so they were probably on their way to a clubhouse. They took up all four lanes of the road. Everybody else on the street had stopped to watch them too. On the opposite sidewalk, a pedestrian cop in shorts climbed up on a garden planter and raised a walkie-talkie to his mouth, but there wasn't much point. By the time his reinforcements arrived, the bikers would be long gone. As the bikes passed Shanly Street and Wallace Avenue, the oncoming rush-hour traffic squeezed by them. Come to think of it, he had heard about a clubhouse up at Dufferin and Steeles, though he had no idea where the heck that was. The only Toronto he knew well was the Christie Pits area of his childhood.

The colors on the bikers' jackets had been hard to miss, but he didn't recognize the patch. He'd been away from the scene for far too long. There were only three possibilities, though. This club was either an affiliate of the Angels, the Outlaws or the Choice. Right now, he hated them all or he should. The Choice, the Wolfhounds' allies, had just stood there and watched while they were run out of town.

Toronto was on Daylight Savings Time, so it got dark early now, but there were still way too many people out on their Dufferin Street verandas watching the bikers put on their show. Lights were coming on in front room windows and he could smell cooking aromas from some of the houses he passed, a lot of tomato sauce with onions and oregano and garlic. He was hungry and lonelier than he'd thought possible, but he'd be seeing Liza soon. She probably had the fixings for spaghetti. He made a sharp right onto Shanly Street and then a left onto Salem Avenue.

On his way, he noted several houses with cardboard signs in their front windows advertising "Rooms to Let." He was going to need a different address from Liza's, wherever he actually slept. He'd have to sneak in and out of her place at night and not go advertising his presence. He didn't like it, but he didn't have much choice. An ad in the *Star* classifieds for a basement room on Southview had already caught his eye that morning, but he didn't have time to check it out now. The closer he got to Liza's house the better, even if he didn't barge in right away.

Salem waltzed him right over Southview into Dovercourt Park, past the playground and the kiddie pool. The pool sported an autumnal arrangement of brown maple leaves and flotsam in a bit of rain water. The park was empty.

If they wanted to, a lot of people could see him from the windows of the houses surrounding the park, but it didn't matter. There were lots of bums downtown, so why not here? At the north end of the park, he sat down on a bench facing Fernbank and waited for the street lights to go on. There was another "Room for Rent" sign on a semi-detached Fernbank house that looked like it might be right behind Liza's place, but he didn't like the looks of the shifty-looking greaser raking the front lawn. The guy wasn't a cop, just a runty little creep, but still. At least there were no other suspicious looking men around and nobody who remotely resembled a police detective, just a couple of people hurrying home from work. It was that time of day. A sheet of newsprint tumbled over on the grass and wrapped itself around his feet. He picked it up and tried to read in the dimming light.

An article about Silverton filled the whole page. Judging by the date in the upper right hand corner of the paper, somebody had held onto it for a while, perhaps to savor the details.

Christ, he hoped that they couldn't do anything for him at Sunnybrook and that Silverton just up and died. What the hell did he care. It would make his own life so much easier. No way he wanted to tell his father or Liza any more than he already had. Or anybody else. And no way he was going to let on what really happened at St. Matthew's. People didn't have to know all that shit. It was none of their business, he figured. As for the other kids at St. Matthew's — who had come to far worse harm at Silverton's and Danby's hands and he knew this for a fact — well, most of them were already dead. His disclosures wouldn't help them or their families. Telling stories — especially true stories — would just make everybody feel a hell of a lot worse.

Chapter 47
Homecoming

By the time Dace landed the plane at Toronto Island Airport, Liza had almost completely settled into the little house on Hallam Street, just far enough from her mother's place on Clinton. Library books filled her house, fallen maple leaves littered the sidewalks and Cubs and Scouts sold apples and red poppies at the end of her street. All the monarch butterflies had flown south—down the Lakeshore and over the lake— great hordes of them from her south-facing yard and the little park around the block.

She had seen nary a butterfly for two or three weeks, but she met up with her good friend Val Jaffe in the playground at Dovercourt Park practically every day. Val made up for a lot. Liza loved everything about her: her pixie haircut, her self-deprecating humor and the fact that she was a married woman with a husband who adored her. *Oh, God*, Liza thought, *I want to be a married woman and if I ever get enough money, I'll get all my hair chopped off too*. Both Val and her husband worked for magazines. And they wrote! Val wrote mostly articles for a women's magazine and she was an impeccable editor, but she was planning a book too.

Val's three-story Victorian on Southview Avenue fronted onto the park, way on the opposite side from Liza's perverted neighbor. When the two young women met in the playground, it was always the dinner hour and they had the place to themselves. Both Liza and Val ate late so they could push their children on the swings after daycare. Sometimes Val had an open bottle of beer in her coat pocket and offered Liza a swig. On alternate nights, Val's husband was in their house cooking dinner, so she could stay longer.

After she had sung Micah to sleep, Liza found the long evenings lonely, though she had plenty to do. For the past two months, she had read and written her papers at the kitchen table under a yellow light, ignoring the laundry shoved into a hamper and the dust bunnies all over the house. She didn't have a vacuum cleaner anyway, just a broom and a mop. Her neighbor Mrs. Campione took her small garbage can up and down from the curb every Tuesday and Friday. Liza felt a little guilty, but she could never take her garbage out fast enough to stop her.

Liza would have given anything to have what Val had: a husband to share her life. The two women talked about almost everything. Liza couldn't believe the stuff she told Val, the secrets that spilled from her mouth. Her fears about Micah's motor skills, her academic dreams and the backstreet abortion she'd had in Dublin when she was sixteen.

She even told Val a little about Dace, stringing out his story a bit at a time. She told her about the monarchs first.

"Oh, but he must get some credit for the discovery and you too — you guys and Dr. Sheridan — not that horrible PhD girl," Val had insisted when she heard. "What the hell is taking Sheridan so long to publish his results anyway? I haven't seen anything in the news."

Liza shrugged. "I don't know. Dr. Sheridan found a tagged butterfly the day we were there, but maybe he hasn't found any of *his* tagged butterflies yet. He has to find some to prove that monarchs fly all the way from Canada to Mexico."

Val was smart though. On her lunch hour, she'd gone to the newspaper archives at Central Library and looked up Dace and formed her own opinions, just like Liza had so long ago. When she heard, Liza had felt horrified and protective and a bit betrayed. Not that Val was likely to betray her, but still. God, oh, God, why had she told her so much? A woman like that would confide in her husband too. Sure, he sounded like a nice guy, but Liza hadn't even met him yet. And the Jaffes had the occasional renter and a live-in nanny — what if she overheard something? It was Liza's impression from reruns of *Upstairs, Downstairs* that the help figured out everything.

Worse, there was a lot more about Dace in the newspaper archive than there had been when Liza first researched him when she was fourteen. All those nasty stories about his participation in the Maitland Penitentiary Riot—those two murdered men!—his painfully short parole and then his escape.

When Val told her what she'd found out about Dace, they had both blushed. "I'm sorry," Val said, "it must be hard for his family when there's so much about him in the news."

"Higher, higher," Val's daughter shrieked and kicked in her swing, while Micah rattled the chains on his seat and tried to say "higher" too.

"He's Micah's father," Liza blurted, grabbing the swing so she could pull up one of the baby's dangling socks.

Val looked confused. "But you said he's your cousin—so he's not a first cousin then?"

Liza looked away. "Yes," she said, feeling a bit sick. *Please still like me*, she thought.

"Well, that's certainly a bit unusual, especially here, now, in these times," Val said, but much to Liza's relief, she was smiling. "You know my great-grandparents were first cousins and their children turned out alright or I wouldn't be here today. Not that everybody thinks I'm alright, but..."

"Yeah, I bet," Liza said, her tension starting to ease a little, but then Val spoke again.

"So he's still in Mexico then?" she asked.

"Who, Dace?"

"Who else?"

"Well, he was last February," Liza hedged. "I'm not sure where he is now—and Judge Silverton—oh, but you've got to go now!" she added, feeling even more relieved. Val's husband had just come out onto their veranda, thank God, and was waving at them from across the road.

Val picked up her protesting daughter and put her mouth to the four-year-old's ear. "We'll come back to the swings tomorrow, Sunshine," she promised, dodging a kick from the child's running shoe. "Some of the stuff in the papers is true," she said as she backed away from Liza, with her daughter still flailing in her arms and almost dwarfing her, "but I'm a journalist too. I've got other sources and I can read between the lines. And I know that fellow Herbert Yonge. I'll talk to him."

*****

Val told Liza stories too: even about how she'd had a therapeutic abortion, after she'd had her daughter and it was finally legalized in Ontario. She had gotten the abortion for medical reasons, but she couldn't have another child, not with the bastard of an editor she worked for or she would have gone stark raving mad. "And I'm mostly grateful, well, I'm relieved that I could," she confessed. "I had my daughter to think about too. She didn't need a crazy mother."

In spite of her demanding job, Val always got home from work before her husband, partly to relieve their live-in nanny, but mostly to keep her mother off her back.

"You're neglecting your daughter," Val's mother always said. Liza had caught sight of the mother once as she flounced off the veranda and she was rather scary: a large, opinionated woman of eastern European origins. Val must have taken after her father, for she was rail thin or maybe she just didn't get enough time to eat.

With their academic backgrounds, she and Val discussed literary matters too: they both loved books and authors by extension. Val was really into Marshall McLuhan.

"The medium is the message," she liked quoting. When Liza mentioned Dr. Diamond and his friendship with Marshall McLuhan, Val had been fascinated.

"When I fly up from Texas to Toronto to visit my friend Marshall McLuhan, I'll come visit you too," Dr. Diamond had promised when Liza first told him about her move. *You'd better not*, she often thought, especially when she was doing a chore or putting up a sunny yellow wallpaper on one wall of Micah's new room, which looked out over the backyard and was just off of her room.

Whenever she did mind-numbing household chores, memories of the past filled her mind, which was another reason she avoided housework, much as she loved the house on Hallam. It was a doll's house, really, a place where she could playact a real family life. To have made a new friend and to have a house for Micah, a place where Dace could slip in the backdoor! Or maybe he'd just boldly saunter up to her veranda after he'd stashed his plane at the little Toronto Island Airport, just twenty minutes from her new home. He'd take the subway to her house or walk. Because he was coming back. He had to! They'd figure out what to do with him then, find him someplace to "stay" in the neighborhood. Maybe at Val's? She and her husband rented out a basement room. Dace could have his mail sent there, his Social Insurance number, whatever, but he'd slip into Liza's bed when it got dark. He'd have to apply for his SIN number under his assumed name…Christ, she was getting way ahead of herself. One thing at a time.

He couldn't phone her because her line was probably tapped, but he had her new address and she got little notes from him all the time. The notes didn't say much, but they kept her going, they really did. With his dark eyes and his hair, he'd fit right into this Italian neighborhood for sure. Like she had, until she opened her mouth and people realized she was an Anglo and not really one of them.

Her mother had spotted the ad for the house on the bulletin board of the Loblaws where she worked part-time. Maeve Magill lived in a one bedroom flat on the top floor of a three-story house, so she hung out at her daughter's brick house on Sundays like she owned the place. The house with the big veranda was in a rough working-class neighborhood, close to the Annex, but not central enough to attract other students or exact an exorbitant downtown rent. The rent was cheap, real cheap, two hundred dollars a month, not including utilities or Liza couldn't have afforded it. She'd get a roommate if Dace didn't come home to help out with the rest, but he was, he was. In any case, she had total control over the amount of money she spent on heat and electricity and she didn't have a TV. At night she layered her winter coat over Micah's blankets and sometimes took him into bed with her to keep them both warm.

She'd splurged on a secondhand washer and dryer, though, delivered from a local store. She didn't have time to hang baby clothes out in the yard and entertain that little man with the lawnmower. The man who owned her house had moved his family to the suburbs twenty years earlier, but he had never been able to let their first home go.

The little house's backyard was huge and the small park around the block attached to the Dovercourt Boys Club was another bonus. Micah would play soccer and hockey there someday if their luck held out, though they might have to move to a bigger house down the street if she had another child and she wanted one more baby, although how the hell she'd manage, she didn't have a clue. *Oh, Liza,* that annoying little voice inside her said. *You can't do that. Dace will kill you. And think about Micah and all of the things you still want to do.* There was only street parking, but the backyard had two abundant peach trees, a perennial garden with grapevines and strawberries that came back year after year. The courtyard style park around the corner had a playground and a wading pool that became an ice rink in the wintertime. She could walk to stores at the Galleria Mall and on Bloor Street and to the subway and often did.

She walked unmolested, a mother in a neighborhood where idle old men viewed any girl over the age of eleven as fair game, but who revered motherhood. "Madonna," they still whispered under their breath when she walked by. She heard them and it didn't bother her because she had grown up on Grace Street near Christie Pits, just blocks away and she'd heard the same things there. She provided endless entertainment for her mostly Italian neighbors, walking with Micah strapped to her front or her back in his baby carrier. When she carried him this way, Micah was so big now that his feet tapped the middle of her thighs.

On Thursday mornings, she took him to a babies' story hour at the Gladstone Public Library before they went to daycare, something none of her neighbors could understand. Mary Mother of Jesus, he was just a baby! What did he want with books?

The moment the black dressed women spotted Micah on the street, they descended on him and pressed sweets into his fat little hands, which Liza swiped as soon as they were out of sight.

"Corduroy," Micah tried to say and "Runaway Bunny."

Liza could almost read her neighbors' minds. *So this is how a Canadian girl, an educated girl looks after a baby*, they thought. *She needs help, a mother to tell her what to do.*

Micah was a long baby and a good size for his age, but he could never be fat enough for them. "Too skinny! You too!" they said, frowning when she said she was still breastfeeding him and then asking, "Where Papà?

"At work," Liza always said, her stomach plummeting while she wondered what the hell kind of work Dace was doing now. On Halloween, she had witnessed the men and boys on Hallam dealing with a couple of bikers who wanted to rent a flat across the street. The renters hadn't looked like outlaw bikers, maybe just a couple of homosexual guys who fancied riding motorbikes. Fortunately nobody had been hurt. "Gays," they were starting to call guys like that now. What if Dace came and her neighbors went after him with chains too? Well, it didn't bear thinking about. Dace could handle a bunch of old guys anyway.

"Um, he's working in Mexico, flying planes for mining contractors to remote sites, but he's coming home soon," she told her neighbors. She didn't know what else to say. *Oh, God, please don't let Dr. Diamond show up instead Dace,* she thought. They'd probably think he was her Sugar Daddy, which he was in a sense. He had got her into the University of Toronto, something she couldn't have done by herself, qualified or not.

The older women stared back at her, unable to relate to her blather about Mexican mining contractors. They weren't even sure where Mexico was and they had trouble with her English too. They had arrived from Italy in the late fifties and early sixties, but they didn't get out of the house much and they watched mostly Italian television.

"I'm not on welfare," she felt like adding, but she didn't. Even as a grad student with a baby, she was richer than most of the people on Hallam. The men relied on unemployment insurance in the wintertime, while the women toiled in backyard vegetable gardens and basement kitchens and made everything from scratch. It was a rare family where the teenagers didn't drop out of high school by grade ten to help out too. In their world, she would have been supporting her poor mother. Well, at least her mother wasn't supporting her.

"Is Papà Canadian?" people also asked her, "English Canadian like you?"

My God, at least I'm trying, she thought as she collapsed into bed at midnight, so overcome with exhaustion and longing for Dace that she didn't have enough energy left over to fear the noises she heard in the dark — mostly the barking of the German shepherd and the cooing of the pigeons next door.

The money she got from teaching three tutorials and grading first-year papers was just enough to cover her rent and her tuition. Since she was a university employee and Micah was over a year old, he'd qualified for free daycare, a real plus or she never would have been able to manage. She hated leaving him with the rest of the babies — some of them the aggressive brats of laidback hippie types — but the daycare at the University of Toronto was supposed to be topnotch. "Use your words, not your hands," was all one mother said when her daughter hauled off and smacked another toddler in the face. Liza would have felt better if Micah had been walking and able to fend for himself, but he was still crawling or scooting along, mostly on his bum.

Carting him in the Snugli baby carrier, she hiked with him from Hallam and Dufferin Street, all the way to St. George Street and Bloor where the University of Toronto began its spread.

Passing all the stores strung out on Bloor Street, she sometimes recalled the pretty campus in Maitland where she had finished her Honors BA, but Toronto was where she had spent her formative years. She felt at home here. Her uncle Norm sent her a hundred dollars a month for extras, a sum she was powerless to refuse. At the end of each month, she had nothing left over. She had no choice but to ignore the panhandlers she met along the way whose signs read things like: "Lady, I have nothing to eat." Dace used to give them his spare change, even if it all went for booze. But she could barely afford Tempra for Micah when he caught something at daycare.

"I can do this by myself," she told everybody, including her mother who was ambivalent about helping out with the baby — especially at her advanced age and with her terrible nerves. Maeve Magill Devereux worked part-time anyway. She had to if she wanted to eat. Liza's younger brothers, the twins, were in and out of Maeve's ex-husband's house. The boys were always up to no good and he was always kicking them out. He had a new family, a pair of girls. He couldn't or wouldn't give his sons a streetcar ticket. They were big enough and old enough to work like he had ever since he graduated grade eight. But he claimed them on his income taxes and would have claimed his daughter Liza too if he'd seen her just once in the past seven years.

"You can't," her mother said, when Liza finally ended up with the flu too. It hadn't been Maeve Magill's mother's style and it wasn't hers to tell an adult child what to do, but she didn't have much choice. Not with the baby involved. It was funny, wasn't it? Smart, educated girls were all the same, real stupid about basic stuff.

Maeve stared at her daughter lying in bed with a seventeen-month-old boy — still not walking! — playing at her feet and added: "Your father was useless, so I did everything by myself — had three children in three years and took care of you and him and the twins — but you can't.

You're still going to school. What about welfare? Lots of girls in your situation are getting it now. They come into Loblaws all the time. Listen, these girls get lots of money and their prescription drugs and their dental work paid. Welfare even gives them a clothing allowance! I didn't even get that with your father. It's not like when I was young when you had to marry the guy or do something—you know what I mean!—or give the baby away, if you were stupid enough to get caught doing stuff you shouldn't be doing. And Micah's not walking yet. Maybe you should take him to the doctor."

When Liza kept her eyes closed and failed to respond, her mother paused for a moment and picked up her teacup from the bedside table. Liza wasn't fooled though. Her mother had more to say and she had hoarded this next question for a long time, longer than most people would. "Who's the baby's father, anyway?" Maeve asked. "You should tell. My landlady's daughter did and the father had to pay. It's not like when I was young," she repeated, "Micah's father has to help!"

Liza pulled the bedspread up to her chin, shivering and stared at the bay window, even though all three blinds were pulled down and she couldn't see anything. "There's nothing wrong with Micah," she said.

"His father still has to pay," her mother persisted.

Oh, no, he doesn't, Liza thought. *Thank God, you and Uncle Norm don't talk and that I'm such an accomplished liar.* "His father is a student," she lied effortlessly, imagining Mel the medical student. It would have been so nice—oh, she couldn't do this, she couldn't do this, she couldn't raise Micah by herself. It was just too goddamn hard. Suddenly hot, she sat up, flung the bedspread back off and shoved her hair behind her ears. "He's not interested, anyway."

"Who?"

"The dad for God's sake! And I don't have the time or the energy to make him pay. Can you please, please just take Micah back to your place for today?" Liza paused, longing for her friend Val. Maybe Val's nanny could take Micah too? No, it wouldn't be fair. Val's little girl Sunshine was such a handful. Spoiled rotten by so much attention from three or four doting adults, she always had to be the whole show. "You can use that little folding stroller you found at the secondhand children's store on Bathurst last week," Liza coaxed.

Her mother wouldn't though. "I can't take him back there—my

landlady would have fits. But maybe I can stay downstairs on that old couch for the night. I'm not working tomorrow."

******

And so it was that Liza's mother was there when Dace finally arrived. Alerted by the German shepherd barking next door, Maeve was wide awake on the couch when she heard the backdoor creak open and then something dark filled the living room door. How on earth—she was sure she had locked both the back and the front door! In terror, she sat up on the lumpy couch, her fist crammed into her mouth. Liza was awake too, upstairs in bed rereading *Jude the Obscure* which was about a couple of doomed cousins and trying not to listen to the damn dog bark.

Maeve hadn't seen Dace since he was an eighteen-year-old boy at her in-laws' farm and he and Liza were mooning about, so she didn't recognize him right away.

He was a cutthroat murderer come to get her for sure.

A shriek tried to burst from her throat, but nothing came out. It was her worst fear, she told Liza and Dace later—that she'd be raped and murdered, because she was a woman on her own without a man. It happened in Toronto all the time. In fact, if you read the newspapers and watched enough television, it happened everywhere. The world was full of people who hated women. Misogynists, Liza had called them, using one of her big words.

"Auntie Maeve?" a deep voice said and then without seeing his face clearly--maybe because it was covered in hair--she recognized her ex-husband's nephew D'Arcy or Dace as all his bad friends had taken to calling him. Maeve was good with voices, and besides there was just something about the boy's size and shape, the way he filled the doorway or maybe just the way he smelled, like a Devereux man.

"What are you doing here?" she asked straight away.

Oh, that Liza was a closemouthed one and there had been a couple of family rumors and that funny business out at the farm, but they were cousins for God's sake and nobody had heard from this devil for years. The police had called her about him a couple of Christmases ago, scared her half to death.

Dace held up his hands in the air like a man in front of a pointed gun. "Shhh," he said, "It's alright. I've come to see Liza," he said, "and my son."

"Your son?" she asked, bewildered. "Where is he? And why, oh, God, Liza's sick in bed! She can't help you with whatever trouble you've gotten yourself into this time. She's got her own life."

"Well, she's up now," Dace said, backing up in the doorway and staring up the suddenly light-filled stairs. You looked like an angel, he told her later. An angel I wanted to fuck, except your mother was standing there and even I have some principles, darling…

"Hello, Dace," Liza said, standing at the top of the staircase with a housecoat pressed up against her bare chest and her hand to her throat. When he came home, she had never imagined it would be like this. That she'd be tongue-tied, that her mother would be tidying up the couch in the living room and eyeing the phone on the end table like it was high time she called the police.

That she herself would be thinking: *Look at you! I hate all that hair and that beard! You look like one of those panhandlers down on Bloor Street.*

As if any of that mattered.

"I'm still calling myself René Gagnon," he said. "I've got a birth certificate and everything, well, a baptismal certificate from a church in Quebec. You don't need a birth certificate from there. What do you think?"

"Well, the name's kind of sissy. But I like the beard," Liza smiled, pulling on her robe for her mother's sake and flying down the stairs straight into his arms.